SHADOWED PAST

Dedication

For Jaime, Erika, and Deena

Daughters of my heart,
bright as dawn upon the hills—

Thank you for believing in me
when the road was shadowed.

This tale carries your light,
woven through each word
like ancient song.

—J.K. Lane

Contents

Chapter 1

"Crown of Shadows"

A MIDST THE SILENT, SNOW-BLANKETED cemetery, Theodora's vibrant red hair blazed against the stark white landscape. Her boots broke through the crisp snow with each step, the soft crunch echoing through the still air, mirroring the grief that burdened her soul.

She wandered through the maze of tombstones. The watchful eyes of stone angels and twisted, bare trees seemed to follow her every move. The biting cold seeped into her lungs with each breath, a stark reminder of the fleeting nature of life and the inevitability of death.

As she approached her parents' graves, Theodora hesitated. The simple, elegant headstones of King William and Queen Amara stood out among the rest, a crown etched above her father's name and a delicate primrose adorned her mother's, a symbol of her grace and beauty.

Sinking to her knees, Theodora felt the icy dampness of the snow seeping through her pants. With a deep breath, she removed one glove and placed her warm hand on the frigid stone. As her fingers traced the engraved names of her parents, a shiver ran up her arm, the chill reaching deep into her already aching heart. Fragmented memories danced through her mind—the sound of her mother's gentle laughter, the comforting strength of her father's presence, but they remained distant, shrouded in an impenetrable haze.

A solitary tear slipped down her cheek, freezing in the bitter winter air like a small, crystalline jewel. Theodora allowed her eyes to drift closed. The soft whispers of the wind carried away some of her pain, yet left the unanswered questions that haunted her still.

"Why can't I remember?" The words fell from her lips, barely audible, laden with a desperate longing. The sorrow she had carried for so long, its origins a mystery, had brought her to this place of silence, where the boundary between the living and the dead seemed to blur.

As the sun climbed higher in the sky, chasing away the shadows, an unsettling feeling washed over her. The hairs on the back of her neck stood on end as a faint whisper drifted through the air.

Theodora's eyes flew open; she scanned the rows of gravestones for any sign of movement or the source of the eerie sound.

"Ye grieve for the departed, Princess," a voice murmured from the shadows at the edge of the graveyard. A figure cloaked in darkness stood just beyond reach of light. "But do ye truly be knowin' their fate?" His words sent a shiver down her spine as his cloak rippled in an unseen breeze; his face obscured beneath a dark hood.

"Who are ye?" Theodora demanded, keeping her voice steady despite the trembling of her heart. She slowly rose to her feet, her gaze never leaving the dark figure before her.

The air was thick with tension, charged with an unspoken challenge that hung between them like an invisible barrier.

The stranger moved forward with steps fluid yet purposeful. Piercing green eyes met hers from beneath his hood; their intensity unsettled.

"I am but a messenger," he replied smooth as silk yet cold as steel hinted at hidden dangers. "A bearer of truths long buried."

Theodora's heart pounded in her chest, but she squared her shoulders, determined not to show any weakness in front of this mysterious stranger.

In that instant, the world around her seemed to warp and twist; reality itself bent. A vivid, fleeting vision flashed before her eyes—a dimly lit chamber within the cold stone walls of Donaglen Castle. Sinister shadows danced along the walls; their movements fluid and disturbing. The echoes of tortured screams filled the room, sending icy tendrils of fear down her spine.

For a heartbeat, Theodora felt transported to that very chamber, immersed in the tangible atmosphere of terror and anguish. Shadows swirled around her, their whispered secrets just beyond her grasp. Her heart raced as she struggled to maintain her hold on what was real, fighting against the pull of the unsettling vision.

As swiftly as it had appeared, the vision faded, leaving Theodora unsteady and breathless. The enigmatic figure observed her with a perceptible smirk, a flicker of dark amusement in his haunting gaze.

"Enough with yer riddles," Theodora demanded, her voice quivering slightly despite her efforts to maintain composure. "Tell me straight, what do ya know about what happened to me parents? And why come to me now after all this time?"

The stranger cocked his head to the side, his faint smile visible in the light of the sun. "All in good time, Princess Theodora," he replied, his tone maddeningly calm. "Look not only to the past for answers, but keep watch on the shadows that lurk in the present. Trust not what yer eyes behold, but seek the truth that lies beneath the surface."

As he uttered these cryptic words, his form began to fade, melting back into the shadows.

"Wait!" Theodora cried out, her voice reverberating through the silent graveyard. "How is it ya know me name?" But the mysterious figure vanished without a trace, leaving her plea to echo into silence.

A biting wind tore through the cemetery, its icy caress sending a shiver down her spine as she huddled deeper into her cloak.

Unanswered questions about her parents' fate gnawed at her, close yet frustratingly out of reach. She scanned the treeline one final time, but only the dancing shadows greeted her, mirroring the unresolved mysteries that hung heavy in the crisp morning air.

Ms. Whoo's soothing voice pulled Theodora from her thoughts, a welcome respite from the eerie encounter. Turning to face her guardian, she found comfort in the familiar presence.

"What troubles ya, child?" Ms. Whoo asked, her hand a reassuring weight on Theodora's shoulder. "I felt a disturbance in the air."

Theodora recounted the unsettling meeting with the stranger, her words tinged with both relief and unease. Ms. Whoo's eyes flickered with recognition as she listened intently.

"Fate has set its sights on ya, it seems," Ms. Whoo said, her tone grave. "This stranger's appearance is a sign that the mysteries of yer past are resurfacing."

Theodora's mind swirled with conflicting emotions as Ms. Whoo spoke. "What do ya know about this figure?" Theodora asked.

Ms. Whoo's face grew somber as she considered the question, her timeless eyes holding secrets untold. Before she could answer, the sound of footsteps crunching through the snow drew their attention.

Cornelius quickened his pace as he approached Theodora and Ms. Whoo, his brow furrowed in worry. Theodora could sense the tension in his every step, the unspoken concern hanging heavy in the air.

"Princess Theodora, is everything alright?" Cornelius inquired, his voice laced with a mixture of protective instinct and genuine care. His eyes swept over Theodora's face, searching for any sign of distress or discomfort.

Theodora straightened her posture, meeting Cornelius' gaze with a determined look. Despite the lingering unease from the encounter with the mysterious stranger, she mustered a small smile to reassure him.

"I am well, Cornelius," she replied, her voice steady despite the tumult of emotions swirling within her. "Just a momentary disturbance in the graveyard, nothin' more."

Cornelius nodded, his expression softening slightly at Theodora's words. He was not only the head of the guards but also her archery instructor, a role he took with utmost seriousness. His rugged exterior belied a deep sense of care and responsibility towards the young princess under his protection.

"Good ta hear, Princess," Cornelius said, his tone gruff yet reassuring. "Shall we proceed with yer morning archery lesson, or do ya need more time?"

Theodora nodded, appreciating the comforting routine that provided a sense of stability amid the chaos around her. "I'm ready, Cornelius. Let's not be dilly-dallyin'." She stood confidently, determined not to let the previous events affect her resolve.

Theodora breathed in the crisp air, the scent of pine and distant hearths filling her senses as Cornelius led her through the winding paths of the cemetery.

As they walked, Cornelius remained by Theodora's side, his eyes scanning their surroundings with a protective gaze. Theodora couldn't help but feel grateful for his presence, knowing that he was always ready to defend and guide her.

"Ya seem tense," Cornelius remarked, breaking the peaceful silence between them.

Theodora sighed, her mind still reeling from her encounter with the mysterious stranger. "I can't shake off this feeling of unease," she admitted. "Ms. Whoo said it was a sign from me past resurfacing."

Cornelius furrowed his brow in concern, but didn't press further. He knew that Theodora would tell him what she needed when she was ready.

Theodora pushed against the rusty gates, their hinges protesting as she stepped out into the snow-covered field. Ms. Whoo followed closely, her parting words a gentle reminder. "Trust yer instincts, lass. They'll guide ya true." With a final glance towards the shadowy treeline, she headed back to the castle.

"Ya think we should be worried?" Theodora asked Cornelius.

"Aye," he nodded, watching Ms. Whoo's retreating form. "Her senses are sharp, always ahead of trouble. Best we stay alert."

As they crossed the field, Theodora felt a surge of energy beneath her feet, the land itself seeming to acknowledge her presence.

On the archery range, the snow-dusted targets beckoned. Cornelius offered guidance as Theodora prepared to shoot.

"I've never been good at this," Theodora admitted. "Not sure I'll ever get the hang of it." Even after a year, she still felt out of place with the bow compared to the weight of her crown.

Cornelius smiled warmly. "Patience, lass. Even the greatest archers started as beginners."

With determination etched on her face, Theodora's mind drifted to the enigmatic stranger she had crossed paths with in the cemetery. Memories of his piercing gaze and cryptic utterances lingered, giving rise to a whirlwind of inquiries: Who was he, really? What did he want from her? Her arrow veered off course, urging her to reload and try again. The perplexing enigma surrounding their chance meeting shrouded her thoughts, casting a veil over her concentration.

Now that she was beginning to uncover fragments of her own past through dreams and strange encounters like this one, it only intensified her desire to unravel the secrets surrounding her parents' death.

"Ya think Ms. Whoo's quick exit had something ta do with that stranger?" Theodora asked, releasing the arrow. It flew closer to the center this time, but was still not quite on target.

Cornelius pondered the question, scanning the snowy landscape. "She's a wise one, and wouldn't leave without cause. There must be danger afoot," he replied, a hint of concern in his voice.

Ms. Whoo's boots struck the cobblestones with urgency as she dashed back to the castle, her crimson cloak billowing behind her in the biting wind. The hairs on the back of her neck prickled, an unsettling sensation of being watched accompanying each step. From atop the castle turret, a raven's piercing caw echoed, its beady eyes following her every move with unnerving precision.

Ms. Whoo's keen gaze swept over the castle walls, the weight of hidden truths bearing down upon her. The everyday sounds of laughter and clanging armor from the grounds below seemed to mock the insidious danger lurking just out of sight.

An oppressive sense of dread permeated the air, growing thicker with each passing moment, despite the mundane activities of the maids and knights going about their duties. Undaunted, Ms. Whoo forged ahead, delving deeper into the castle's shadowy heart. Her purposeful footsteps reverberated through the dimly lit corridors, a whispered promise of secrets waiting to be unveiled. With every step, she drew closer to the long-forgotten chambers where the answers to age-old enigmas lay entombed, beckoning to be unleashed.

Stepping into the room, her boots barely whispered against the intricate rugs adorning the floor. Each footfall resonated in the expansive space, harmonizing with the ethereal whispers of magic that permeated the air.

The tapestries along the walls seemed to come to life in her presence, the legendary heroes depicted upon them appearing to shift and dance as if drawn to her energy. Ms. Whoo raised her hand, a soft luminescence emanating from her palm and casting intricate shadows on the chamber walls. The room pulsed with an ancient, tangible power that vibrated through every stone.

In the center of the room, a radiant orb glimmered with enigmatic symbols, its surface alluring like a distant mirage promising untold wonders. As Ms. Whoo placed her hands upon its cool, smooth exterior, a surge of energy coursed through her veins, igniting every nerve ending with a tingling sensation.

A misty veil materialized before her, blurring the lines between realms, beckoning her to step into the unknown. The air carried the faint aroma of ancient herbs and aged parchment, heightening the sense of entering a world steeped in history and magic.

In the earthly realm, Aris, the sleek black cat, stretched languidly. Peculiar symbols glowed beneath her paws, emitting a mysterious hum. As if pulled by an unseen force, she ventured into the kitchen where similar markings illuminated the floor.

The once comforting atmosphere now crackled with an impending sense of danger. As Aris gingerly stepped on the glowing symbols, they clung to her paws, inviting her to join in a mystical dance with destiny.

"Aris, time is of the essence," Ms. Whoo's voice echoed telepathically within their shared consciousness, her wise eyes reflecting concern and urgency. The flicker of worry in her gaze mirrored the gravity of the unfolding situation.

"The dark forces have made their presence known today," Ms. Whoo continued. "I fear our dear Theodora may be in grave danger. Gather yer belongings and prepare to return home before that sorcerer finds a way ta unleash his Shadow Walkers upon the mortal world."

"I understand," Aris replied, a frown creasing her brow as the weight of the situation settled upon her small shoulders, spurring her into action.

The ominous sense of foreboding that lingered in the kitchen now hung heavy in the air, casting shadows where light once shone. Aris moved with quiet resolve across the tiled floor, each step leaving behind faint luminescent traces from her paws.

In Kandella, Ms. Whoo's mind raced with thoughts of Alexandria's impending return. She knew that Aris, too, could sense the shift. "Will she be ready for the challenges that await her? Can she unravel the mysteries intertwined with her destiny?"

Back in the mortal world, Aris braced herself for the trials ahead, her heart beating in unison with Ms. Whoo's, a testament to the connection between their worlds.

The trees swayed ominously, their creaking branches sending a chill through Theodora's very core. An inexplicable sense of dread crept over her, a primal instinct warning of impending danger.

Her arrow flew wide, burying itself in the snow-covered ground with a soft thud. Frustration bubbled within her, escaping in a puff of frosty breath. She lowered the bow, its weight oppressive, a tangible reminder of her own perceived shortcomings.

Cornelius stroked his grizzled beard, his eyes glinting with hard-earned wisdom. "Ye've got the fire within ye, lass. Ye just need to trust yerself and let it loose."

"Fire?" Theodora let out a bitter laugh. "All I feel is a bloody chill in me bones."

"Mayhaps we're goin' about this the wrong way," Cornelius mused, taking the bow from her hands. "There's more troublin' ya than just yer aim. What's weighin' so heavy on yer mind?"

Theodora hesitated, uncertain whether to bare her soul. But the genuine concern etched on Cornelius's weathered face compelled her to speak.

"It's just... with Ms. Whoo runnin' off and that eerie stranger appearin', it feels like pieces of a puzzle I can't quite figure out," Theodora confessed, her voice tinged with frustration and vulnerability. "What if I'm not strong enough or clever enough to face the darkness that's comin'? I don't want to fail the people I care about."

Cornelius listened intently, his calloused hand coming to rest on Theodora's shoulder. "Ye're not alone in this fight, lass. The road ahead may be dark and uncertain, but remember, even the longest night eventually gives way to dawn," he said, his words a soothing balm to her troubled spirit.

Theodora blinked back the tears that threatened to fall, drawing in a shaky breath of crisp winter air. Bolstered by Cornelius's unwavering support, she straightened her spine, feeling the weight of her doubts begin to lift.

"Yer right, Cornelius," she said, her voice gaining strength and resolve. "I can't let me fears hold me back. There's a mystery unfoldin' before us, and I'll be damned if I don't face it head-on."

With renewed determination, Theodora took up the bow once more. She nocked an arrow, drawing back the string with focused intensity. Letting go of her doubts, she released the arrow.

This time, it flew true, striking the heart of the target. Elation surged through her as Cornelius let out a whoop of approval. "That's it, lass! Ye've found yer fire!"

A triumphant grin spread across Theodora's face, a beacon of hope amidst the winter's chill. Purpose thrummed through her veins as she gathered her arrows, eager to continue honing her skills.

But as she prepared for another round, an unsettling shift in the atmosphere made her pause. The once peaceful surroundings now crackled with an eerie, palpable tension.

Cornelius sensed it too, his bow at the ready as he scanned the groaning trees that seemed to whisper warnings.

"Dark forces," he growled under his breath.

Shadows gathered at the edge of the field, and ancient whispers rode the wind. The very air shimmered with unnatural energy as Theodora moved to stand beside Cornelius.

Despite her newfound resolve, Theodora felt her confidence waver in the face of this unseen threat. A bone-chilling shiver raced down her spine, making her hair stand on end. Her breath caught in her throat, and every instinct screamed at her to run, her heart pounding a frantic rhythm against her ribs.

"Ya sense that too?" Theodora asked, her voice barely audible above the howling wind.

"Aye, lass. Ancient, dark magic be stirrin' in the depths," Cornelius replied. A sharp crack pierced the air, followed by a foul stench that assaulted their nostrils. Instinctively, they lunged aside as their once-peaceful surroundings turned hostile.

"We've gotta move, Theodora. Now!" Cornelius shouted, recovering from the initial shock.

Sprinting down the path towards Donaglen's gates, they watched in horror as menacing storm clouds swirled overhead. "What is goin' on?" Theodora yelled, the wind's fury nearly drowning out her words.

"This ain't no regular storm, lass," Cornelius responded, wincing as the icy rain pelted them relentlessly.

Theodora stumbled but quickly regained her footing, pressing forward alongside Cornelius. The earth trembled beneath their feet as a deafening roar filled the air, signaling the approach of an unknown danger.

"Cornelius!" she hollered over the bedlam. "What do we do now? How can we be defendin' ourselves against this?"

Meeting her gaze, Cornelius spoke with unwavering determination. "The castle, lass. If we can make it inside those ancient walls, we might have a fightin' chance against whatever evil's comin' our way."

Fueled by renewed resolve, they battled through the raging tempest, their only goal to reach the safety of the castle before the sinister storm consumed them.

The heavy gates clanged shut behind them as Cornelius' commanding voice sliced through the chaos. "Secure the gates, lads! Double the patrols along the walls, ye hear? We don't know what kind of darkness is comin' our way, so get the defenses ready!"

Theodora stood beside him, her heart pounding in her chest as the castle bustled with frantic activity. A chill seeped into her bones as they descended into the castle's depths.

Suddenly, a dizzying flash of memories assaulted her mind. Ancient books lined endless shelves, and a faint voice whispered the importance of seeking knowledge and power. Theodora stumbled back, her body colliding with the cold stone wall.

"Princess, what's the craic?" Cornelius asked, his brow furrowed with concern.

"Nothing, just some old memories," Theodora replied, shaking her head as the images faded.

Beyond the castle walls, the storm continued its furious assault, with fierce winds and unyielding hail. Inside, the strange tranquility that enveloped them struck her, as if time had come to a halt.

They turned their attention to a lone guard standing at the end of the corridor—a symbol of unwavering duty and sacrifice amidst the chaos. Just then, the distant hoot of an owl pierced the air, serving as a foreboding warning of the danger that lurked ahead.

Theodora and Cornelius exchanged a knowing look, a silent acknowledgment of their readiness to face whatever challenges lay before them. As daylight cast an ethereal glow on the castle grounds and the storm showed signs of subsiding, an unshakable feeling lingered that unseen threats still lurked in the shadows.

"Alright, lass, stay put," Cornelius whispered, guiding Theodora behind a tapestry-covered alcove.

Theodora pressed her back against the cold stone, the musty air heavy with the scent of age and neglect. Her senses sharpened, attuned to the slightest sound or movement. Shadows danced on the walls, playing tricks on her mind as her heartbeat echoed through the empty hallway.

A knot of unease twisted in her gut. The faint whisper of movement caught her attention, sending a shiver down her spine. Theodora spun around, ready to confront whatever lurked in the darkness. As her eyes adjusted to the dim light, she realized it was just a tattered tapestry, its ancient fibers brushing against her fingertips.

Stepping out from her hiding spot, Theodora recalled her father's warnings about the hidden threats that could test her strength when she least expected it.

As she walked down the corridor, servants and knights scurried about, their movements tinged with urgency and nervousness. The echo of their footsteps on the stone floor mirrored the collective unease that hung in the air.

Theodora caught a glimpse of a knight's tense expression, a hint of the trust issues that plagued the castle. Pushing the thought aside, she pressed on, knowing that understanding the castle's dynamics could be just as crucial as facing any physical threat. The sounds of laughter and bustle grew louder as she approached the grand hallway.

Ms. Whoo stood among the crowd, her eyes meeting Theodora's with a look of concern. The young princess hurried to her nanny's side. "What in the blazes is going on? Where did those buggers run off to?" Theodora asked, confusion written on her face.

"There are things afoot we can't fully understand." Ms. Whoo replied. "Remember, child, the answers you seek often lie where the past and present intersect."

Theodora's confusion only deepened as Ms. Whoo's cryptic words echoed in her mind. What did she mean by the past and present? The castle walls had always sheltered the princess, and her life revolved around court etiquette and lessons on being a proper lady.

But now, as the world outside seemed to crumble, Theodora faced a harsh new reality. She needed answers, and she needed them now.

As if sensing her thoughts, Ms. Whoo spoke again. "I know it's a lot to take in, but trust that everything will become clear in time."

Theodora felt an irresistible pull towards the library, as if some unseen force was guiding her there. An urgency burned within her, compelling her to uncover the long-buried secrets that seemed to whisper just out of reach.

Stepping away from the lively chatter of the gathering, Theodora made her way to the library. The ancient doors groaned in protest as she pushed them open, revealing the dimly lit room beyond.

Time seemed to stand still within those hallowed walls. The scent of aged parchment enveloped her, and dust motes danced in the waning light that filtered through the high arched windows.

As Theodora wandered through the labyrinth of bookshelves, her fingers brushed against countless tomes filled with forgotten tales and knowledge waiting to be rediscovered. Each volume held the promise of answers, sending shivers down her spine. After the recent upheavals in her life, these were the answers she desperately craved.

"What secrets do these books hold?" she wondered, her mind swirling with grief and unresolved questions. Memories of her past flickered like shadows. Losing her parents, leaving a gaping void and the uncertainty surrounding her family's legacy tugging at her heart.

Theodora's gaze fell on a peculiar section, where the books were older and more weathered than the rest. One volume in particular caught her eye, its ancient leather cover bearing an intricate insignia visible beneath layers of dust. She felt an inexplicable pull towards it, as if an invisible thread connected them.

Ms. Whoo's cryptic words echoed in her mind: "Your past holds the keys to unlock hidden treasures." Those words etched themselves into Theodora's memory like a mantra, pushing her forward into a realm of forgotten knowledge. Yet, self-doubt gnawed at her—could she truly uncover what lay buried within?

With a trembling hand, Theodora reached for the book. As her fingers grazed its ancient cover, she felt a surge of energy pulsing from its pages, awakening something deep within her. It was an instinct honed by years of feeling out of place in both the mundane world and the magical one she had only begun to explore.

Strange whispers filled the air around her, seeming to come from another realm. Memories of long-buried secrets flickered through her mind, conversations with Ms. Whoo about lineage and legacy that she had once dismissed as mere fanciful stories. But now she wondered, "Was there more to those tales than she realized?"

In that moment, Theodora knew this ancient tome was far more than just another dusty volume. Whether by fate's design or sheer happenstance, she found herself standing before it, the weight of the decision pressing upon her like a physical force. The secrets within its pages held the power to either cast light upon the shadowed paths of her past or plunge her deeper into the abyss of uncertainty.

With trembling hands, Theodora grasped the worn leather book, feeling its weight grow as she pulled it from the shelf. The library around her disappeared, leaving her focused on this crucial object. In her hands, she held not just a book, but a key to the secrets of her identity and her family's legacy.

Chapter 2

"When Shadows Stir"

ALEXANDRIA'S EYES SNAPPED OPEN, her heart racing, and her breath coming in ragged gasps. Beads of sweat trickled down her face, plastering strands of her auburn hair to her damp forehead. As she blinked away the lingering confusion, the sinister shadows from her nightmare seemed to dance along the walls of her dimly lit bedroom.

Sitting up, Alexandria ran her trembling hands through her tangled locks, trying to calm her frayed nerves. The suffocating room felt laden with the oppressive weight of past anxieties, and the distant hum of urban life provided little comfort. Taking a deep breath, she inhaled the familiar scent of her surroundings, hoping it would ground her, but the unease in her mind persisted.

Echoes of the phantom forest from her dream clung to her, blurring the line between slumber and wakefulness. Her skin crawled with the sensation of unseen frost, and the ghostly sound of crunching leaves seemed to follow her, as if she were still frantically running through that ominous woodland. Even in the faint morning light filtering through the curtains, Alexandria couldn't shake off the vivid remnants of her nightmare.

Squeezing her eyes shut, she tried to piece together the fragmented images from her dream, but they slipped through her grasp like wisps of fog. Her heart still pounded in time with the phantom rhythm of desperate footsteps on freshly fallen snow. Shadows lurked at the edges of her mind, just out of reach. A chilling image flashed before her: a dark, cloaked figure with piercing green eyes that seemed to stare straight into her very being.

Was this vision a shard of forgotten memories or an omen of troubles to come? Her mind raced, desperately trying to make sense of the jumbled pieces, but clarity eluded her.

Glancing towards the door, she considered fleeing from the suffocating uncertainty, but hesitation gripped her. Should she run from her fears or confront them head-on? Just then, a sharp knock at the door shattered the silence, making her jump.

"Alexandria? Are you awake in there?" Her mother's grating voice called out, setting her teeth on edge.

"Yeah, I'm up," she muttered under her breath, a hint of sarcasm lacing her words as she tried to push down the inner turmoil with a heavy sigh. She hoped her exhaustion would conceal her true emotional state.

With a weary groan, she threw back the covers and swung her legs over the side of the bed. As she stood up, a wave of vertigo washed over her, forcing her to reach for the bedpost for support. The rough wood dug into her palm as she closed her eyes, waiting for the dizziness to pass. The scent of pine and varnish intermingled with the coppery taste of fear in her mouth.

Throwing on some clothes, Alexandria stumbled into the bathroom. She splashed cold water on her face, hoping to cleanse herself of the nightmare's persistent grip, but the unsettling sensations refused to be washed away so easily. Yanking a brush through her knotted hair, she winced with each painful snag, the physical discomfort mirroring the unresolved tensions within her.

She dragged herself down the stairs, struggling with each step as if concrete weighed down her feet. The kitchen buzzed with the typical morning commotion, but beneath the surface, an undercurrent of tension crackled like static electricity. Her parents' worried glances and hushed conversations clashed with Liam's oblivious good mood, only amplifying her discomfort.

Slumping into her chair at the breakfast table, Alexandria inhaled the comforting scents of pancakes and scrambled eggs, a momentary reprieve from the suffocating atmosphere. The air felt thick and oppressive, as if she were breathing through a damp cloth. Drawing a full breath seemed nearly impossible.

"Honey, are you alright? You're looking a bit under the weather," her mother asked, her brow furrowed with concern.

Alexandria forced a weak smile and pushed her plate away. "Yeah, I'm okay. Just had a rough night, that's all." The half-truth rolled off her tongue with practiced ease.

Her father's warm hand engulfed hers, his touch a lifeline in the tempest of her emotions. "Remember, you can always come to us if something's bothering you," he reminded her, his eyes brimming with unconditional love and support.

Alexandria's heart ached to confide in him, to pour out the fears and doubts that plagued her, but the words lodged in her throat. How could they possibly relate to the nightmares that haunted her sleep and the constant struggle to maintain her grip on reality?

She managed a nod, avoiding direct eye contact with her parents. Their well-meaning expressions only heightened her guilt for keeping them in the dark.

"Listen, kiddo, I've gotta head out early for work today," her father said, shattering the uneasy quiet. "But I'll be back in time for dinner. If you need to talk, I'm all ears."

As Alexandria fought to maintain her mask of normalcy, a subtle shift in the atmosphere sent a shiver down her spine. Glancing up, she caught her parents exchanging a loaded look, their faces etched with unspoken concerns and worries.

Her father cleared his throat, breaking the tension. "Hey, why don't you and Liam go for a hike after school? Get out in the fresh air, you know?"

Alexandria and Liam shared a surprised glance at the sudden suggestion. "Uh, yeah, sure Dad. Sounds good," she replied.

A blaring car horn shattered the moment. "Oh, that's my ride!" Liam jumped up from his chair. "Catch ya later, Lex." He messed up her hair playfully as he rushed past, leaving her longing for the carefree attitude that seemed to come so easily to him.

As the door slammed behind him, a heavy silence settled over the kitchen once more. Alexandria stared blankly at her untouched breakfast, her mind a tangled web of unanswered questions and growing unease.

Her gaze drifted to Aris's empty food bowl near the back door. "Hey, where's Aris?" Alexandria asked, breaking the quiet. "She never skips breakfast."

Her mother took a slow sip of coffee, trying to play it off. "Oh, you know cats. She probably found a sunny patch under a tree and passed out." But the flicker of worry in her eyes said something else.

A weight settled in Alexandria's chest—slow, creeping. Something felt off. She hadn't noticed it at first, just a strange stillness in the house, the kind that didn't belong. Now that she was thinking about it, she realized she hadn't seen Aris at all since waking up.

Had she slipped out early this morning? Or was it last night?
She frowned. Either way, Aris always circled back by now.

Her eyes shifted to her father, studying his face. Looking for anything that might give him away. "Is everything okay?" she asked. "Like... really okay?"

Elmer met her eyes and smiled, easy and warm—but it didn't quite reach. "Everything's fine, sweetheart."

She didn't buy it.

A memory stirred—brief but vivid—of Aris disappearing between trees, her silhouette melting into the shadows. It felt more like a dream than something real, but it clung to her anyway. The house felt different without her. Hollow. Like it was holding its breath.

There have been other strange things lately, too. Fleeting sounds. Whispers that never formed full words. She'd brushed it off—stress, maybe. Not enough sleep.

But this morning was different.

A whisper had cut through the silence. Clear. Name-shaped. Ms. Whoo.

Alexandria hesitated. Her lips parted, the question slipping out before she could stop it. "Wait... who's Ms. Whoo?"

Her mother turned sharply, eyebrows knitting. "What are you talking about, hon?"

"I..." Alexandria shook her head. "Thought I heard someone say that. Never mind." She forced a smile, but her skin tingled with unease.

Something was off. And whatever it was, it wasn't going away.

She was about to press again when the sharp honk of the school bus cut through the moment. Grabbing her backpack, she backed toward the door. "I've got swim practice after school."

She didn't wait for a reply. Just left the house and the silence behind her.

As the bus vanished around the bend, Diana and Elmer exchanged a loaded glance, their faces etched with worry. They headed inside, the door clicking shut behind them with an ominous finality.

"Damn it, Elmer, she's not ready," Diana said, her voice strained. "We need more time before going back to Kandella."

Elmer's grip tightened on his mug, his knuckles turning white. "I know, but the prophecy is in motion. Valendor knows about the girls now. His Shadow Walkers won't hesitate to cross over."

"And Theodora... she could already be in danger," Diana added, her eyes shadowed with fear.

Elmer placed a comforting hand on Diana's shoulder. "We have to tell Alexandria the truth tonight. About who she really is and what's coming."

Diana met his gaze, her expression resolute despite the gathering storm clouds outside. "You're right. But what if it's too much for her to handle? This normal life is all she's ever known."

They fell into a tense discussion, planning how to prepare Alexandria for the memories she'd need to reclaim, the magic waiting to be awakened within her, and the looming threats they'd face in Kandella.

Suddenly, a chill raced through the room, and Diana's amulet flared with an eerie light. Aris appeared before them, her wolf form radiating urgency.

"Aris, what's wrong?" Diana asked, her hand instantly reached for her necklace.

Aris's mental voice cut through their minds like a blade. "Valendor's Shadow Walkers have breached the portal. They're coming for Alexandria!"

The air grew heavy, crackling with dark energy. Aris continued, her tone grave, "You must listen to me. The Shadow Walkers are relentless. They'll corrupt and destroy everything in their path to get to her."

Elmer growled, his jaw clenched with determination. "We'll keep her safe, no matter what it takes."

Diana nodded, striding towards the ornate mirror on the wall. "I'll cast a protection spell over her."

Ancient words spilled from her lips as she focused on Alexandria, the mirror thrumming with power. In her mind, she saw her sitting on the bus, unaware of the encroaching danger. With a final intonation, Diana wove a shimmering shield around her, light flaring before settling into a subtle, protective glow.

"That'll hold for now," Diana said, her voice steady. "But Valendor's minions won't give up."

Elmer stared out into the gathering storm, his expression grim. "Then neither will we. Whatever it takes, we'll keep Alexandria safe."

Diana's powerful incantation had set in motion a chain of events that would irrevocably shape Alexandria's destiny. As they braced themselves for the impending storm, Aris nuzzled Elmer's hand, her playful gesture momentarily easing the tension that hung heavy in the air. Elmer couldn't help but crack a smile, grateful for her unwavering loyalty and support.

With a solemn nod, Aris acknowledged his gratitude before turning her piercing gaze towards the ominous horizon, a stark reminder of the looming battle that threatened to shatter the delicate balance between realms. Elmer's brow furrowed as he sensed the growing unease permeating the atmosphere. "You feel that too, don't you?" he murmured, his words tinged with apprehension.

Diana inhaled sharply, the electric tension causing her shoulders to stiffen. "The shadows are getting bolder, more restless," she whispered, her voice quivering slightly.

A low growl rumbled in Aris's throat as she readied herself for the imminent confrontation. The very air seemed to thicken with a sense of foreboding, as if even the earth itself was holding its breath, bracing for the profound impact these events would have on Alexandria's journey.

"We can't afford to waste any more time," Elmer declared, his resolve unwavering in the face of the encroaching darkness. "The wheels are in motion now," he added grimly, his words nearly swallowed by the subtle disturbances that seemed to grow more insistent with each passing moment.

Aris froze, her ears twitching as she detected distant sounds that human senses couldn't perceive. It was a telltale sign that danger was fast approaching. Without a word spoken between them, they all understood the gravity of the situation—time was running out, and their fight against the relentless darkness had reached a critical juncture.

Chapter 3

"The Unveiling"

THEODORA'S PULSE RACED AS her fingertips grazed the ancient tome's insignia one last time before relinquishing her grip. She inhaled, steadying her nerves, when an unexpected sight caught her eye, stealing her breath—a luminous crystal orb pulsing with an ethereal glow at the heart of the library.

Captivated by its mesmerizing radiance, Theodora approached the orb cautiously, her eyes mirroring its shimmering hues. The air crackled with enigmatic energy, drawing her closer, as if attuned to her presence.

The world around her blurred into a hazy backdrop. It became the sole focus of her attention. Fingers outstretched, hovering just mere inches away from its surface, Theodora wavered momentarily, a flicker of doubt in her eyes.

With shaky hands, she extended her arms and rested her palms on the orb. The instant her skin connected, a surge of energy coursed through her veins, igniting every nerve ending. The bond was instantaneous and profound, sending a shockwave down her spine. Deep within her core, a dormant spark roared to life, as if it had awakened a slumbering part of her soul.

Long-buried memories seeped through the cracks, piercing the protective veil Ms. Whoo had woven. A majestic castle emerged from swirling mists, its spires stretching towards an azure sky. Familiar faces moved within its shadowed halls, their expressions a tapestry of hope and urgency. Amidst it all, Theodora saw herself standing at the castle's core, realizing her pivotal role in a tale woven with magic and mystery.

Theodora's breath caught as the visions intensified, each more powerful than the last. An otherworldly light flooded the room, casting an ethereal glow. The images continued to flow, overwhelming her senses.

As the scenes unfolded, Theodora's heart thundered in her chest, her breath shallow and rapid. Tears pricked the corners of her eyes, threatening to spill over. A tidal wave of emotion crashed over her, threatening to sweep her away.

Her parents appeared vibrant and full of life, engaged in fervent discussion with indistinct figures. Her mother's tender smile and her father's eyes crinkling with laughter were achingly familiar yet surreal. Theodora's heart clenched, a searing pain that threatened to shatter her.

Hands quivering, she clung to the connection with the orb, desperate to hold on as the air around her grew heavy, crackling with energy. The scent of ancient wood and earth mingled with the distant drone of insects, intensifying her longing. She yearned to feel the warmth of her parents' touch, to hear their voices intertwined with her own, and to never let go.

Memories shifted again. The library transformed before her eyes into a vibrant hub of scholars and magicians, alive with activity. Animated discussions echoed through the halls, accompanied by the whisper of turning pages. At the center of it all stood her parents, their presence commanding and comforting. The love and pride that shone in their eyes as they looked at each other was almost too much to bear.

A strangled sob tore from Theodora's lips as she drank in every detail, a stark contrast to the cold reality she had endured. The weight of the years without them crushed her, the emptiness in her heart a constant ache. But now, seeing them here—so full of life and passion—a fierce mix of grief and joy surged through her. Tears ran down her cheeks as her chest clenched, the lost moments unfolding before her, their love, hopes, and fears cutting deep.

In the whirlwind of youthful vitality, Theodora found herself twirling through a surreal dance with a familiar yet elusive figure. As the fantastical imagery melted away, leaving her breathless and trembling, the library seemed to pulse with a rejuvenated energy, repelling the encroaching darkness with the orb's radiant beam. Her heart pounded with a blend of apprehension and fascination, yet the resolute spirit ignited by the mysterious visions held firm, grounding her in a renewed determination.

Amidst the swirling chaos of memories and emotions threatening to overwhelm her, a soft rustle of fabric, barely discernible, caused Theodora to still. There was a presence—a familiar one—that enveloped her, creating an atmosphere she could feel in the very air around her. With no need to turn or seek physical confirmation, Theodora instinctively knew that Ms. Whoo had entered the room.

As if in response to this arrival, the energy in the chamber shifted, acknowledging the silver-haired guardian's presence. An unseen force tugged at Theodora's senses, drawing her attention to where she knew Ms. Whoo stood. It was a subtle shift, imperceptible to most, but for Theodora, it was as clear as day.

Whirling to face her nanny, Theodora demanded answers, her voice trembling. "What in all that's holy is going on? What are these bleedin' visions?"

Theodora's voice wavered with a mixture of frustration and desperation, her eyes pleading for clarity amidst the whirlwind of emotions that threatened to consume her. Ms. Whoo observed the Princess with a steady look, her face expressing a deep understanding mixed with a touch of sadness.

Emerging from the shadows with a serene and composed presence, Ms. Whoo spoke. "The visions ye've seen, dear Theodora, are remnants of yer past, pieces of a reality that is no more," her voice echoed the sorrow reflecting Theodora's inner turmoil. "A powerful spell concealed these memories from you, hiding them away."

The princess felt a surge of anger blossom within her chest, mingling with the overwhelming sadness and confusion that gripped her soul. "But why show them to me now? Why torment me with glimpses of a life I can never reclaim?" Her words trembled with raw emotion, echoing through the chamber like a haunting melody.

Ms. Whoo's gaze softened, a glint of compassion shining in her eyes. "Theodora," she said, "the time has come for ya to uncover the truths hidden from ya. The past holds the key to yer future, and only by confrontin' the shadows that linger there can ya step into yer true destiny."

Her brows furrowed in frustration, her hands clenched into fists at her sides. The weight of her lineage bore down on her like an unyielding burden, the unanswered questions swirling in her mind like a maelstrom. "I want ta understand, Ms. Whoo. I need ta know the secrets that've been kept from me," she implored, her voice a mixture of vulnerability and determination.

Ms. Whoo nodded, her hair catching the dim light of the chamber as she moved closer to Theodora. "There are forces at play far beyond our understandin', me dear, as painful as it may be."

The aroma of freshly baked bread and roasting meat filled the air, intensifying Theodora's unease. She felt torn between the comfort of the old walls and a longing for something beyond them. Though questions filled her mind, she knew pressing Ms. Whoo for answers was pointless; the nanny was enigmatic and would reveal her secrets in her own time.

With a heavy heart and a storm of unresolved thoughts, she turned from Ms. Whoo and went to a small table lit by the window. Sitting in the well-worn chair, Theodora traced the carved designs, memories of countless hours spent there flooding back.

She wanted answers, but a part of her hesitated, knowing some truths were better left buried. Still, her curiosity won out. Ms. Whoo had been there through everything - the nightmares, the confusion, the loss. If anyone could help her make sense of it all, it was her.

Soft footsteps drew closer as castle servants arrived with lunch. The rich smell of roasted meat and fresh bread pulled Theodora from her thoughts. Steam rose from bowls of hearty stew as the servants arranged the meal, careful not to disturb the heavy mood that hung over their princess. They moved with gentle purpose, hoping the warm food might bring some small comfort to the tense atmosphere.

Silverware clinked against earthenware as Theodora pushed her food around her plate, too preoccupied with Ms. Whoo's revelations to eat. The rich stew barely registered on her tongue as her mind churned over the cryptic conversation. Despite her unease, she found herself looking forward to their upcoming lessons. Ms. Whoo's tales had always been her escape from the castle walls, offering glimpses into distant lands and extraordinary adventures. Each story resonated deep within her, awakening something that craved more than the sheltered life she knew.

One story in particular captured Theodora's imagination—a captivating saga of three kings, their paths woven by the threads of destiny. As Ms. Whoo's voice filled the room, the young princess leaned forward, her eyes sparkling with rapt attention.

"Tell me more about these kings, Ms. Whoo," Theodora urged, her voice brimming with enthusiasm. "I want to know everything!"

Ms. Whoo smiled, a knowing twinkle in her eye. "Ah, child, their tale is one of great courage, sacrifice and the power of unity. It all began in a time of darkness..."

'*They say the third king of the island pioneered the Flight Project, after losing the first and second kings—his father and brother—to the lanky swimmers of the sea. He had great faith that the answers lay in the skies, after far too many sailors and tradesmen met their doom in the dark waters and ended up in the bellies of the mermaids. His ideas seemed preposterous, but so eager he was to inspire his people that he himself piloted the inaugural flight of the very first flying machine. He inspired them, and thus his work continued.*'

'*But that was the work of the fourth king, as the first flying machine had considerable design flaws, and the brave third king ended his brief reign in the bellies of the mermaids.*'

Theodora hung onto every word as Ms. Whoo regaled her with stories of daring aerial escapades, treacherous merfolk and the rich tapestry of their kingdom's past. The young princess's eyes sparkled with wonder, her mind alight with visions of soaring machines and depths unexplored. As the tales drew to a close, Theodora eagerly embraced their guessing game, relishing the chance to set aside the day's heavier conversations for a spell of lighthearted fun.

With each beautifully illustrated card, something stirred deep within Theodora—an awakening of dormant senses, a sharpening of intuition that defied explanation. Her uncanny knack for guessing the hidden images astounded even herself, hinting at latent telepathic gifts intertwined with the resurfacing memories that danced at the edges of her consciousness. A destiny far grander than she had ever dared to imagine seemed to beckon from just beyond the veil.

As they delved deeper into the game, Theodora found herself mesmerized, her focus unwavering. Each card revealed felt like a key turning in an ancient lock, the creaking of long-sealed doors echoing through the chambers of her mind. The scent of time-worn parchment and delicate lavender wafted through the air, evoking a kaleidoscope of half-remembered sensations and emotions.

Energy coursed through Theodora's fingertips as she touched each card, like static electricity but deeper, more meaningful. The images sharpened before her eyes, their details suddenly crystal clear. Each one felt like a piece of her past clicking into place, hinting at a greater destiny she was only beginning to understand. The path ahead both thrilled and terrified her, if only she dared to embrace it.

Theodora abandoned her game, driven by a restlessness she couldn't shake. She made her way through the castle corridors, sunlight streaming through stained glass windows and casting colored patterns across the stone floors. Something pulled her toward the castle doors - maybe it was the quiet after all those visions, or maybe it was just the need to clear her head.

When she stepped outside, her breath caught. Fresh snow had transformed everything into winter silence, unmarked white stretching as far as she could see. The familiar castle grounds looked different under their pristine covering, and for a moment, Theodora forgot about the weight of destiny and prophecy. Out here in the crisp air, watching her breath mist in front of her, she felt oddly at peace.

Rabbits emerged from their burrows to play in the fresh powder while birds called from snow-laden branches, drawn to Theodora's calm presence. The peaceful winter scene made her forget her troubles for a moment as she watched nature unfold around her.

Finding her usual spot on the weathered bench, Theodora relaxed among her woodland friends. Then she spotted it - a baby Unari padding through the snow toward her. Its silvery fur caught the light like moonbeams, and when their eyes met, she saw an innocence that made her heart melt. The tiny creature's gentle gaze held her transfixed.

The Unari moved with an otherworldly grace, its presence making the winter garden feel alive with magic. When Theodora extended her hand, the tiny creature padded over and leapt into her lap without hesitation, curling up against her with a contented purr.

Unari were creatures of myth and legend, renowned for their extraordinary rarity and awe-inspiring magical abilities. A perfect fusion of unicorn and Kitsuné, the baby Unari boasted a magnificent horn that caught the sun's rays and nine resplendent tails that flickered like living flames in the crisp winter air. Each tail displayed its own unique hue, creating a mesmerizing kaleidoscope of amethyst, emerald, and sapphire that danced and swirled with every movement.

History had long whispered of the Unari's supposed extinction, making their presence in Theodora's sanctuary even more astonishing and precious. Ancient tales spoke of the incredible good fortune and blessings that befell those lucky enough to encounter these mythical beings, and as Theodora cradled the baby Unari close, she couldn't help but feel truly blessed by its presence in her life.

Running her fingers through the Unari's fur, Theodora remembered the night they first met. A fierce blizzard had driven a group of travelers to seek refuge at the castle. As she led them inside, she spotted the tiny creature bundled in their arms - a baby Unari, separated from its family in the storm. The moment their eyes met, she knew she had to protect it. Something about its lost, vulnerable state called to her very soul.

Their connection deepened with each passing day. As Theodora's own abilities awakened, she began sensing the Unari's thoughts and feelings without words. Sometimes she'd catch glimpses of its memories - flashes of running with its herd through moonlit forests before the storm tore them apart. Those moments only strengthened her resolve to give it the home it had lost.

Now, as the Unari purred in her lap, Theodora felt that familiar warmth spread through her chest. More than just guardian and ward, they had become family. Their bond went beyond mere companionship - they understood each other in ways that needed no explanation. And as her powers grew stronger, so too did their silent conversations, a dance of thoughts and feelings that felt as natural as breathing.

She named the Unari "Kimi Rei," feeling it captured both its noble spirit and their unique bond. Together, they formed an inseparable pair, their destinies intertwined as they navigated the mysteries and wonders of the world around them.

Khadall, Theodora's faithful owl, watched over the enchanting garden scene. Perched on a branch, his gleaming feathers reflected his wisdom and strength. With a piercing gaze, he silently reassured Theodora of her safety within her sanctuary. His presence promised protection for her and the delightful creatures around her.

As Theodora found herself in the midst of the bustling courtyard on this particular day, she couldn't help but notice the mice scampering around her feet, their tiny bodies filled with a sense of urgency and excitement. The sudden flurry of activity piqued her curiosity, and she knew that something out of the ordinary had occurred.

Instinctively, Theodora ventured further into the garden, her attention drawn to a small, lifeless form lying on the ground. As she approached, she realized it was a mouse, its tiny body still and unresponsive. In that instant, a wave of compassion washed over Theodora, and an overwhelming desire to help the helpless creature consumed her. Little did she realize that this chance encounter would be the catalyst for an extraordinary adventure, one that would forever change the course of her life.

Theodora dropped to her knees without thinking, gathering the tiny mouse into her trembling hands. A strange warmth tingled through her fingers as she cradled it, and impossibly she felt something shift. The mouse twitched, then squeaked softly, its whiskers quivering as it drew a breath. Theodora stared, daring to breathe herself as the creature stirred to life in her palms.

Magic shimmered from her hands, wrapping around the mouse and filling it with vitality until it sat up, very much alive. Theodora gaped at her own fingers, her mind reeling. How could this be possible?

Overwhelmed by the myriad of questions that flooded her mind, Theodora realized she needed advice from the one person who had consistently supported her—Ms. Whoo. The wise owl who had comforted her through scraped knees and chased away the monsters that lurked in her nightmares.

With a sense of determination, Theodora returned to the castle and searched the lively halls and the bustling kitchen, hoping to find her trusted mentor, but to her dismay, she was nowhere to be found. Undeterred, she climbed the stairs leading to the dimly lit chambers, her urgency growing with each step.

Little did Theodora know that high above, in a hidden chamber, Ms. Whoo was making preparations for Alexandria's imminent arrival, steeling herself for the profound revelations to come.

Disappointment weighed on Theodora's heart as she emerged from Ms. Whoo's chambers empty-handed. The silence of the castle seemed to press in on Theodora, amplifying the turmoil that raged within her. She yearned for the comforting presence of her nanny, longing for the wisdom and guidance that had always been a constant in her life.

As Theodora approached her own chambers, her steps faltered, a sense of uncertainty gripped her. Taking a deep breath to steady herself, Theodora pushed open the door to her room, seeking solace in the familiarity of her surroundings.

In the wake of her parents' tragic passing nine years prior, Theodora sought solace within the pages of her journal. Initially a vessel to safeguard cherished memories and navigate the depths of grief, it transformed into a trusted confidant, a sanctuary for her thoughts steeped in both sorrow and hope.

The candlelight flickered as Theodora bent over her desk, her hand shaking slightly as she gripped the quill. Words spilled onto the parchment as she poured out her chaotic thoughts, each line helping to untangle the mess of emotions churning inside her. The familiar act of writing brought a strange sort of peace, even as she struggled to make sense of everything that had happened.

Her script, though refined, bore the marks of urgency as she penned:

'Two cycles have passed since I first began to chronicle my deepest thoughts and feelings. On this day, I have uncovered within myself extraordinary abilities, bestowed upon me by forces divine. The awakening of these arcane powers fills me with both exhilaration and trepidation. Destiny's weight bears down upon my shoulders, compelling me to embark on this uncharted journey with courage. And yet, my mind is awash with questions: What is the source of this power? Why has it chosen to manifest now, after lying dormant for so long? But most unsettling of all, why am I gripped by this overwhelming fear of losing those I hold dear?'

Theodora squeezed her eyes shut, desperate for a moment's peace. When she opened them, her heart nearly stopped - there, hovering before her desk, was a translucent figure wreathed in silvery light. An otherworldly voice drifted from it, the sound making her question everything she thought she knew. Something pulled at her, urging her toward darkness and mystery. Theodora's mind raced as she stared at the apparition, wondering if exhaustion had finally caught up with her or if this was truly happening. The line between reality and imagination blurred as she tried to make sense of what stood before her.

"Ah, I've been waitin' for ya," the Figure whispered, its words drifting through the air like tendrils of mist. "Deep within ya lies an ancient power—a legacy steeped in magic and destiny awaits ye."

The Figure's voice echoed through the chamber like distant thunder, making Theodora shiver despite herself. Though fear and wonder battled within her, she forced herself to look up, meeting the entity's shadowed gaze head-on.

The air itself seemed alive with power, and a soft light radiated from the Figure, casting an eerie glow across Theodora's face. She straightened her back, chin lifted in defiance.

"Who... who are ya? What do ya mean by 'legacy' and 'destiny'? What is this power that lies within me?" Theodora demanded, her voice unwavering despite the urgency that laced her words.

The Figure bowed its head, an act that conveyed both reverence and the wisdom of ages past. "I am but a remnant of what once was, a murmur of what is yet to come," it replied. "The very essence of an ancient magic flows through yer veins, Princess Theodora.

The power that slumbers within ya is no mere coincidence—it is yer birthright, a legacy handed down through the generations."

As the gravity of the Figure's words settled upon her, Theodora felt her breath catch in her throat.

The Figure hushed its voice and said, "There be an old prophecy that tells of a time when something rises to threaten the balance of Kandella. In that hour, those born of the Carrington bloodline shall wield powers long forgotten and shape a new destiny for our world."

As it rambled on, the Figure's image flickered and wavered, like a candle in the breeze. "Yer path intertwines with forces beyond yer understandin', but mind this: true power lies not just in magic, but in the bonds ye make and the choices ye take. Trust in yerself and those who stand beside ye, and ye can conquer any obstacle that lays ahead."

Theodora's emotions churned wildly as she tried to process what she'd witnessed. Fear and excitement warred within her, but beneath it all burned a fierce determination. She kept her eyes locked on the ethereal figure, refusing to look away even as her mind reeled from its revelations.

As the ghostly figure started to vanish, dissipating like the mist at dawn, she extended her quivering hand, clutching at nothingness.

Questions raced through her mind, demanding answers she couldn't find. The room felt different now - colder, emptier without the figure's presence. Only the gentle stirring of the tapestries in the breeze remained, a final whisper of the otherworldly encounter that had shaken her to her core. Despite her fear, something about the mysterious visitor had awakened a yearning in her soul, calling to something deep within that she was only beginning to understand.

Theodora's fingers trembled, dropping the quill to the floor. She stared at the parchment, now marred by a dark smudge. The scent of candle wax and old parchment filled the air as she slumped back, her green eyes troubled by the Figure's cryptic words. Her heart raced, mirroring her chaotic thoughts.

The Figure's message still rang in her ears, haunting her as it echoed through the oppressive quiet of her chamber. Its absence left an unsettling emptiness that seemed to press in around her.

She had just reached for her fallen quill, desperate to write down everything before it slipped away, when a soft knock at the door jolted her back to reality.

Drawing in a shaky breath, Theodora managed a quiet "Come in."

The hinges groaned as the door swung open, and there stood Ms. Whoo, her familiar presence instantly calming. "There ye are, dear child," she said warmly in her thick brogue, bringing with her the comforting scents of lavender and spice that seemed to chase away the room's heaviness.

Relief flooded through Theodora at the sight of her nanny, a beacon of stability amidst the churning uncertainties. Questions tumbled from her lips as she approached, her voice laced with concern, "Where have ya been? I searched every nook and cranny of this bloody castle. Are ya alright?"

Ms. Whoo's eyes twinkled with amusement as she patted Theodora's hand, her touch a reassuring anchor. "My dear Theodora, I'm always precisely where I need to be—even when ya can't see me," she replied, her words carrying a wisdom that extended far beyond their surface meaning.

Shadows danced on the walls as candlelight flickered across Ms. Whoo's weathered face. Her presence alone seemed to calm the chaos in Theodora's mind, like it had so many times before. Though Ms. Whoo could sense the change stirring within the young princess - an awakening that would reshape her destiny - she offered a knowing smile. Some revelations could wait for another day.

"Dinner be comin' round, Theodora," Ms. Whoo announced, her melodic lilt serving as a balm to Theodora's frayed nerves. Still reeling from the ghostly encounter, Theodora hesitated, a rare vulnerability seeping into her words, "Can ... Can I dine in me chambers tonight?"

Ms. Whoo's expression softened further, her understanding evident as she nodded. "Aye, me dear. Yer meal'll be up shortly." With a comforting squeeze of Theodora's shoulder, she glided towards the door, her movements imbued with an otherworldly grace. As she reached the threshold, Ms. Whoo paused, turning back to fix Theodora with a gaze filled with unwavering reassurance.

"Remember always," Ms. Whoo's voice resonated with profound wisdom and comfort, each word a guiding light in the darkness, "Even amidst the shadows, let yer own inner fire light the way."

Ms. Whoo's words lingered as she closed Theodora's door behind her. Walking the dim castle corridors, memories of her own past weighed on her mind. The stone walls held echoes of her childhood, when she'd watched her mother serve as nanny to the Carringtons before her.

Her mother had been something special - eyes bright with joy, always ready with a story or song. Together they'd celebrated the old ways, dancing at Saint Brigid's Day festivals and lighting Bealtaine fires under starlit skies. Simple moments that had bound them close, just as Ms. Whoo and Theodora were bound now.

But her mother had carried darker knowledge too. She'd whispered of ancient prophecies, of evil stirring in forgotten places. The magic that once flowed through Kandella was weakening, leaving gaps where shadows could seep in. Even the castle's brightest halls felt dimmer these days.

"Guard them well," her mother had said on her deathbed, entrusting her with a duty passed down through generations. "Protect the Carringtons." Some days, the weight of it felt like too much to carry—but she had never once considered walking away from what had to be done.

With each footfall echoing through the corridor, Ms. Whoo drew strength from memories of her mother's teachings. Years of rigorous training under the castle's sorcerers had honed her abilities, though the weight of duty never lessened. Her ancestors' sacrifices remained a constant reminder of what was at stake.

The deeper she went into the castle's ancient passages, the colder the air grew around her. An unsettling feeling crept up her spine as her mother's warnings seemed to whisper from the weathered stones themselves. Pushing aside her unease, Ms. Whoo steeled herself for what lay ahead. The tasks before her couldn't wait - darkness was gathering, and she needed to be prepared.

The heavy door clicked shut behind Ms. Whoo, leaving Theodora alone with her thoughts. Shadows from the flickering candles danced across stone walls that suddenly felt too close, too confining. Her pulse quickened as uncertainty crept in.

The familiar scents of her chambers - lavender, spices, and dried roses - did little to calm her racing mind. Outside her room, the sunset painted the sky in deep reds and golds as night approached.

Unable to sit still, Theodora stood at the door to her balcony, staring out at the world she'd never truly known. A rustling caught her attention, and she turned to find Khadall perched nearby, his striking figure dark against the dying light. His amber eyes held a wisdom that seemed ancient as he moved closer, gently nudging her outstretched hand.

Something about the owl's presence steadied her. With a soft, reassuring hoot, Khadall spread his wings and took flight, disappearing into the growing darkness.

Theodora leaned against the railing, watching the first stars appear in the darkening sky. The Figure's words from earlier still echoed in her mind, filled with riddles she couldn't quite grasp. Her fingers drummed against the stone as she considered what lay ahead. The thought of leaving everything she'd ever known behind made her stomach flutter with equal parts excitement and fear.

As she contemplated the mysteries that lay ahead, a knot of apprehension tightened in her chest. Could she muster the courage to face the perils that awaited her beyond the castle gates?

A soft tap at the door announced her evening meal. Theodora's attention shifted to the rich aromas drifting into her chamber as servants glided in with covered dishes. For a brief moment, the enticing smells of roasted meats and fresh bread distracted her from her worries. With a nod of gratitude, she watched as they departed, leaving her alone in the flickering glow of candlelight.

Before her sat a feast fit for royalty—a perfectly roasted chicken gleaming at the center, surrounded by vibrant vegetables that caught the candlelight. Her stomach growled, reminding her she hadn't eaten all day. The familiar routine of dining alone in her chambers provided a strange comfort amid the chaos of the day; however, tonight was different. Though the spread looked tempting, she couldn't shake the unsettling feeling that clung to her, making even the comfort of dinner feel somehow strange and distant.

The cool touch of the silverware grounded her as she eased into her seat. With the first bite of chicken, a fleeting sense of normalcy washed over her, briefly dispelling the day's chaos. However, the Figure's warnings resurfaced, overshadowing the meal with questions about her destiny. Her hunger waned as the meal felt unfamiliar and odd.

Her fork stopped halfway to her mouth, a piece of chicken dangling forgotten as she stared into space. The thought of venturing beyond everything she'd ever known terrified her, yet something deeper than fear stirred within - a quiet certainty that she had to face whatever waited ahead, no matter how daunting the path might be.

Overcome by an unexpected urge to go outside, Theodora wrapped herself in a heavy shawl and ventured onto the balcony once more. The chilly night air bit at her cheeks, and a sharp wind pulled at her clothing. Khadall's eerie hoot resonated through the night, breaking the silence that enveloped her like an enchantment.

She found her eyes irresistibly drawn to the dense forest beyond, where moonlight danced with shadows in an otherworldly rhythm—captivating yet tinged with something unsettling. Wisps of mist began to rise from the earth like ethereal fingers, wrapping slowly around the ancient stone walls of the castle and filling her senses with prickling unease.

The wind carried whispers through creaking timbers, each sound a warning of what lurked beyond the castle walls. An unseen weight pressed against her chest, both thrilling and terrifying. Though the night's mysteries beckoned, Theodora turned away, retreating to her room. She closed the door with quiet determination, choosing the safety of familiar walls over the darkness that called to her.

Seeking comfort, she settled on the couch beside the crackling fire, her gaze falling upon the well-worn book "Echoes of Elysium" that rested on the nearby table. The tale of mythical lands and forgotten magic had always captivated her imagination, and with a wistful sigh, she reached for its familiar pages, losing herself in the lyrical prose and vivid landscapes.

For an hour, she immersed herself in the world of myth and mystery, the story weaving a tapestry of wonder and adventure that quieted her restless spirit. The characters became her companions, the settings a sanctuary far removed from the confines of Donaglen Castle.

At last, Theodora closed the book, a reluctant sigh escaping her lips. The echoes of the tale lingered in her mind, whispering of untold secrets and untamed magic. With a touch of melancholy, she set the book aside, vowing to return to its enchanting pages another time. The room was quiet now, the only sounds were the soft crackle of the dying fire and the muted whisper of the wind beyond the walls.

Alone in her chamber, bereft of Khadall's comforting presence, a sense of melancholy crept over her, settling like a shadow upon her heart.

Theodora tried pushing the dark thoughts from her mind as she climbed into bed, tugging the covers close. Despite the crackling fire, a chill crept through the room, raising goosebumps on her arms. Her eyes darted to the door; she swore she locked it, but now it hung slightly ajar, revealing the night beyond.

Something moved at the corner of her vision. She held her breath, straining to hear anything in the pressing silence that filled her chambers. The quiet felt wrong, heavy in a way that made her skin crawl.

Her heart pounded furiously as she hurried to close the door. Just as her fingers grasped the doorknob, an eerie scream shattered the silence of the night, reverberating from the depths of the forest. She had never encountered such a sound before—it chilled her to the bone. With trembling hands, she slammed the door shut and secured the lock.

Though trembling, Theodora squared her shoulders, refusing to let fear master her. The silence that followed pressed in around her like a physical weight, as if warning her of unseen dangers. Every instinct screamed at her to stay safe in her room, yet she couldn't ignore the strange pull she felt toward the forest - like destiny itself was calling.

She stared out the window, her breath fogging the glass. A single droplet trickled down the pane. From somewhere in the depths of the castle, an old lullaby began to drift upward, its familiar melody both comforting and eerie as it wound through the corridors and under her door.

Seeking refuge in her bed, Theodora's eyes darted around the once comforting confines of her chamber, now distorted by an unsettling aura that clung to every corner. She burrowed beneath the covers, desperately clinging to the notion that sleep would chase away the unease that gripped her heart. As her eyelids grew heavy, surrendering to the pull of exhaustion, a shapeless figure darted past her balcony, vanishing into the night before she could comprehend its presence.

The fleeting encounter left an icy fear coiled tightly within her chest, and as unconsciousness finally overcame her resistant thoughts, a chilling realization formed in Theodora's mind: an ancient force had stirred from its slumber, and something had irrevocably altered the very fabric of her existence.

Chapter 4

"Awakening the Forgotten"

THE GRAVEL CRUNCHED BENEATH Alexandria's worn sneakers as she trudged towards the bus stop, each step a reminder of how out of place she felt. Sideways glances from passersby made her stomach churn with anxiety, the unease twisting her insides into knots. She quickened her pace, desperate to reach the comfort of familiarity.

Vivid snippets of her dreams danced at the edges of her mind, their startling clarity sending a chill down her spine. Visions of writhing flames and shadowy figures blurred the boundary between nightmare and reality. The haunting echoes of their whispers seemed to follow her, just out of reach.

The school bus emerged from the dreary morning like a vibrant lifeline. As Alexandria climbed aboard, she noticed Mr. Gresham's customary nod of acknowledgment. Grasping the metal railing, she couldn't shake the eerie sensation of being watched, as if invisible hands were closing around her neck.

"Morning," Alexandria mumbled to Mr. Gresham, her voice quivering slightly.

His gruff exterior softened momentarily. "Everything okay, kid?"

She plastered on a weak smile. "Yeah, I'm good. Thanks."

Sinking into her regular seat, Alexandria rested her head against the cool window. Try as she might, the unsettling feeling continued to seep into every crevice of her mind. Harper glanced up from her phone, instantly attuned to her friend's troubled state.

"The dream's back, isn't it? You're acting weird," Harper remarked, scrutinizing Alexandria as she leaned closer.

Alexandria fidgeted with a frayed thread on her sweater, avoiding eye contact. "What dream?" she asked.

Harper's eyes widened, realizing her mistake. She quickly covered with a comforting grin. "You know, the usual - magic, other worlds, ancient prophecies. Totally normal stuff."

Rolling her eyes, Alexandria retorted, "Yeah, because dreaming about mythical beings and cosmic destinies is so ordinary."

Harper laughed uneasily, scooting nearer. "Alright, you got me. I might've heard you sleep-talking when I crashed at your place last weekend."

A wave of relief washed over Alexandria, grateful for Harper's steadfast support. "I just don't get why I keep having these dreams," she confessed.

Harper took Alexandria's hand, giving it a gentle squeeze. "Dreams can be meaningful, Lex. Maybe there's something inside you trying to break through."

A faint smile tugged at the corners of Alexandria's mouth. Sighing, she gazed out at the rain-spattered landscape. "This time felt different, more real than ever. I can't shake this feeling that something bad is coming."

Concern etched Harper's features, but she offered a reassuring pat on Alexandria's arm. "Hey, we've been best friends forever. I know this is scary, but I also know you've got the strength to handle whatever comes your way."

Blinking back tears, Alexandria nodded. She wanted to trust in her own resilience, to believe these dreams were nothing more than the workings of a hyperactive subconscious. Yet, a persistent whisper deep within hinted otherwise.

Were these visions revealing a hidden part of herself? A truth she had long suppressed?

Lost in their conversation, Alexandria noticed the shadows outside taking on menacing forms, as if something from her worst nightmares was trying to break through into reality. A shiver ran down her spine as the bus jerked and shook, sending a chill through her body. Meanwhile, Mr. Gresham grumbled curses while struggling to control the unruly steering wheel.

Without warning, shadows converged towards the bus—their forms solid enough to chill Alexandria's bones. Her heart raced in her chest, a dread building in the pit of her stomach. She glanced around the bus, but everyone seemed oblivious to the encroaching darkness. The air inside grew colder, a tangible fear settling over her like a suffocating blanket.

Harper turned to Alexandria, concern etched on her face. "What's wrong?" she asked, following Alexandria's gaze out the window.

"Can't you see them?" Alexandria asked, her voice barely above a whisper.

Harper's eyes searched the trees as she glanced out the window. "See who, Alex?" she asked.

The shadows crept closer, their malevolent presence seeping into the bus like a poison. Alexandria felt a surge of panic rising within her, but she forced herself to stay calm. There was something familiar about these shadows, a resonance deep within her that stirred memories she couldn't quite grasp.

As they drew closer, their dark tendrils reached out as if to ensnare her in their grasp. But she refused to cower before them.

Malachai's piercing gaze bore into Alexandria's soul. "I am Malachai," he snarled, his voice dripping with venom. "Your time has run out, Princess. The ancient power flowing through your blood is ours for the taking."

Alexandria stared at him, her mind reeling. Princess? Ancient power? She couldn't make sense of his cryptic words. The absurdity of being called a princess, let alone one with magical abilities, left her questioning her sanity.

"Listen, I don't know what you're talking about," Alexandria shot back, mustering every ounce of courage she had. "I'm no princess, and I sure don't have any special powers. Just leave us alone."

To her surprise, Malachai let out a grating laugh that sent shivers down her spine. "Oh, how naïve you are, Alexandria Carrington," he taunted, his tone laced with contempt. "Denying the truth won't save you now." His shadowy minions pressed closer, their twisted forms and glowing eyes filling the air with a suffocating darkness.

Alexandria found herself cornered, the sinister figures closing in from all sides. As they lunged forward, their razor-sharp claws outstretched, a primal instinct took over. Without understanding how, she unleashed a burst of blinding light that sent the creatures reeling back, their agonized shrieks piercing the air.

Stunned by the sudden display of power emanating from her own body, Alexandria whirled around to face Harper. "Did you see that? What the hell just happened?"

But with her eyes glued to her phone screen, Harper, oblivious to the supernatural drama unfolding mere inches away, absorbed herself in her own world. The realization that she was facing this terrifying ordeal alone sent a wave of icy fear through Alexandria's veins.

As the initial shock subsided, a flicker of determination ignited within her. She couldn't count on anyone else to save her from this nightmarish situation. Steeling herself, Alexandria took a deep breath and focused on the strange, tingling sensation that danced at her fingertips. Whatever this newfound power was, she knew it was her only hope of survival.

Brushing aside the nagging doubts that threatened to undermine her resolve, Alexandria closed her eyes and delved deep within herself, latching onto the pulsing strands of power that thrummed just beneath the surface. It was as if a hidden gateway had been unlocked, granting her access to an ancient, primal force that demanded to be acknowledged.

The shadows pressed forward once more, their insidious whispers designed to unnerve her. Alexandria fought back the rising tide of fear, refusing to let it consume her.

Calling upon the untapped wellspring of magic that now flowed through her, Alexandria summoned forth a surge of energy that wrapped around her like a shimmering shield, driving back the dark shadows.

Malachai unleashed a roar of rage as his minions cowered before the blinding brilliance that poured from Alexandria. The shadowy entities writhed and shrieked, their forms wavering as if the sheer intensity of her magical aura was too much for them to bear. For a fleeting instant, light, and darkness clashed, the very air crackling with the raw power of their confrontation.

Every instinct screamed at her to flee, to escape while she still could. But deep down, Alexandria knew that she had the strength to confront whatever trials lay ahead. The murmurs of uncertainty faded into the background as she embraced the newfound power that surged through every fiber of her being.

The creatures let out agonized wails, their misshapen bodies contorting in the face of the searing radiance before they dissolved into tendrils of smoke that scattered on the wind.

Squaring her shoulders, Alexandria confronted Malachai, her voice ringing out with unwavering conviction. "You and your shadows can keep coming, but I won't let you threaten the people I love. Whatever twisted scheme you've got planned, I'm going to stand in your way."

Malachai's eyes flashed with contained fury, the malice within them smoldering even as his form appeared to flicker at the edges. "You may have scratched the surface of your power, Princess, but you haven't got a clue about what you're truly capable of," he spat, a tinge of vexation coloring his tone.

Alexandria met Malachai's piercing stare unflinchingly, the power still surging through her veins imbuing her with newfound courage. "I might not have all the answers about who I am or what I can do, but that won't stop me from protecting the ones I care about," she declared, surprised by the steely edge in her own voice.

Malachai's face contorted into a vicious sneer as he lifted a hand, wisps of dark energy swirling around his fingertips. "You'll live to regret crossing me, Alexandria Carrington. One way or another, the shadows will have you," he snarled, his words dripping with icy malevolence.

As he spoke, his form began to unravel until only a pair of baleful, glowing eyes remained, gradually fading from view. Alexandria slumped back into her seat, a wave of relief and fatigue crashing over her.

Amid the other students on the bus, Alexandria found herself enveloped in a cacophony of chatter and laughter, a poignant contrast to the tranquility she craved. Nostalgia tugged at her heart, whispering tales of a simpler time when she measured worries in poor grades and relationship drama, now mere echoes in the recesses of her mind.

Observing her peers engrossed in their digital worlds, she felt a sudden disconnect, as if she had outgrown the very fabric of familiarity that once bound them together. A swell of conflicting emotions surged within her, mingling sweetness with sorrow as she gazed out the window, feeling the weight of her altered existence settling like a heavy cloak upon her shoulders.

Clutching her backpack like a lifeline, Alexandria watched as the bus left the shadowy forest behind. The magic that had moments ago pulsed through her was subsiding, leaving a chilling wake of awe and apprehension. Her classmates remained ignorant of the otherworldly battle that had just taken place, and Alexandria was determined to keep it that way.

Noticing Harper's worried gaze fixed upon her, Alexandria forced a faint smile. "Just tired," she mumbled, praying her friend wouldn't pick up on the slight quaver in her voice.

As the bus rolled to a stop in front of Shay High, Alexandria hugged her arms close, the weight of her secret pressing to the surface. Harper's hand found hers, squeezing gently as if trying to siphon away some of the burden. Alexandria managed a stiff nod, her gaze distant and unfocused. Inside, a tempest of emotions swirled, fragments of her inner world that only she could piece together.

Navigating the throngs of students, they made their way to the familiar red brick facade. Near the entrance, a cluster of seniors in black leather jackets emblazoned with a silver wolf logo caught Alexandria's eye. The Pack, in all their swaggering glory.

Blake Harrison, their ringleader, flashed her a cocky grin as they passed. "Looking good, Alex," he called out, his cronies snickering like hyenas.

Alexandria pointedly ignored him, her pace quickening. Harper linked arms with her, murmuring, "Just keep walking. They aren't worth your time."

Inside, the scent of chalk and musty textbooks wrapped around Alexandria like a comforting blanket. The mundane rhythm of slamming lockers and hurried footsteps grounded her, a reminder that life marched on, oblivious to the supernatural chaos that had invaded her world.

Someone pushed Alexandria unexpectedly, causing her to slam into her locker, the cold metal stinging her skin. She spun around to see Robert, the star quarterback, towering over her with a sneer.

"Watch where you're going, your highness," he mocked, his teammates guffawing at the jab.

Harper stepped forward, her eyes flashing. "Back off, Robert. Why don't you throw a ball around and leave her alone?"

Robert's gaze narrowed, but he shrugged and sauntered off, his posse trailing behind him.

"Idiots," Harper muttered. "You okay, Alex?"

Alexandria nodded, the sting of Robert's words fading. "Yeah, thanks for having my back."

Harper bumped her shoulder playfully. "That's what best friends are for. Besides, they're all bark and no bite."

Drawing in a steadying breath, Alexandria met Harper's gaze, a flicker of determination sparking to life. "You know what? I'm done letting them get to me. They can take their remarks and shove it."

A grin spread across Harper's face. "Damn straight. That's my girl."

As Alexandria turned to her locker, her hands shook slightly as she fumbled with the combination, the weight of Robert's malicious stare still prickling her skin. But she refused to let it shake her newfound resolve. She had faced down literal shadows - a bunch of high school bullies were nothing in comparison.

The shrill ring of the first bell echoed through the halls as Alexandria gathered her textbooks, slamming her locker shut with a satisfying clang. Out of the corner of her eye, she spotted Robert and his lackeys strutting towards the gym, their screeching laughter grating on her nerves. The memory of their earlier confrontation burned in her mind, igniting a fierce determination within her.

"I'm not gonna be their punching bag anymore." Alexandria muttered under her breath, her grip tightening on her books.

As she turned to head to class, her gaze fell upon the garbage can near the gym entrance. As if guided by an invisible force, the can toppled over directly in Robert's path. He stumbled, his arms flailing comically as he face-planted onto the linoleum floor with a resounding thud.

The hallway erupted in a chorus of laughter and cheers, the sound bouncing off the walls and lockers. Students whipped out their phones, eagerly capturing the moment for posterity. Alexandria couldn't help but let out a shocked gasp, her eyes wide as she watched Robert scramble to his feet, his face beet-red with humiliation and anger.

As the laughter continued to swell, Alexandria hurried down the hallway, her mind reeling. Had she somehow caused that garbage can to fall? Was this connected to the strange powers that had manifested on the bus? The uncertainty gnawed at her, mingling with the whispers and snickers that trailed in her wake.

Slipping into her first-period classroom, Alexandria made a bee-line for her usual seat by the window. Harper plopped down beside her, her eyes alight with curiosity.

"Okay, spill. What was that all about?" Harper demanded in a hushed whisper.

Alexandria fidgeted with her pen, avoiding her friend's probing gaze. "I have no idea," she admitted.

As Mrs. Larkin launched into her lesson on ancient civilizations, Alexandria found herself adrift in a sea of her own thoughts. The droning lecture faded into background noise as she grappled with the implications of her newfound abilities. Should she embrace these powers, harness them to stand up to the bullies who had tormented her for so long? Or should she bury them deep, keep them hidden like a shameful secret?

The minutes ticked by at an agonizing pace, each second weighing heavily on Alexandria's mind. The prospect of being different, of standing out in a sea of judgmental peers, tied her stomach in knots. Yet, beneath the fear, a flicker of excitement stirred within her. The notion that she might possess something extraordinary, something that set her apart, was as thrilling as it was terrifying.

When the bell finally rang, signaling the end of class, Alexandria gathered her things with a mix of relief and trepidation. As she and Harper filed out of the room, the lingering unease clung to her like a second skin, a constant reminder of the strange new world she had stumbled into.

Later at lunchtime, Alexandria, and Harper settled into their usual spot in the bustling cafeteria. The air was thick with the scent of fried food and the chatter of students. Alexandria picked at her orange chicken, her appetite dulled by the morning's events.

"I think something weird is happening to me," she confided, her voice barely audible over the noise.

Harper leaned in, eyebrows raised. "Like the thing with Robert earlier?"

Alexandria nodded, pushing her food around the plate. "Yeah. These... abilities, or whatever they are. I need to figure out what's going on."

"Maybe you should talk to your parents about it," Harper suggested.

Alexandria frowned, thinking of her family's secretive nature. Could their past hold answers to her current predicament? "You might be right," she conceded, setting down her fork.

The rest of the school day passed in a haze. After the final bell, Alexandria, and Harper headed to swim practice, a routine that had become a welcome constant since freshman year.

"Ready to dominate those laps?" Harper grinned, her competitive streak shining through.

Alexandria managed a smile, grateful for the distraction. As they swam, she pushed herself harder than usual, focusing on each stroke and breath to keep her troubled thoughts at bay.

The rhythmic splashing filled the pool as they powered through their laps. Despite the burn in her muscles, She found comfort in the familiar motions. Harper's presence in the next lane was a reassuring reminder that she wasn't alone in all this.

As they neared the end of practice, Alexandria gasped for air, giving one final push. She touched the wall, a sense of accomplishment washing over her as she caught her breath.

Harper popped up beside her, flashing a triumphant smile. "We crushed it today!"

Alexandria chuckled, feeling some of the day's tension melt away. "Yeah, we did. Thanks for always pushing me."

They hauled themselves out of the pool, muscles aching but minds clearer. As they grabbed their towels, Harper turned to Alexandria. "So, have you decided how you're going to bring this up with your parents?"

Alexandria nodded, a determined look crossing her face. "I'll talk to them at dinner tonight. It's time to get some answers."

Changing the subject, Harper asked, "So, any big plans this weekend?"

"Mom wants to go shopping for my party stuff," Alexandria replied with a shrug.

Harper's eyes lit up. "Oh yeah, the sweet sixteen! It's going to be epic."

Alexandria playfully shoved her friend. "Oh, stop. You better show up, by the way."

"As if I'd miss it," Harper scoffed. "Wild horses couldn't keep me away."

Their laughter echoed through the locker room as they gathered their things. As they stepped outside, the late afternoon sun cast a warm glow over the school grounds. A group of students hung out near the old oak tree, their voices carrying on the breeze.

Harper's mom pulled up, honking the horn. "That's my ride," Harper said, giving Alexandria a quick hug. "Text me later, okay?"

As Harper's car drove off, Alexandria found a nearby bench and sat down, tilting her face towards the sun. The sounds of kids playing in a nearby park and a distant lawnmower created a peaceful backdrop. For a moment, she let herself enjoy the calm before facing whatever challenges lay ahead.

The peaceful moment shattered as Diana's car pulled up. Alexandria snatched her backpack and slid into the passenger seat, immediately sensing the tension in her mother's posture.

"Everything okay?" Alexandria asked, eyeing Diana's white-knuckled grip on the steering wheel.

Diana forced a smile that didn't reach her eyes. "Just work stress. How was your day?"

"Weird," Alexandria replied, hesitating. "Really weird, actually."

As they merged into traffic, Diana glanced over. "Weird how?"

Alexandria took a deep breath. "I think... something's changed in me."

Diana's knuckles tightened further, her face paling. "What kind of change?"

Struggling to find the right words, Alexandria stared out the window. "It's hard to explain. On the bus, I felt this... power. Like I could do things I shouldn't be able to."

Diana's eyes widened before snapping back to the road. "What do you mean by power?"

"I don't know," Alexandria sighed, frustration creeping into her voice. "There was this darkness, and I fought it off somehow. It doesn't make any sense."

A flicker of recognition crossed Diana's face before she masked it with concern. As they turned onto their street, she took a shaky breath.

"Alexandria, there's something you need to know about where we come from." She parked in the driveway and turned to face the young girl. "We're not from this world. There's another realm called Kandella."

She stared at her, searching for any sign of a joke. Finding none, her mind reeled. Magic? Other worlds? It sounded insane, yet Diana's grave expression left no room for doubt.

As the words sank in, fragments of memories began to resurface—strange lights, whispered secrets, symbols that seemed to glow. Childhood imaginings suddenly felt real, tangible.

"There's more," Diana said.

Alexandria's heart raced. "What else?"

"You're not just from Kandella. You're also a princess."

Alexandria felt the blood drain from her face. "What? Why didn't you tell me?"

"Ms. Whoo erased your memories to protect you," Diana said. "The Shadow Walkers attacked Donaglen Castle and took your real parents."

"My parents?" Alexandria's voice cracked.

"Kidnapped when you and your sister were small," Diana said, her own voice shaking. "Ms. Whoo hid your identities from Lord Valendor.

"She loved you as her own," Diana added, "carrying the burden of your past alone."

A name floated to the surface of Alexandria's mind. "Theodora?"

Diana nodded. "Your twin. To keep you both safe, we separated you. She stayed with Ms. Whoo in Donaglen, and we brought you here."

Alexandria's breath caught as the revelation hit her - she had a twin sister. The knowledge struck something deep within her, filling an emptiness she'd never fully recognized before. A storm of emotions crashed through her: rage at being kept in the dark, betrayal that cut to her core, yet underneath it all flickered a desperate spark of hope.

Then, like a photograph snapping into focus, a memory surfaced - a girl with brilliant red hair and eyes identical to her own staring back at her. Theodora. The name echoed in her mind as an inexplicable sense of completeness washed over her, like finding a crucial piece of herself she never knew was missing.

"Why did you lie?" Alex's voice cracked, tears welling up. "How could you and Elmer pretend to be my parents all this time?"

Diana's eyes filled with remorse. "We thought we were protecting you, giving you a chance at a normal life away from Valendor's reach."

"A normal life built on lies!" Alex shot back, her hands clenched into fists.

"I know it's hard to understand," Diana said, her own eyes glistening. "Ms. Whoo believed it was the best way to keep you and Theodora safe."

Alex shook her head, overwhelmed by the weight of the revelations. "I don't know how to process any of this. How am I supposed to trust you now?"

Diana reached out hesitantly, her hand shaking. "Please, Alex. Everything we did was to protect you. We love you like our own."

Alex stumbled out of the car, her legs shaky beneath her. The words echoed in her mind - sister, princess - like fragments of a half-remembered dream. They should have felt foreign, ridiculous even, but something deep within her resonated with an uncomfortable certainty. These weren't just words. They were who she was.

She made her way towards the house, tears streaming down her face as she struggled to catch her breath. The damp grass squelched beneath her feet, grounding her in the moment. Her emotions were a tangled mess—anger, confusion and a strange sense of clarity. All those years of feeling like she didn't quite fit in now made perfect sense.

Diana's final words echoed in her mind: "Your powers are awakening. It's time to face your destiny. Kandella needs you."

Alexandria stumbled through the front door, her mind a whirlwind of confusion. Diana followed close behind, steadying her with a gentle touch.

"I know this is a lot to take in," Diana said, guiding Alexandria to the living room. "But you need to understand who you really are."

Alexandria collapsed onto the couch, her legs giving way. She stared at her hands, struggling to reconcile the ordinary girl she thought she was with the princess Diana claimed her to be.

"Tell me about Kandella," Alexandria whispered.

Diana sat beside her, a wistful smile on her face. "Kandella is a place of wonder and magic. There are vast forests, glittering lakes, and towering castles. The flowers chime in the breeze, and trees bloom with ever-changing colors. Birds sing melodies while butterflies dance through the air."

As she spoke, Alexandria felt a strange longing for this place she'd never known. She could almost smell wildflowers and pine, as if Kandella was calling to her.

"Kandella is a land where the veil between the mortal world and the mystical is thin," Diana continued. "Fairies laugh in sunlit glades, druids cast spells in ancient groves, and unicorns graze in glowing meadows."

Alexandria closed her eyes, picturing emerald forests whispering secrets of old, cascading waterfalls shimmering with ethereal light, and mountains cradling the heavens, crowned with swirling mists. The image painted by Diana's words felt like a dream, yet somehow familiar.

Her heart raced as she absorbed Diana's words, painting a vivid picture of her birthplace. The room fell silent, broken only by the ticking clock. Alexandria took a deep breath and met Diana's eyes, bracing herself for more.

"What happened to my parents?"

Diana's expression darkened. "Lord Valendor took them. He wanted the kingdom for himself and he also controls the Shadow Walkers."

Alexandria's chest tightened with a mix of anger and fear for her parents and the sister she couldn't remember.

A soft sound caught her attention. She looked up to see Aris, her feline guardian, padding towards her. The cat's presence was oddly comforting.

Aris moved with quiet grace, her black coat gleaming. Each step she took was deliberate and purposeful, a silent dance that exuded unwavering loyalty. She jumped onto the couch and curled up next to Alexandria, purring softly. Her golden eyes locked onto Alexandria's gaze, conveying a deep understanding. Despite her turmoil, Alexandria felt grounded by Aris's warmth.

Diana watched them with a smile, stroking Aris's fur. "Aris has been with you since you were born," she said. "She'll guide and protect you when you return to Kandella."

Alexandria clenched her fists, her voice surprisingly steady. "I have to find Theodora. And we need to rescue my parents and Kandella from Lord Valendor."

Diana's eyes softened. "Your connection with Theodora runs deeper than any spell. It'll lead you back to each other."

A mix of fear and determination welled up in Alexandria. The image of her fiery-haired twin burned bright—a beacon of hope amidst the chaos.

"Be careful," Diana cautioned. Your powers are still unfamiliar to you. The Shadow Walkers will stop at nothing."

Alexandria nodded, jaw set. The road ahead was treacherous, but for the first time, she felt a sense of purpose stirring within her.

Diana squeezed her hand before heading to the kitchen. As she left, a tiny silver bell flower slipped from her hair, landing silently on the carpet. Its petals glimmered for a moment, then vanished—as if signaling the upheaval to come.

Left alone with her thoughts, Alexandria stroked Aris, finding comfort in the cat's presence as she mulled over her newfound sister and the daunting task ahead.

Chapter 5

"Before Night Takes Her"

I N THE DIM CHAMBER Theodora jolted awake, her heart pounding as fragments of a nightmare clung to her consciousness. Shadowy figures scaling fortress walls, her parents' desperate cries - the images felt too real, too vivid. She sat up, clutching the silk sheets as she tried to steady her breathing.

The imminent danger outside the palace walls weighed heavily on her mind. Throwing off the covers, Theodora rose and padded across the cool stone floor to the balcony. She swung open the wooden doors, stepping out into the crisp morning air.

Dawn's light bathed Primlow in a soft golden glow, highlighting the snow-dusted landscape below. Theodora's eyes swept over the familiar scene - distant mountains, glistening village rooftops, the winding river. It was beautiful, but even this couldn't erase the lingering unease from her dream.

Her gaze drifted to the fortress walls. For a moment, she could almost hear the phantom echoes of battle - clashing steel, desperate shouts. Though hazy, she felt a profound connection to these very real memories, as if they were remnants of a past she couldn't quite grasp.

Theodora shivered, wrapping her arms around herself against the chill. "I must be strong," she whispered, her breath visible in the air. "For Kandella, for my family."

Theodora lingered on the balcony, allowing the serene beauty of the kingdom to fortify her resolve. From her vantage point, she watched the village come to life. Women at their wash tubs, children chasing chickens, men chopping firewood. The familiar bustle should have been comforting, but she couldn't shake the feeling that danger lurked just out of sight.

She retreated to her chamber to prepare for the day. Her archery lesson with Cornelius awaited. As she fastened her leather arm-guards, her hands trembled slightly. The dream's effects lingered, but she pushed the thoughts aside, focusing on the training ahead.

She made her way to the kitchen, hoping a quick bite would settle her nerves. The bustle and aromas enveloped her as she entered - fresh bread, sizzling bacon, and strong coffee. Miss Brigit, the chef's assistant, greeted her with a warm smile.

"Here you go, deary," she said, offering a steaming bowl. "A hearty breakfast to fuel your day."

Theodora accepted gratefully, settling at the oak table. As she ate her honey-sweetened porridge and fresh berries, the familiar flavors grounded her, easing the remnants of her troubled night. The kitchen's rhythms - the chopping, sizzling, and Miss Brigit's cheerful humming - added to her sense of comfort.

She moved with surprising grace despite her plump figure, her flushed cheeks a testament to both the ovens' heat and her passion for cooking. Each step caused her silver curls to bounce, creating a halo around her face. A smile tugged at Theodora's lips as she admired Miss Brigit's vibrant dress, its swirling patterns dancing in harmony with her movements. The flour-and-spice-stained apron spoke volumes of her dedication to nourishing the castle's inhabitants.

Finishing her meal, Theodora exchanged a smile with Miss Brigit before heading out. The simple breakfast had done its work, providing both nourishment and a much-needed sense of normalcy. She felt ready to face whatever challenges the day might bring.

Theodora shivered as she stepped into the frosty morning air, her breath clouding in front of her. The sky painted itself in soft hues of purple and pink, heralding the dawn. Snow crunched underfoot as she made her way to the training field, her footprints the only blemish on the pristine white blanket.

Theodora paused, tilting her head back to feel the snowflakes caress her skin. As they melted on her lashes, tiny droplets sparkled like liquid diamonds.

Cornelius stood in the distance, a lone figure silhouetted against the rising sun. His bow was at the ready, a familiar sight that calmed Theodora's nerves. With determined steps, she trudged through the snow-covered field, eager to begin their practice.

Without a word, Cornelius passed her the bow, a silent exchange that spoke volumes in its familiarity. As she notched an arrow and raised the weapon, muscle memory took over like an old friend guiding her hand. She exhaled slowly, focusing on the distant target.

The arrow sliced through the air with precision, but landed just shy of its mark. Theodora frowned, determined to improve with each shot.

"Let's work on that accuracy today," Cornelius said, his voice gruff but encouraging.

Arrow after arrow, Theodora honed her skills. Beads of sweat glistened on her forehead as she tirelessly aimed and released, each moment a testament to her unwavering resolve to excel.

"Good stance, lass. Just need to fine-tune that aim," Cornelius noted.

As evening approached, fatigue set in. Theodora summoned every fiber of strength within her for one final shot. With steely focus and unwavering determination, she drew back the string, feeling time slow to a crawl around her.

A hush fell as the arrow whistled through the air, striking dead center. Cornelius gasped, a proud smile tugging at his features. "A perfect bullseye! Ya done well, Princess," he exclaimed.

Pride swelled in Theodora's chest. "I couldn't 'ave done it without ya." she grinned.

A distant rumble interrupted their celebration. The ground trembled beneath them, sending warning signals through the air. They quickly gathered their equipment and hurried towards the castle.

Hail pelted the courtyard as they entered. Lightning flashed, casting eerie shadows. Theodora's heart raced, both from exertion and growing unease.

The storm raged outside as Theodora hurried to her chambers, a blinding flash illuminating her path followed by thunderous rumblings echoing through the corridors. Pausing to take a deep breath, she entered her room, where firelight cast long shadows on the walls. As she fastened her gown and turned toward the window, the lightning filled the space with eerie shapes, intensifying the storm and shaking the castle's foundation.

A knock startled her. Chloe entered, eyes lowered. "Evening, Miss. You're needed in the library."

"Thank ye kindly, Chloe. I'll be down in a jiffy." Theodora replied. The maid curtsied and left.

Theodora took a deep breath, steeling herself for whatever awaited her.

Ms. Whoo hunched over an ancient tome in the library, the musty scent of old parchment filling her nostrils. Her eyes lit up as she found the Memory Reversal spell. "Well now, here it is," she whispered, her excitement tinged with apprehension.

Ms. Whoo's eyes narrowed as she read the intricate incantations and delicate instructions needed to perform the spell. Time was slipping away—only seven days remained.

Her hands trembled as they hovered near an ivory box. Inside lay a silver bracelet adorned with an Opalite crystal, a relic of sisterhood between Theodora and Alexandria. She contemplated its new purpose as a shield against Lord Valendor when Theodora silently entered the room.

"What's in the box?" Theodora asked, peering curiously.

Ms. Whoo quickly shut the lid. "Ah, there ya are! I've been waitin' for ya."

"Chloe said you needed me?"

"Aye, thank ye fer comin'. There's important matters we need to discuss."

Theodora nodded. "I've been meanin' to talk to ya about some things meself."

Concern flashed across Ms. Whoo's face. "What's troublin' ya, lass? Has somethin' happened?"

Theodora recounted the event the day before involving the small mouse and confessed to wielding powers beyond comprehension.

She felt a sense of discord within her, like a whispered secret seeking light.

"No more beatin' around the bush," Theodora said. "I want the truth, now."

Ms. Whoo's expression softened. "And ye shall have it, dear. But ye might want to sit for this."

As they settled, Ms. Whoo took a deep breath. "Ah, lassie," she said, "they kept truths about yer past from ya fer far too long." She spoke with steady conviction, making sure the weight of her words sank in. "These hidden realities will lead ya down uncharted paths and awaken dormant powers within ya."

Ms. Whoo explained the inherent connection between Theodora's lineage and her abilities. "The magic that flows through yer veins and the memories lingering on the outskirts of yer mind - they're more than mere coincidence," she revealed. "Yer past and present are interconnected in ways ya can't even begin ta imagine."

As the weight of Ms. Whoo's revelation settled upon Theodora, a tempest of emotions stirred within her. Her hands trembled as she met her nanny's gaze, her eyes reflecting a mixture of astonishment and wonder. Each breath felt like a battle against the truth that now consumed her, unraveling the very fabric of her existence.

The library walls seemed to close in, crackling with an electric energy that pulsed through the air. Questions flooded her mind, unlocking hidden memories and unfurling unforeseen possibilities that danced at the edges of her consciousness.

A softness crept into Ms. Whoo's expression as she observed the young princess, noting the furrow of her brow as she grappled with this newfound knowledge. The weight of truth hung between them, mingling with the undercurrent of confusion and fear that flickered across Theodora's features.

Despite her best efforts, Theodora battled against a tide of disbelief. While she had always sensed an innate difference within herself, the reality revealed now eclipsed even her most extravagant fantasies. In this moment, the significance of her title as princess paled compared to the enormity of what she had just learned.

As the realization of her true identity and latent powers sank in, Theodora felt a surge of both excitement and trepidation. The world she thought she knew had expanded, revealing hidden depths and untold possibilities.

"Listen closely, lass, this might be hard for ya to wrap yer head around, but it was all done to keep ya safe and hidden." Ms. Whoo explained, her voice gentle yet firm.

"Safe? From whom, exactly?" Theodora asked, her eyes a tempest of alarm and curiosity.

"Ah, there's a wicked force out there, Theodora. A devilish creature that seeks control over all. Calls himself Lord Valendor."

Theodora's brows furrowed in confusion. "What does he be wantin' with me?"

"He's after ya powers, lass," Ms. Whoo replied. She explained how the magic coursing through Theodora's veins, a gift passed down from her ancestors, binds her to the fate of Kandella and can change the tide in their battle against evil. "I cast a spell to hide yer true identity and stop them from findin' ya," she continued. "I blocked yer memories and hid ya right under their noses." Urgency tinged her voice as she added, "But now, as yer 16th birthday approaches, time is runnin' out. It's time for ya to embrace yer true self."

Ms. Whoo's words settled on her shoulders. Disbelief, apprehension and newfound resolve whirled through her mind. Gripping the velvet couch's armrest, she searched her familiar eyes for deceit but found only unwavering honesty.

"I don't know if I'm strong enough fer this," Theodora whispered, her hands shaking.

Ms. Whoo squeezed her hands reassuringly. "Ye're stronger than ye know, lass. What happened in the courtyard was just the beginnin'."

Their conversation about Theodora's powers ended abruptly when the library door burst open. Nala, one of the newer servants, stumbled in, breathless and pale with fear. She gripped the doorframe, her hands trembling as she fought to catch her breath.

"Beggin' yer pardon ma'am," she gasped, "but I've an urgent confession!"

Ms. Whoo stood, alarmed. "Can't this wait?"

"No ma'am, It can't. 'Tis about the girls."

"Speak up then," Ms. Whoo commanded.

"Ya see, I was under Lord Valendor's cursed spell," She began, wringing her hands. "He made me do his dirty work. He sent me here ta find out if the prophecy was true. Ta see if the girls lived."

"This mornin' I heard yer chatter confirm their existence," she continued. "I passed the information on to him, and it immediately broke the spell he had over me. When I realized what I'd done, I knew I had to warn ya!"

"Warn us of what?" Theodora demanded.

"The Shadow Walkers, miss! He's sendin' them tonight ta destroy ya!" she cried, tears streaming down her face.

Ms. Whoo's eyes hardened. "We must act now. Theodora, go to yer room and pack what ye can carry. I'll be there soon."

With her heart pounding, Theodora hurried from the room, the weight of her destiny pressing upon her.

Theodora raced up the winding stone staircase, her fiery locks bouncing behind her. Her heart pounded in her chest as she climbed, each step taking her deeper into the ancient castle. The flickering torchlight cast eerie shadows that seemed to reach for her like ghostly fingers.

As she ascended higher, anxiety gnawed at her insides. This once-sanctuary now felt like a treacherous battleground where uncertainty loomed at every turn. Her breath came in quick gasps clutched at the cold stone walls for support.

Finally, she reached her room - a place that had once brought her comfort but now felt more like a trap. Every creak of the floorboards echoed through the hollow space, making her skin crawl with fear. The tapestries rustled in the draft, as if whispering long-forgotten secrets that threatened to unravel her very being.

She winced at every sound, hyper-aware of potential dangers that lurked in the shadows. With trembling fingers, she lit a single candle, casting a flickering light across the room. Its warm glow provided little solace against the encroaching darkness.

A sudden gust of wind blew through an open window, making the candle flame dance. Theodora's pulse raced as she hurried towards her bed, each heartbeat thundering in her ears. As she grasped the bedpost for support, the room began to swirl around her - a disorienting sensation that left her feeling dizzy and help-less.

Just when she thought she might pass out from fear or exhaustion, something inside her snapped. A surge of energy coursed through her veins like molten fire, awakening something primal and powerful within. With renewed determination, she took a deep breath and gazed out into the night sky through the open window.

The wind murmured, bringing with it a hint of danger that made her skin tingle. Every breeze seems to hint at unseen threats hiding in the darkness. As Theodora's determination faltered, a shiver ran down her spine, with the candlelight flickering and creating long shadows that appeared to move with a menacing purpose. The weight of her impending destiny settled upon her like a leaden cloak, suffocating the spark of determination that had flared within her moments ago.

The castle walls, once a familiar bastion of safety, now loomed ominously around her, their ancient stones whispering foreboding secrets that made her heart race with fear. Uncertainty gripped her like icy claws, and she trembled at the thought of what awaited her beyond those looming gates. The truth she sought suddenly felt like a treacherous labyrinth, with unseen dangers lurking in its dark corners, ready to ensnare her in their malevolent embrace.

In the library's hushed stillness, Ms. Whoo paced, awaiting Cornelius. She paused at a dusty chest, kneeling to extract items into a small pouch before securing it again.

Crossing back to the mahogany desk, she selected a faded sheet of paper and plucked up an old-fashioned ink pen from the cobalt-blue inkwell. With swift strokes, she penned a few quick messages before folding and storing one of them in the velvet pouch.

Moments later, the library door creaked open. "Ah, there ye are," Ms. Whoo said. "Close the door, would ya?"

"Ya called for me?" Cornelius asked.

"Aye. Is Finnegan O'Leary still lingerin' about?" Ms. Whoo's eyes darted to the window. She clung to the hope that the druid, a living link to her past, would remember their shared history.

"I reckon he's at O'Connor's pub." Cornelius replied, sensing the tension.

Ms. Whoo whispered, "Shadow Walkers are comin' tonight—Lord Valendor knows about the girls. Take this message, quietly now."

Cornelius nodded, taking the note and leaving swiftly.

Alone, Ms. Whoo exhaled, her gaze falling onto the ivory box. As she picked it up, she traced its carvings, each line a reminder of her own past. Gathering the box and the blue pouch, she strode through the empty corridors, her steps echoing.

A shudder stopped her. "Theodora," she murmured, worry creasing her brow.

In her room, Theodora sat rigid on her bed, grappling with her newly revealed identity. Fear pulsed through her veins as questions raced through her mind. How could everything she had ever known crumble so quickly? Would her life ever be the same? Cold tendrils of uncertainty wrapped around her hammering heart.

Yet, beneath the terror threatening to overwhelm her, a small ember of curiosity flickered to life. The strange power she had felt in the courtyard intrigued her, as did the whispered secrets that had always shadowed her existence. Could this be the key to unlocking the truth of who she really was?

The bedroom door swung open as Ms. Whoo entered, her presence filling the room. She knelt before Theodora, concern in her eyes as the intricate patterns on her robe swirled with a subtle magic that whispered of ancient secrets.

"Are ye alright, lass?" she asked. "I know it's a lot, but we've no time to waste. The Shadow Walkers are comin'."

Theodora locked eyes with Ms. Whoo, her fear mirrored in the woman's gaze. "Shadow Walkers," Theodora muttered, her voice trembling. The myths she'd heard as a child were terrifyingly real.

Ms. Whoo cradled Theodora's face, her warmth offering reassurance. "You've been so brave," she said. "But we need ta keep moving. There's danger ahead and we're running out of time."

Feeling a surge of strength from Ms. Whoo's encouragement, Theodora got up from the bed, her resolve clear on her face. "What do I need ta do?" she asked, steadier now though her hands still shook slightly.

"Ye must leave the safety of Donaglen Castle and venture beyond its walls. Ms. Whoo said, her eyes never leaving the princess's face.

Theodora's heart raced. *Leave Donaglen? It was all she'd ever known.* "I-I can't," she stammered. "Please, Ms. Whoo, I beg of ye. Let me stay here, let me hide in the safety of the castle walls. I'm not ready ta face whatever lies out there."

Ms. Whoo's expression softened, sympathy glinting in her wise eyes. She reached out and took Theodora's hands in her own, the touch grounding and familiar. "I know yer fear, me dear Theodora," she said. "But ye must go. It's yer destiny, and the Shadow Walkers won't be stoppin' until they find ye."

Theodora felt a surge of conflicting emotions course through her. The desire to cling to the familiarity of the castle warred with the knowledge that she could not escape her fate. With a heavy heart, she looked back at Ms. Whoo, her eyes shimmering with unshed tears. "Is there really no other way?" she pleaded, her voice cracking with emotion.

Ms. Whoo's gaze softened even further, her features full of understanding and compassion. She knew the weight of the burden Theodora carried, the struggle between the safety of the known and the uncertainty of the unknown. With a gentle smile, she squeezed Theodora's hands reassuringly.

Ah, me dear lass, I wish there were a simpler road fer ye to walk," Ms. Whoo replied, her voice filled with ancient wisdom. "But the hands of fate have entwined themselves 'round ye, binding your destiny to that of Kandella and all who call it home."

Theodora bowed her head, strands of fiery hair falling like a curtain around her face as she absorbed Ms. Whoo's words. A sense of resignation washed over her, mingling with a flicker of determination that burned bright in her chest. This was her moment of truth, the pivotal crossroads where she had to decide whether to cower in fear or rise to meet the challenges that lay ahead. With a deep breath, she lifted her chin and met Ms. Whoo's gaze once more.

"I'll do it," Theodora said, her voice laced with a fierce determination. "I'll take on whatever comes me way and embrace the journey that fate has laid out fer me."

A glimmer of pride shone in Ms. Whoo's eyes as she nodded, her expression a mix of sorrow for the hard road ahead and unwavering support for the princess she had watched over since birth. Rising to her feet, she clasped Theodora's hands. "Ye've got the spirit of yer ancestors within ye, Theodora Carrington," Ms. Whoo said. "Believe in yerself, and remember ye are never truly alone, no matter how dark the road ahead may be."

Strengthened by Ms. Whoo's words, Theodora straightened up and asked, "Tell me what I need tae do."

"Ye'll need ta dress like a commoner," Ms. Whoo said. "Blend in with the folk in Primlow. Ye'll find friends there ta help ya."

With those words lingering in the air like a whispered promise, Theodora picked out simple clothing—a plain tunic and durable boots—to avoid drawing attention to herself as royalty. As she changed, the weight of her journey settled on her shoulders.

Ms. Whoo handed her a shimmering cloak woven from threads of moonlight and starlight, its protective enchantments weaving a shield around her.

As Theodora fastened it around her shoulders, a sense of power surged through her veins, mingling with the fear that still lingered in her heart. The cold realization that she was stepping into the unknown, shedding the safety of her familiar life for the uncertainty that lay beyond the castle walls, sent a shiver down her spine.

Watching her get ready to leave the security of all she knew for the uncertain world outside stirred mixed feelings in Ms. Whoo too—pride for Theodora's courage but sadness at the inevitable hardships. With a steady hand, Ms. Whoo grasps Theodora's shoulder, her touch grounding and filled with unspoken reassurance.

"Remember, me dear Theodora," Ms. Whoo's voice was a gentle murmur, "yer strength lies not just in yer magic or lineage, but in the courage of yer heart and the bonds ye forge along this path."

Theodora met Ms. Whoo's gaze, the flicker of fear in her eyes now tempered by a growing resolve. She nodded, a silent promise to herself and to the mentor who had guided her with unwavering care and love.

"Ah, let's not be dawdling then. A druid friend is waitin' at O'Connor's Pub in the village."

"A druid?" Theodora questioned with curiosity cutting through some of her apprehension.

"Aye, his name be Finnegan O'Leary," Ms. Whoo replied, her voice steady and laced with a hint of urgency. "He'll guide yer training, teach ya how to wield yer magic, and help keep ya safe. Time grows short, lass. Ye'll need his wisdom as much as his protection."

Theodora took a deep breath, trying to absorb the gravity of Ms. Whoo's words while suppressing the trepidation tightening her chest. A druid—an ancient being of expert knowledge and power—felt like both an intimidating figure and a glimmer of hope in these uncertain times. She nodded, determination flickering across her features.

"Will I—will I be comin' back here?" she asked, her voice barely above a whisper.

Ms. Whoo's expression softened into something between sorrow and pride. She gently cupped Theodora's cheek as though committing the moment to memory. "I cannae say fer certain what lies ahead," she admitted with a tenderness that sent a pang through Theodora's chest. "But know this: no matter where this journey takes ye or how far ye stray from these walls, Donaglen is always in yer heart... because it's part o' who ye are."

The words carried an aching truth that settled over Theodora like a bittersweet embrace—a reminder of both home and the sacrifices required to protect it.

A sudden gust rattled the windowpane behind them, drawing their attention to the ominous shadows stretching long across the castle walls. The storm outside surged with unrelenting vigor, lightning illuminated the chamber in harsh flashes as if Kandella itself were crying out against the darkness encroaching upon it.

Chapter 6

"Crossing the Veil"

A LEXANDRIA LAY IN HER bed, heart pounding as the day drew to a close. A cold sweat coated her skin as the weight of her royal heritage bore down on her. She was no ordinary teenager; she was a princess, magic thrumming through her very being. Her fate demanded she face an unknown future, to master the untamed abilities churning inside her, and journey back to Kandella where her sister waited, likely caught in unthinkable dangers.

Bolting upright, Alexandria felt the harsh reality engulf her. Even with the murmurs of uncertainty and threads of dread twisting her thoughts, one undeniable fact persisted - this path was hers to tread. Recollections drifted in like dawn's haze over dewy meadows. She could almost hear the peals of laughter echoing through palace corridors and feel the tender gazes of her parents, their eyes filled with adoration and worry.

Alexandria wandered to the window, gazing out at the fading sunlight that cast lengthening shadows across the garden. The tranquil scene stood in stark contrast to the tempest raging within her. How could she possibly leave behind everything familiar? Was she prepared to venture into a world teeming with untold perils at every turn?

Amidst the storm of emotions, memories of her sister flickered like a distant beacon of hope in the darkness. Despite the mystic spell that had erased their shared past, the unbreakable bond between them remained unscathed. The mere thought of reuniting with Theodora fueled Alexandria's resolve, lighting a fire within her wavering heart.

A myriad of questions inundated her thoughts: *What perils awaited her in Kandella? Would she find the strength to shield her loved ones from harm? Could she navigate the treacherous path that lay ahead?*

Alexandria wiped away a tear as the weight of her newfound destiny pressed down on her. By the window, reality hit hard - she wasn't just leaving behind her normal life, she was walking into something far bigger than herself. The comfortable world she knew, with its predictable days and friendly faces, felt like it was slipping through her fingers.

A dark lord threatening an eternal winter sounded like something from her storybooks, not her actual life. Just yesterday she'd been worrying about math homework, and now this? She wasn't sure if she had what it took to face whatever waited for her. But deep down, she felt Theodora's presence calling to her, pulling her toward Kandella like an invisible thread she couldn't ignore even if she tried.

With a final glance out the window, she whispered a silent promise to herself and Theodora. "I will find you. We will face this together."

During dinner that evening, Elmer recounted how Kandella had fallen into darkness after they left for the mortal world. He described Lord Valendor's sinister plan to trap the villagers and cover Kandella in an unending winter. Outside, thunder growled, adding to the tension of the story.

As his words sank in, Alexandria felt a shiver go down her spine. The idea of her birthplace, once a magical haven, now frozen in time, filled her with dread. She looked around the table and saw the same solemn expressions reflected on her family's faces.

"It's up to Alexandria and Theodora to stop Lord Valendor," Diana declared. "They're the only ones with the power to defeat him and restore Kandella to its former glory."

Alex shook her head in disbelief. "Wait, hold up. Why does it have to be us? We're just teenagers! There must be someone more qualified for this hero stuff."

Elmer leaned forward, his expression serious. "An ancient prophecy foretold this very moment. It states that only the princesses born of the Carrington bloodline possess the magic necessary to overthrow Lord Valendor and save our homeland."

Diana reached across the table, placing a comforting hand on Alexandria's arm. "I know it seems overwhelming, sweetheart, but you and Theodora have a strength within you that even you haven't fully realized yet."

Alexandria shook her head, pushing her chair back from the table. "I don't know if I can do this. I mean, I just found out I'm a princess from another world, and now I'm supposed to save it? It's too much."

Elmer leaned forward, his eyes filled with understanding. "Alexandria, I know it's a heavy burden, but you won't be facing this alone. You have Theodora, and you have us. We'll be with you every step of the way."

Alexandria stared at her plate, pushing food around with her fork as her mind raced. The sounds of dinner faded into the background while the reality of her situation pressed in. Being told you're a princess with magical powers who needs to save an entire realm wasn't exactly easy to process.

Liam glanced up from his sketchbook where Donaglen Castle was taking shape. "Look, I get that this is crazy," he said, adding details to one of the towers, "but if anyone can handle being some legendary princess warrior, it's definitely you. You've got this, Alex."

His pencil moved across the paper as the castle emerged beneath his hand, each carefully drawn stone bringing the fortress to life. The ancient stronghold seemed to rise from the page, a testament to the heritage Alexandria would have to embrace, whether or not she felt ready.

Diana leaned in, marveling at the intricacy of Liam's sketch. It was as if he had walked the castle's halls himself, every detail rendered with uncanny precision for someone who had never set foot in Kandella.

"Liam, this is incredible," Diana breathed. "How do you know what Donaglen Castle looks like?"

Liam glanced up, his eyes holding a depth that seemed to reach beyond his years. "I just see it, Mom. It's like I get these flashes, these glimpses into places I've never been and people I've never met. It's as if I'm piecing together a giant puzzle, one vision at a time."

The room went quiet as everyone absorbed Liam's words. He fixed his gaze on Alexandria, examining her so intently that she squirmed uneasily in her chair.

"What do you see when you look at me, Liam?" Alexandria asked.

Liam's expression softened, a gentle smile playing on his lips as he set aside his sketchbook and moved closer to her. "I see you, Alex. Not just the prophecies or the royal bloodline, but the real you. The fire in your eyes, the bravery in your heart. You've always been more than just my sister - your family in every way that matters." His violet eyes gleamed with an otherworldly light. "And I know, without a doubt, that you hold the key to unlocking the magic within yourself. It's woven into the very fabric of your being."

Alexandria's brow furrowed. "How can you be so certain?"

"Because I see things differently," Liam said, but with conviction. "My autism lets me notice things others don't. Where they see problems, I see a way through. And when I look at you, I see something powerful—something waiting to rise. You're closer than you think."

Diana's chest tightened. She'd always known Liam was different—brilliant in ways that didn't fit neatly into the world. But hearing him speak like this, with such clarity, stirred something deep in her.

He took a breath. "People don't really see me. I don't fit what they expect, so they assume I'm broken. But I'm not. What makes me different is exactly what makes me strong. I just... see the world differently. And that matters."

Alexandria leaned over and gave Liam a quick hug. Across the table, Diana, and Elmer exchanged a meaningful glance, etching pride and concern on their faces for the path that lay ahead for their exceptional son.

Diana spoke to Liam with a warm, reassuring voice. "Sweetheart, your visions, and insights shine like a guiding light in a world often shrouded in confusion." They're an integral part of who you are, intertwined with your fae heritage. Embrace them, and let no one make you feel you need to hide or fear them."

Elmer nodded in agreement, his violet eyes shining with fierce love. "Liam, you may have been born in this mortal realm, but you're every bit as fae as your mother and I. Just as Alexandria is both a Carrington princess and royalty of Kandella's Kingdom of McKuilly. You too carry the essence of our people within you."

As the truth of his identity settled over him, Liam's eyes widened, a myriad of emotions playing across his face. Each word from his parents seemed to click into place, like pieces of a long-lost puzzle finally coming together.

Diana leaned forward, her voice gentle but unwavering. "Being fae isn't just about magic or living between worlds. It means carrying responsibilities that shape the future. Your gift of seeing what others can't - it's meant to help guide people, Liam. To light the way when paths grow dark."

Liam sat still, absorbing her words as understanding settled over him. For the first time, he felt truly at home in his own skin. Around them, the dining room took on an otherworldly quality, the lamplight casting strange patterns on the walls that seemed to move of their own accord.

Night crept in around them as Diana stood up. She gripped Liam's shoulder, steadying him as the weight of ancient prophecies and modern truths settled around them. Her touch bridged two worlds - the ordinary life they'd built here and the extraordinary destiny that called to them all.

"It's getting late," Diana said. "Today's revelations have been a lot to process. Let's get some rest and allow these truths to settle in our hearts."

Elmer rose to his feet, his expression a mixture of determination and solemnity. "Alright, everyone, it's time to hit the hay. We've got a big day ahead of us tomorrow, prepping for our journey back to home. So get some shut-eye while you can." His eyes gleamed with an intensity that seemed to crackle through the room like an electric current.

Alexandria and Liam exchanged a look of shared curiosity, the weight of the road ahead of them settling upon their shoulders. The mere mention of returning to Kandella sent a shiver down Alexandria's spine, awakening long-dormant memories of a mystical realm she had only ever dreamed of—a realm where she hoped to finally reunite with her sister.

Elmer's voice cut through the silence, commanding their full attention. "The time has come for us to embark on this journey as a family, to bring the Carrington twins back together and unleash the ancient magic that binds their fates. Kandella is waiting for us, and we must be prepared to face whatever challenges lie ahead. It won't be easy, but together, we can overcome anything."

As night descended and weariness took hold, everyone sought refuge in their rooms. Just as Alexandria was about to shut her door, a gentle meow caught her attention. She turned to find Aris in the hallway, her eyes glimmering with an unearthly luminescence.

The feline entered the room, gracefully settling on the bed. Alex couldn't help but smile at her furry friend's antics. "Got something on your mind, Aris?" she whispered.

However, as she moved to close the door, a voice echoed within her mind. Startled, she glanced back at Aris, catching a brief flicker in the cat's form.

Alexandria stood frozen in the doorway, one hand still on the knob.

"While I may not speak in the conventional sense," Aris' voice echoed in her mind, smooth and certain, "the connection we share surpasses the limitations of this world. Follow your instincts, for they shall be your compass on this journey."

Her breath caught. She stared at Aris, sprawled casually across the bed like any ordinary cat—but nothing about this was ordinary. Her fingers tightened on the doorknob. Her pulse pounded in her ears.

She took a step back, eyes wide, her mouth parting as if to speak, but no words came. A voice—his voice—had spoken directly into her thoughts. That wasn't possible.

Yet Aris simply lay there, still and calm, watching her with eyes that seemed far too knowing.

"I don't understand," Alexandria breathed, her voice trembling. "How is any of this possible?"

Aris' eyes shimmered with an otherworldly light as she blinked. "Our connection spans lifetimes, transcending the boundaries of time and space," the voice whispered once more. "In the realm we come from, such bonds defy the constraints of the physical world."

As Alexandria absorbed the cat's words, a whirlwind of emotions surged within her—wonder intermingled with apprehension. The realization that their relationship held depths she had never fathomed settled upon her, both exhilarating and daunting.

Cautiously, Alex approached Aris, reaching out to stroke her soft fur. As their connection intensified, a comforting warmth emanated from the cat, enveloping Alexandria in its gentle embrace.

"Remember, you do not face these trials alone," Aris reassured her. "Together, we shall unravel the mysteries of your past and unlock the potential that lies within you." The cat's unwavering confidence washed over Alex like a soothing balm, quieting her fears and instilling a sense of tranquility.

Exhausted, Alex climbed into bed, her fingers caressing Aris' fur as the cat's purrs filled the room with a calming rhythm. As sleep slowly claimed her, she found solace in Aris' comforting presence, drawing strength from their extraordinary bond.

Hours later, the sound of Aris' menacing growls jolted Alexandria awake. The once sleek, black fur now stood on end as the cat leapt from the bed, darting towards the door with a sense of urgency. Her sharp claws scratched at the wood, demanding to be let out. Still disoriented from sleep, Alexandria stumbled over and opened the door.

Pulse racing and adrenaline pumping, Alexandria followed Aris down the shadowy hallway, the darkness seeming to reach out with spectral fingers. An oppressive sense of foreboding hung in the air as they hurried towards the living room, guided only by the moonlight spilling through the window.

Aris stood guard by the window, her black fur bristling as she fixed her piercing gaze on a shadowy figure lurking outside. Though darkness hid its features, the figure emitted an unmistakable aura of evil, chilling Alexandria to the core.

Crash! The sudden sound of shattering glass ripped through the eerie silence, jolting Diana and Elmer into action. They raced down the stairs to join Alexandria, their faces etched with fear as an invisible, malevolent force closed in around them. The air grew thick and oppressive, crackling with dark energy that made each breath a struggle.

They've tracked us down," Diana hissed, her voice laced with panic. She gripped Alexandria's shoulders, her eyes wild with urgency. "Alex, you need to get out of here, now! Elmer and I will hold them off as long as we can."

"Run upstairs," Diana continued, her voice steady despite the fear in her eyes. "Pack light and stay with Aris - she knows where to go."

Alexandria raced up the stairs, each footstep echoing through the darkened hallway. Her hands trembled as she burst into her bedroom, mind racing as she tried to focus on what to bring.

She grabbed her backpack, stuffing in the basics - clothes, water, a few precious keepsakes. Her hand brushed against the old journal on her nightstand. After a moment's pause, she tucked it away too, drawing comfort from its familiar weight.

In the hallway, Aris waited at the top of the stairs, eyes fixed on Alexandria with unmistakable urgency. The cat's tail twitched impatiently as Alex hurried down the steps, her heart hammering against her ribs as chaos erupted around them.

She fought back the tears, knowing she couldn't stop for proper goodbyes. Following the cat's lead, she slipped out the back door into the biting night air, leaving behind the only home she'd ever known.

Alexandria's chest constricted as they fled deeper into the woods, guilt and anguish threatening to overwhelm her. Everything inside her screamed to turn back, to fight alongside her family against whatever was coming. But she knew why they'd sent her away -

their sacrifice kept her safe. Understanding this didn't make it hurt any less as she pushed forward, her heart breaking with each step that took her further from home.

Darkness pressed in around them as they ventured further into the forest. While Alexandria stumbled over roots and branches, Aris moved with fluid grace through the shadows, leading her along hidden paths with unwavering certainty. The night seemed alive around them - leaves rustled overhead and twigs snapped underfoot, each sound amplified by Alexandria's heightened awareness of their surroundings.

The forest opened up to a clearing bathed in moonlight, where a vast lake mirrored the starlit heavens. Alexandria strolled beside Aris along the shore, her eyes locked on the majestic waterfall towering ahead. As they walked beside the water, she spotted it—a subtle, otherworldly glow coming from behind the waterfall. It flickered over the nearby rocks and plants.

Alexandria's breath caught as she stepped closer, mesmerized by the strange lights. The waterfall's roar mixed with an otherworldly hum that seemed to vibrate through her bones. Mist sprayed their faces as they approached, the cool droplets a stark reminder that this was real, not some fevered dream. Aris stayed close, her presence steadying Alexandria's nerves as they ventured forward.

Behind the curtain of water, a cave entrance slowly emerged from the darkness. Wisps of fog danced around the opening, creating strange patterns in the dim light. Alexandria felt a pull toward the mysterious space - like stepping into one of her childhood stories, where magic wasn't just imagination but breathtakingly real.

"Strange, I've never noticed this before," Alex murmured, her voice an uncertain blend of wonder and apprehension.

Aris responded with gentle resolve. "This has always been here, hidden to shield you."

Alexandria gazed at the flickering lights, her mind torn by conflicting feelings. A part of her was eager to explore what lay beyond the doorway, yet another part urged her to flee. Having lived her entire life in the mortal world, was she truly ready to abandon it all? As she watched the enchanting glow, the gravity of her decision pressed down on her, knowing that her next move would alter everything.

Aris leaned her head against Alexandria's palm, offering comfort that went deeper than physical touch. Their connection hummed between them, built from years of shared moments. When Alexandria's eyes met Aris's piercing gaze, she saw something ancient and knowing in those golden depths.

"I need to show you something," Aris's voice whispered in Alexandria's mind, clear as a bell. "Though first - and this may not shock you at this point - I should mention I'm not exactly your average house cat."

Aris stepped back gracefully, her body beginning to shift before Alexandria's eyes. Her black fur rippled as she grew larger, paws expanding into powerful feet with sharp claws. Her ears length-ened and turned pointed while her face stretched into a wolf's muzzle. In seconds, where Alexandria's cat had stood now towered a massive white wolf, its coat bright against the darkness. Those familiar golden eyes still watched her intently, carrying the same knowing look Aris had always had.

"Aris?" she murmured, her voice shaking with both wonder and disbelief. She extended a cautious hand, her fingers lingering mere inches from the wolf's snout.

The wolf nodded, "Yes, Alexandria. I am a shapeshifter." Aris's voice echoed in her mind, rich with warmth and wisdom.

Alexandria's fingers finally made contact with Aris's fur, sinking into the thick, silky coat. A jolt of energy coursed through her at the touch, as if the very essence of magic flowed between them. The scent of pine and wild herbs filled her nostrils, mingling with an otherworldly musk that spoke of ancient forests and moonlit nights.

"A shapeshifter?" Alexandria breathed, her eyes wide as she took in every detail of Aris's new form.

Aris's tail swished, stirring the air around them with a slow, deliberate flick.

"In Kandella, many things are possible that your mortal world would deem impossible," she said, her voice threading into Alexandria's mind. It still carried that familiar calm and amusement, but now there was a shift—a new weight behind it. The tone had deepened, roughened slightly, like a distant echo of a wolf's growl wrapped in velvet.

"Shapeshifting is but one gift bestowed upon guardians like myself."

The words hung in the air, heavier than before, as if they came not from the small black cat on the bed, but from something much larger just beneath the surface.

Alexandria's mind reeled, struggling to process this new revelation. All the years she had spent with Aris, confiding in her, seeking comfort in her presence—and yet, there was still so much she didn't know about her faithful companion.

"Why didn't you tell me before?" she asked, a note of hurt creeping into her voice.

Aris flattened her ears slightly. "I didn't choose to keep this from you. They sealed your memories to protect you—and with them, the knowledge of my true form."

A cool breeze rustled through the cave, carrying with it the faint, eerie howls of distant creatures. Alexandria shivered, aware of the dangers that lurked in the shadows beyond the safety of the moonlit glade.

"We don't have much time," Aris said, her mental voice cutting through Alexandria's swirling thoughts. "The Shadow Walkers draw near, and we must get to the other side of the portal before they find us."

Alexandria's heart leaped into her throat at the mention of the Shadow Walkers. She could almost feel their malevolent presence creeping closer, threatening to engulf them in darkness.

"But what about Diana, Elmer, and Liam?" she asked, panic rising in her chest. "We can't just leave them behind!"

Aris moved nearer, her warm breath brushing against Alexandria's skin. "The others are strong and capable, Alexandria. They'll delay the Shadow Walkers for as long as possible, but our focus must be ensuring your safety."

Alexandria's hands tightened into fists at her sides. "I can't leave them behind," she murmured, her voice trembling.

"You're not abandoning them," Aris assured her. "By going through the portal, you're taking the first step towards fulfilling your destiny—and ultimately, towards saving us all."

Alexandria took a deep, shuddering breath, trying to steady her nerves. She looked into Aris's eyes, finding strength in the unwavering trust and loyalty she saw there.

With a final look at the world she was about to leave, Alexandria gathered her courage and moved ahead, prepared to confront the challenges that awaited her beyond the portal.

Acknowledging Alexandria's readiness with a nod, the wolf turned towards the shimmering lights. Side by side, the princess, and her guardian approached the mystical gateway, their steps guided by the luminous promise of her fate that beckoned from beyond the veil.

Chapter 7

"Into The Shadows"

Ms. Whoo's nimble fingers retrieved the intricate ivory box from the folds of her dress. In the flickering candlelight, the box's delicate carvings seemed to dance, casting mesmerizing shadows across its surface.

Cradling the box with the utmost reverence, Ms. Whoo's brow furrowed in concentration as she extended it towards Theodora, a faint smile playing upon her lips.

The box immediately caught Theodora's attention. "What've ya got there, Ms. Whoo?" she asked, her voice tinged with intrigue. As she took the box into her hands, a barely audible whisper seemed to emanate from within, as if the contents held a secret yearning to be revealed.

With delicate fingers, Theodora flicked open the top, revealing a stunning silver bracelet nestled inside. The sight took her breath away, and a wave of long-buried memories washed over her, stirring something deep within her soul.

"Did... did me mother give me this?" Theodora wondered aloud, her fingers caressing the intricate designs adorning the bracelet. In that moment, she realized that this was no ordinary piece of jewelry; it was a symbol of enduring love, a tangible connection to her past.

Ms. Whoo arched her brow, a knowing glint in her eye. "And how would ya be knowin' that, lass?"

As Theodora slid the bracelet onto her wrist, a jolt of electricity coursed through her body, igniting a sense of familiarity and be-longing. "I remember a woman with fiery red hair... she gave this ta me," Theodora replied, her voice distant as the memory took hold.

Tracing the delicate patterns with her fingertips, Theodora found herself transported back to a distant moment from her childhood, the vivid images flooding her mind.

'Warm sunlight poured through the castle windows, bathing the stone walls in a golden glow. A young Theodora sat cross-legged on a plush rug, her auburn curls bouncing as she leaned forward, wide-eyed with wonder. "Ma, what's that?" she asked, pointing to the silver bracelet in her mother's hand.

Queen Amara's emerald eyes sparkled with affection as she smiled down at her daughter. "This, my darlin' Theodora, is a very special bracelet," she explained, unclasping it and holding it out for the young princess to see. "I had it made just for you."

Theodora reached out, her small fingers tracing the intricate patterns etched into the metal. As she touched the bracelet, a faint tingle of energy danced across her skin, igniting a sense of wonder within her. "It's magic, isn't it?" she whispered, her voice filled with awe.

"Indeed it is," Queen Amara confirmed, her tone gentle yet firm. With a loving touch, she clasped the bracelet around Theodora's wrist, the silver gleaming against her fair skin. "Remember ya carry the legacy of our family within ya. No matter what challenges ya face, ya have the strength to overcome them."

As the memory faded, Theodora found herself back in the present, her mother's words echoing through her mind like a gentle reminder of the courage and resilience that flowed through her veins.

A shadow flickered across Ms. Whoo's features, a hint of sorrow in her eyes. "Aye, yer ma entrusted ye with that bracelet," she confirmed. "And truth be told, I be the one who crafted these pieces at her request."

"Pieces?" Theodora questioned, her brow furrowing as she tried to focus on her nanny's words. "What d'ya mean? Who else did ya make 'em for?"

Ms. Whoo felt her heart grow heavy under the weight of untold secrets. In a cryptic whisper, she said, "Don't ya be worryin' about that now, child. The truth will come to light in due time."

Theodora's gaze remained fixed upon the bracelet, its presence stirring a whirlwind of memories and questions within her. While grateful for her mother's meaningful gift, the revelation of other pieces created by Ms. Whoo left her with a growing sense of unease.

Sensing Theodora's troubled thoughts, Ms. Whoo's expression softened, her wrinkled brow etched with empathy. She laid a reassuring hand on the princess's shoulder, her touch a gentle comfort. "Fear not, me dear," Ms. Whoo said, her voice low and soothing. "Though mystery shrouds the path ahead, trust that yer journey will unfold as it's meant to." Her words, like a flickering candle in the darkness, brought a glimmer of comfort to Theodora's heart.

Cornelius burst into the room and shattered the tranquil moment. "Madam! Princess! The guards spotted movement near the woods! We must leave at once!"

Hearts pounding in unison, Theodora and Ms. Whoo raced down the dimly lit corridor, their footsteps muffled against the stone as they navigated the shadowy halls.

Ms. Whoo's grip tightened on Theodora's arm, her whispered words tumbling out in a desperate stream. "Stay out of sight and move quickly, lass. There's danger lurkin' at every turn."

Theodora found solace in Ms. Whoo's embrace, drawing strength from their unspoken bond as they followed Cornelius down the spiral staircase. "Ya have the power within ya, child," Ms. Whoo reassured her. "Trust in yerself, and ye shall find yer way."

Determination surged through Theodora as they descended. At the landing, she caught Cornelius's eye, drawing silent strength from his steadfast presence. In his unwavering loyalty, she found the resolve she needed for whatever lay ahead.

Amidst the chaos, Khadall swooped down from the shadows above, his graceful wings carrying him to Theodora's shoulder. His presence brought a calming stillness, his voice filled with solemn conviction. "Fear not, me princess," he declared, his words a steadfast vow. "I'll be stayin' by yer side throughout this perilous journey, guidin' ye with unwavering devotion."

Theodora's heart skipped a beat, the moment's gravity washing over her. For years, she and Khadall had shared something wordless—a bond of silent protection and trust. Now, hearing his actual voice—rich and deep with that familiar accent that mirrored her own—sent an unexpected shiver through her. She glanced at the owl, seeing him anew. Their quiet companionship had suddenly transformed into something different, something more tangible. The friend who'd watched over her in silence all these years was now offering his wisdom aloud, making their connection even more real in this moment of danger.

Almost unconsciously, Theodora lifted her hand, fingers grazing Khadall's downy feathers and relishing the comforting warmth that radiated from his owl form. "How... how can this be, Khadall?" she breathed, her voice scarcely above a whisper.

Khadall's eyes softened, ancient knowledge glimmering in their depths. "The veil o' secrecy must now lift, Princess. Kandella stands on the precipice of significant change, an' it's time we fully embrace the connection we share." His words settled heavily over the room, thickening the air with the gravity of the moment.

Ms. Whoo stepped forward, her presence soothing Theodora. "Heed Khadall's counsel, child. Forces move beyond our understandin', and yer fate weaves tightly with the destiny of Kandella itself."

Drawing in a steadying breath, Theodora squared her shoulders, a fierce determination flickering to life in her eyes. "Very well, Khadall. Show me the way," she declared, her voice unwavering despite the fear that still thrummed through her veins.

With a powerful sweep of his wings, Khadall launched himself into the air, gliding through the open door and vanishing into the moonlit night beyond. Theodora hastened after him, her cloak flaring out behind her as she plunged into the darkness. The chill night air whipped past her face, carrying with it the earthy scents of the forest—a stark reminder of the untamed world that awaited her beyond the castle walls.

Theodora's boots pounded against the weathered stone bridge, each hurried step reverberating through the charged atmosphere. Khadall soared above, his powerful wings stirring the air as he maintained a vigilant watch for any signs of danger. The night sky crackled with lightning, an ominous reminder of the perils that lay ahead.

Navigating the twisting alleyways of Primlow with purpose, Theodora made her way towards O'Connor's Pub, a sanctuary of warmth and kinship amidst the gathering gloom. Her cloak billowed behind her, the rich fabric whispering against the biting wind that carried the distant sounds of the village's hidden inhabitants.

As she approached the pub, its welcoming glow spilled onto the cobblestones, beckoning her closer. Theodora's heart raced with a mixture of apprehension and anticipation as she reached for the heavy oak door, its ancient hinges creaking as she stepped inside.

The pub's interior enveloped her in a cocoon of comfort, the evening chill retreating in the face of crackling hearths, lively conversation, and the soothing strains of music. Theodora's emerald eyes swept the room, taking in the faces of the patrons, their expressions alight with camaraderie and contentment. The mingled scents of hearty fare and rich ale suffused the air, wrapping around her like a familiar embrace.

Amid the pub's revelry, a spirited 'Seisiun' was underway, the villagers united in song and merriment. As Theodora wove her way through the crowd, a barmaid narrowly avoided colliding with her, expertly balancing a tray laden with frothing mugs and steaming plates.

"Watch yer step, lass!" the barmaid cautioned, her voice carrying over the din.

"Sorry about that," Theodora offered apologetically, side-stepping to allow the server to pass.

At the bar, a burly bartender greeted her with a warm smile. "What can I get for ye, miss?"

"An ale, please," Theodora requested, hoping to blend in with the local patrons while trying to quell the nerves that fluttered beneath her calm facade.

"Comin' right up!" The bartender chuckled, filling a glass with practiced ease and sliding it across the counter to her. "Enjoy, lass."

Theodora took a tentative sip, the ale's bitter flavor masking her unease as she scanned the room, searching for the druid amidst the sea of faces illuminated by the flickering candlelight. With each passing moment, the knot of fear in her stomach tightened, her inner turmoil concealed behind a veneer of composure.

Suddenly, a drunken sailor stumbled into her space, his ale-soaked breath assaulting her senses as he gripped her arm with clumsy insistence. "Why don't ye join me for a drink, pretty lass?"

Before Theodora could react, a cloaked figure materialized behind the sailor, a glint of steel flashing in the dim light as a dagger pressed against the man's throat. "Let her go if ye value yer life," the stranger growled, his voice low and menacing.

The sailor blanched, releasing Theodora's arm and staggering away, his bravado evaporating in the face of the hooded figure's unspoken threat.

Theodora realized, with a start, the stranger who melted back into the crowd matched Ms. Whoo's description of the druid she was to meet. Finnegan's unassuming appearance belied the quiet strength and unwavering resolve that emanated from his every move, an enigmatic guardian cloaked in mystery.

Three specters slipped through the sinister forest bordering Primlow, their fluid movements unnaturally silent as they approached the village gates. The air around them seemed to chill, leaves shivering in their wake as if nature itself recoiled from their presence.

The sky split open with a ferocious Thundersnow storm as they neared their destination, ice, and lightning crashing down to blanket the land in frozen white. The unnatural storm cast eerie shadows across the landscape, a perfect cover for their midnight approach.

These were the Shadow Walkers, Lord Vallendor's most feared hunters. Once elves, now corrupted vessels bound to their master's will, they existed only to extinguish the final threats to Vallendor's reign—the surviving heirs of King William and Queen Amara.

Nine years had passed since Vallendor had seized the beloved monarchs, driven by his obsession with preventing the prophecy that foretold his downfall. The king and queen remained alive in his dungeons, a calculated cruelty that served his paranoia.

Vallendor's curse had transformed the once-thriving kingdom into a frozen wasteland. His dark magic had spread across the realm like poison, draining hope from the land as surely as it drained warmth from the air.

Lightning flashed, briefly illuminating the Shadow Walkers' features beneath their hoods—hollow eyes, skin pulled tight across inhuman faces. No breath clouded the air before them despite the bitter cold.

They converged at Primlow's center, moving with silent purpose through streets where windows darkened at their passing. The tallest among them produced a crystal sphere, its sickly glow pulsing between bone-white fingers. The orb hummed with malevolent energy—their direct link to Vallendor, who awaited news of their hunt. Through this connection, they would report on their pursuit of Theodora, one of the twin princesses whose mere existence threatened everything their master had built through blood and betrayal.

As Theodora wove through the lively pub, her heart pounded in time with the rumbling thunder outside. The tension in the air was palpable as she scanned the crowd, searching for the enigmatic figure who had come to her aid earlier. Amidst the sea of faces, her gaze settled on a hooded man tucked away in a shadowy corner.

Steeling herself, Theodora approached him with determination, knowing that the answers she sought could upend her world. As she drew near, the man stood, firelight dancing across his chiseled features and piercing blue eyes.

"Princess," he greeted, his rich brogue cutting through the noise. "I've been expecting ya."

Theodora took a seat across from him. "I was told to seek ya out."

Finnegan's inscrutable gaze held equal parts knowledge and mystery. "I'm here to guide ya, to help ya navigate the dangers that lie ahead."

Recent events had plunged Theodora into uncharted territory. Finnegan's presence eased the burden of the unknown, igniting a flicker of hope amidst the encroaching darkness.

Theodora leaned forward, desperation tinging her voice. "I need answers. The Shadow Walkers, the prophecy... what does it all mean?"

Finnegan's expression grew grim. "Ya must be careful, lass. There are those who would seek to deceive ya, to lead ya astray. Shapeshifters walk among us, and it's gettin' harder to know who to trust."

"And how do I know I can trust ya?" Theodora challenged, her emerald eyes boring into his.

A hint of a smile played at the corner of Finnegan's mouth. "Ms. Whoo wouldn't have sent ya to me if she didn't believe I could help. She's a sharp one, she is."

Theodora slumped in her chair, shoulders heavy with the burden of too many revelations. "Ms. Whoo kept mentionin' some prophecy, but I'm still in the dark. What's it got to do with me, anyway?"

Finnegan leaned closer, voice dropping to barely above a whisper. "It speaks of twin princesses," he said, eyes darting to check no one was listening. "Only together can ya defeat the sorcerer who's bleedin' our land dry. Those Shadow Walkers? They're his twisted servants." He took a quick swig of ale. "Their only purpose is huntin' ya down before ya can find yer sister and fulfill the prophecy. Valendor knows the prophecy as well as we do, and he's terrified of what'll happen when ya two finally stand together."

Theodora's head spun as Finnegan's words sank in. Twin princesses? Prophecies? A sorcerer bleeding the land dry? She gripped the edge of the table, trying to anchor herself to something solid while her world tilted sideways.

"I don't have a sister," she said, her knuckles whitening. "I think I'd know if I had a twin runnin' about somewhere."

Finnegan took a slow sip of his ale and kept his eyes fixed on hers. "They built yer whole life on necessary secrets, Princess. What ya know and what's true ain't always the same thing."

The firelight caught the silver at his temples as he leaned forward. Theodora studied his face, looking for any hint of deception in those weathered features. Instead, she found only certainty—the kind that comes from knowing things that cost too much to learn.

"This is madness," she muttered, running a hand through her hair. "Even if what yer sayin' is true—how am I supposed ta fight some all-powerful sorcerer? They didn't exactly train me for magical warfare at Donaglen, ya know."

Finnegan reached across the table, his hand coming to rest atop hers in a gesture of reassurance. "That's why I'm here, lass. To teach ya the skills ya need - magic, bowmanship, the works. Together, we'll find a way to-"

The pub door burst open with a resounding crash, cutting short his words. Nala staggered inside, her face a mask of sheer terror.

"The Shadow Walkers!" she screamed. "They're here!" Flames engulfed her, cutting off her voice mid-sentence.

In an instant, the pub erupted into chaos. Patrons scrambled for cover as tables overturned and glass shattered. Theodora locked eyes with Finnegan, a silent understanding passing between them.

She opened her mouth to speak, but before she could utter a word, an icy gust tore through the room, extinguishing the candles and plunging them into darkness. The shadows seemed to come alive, writhing and twisting like serpents poised to strike.

In that moment, Theodora knew with chilling certainty that the danger Ms. Whoo had warned her of had finally arrived. The battle for her fate, and the fate of all Kandella, had begun.

In the doorway, three silhouettes appeared, motionless and menacing. Their forms seemed to pulse with darkness, radiating malice that chilled Theodora to her core. The Shadow Walkers had found them, their eyes gleaming with an unnatural light that spoke of something beyond human.

Theodora glanced frantically between Finnegan and the advancing threat. The truth hit her with stark clarity—there was no going back to the safety of Donaglen Castle. Whatever path lay ahead had just narrowed to a single, dangerous route through territory she'd never imagined facing.

Blood rushing in her ears, Theodora met Finnegan's steady gaze. His unwavering confidence steadied her trembling hands. In that brief exchange of looks, she made her choice. She would follow where he led, trusting him to guide her through the darkness that now threatened to swallow them whole and toward the answers about her past that had remained hidden for too long.

"Time ta make ourselves scarce," Finnegan muttered, his voice cutting through the havoc as he quickly scanned the room for a way out.

Without wasting a moment, he grabbed her hand—his grip firm but reassuring—and pulled her toward the back of the tavern. He pushed aside a weathered tapestry revealing a narrow passage Theodora hadn't noticed before.

"This way," he whispered, guiding her through.

They burst into the bitter night, ice pellets stinging their faces. The unnatural storm had worsened, hailstones crashing down around them as they splashed through flooded streets and ducked between shadowed buildings.

"There!" Finnegan pointed toward two horses tied at a hitching post, their dark coats catching the blue-white flashes of lightning. They mounted swiftly, the beasts oddly steady despite the surrounding chaos.

"Head low, follow close," he shouted against the storm's howl. "Whatever happens, don't look back!"

Theodora gripped the reins with numbed fingers as they thundered through the winding streets. Each hoofbeat echoed her racing pulse. The freezing wind tore at her cloak and sent needles of ice against her cheeks while she hunched lower in the saddle. Finnegan carved their path with practiced confidence, taking sharp turns without hesitation, revealing his intimate knowledge of every alley and side street.

Buildings streaked past in a blur of shadow and torchlight. Theodora gasped for breath, the frigid air scorching her lungs. She fixed her gaze on Finnegan's back, trusting his lead through the maze of streets as they fled the nightmare behind them.

When they finally broke through the village gates into the open countryside, a rush of wild energy surged through her veins. The vast darkness stretched before them, promising both danger and escape. She pressed forward alongside Finnegan, refusing to look back at Primlow where orange flames now licked skyward, the Shadow Walkers' calling card illuminating the night they'd left behind.

"We've got ta move faster!" Finnegan shouted over the pounding hoofbeats. "Those Shadow Walkers won't be far behind!"

Theodora nodded grimly, spurring her mount onward. "Where are we headed?" she called back, her voice nearly lost in the rushing wind.

"Monaghan forest," Finnegan replied, his gaze fixed ahead. "It's our best chance at shaking them off our trail."

They fled Primlow's smoking ruins, racing toward the forest where ancient trees stood like silent guardians of forgotten secrets. Theodora kept pace with Finnegan, trusting him without hesitation as their desperate escape drove them forward.

Theodora studied Finnegan as he picked their path through the treacherous terrain, his movements decisive despite the darkness. She drew steadying breaths, surprised to find her own panic subsiding. There was something reassuring about his unflinching focus—the way he faced each obstacle without hesitation or doubt. When her own courage faltered, she found herself borrowing from him.

Strange, she thought, how quickly trust could form in desperate times. Just a short time ago, he'd been a stranger—now her life rested in his hands. This wasn't just an alliance of convenience anymore. Their fates had become tangled together by circumstances neither of them controlled but both somehow understood. Whatever invisible thread had pulled them into each other's orbit now bound them to a shared purpose that stretched far beyond this night's escape.

"Finnegan," Theodora called out as they reached the forest's edge, her voice catching on the words, "do ya think there's any real chance? Against Vallendor, I mean. To find me parents and put this right? Or are we just runnin' ourselves ragged for nothin'?"

He glanced over at her, his blue eyes alight with fierce determination. "Aye, lass. I've no doubt in my mind. Together, we'll see this through ta the end, come what may."

Gaining strength from his words, Theodora straightened up in the saddle, her determination solidifying like forged metal. With Finnegan beside her and the force of fate driving her onward, she was certain that nothing could stand in their way.

Chapter 8

"Whispers of Destiny"

THE SWIRLING VORTEX ENVELOPED them in a kaleidoscope of colors, each hue more vibrant and mysterious than the last. Alexandria felt a suspension in time and space; her heightened senses amplified every sound, scent and flicker of light. The air hummed with a melodic resonance that seemed to pulse in tandem with her heartbeat, creating a symphony of unknown origins.

Aris stood steadfast by her side, her fur bristling slightly as they traversed through the portal. The golden gleam in her eyes burned like twin beacons of guidance, reflecting the courage and determination that flowed between them. The sensation of movement was both exhilarating and disorienting, akin to hurtling through a cosmic whirlwind with no end in sight.

As they journeyed deeper into the unknown, glimpses of fantastical landscapes began to materialize around them. The snow-capped peaks gleamed under a blanket of starlit skies, while majestic trees adorned with silver leaves and luminescent crystals cast enchanting hues around them. Delicate snowdrops bloomed like frozen treasures, enhancing the surreal beauty that enveloped the land.

A strange sense of déjà vu tugged at Alexandria's consciousness in this realm of marvels, triggering fleeting memories that slipped through her grasp like wisps of mist.

A flicker of movement drew her gaze. Near a towering Elder tree stood two figures she instantly recognized even in their true forms - Diana and Elmer, resplendent in their fae glory.

Diana radiated raw power, teal hair interwoven with thorns and glittering gems that cast prismatic light. The oak staff in her hands pulsed with ancient magic, each gemstone whispering secrets of the realm's turbulent history.

Elmer too had transformed. Ethereal and regal, his very essence shimmered with pure magic. Midnight hair tumbled down his back in iridescent waves, once emerald eyes now a piercing sapphire. His bearing exuded strength and authority, a silver sword gripped in his hand.

"Welcome, Princess," Diana greeted her. "The time has come for you to accept your birthright and awaken the power within."

She held out a bracelet that seemed woven from moonlight itself, a kaleidoscopic crystal at its center. "This is one of a pair, crafted by your nanny," Diana explained, eyes glinting. "Imbued with powerful magic, these bracelets will lead you and Theodora back to each other. And once reunited, your combined power will be unrivaled."

Alexandria hesitated, hand hovering over the bracelet as she felt its thrumming energy. Uncertainty warred with determination inside her. Meeting Diana's unwavering gaze, she saw the same emotions reflected back.

Pushing aside her doubts, Alexandria grasped the bracelet. Power surged through her veins, igniting the crystal in a blaze of dazzling light. Questions still churned in her mind, but one thing was clear - she was ready to walk this path and uncover her true self.

"Go east along the winding trail," Diana instructed. "And always trust your instincts to guide you."

As she embraced them, Alexandria absorbed their strength and unconditional love. "I'll see you again, won't I?" she asked.

"Of course, my darling," Diana reassured, smiling warmly. "We'll be watching over you from the celestial plane. If you ever need us, simply whisper our names to the enchanted winds."

With a final glance over her shoulder, Alexandria stepped onto the eastern path, icy air filling her lungs and mingling with the apprehension coiled in her chest. Her pulse raced in time with the crunching of snow underfoot as she forged ahead into the unknown.

The forest fell silent around them, making Alexandria hyper-aware of every sound. Wind whispered through branches and trees creaked in the darkness, each noise distinct and unsettling. In the moonlight, shadows seemed to follow their path, watching their every move.

Aris walked beside her, a constant presence guiding her through the snow-covered landscape with quiet confidence.

Their climb steepened as they began their climb up the mountain making Alexandria's lungs burn from the thinning air. She struggled to catch her breath while her exhausted muscles screamed in protest with each step through the heavy snow.

Doubt settled over her as her heart pounded against her ribs. "What if I'm not strong enough?" she whispered, her voice barely audible. "What if my magic fails when we need it the most?"

Aris stopped, turning to face Alexandria. Her eyes seemed to pierce straight into Alexandria's soul, wise and knowing. "It's okay to be scared, princess," Aris said. "But never doubt your own strength. It's there inside you, just waiting to be unleashed. Believe in yourself, and you'll be unstoppable."

Atop the jagged mountain, Alexandria's eyes narrowed against the biting wind. Cresting the ridge, they paused at the unexpected sight below - a perfect lake nestled in a small valley, its surface catching the moonlight like polished silver. Ancient evergreens circled the water, their dark shapes stark against the snow.

The peaceful scene made Alexandria momentarily forget the danger at their backs. She wiped sweat from her brow despite the cold, her muscles aching from the climb.

"Look," she whispered, pointing. "It's beautiful."

Aris dipped her head in acknowledgment before starting down the mountain. The wolf moved with practiced ease down the treacherous slope, paws finding secure footholds in the snow and rock. Alexandria followed more cautiously, her breath clouding the air with each careful step.

The silence pressed in around them, broken only by distant wildlife calls and the soft crunch of snow beneath their feet. Alexandria strained to hear any signs of pursuit as they made their way down toward the sheltered valley.

Once they reached the lake's edge the tension in Alexandria's shoulders finally eased. The water lay still as glass under the moonlight, not a ripple disturbed its silver surface. Aris approached the shoreline, her white fur ghostly against the darkness as she stared across the water with focused intensity.

"We'll stop here tonight," Aris said, her mental voice gentler than it had been during their flight. "You need rest before we continue."

Alexandria let out a long breath, legs trembling with exhaustion now that they'd stopped moving. After hours of pushing through fear and adrenaline, the prospect of sitting down felt almost too good to be true.

"I didn't realize how tired I was until just now," she admitted, dropping her backpack onto a flat stone. "Good call."

Aris padded to the water's edge with quiet confidence, settling herself on the ground. She closed her eyes, tail sweeping once across the snow before growing still. A soft, melodic hum vibrated from her throat as she concentrated. With barely a sound, a small flame sparked to life before them, growing until its warmth pushed back the mountain chill.

Alexandria sat transfixed, watching the wolf work her magic as casually as she'd once jumped onto windowsills. The firelight caught in Aris's fur and reflected in her eyes, casting their little haven in a gentle light that made the snow around them gleam.

Alexandria's stomach growled suddenly, the sound embarrassingly loud in the quiet night. She realized she hadn't eaten since—when? Before everything had changed. Before she'd fled the only home she'd known.

Aris's ears twitched toward the sound, and without a word, she turned her attention from the fire to more practical matters. The wolf rose to her feet, intent on solving this recent problem with the same efficiency she'd shown throughout their journey.

Aris padded a few steps from their camp, eyes sweeping the darkness. "I'm guessing DoorDash doesn't deliver to enchanted mountain hideaways," she quipped, mental voice maintaining its dry humor despite everything.

Alexandria laughed - a startling sound after hours of fear. "What, no pizza guy willing to trek through dimensional portals? That's just poor customer service."

"Can you imagine the reviews?" Aris snorted, circling back to the fire. "'Zero stars. Delivery guy refused to cross the dimensional portal.'"

With graceful movements, Aris began to trace a pattern in the snow with her paw, each motion deliberate and precise. The air shifted around them, growing dense with energy that raised goosebumps along Alexandria's arms.

"Hang on, what are you—" Alexandria began, but fell silent as a weathered iron pot appeared above their fire, suspended by nothing. Steam curled upward from whatever simmered inside, carrying an aroma so delicious her empty stomach clenched in immediate response.

Aris dipped her head toward the pot with an unmistakable smirk in her wolfish features. "Dinner is served," she announced dryly. "One perk of having a magical wolf companion instead of just a house cat."

Alexandria gaped at the impossibly manifested meal, torn between disbelief and hunger as the aroma hit her—rich and savory, with hints of herbs she couldn't even name. After everything she'd witnessed today, somehow this mundane miracle felt the most surreal.

"You could've done this all those times I made us ramen for dinner?" she asked, half-laughing.

Aris's ears flicked back in amusement. "And miss out on your gourmet microwaving skills? Besides, magic has... rules. Even in your world."

"So much I don't know about you," Alexandria murmured, the realization settling in as she reached for the wooden bowl that had appeared as inexplicably as the pot.

"We've got time for that," Aris replied, watching as Alexandria ladled the steaming stew. "Seventeen years as your pet, and I've still got a few surprises left."

Alexandria's hands steady as she lifted the first spoonful to her lips. The flavor burst across her tongue—hearty, complex, and somehow familiar, like a meal from a childhood she couldn't quite remember.

She savored each bite, the warmth spreading through her limbs and settling the jumble of emotions that had plagued her throughout the day. The simple act of eating felt like a balm to her weary soul, grounding her in this moment of respite amidst chaos.

As Alexandria ate, Aris settled beside her, content to watch over her charge with a keen eye. The crackling fire cast flickering shadows around them, painting the clearing in a dance of light and darkness.

With each passing minute, Alexandria felt the tension in her muscles ease, the weight of the day's events slowly lifting. She stole glances at Aris, marveling at the creature who remained a constant in her life, even as everything else turned upside down.

"I wouldn't have made it this far without you," Alexandria said softly, setting her empty bowl aside. "Even when you were just my cat who knocked things off shelves at 3 AM."

Aris's eyes crinkled with amusement. "And to think, all those years I was protecting a princess while you bribed me with tuna."

Alexandria smiled as she leaned back against a nearby rock. The fire crackled, sending sparks dancing upward into the night sky. An owl hooted somewhere in the distance, its call echoing across the still lake. For a moment, the weight of everything lifted - no Shadow Walkers, no destiny, just the peaceful wilderness surrounding them.

She stole a glance at Aris, still marveling at the wolf who'd been her companion all along. The danger hadn't disappeared, but here in this small clearing with the crackling fire and Aris's steady presence, Alexandria drew strength from both her newfound heritage and their unbreakable bond.

As exhaustion finally overtook her, Alexandria's eyes grew heavy. Her last conscious thought before drifting off was of Theodora - the sister she'd never known she had, but somehow felt connected to already. Tomorrow would bring new challenges, but tonight, sleep claimed her completely.

In the realm of her subconscious, something ancient stirred. Alexandria drifted through darkness until a cloaked figure appeared by a gleaming lake. As the stranger approached, their hood fell back, revealing a face that struck Alexandria with immediate recognition.

"Theo?" Alexandria whispered, her voice catching. "Is that really you?"

"Aye, it's me," Theodora responded, her eyes shining with unshed tears. "Been a wee while, hasn't it? Seventeen years too long, I'd say." She gave a half-smile that matched Alexandria's own. "Seems like we've both been through a fair bit, eh?"

Alexandria reached for her sister's hands, a rush of completion washing over her at the contact. The emptiness she'd carried her whole life—the one she'd never been able to name—suddenly made perfect sense.

"We need ta break this thing that's keepin' us apart," Theodora said, squeezin' Alexandria's fingers. "Together, we're strong enough ta fight whatever's comin'. But we don't have much time."

Standing side by side at the water's edge, they faced their reflections—mirror images finally reunited—and something in the shadows seemed to retreat.

They walked the dreamscape together, light rippling outward with each step. Flashes of memory surfaced—two small girls hiding under blankets with a stolen lantern, whispering secrets; racing through castle corridors, laughing; sitting beneath the stars, making impossible promises.

Alexandria felt it then—a presence watching from the edges of her dream. Brief glimpses of a shadow, a figure wielding power that felt suffocating and familiar.

"We're gettin' closer to the truth," Theodora said, her expression hardening. "But be careful. While we're separated in the wakin' world, that thing out there grows stronger."

Before Alexandria could respond, the dream fractured. An unseen force tore her from Theodora's grasp. The dreamscape twisted, colors bleeding into chaos as Theodora's form dissolved into mist.

"Find me!" Theodora's voice echoed as she vanished, leaving Alexandria alone in the collapsing dream.

Alexandria jerked awake, tears still wet on her face as the harsh mountain ground replaced the comfort of her dream. She wiped her cheeks, the hollow ache in her chest more tangible than any pain she'd ever felt. Theodora's absence carved a physical emptiness inside her—a void she hadn't known existed until tonight's connection.

As she blinked away the last tears, her resolve crystallized. Finding her twin had become something far greater now. The shared memories, the lurking shadow at the dream's edge—everything connected their past, their homeland and the darkness threatening both. Their reunion wasn't just personal; it was essential. The dream wasn't a dream, but a deliberate message across whatever barrier separated them. Alexandria knew she would answer it.

Sleep abandoned her for the rest of the night as she tossed on the hard ground, her mind racing through everything she'd learned. A sister she never knew, a homeland in danger, powers she barely understood—it all swirled relentlessly in her thoughts. The moonlight faded as clouds drifted overhead, casting the valley in deeper shadow.

Amid her turmoil, Aris—now back in her familiar cat form—curled against Alexandria's side. Her warm presence and steady purr offered stability when nothing else made sense. Alexandria's fingers found Aris's fur, taking comfort in this one unchanged thing while her entire world transformed around her.

As dawn broke over the horizon, Alexandria stirred from sleep, her mind already racing with memories of the night before. Beside her, Aris purred softly, the familiar sound grounding her when uncertainty threatened to take hold. The black cat stretched lazily, her sleek fur catching the golden morning light that filtered through the trees. All around them, the forest came to life—the songs of waking birds filled the air, and a gentle breeze sent leaves rustling in a whispered greeting.

Aris let out a quiet meow, her golden eyes locking onto Alexandria's with an almost knowing look. Without hesitation, she rose gracefully and padded toward the dwindling embers of last night's fire.

Alexandria watched as Aris circled the flames, her movements fluid and deliberate. With a flick of her paw, the feline conjured a small breakfast for them both. A delicate table appeared, set with an array of golden pastries drizzled with honey and sprinkled with chopped nuts. A bowl brimming with ripe peaches, plump grapes and vibrant oranges added a burst of color and sweetness to the feast.

A steaming pot of oatmeal materialized over the fire, its rich aroma of warm spices blending with the crisp morning air. At the center of the table a pot of herbal tea appeared, its fragrant steam carrying hints of mint and soothing chamomile, accompanied by two waiting cups.

Even after her short time in Kandella, Alexandria still marveled at Aris's abilities. The feline guardian never ceased to surprise her—whether with her shapeshifting prowess or effortless mastery of elemental magic. As she stepped toward the table, Aris tilted her head playfully, as if inviting her to indulge in the meal.

When they had savored the last bites of breakfast, Alexandria watched in quiet fascination as Aris wove more patterns in the air. With practiced ease, she unraveled their campsite, dissolving it into shimmering wisps of magic that swirled briefly before vanishing into nothingness. It was a subtle yet powerful reminder of the fleeting nature of their journey—each step another thread in the ever-changing tapestry of their fate.

Aris transformed into a wolf with a seamless shift, her white coat gleaming in the morning sun. Alexandria watched with quiet amazement, still not quite used to the effortless way her companion changed forms—one moment a cat, the next a powerful wolf standing before her. Aris turned, eyes meeting hers with clear intelligence, and nodded once. Message received. They set off into the snow-covered forest together.

Hours passed as they pushed deeper into the wilderness. Their footprints trailed behind them in the pristine snow—one set human, one set wolf—while towering trees cast long shadows across their path. The forest remained quiet except for the occasional crunch of snow beneath their feet.

Aris stayed vigilant, ears pricked forward and nose testing the air as she led the way. Alexandria found herself lost in thought, memories of childhood surfacing as they walked. She recalled following Theodora through woods much like these, her sister always the fearless one, laughing as she chased butterflies and discovered hidden clearings. Alexandria wondered if Theodora still carried that spark of adventure somewhere inside her, or if years of separation and hardship had dimmed it beyond recognition.

The air turned colder, carrying hints of ancient magic and unseen threats. Alexandria huddled deeper into her cloak, thankful for its protection against the chill. The trees seemed to whisper secrets as the wind rustled through their branches, sending a shiver down her spine. As they neared a small clearing, Aris halted, her ears pricked up and a soft growl escaped her throat. "Stay close to me," she warned. "We need to be on guard."

Alexandria tensed, her eyes darting around to survey the area. "What's wrong? Do you see something?"

"There's something nearby that shouldn't be here," Aris replied, her eyes narrowing.

A sudden rustling drew their focus. From the bushes emerged a mysterious figure. Garbed in shimmering hues of emerald and sapphire, his dark hair framed the angular features that radiated an air of enigma and keen intellect.

"Who are you?" Alexandria asked.

The stranger's laughter echoed with an eerie quality. His intense amethyst eyes seemed to bore into her very soul, causing goosebumps to prickle along her skin.

"Names are fickle things," he responded. "Jasper will do, if ya need somethin' to hold on to." He advanced with an otherworldly grace.

Alexandria regarded him cautiously, her hand poised to grab the hidden dagger Elmer had given her. Aris took a protective stance beside her, a menacing rumble building in her chest.

Jasper held up his hands in a placating manner. "Now now, I come in peace. The strange sorcery of this land led me to this spot."

Alexandria's instincts screamed uncertainty. "This journey is ours alone, stranger. It might be best if you just move along and go your own way," she countered, her tone politely firm but laced with underlying wariness. Aris maintained her vigilant posture, hackles slightly raised in silent warning.

Jasper's grin widened as he noted Aris's defensive stance. "Ah, travelin' solo in these parts can be a real risk, ya know. Your friend there seems to understand that quite well."

Alexandria wrestled with the conflicting urges of caution and curiosity regarding Jasper's motives.

"What's your aim here? Why have you come?" Aris questioned.

"I be seekin' the knowledge that whispers in these old trees and rides on the wind," Jasper replied, his smile broadening at her query.

"We're on our own mission," Alexandria stated with finality, her voice kind but resolute. "There's no time for detours or needless chatter."

Jasper's eyes lingered on her, a glimmer of intrigue and something bordering on admiration in his gaze. "Ah, but isn't it often the unexpected turns o' fate that guide us to our true paths?" His words carried a peculiar wisdom, hinting that he knew more about their quest than he let on.

Aris stayed alert, her unwavering loyalty compelling her to watch Jasper.

"We don't need any added complications," Alexandria said. "If you have nothing to contribute to our goal, then we'll be on our way."

"Steadfast and perceptive, quite the combination," Jasper remarked, his tone respectful despite the intriguing undercurrents in his words. "But ye see, fate has a way o' bringin' together the most unlikely of allies, guidin' them towards intertwined destinies."

Alexandria's jaw clenched at his statement, a flicker of doubt crossing her features. She exchanged a glance with Aris, wordlessly conveying her misgivings about Jasper's enigmatic insinuations. The wolf's eyes reflected a glimmer of caution, but also a spark of interest, as if sensing there was more to Jasper than appearances suggested.

The forest itself seemed to hold its breath, the leaves frozen in midair as if time had stilled in acknowledgment of the stirring magic.

Before they could speak another word, a distant rumble shattered the fragile peace. The ground trembled beneath them, leaves swirling around their feet as trees groaned in protest against an unseen force threatening the forest's foundation.

Aris bristled with an instinctual warning as Alexandria gripped her dagger handle, scanning for the source of the turmoil. Jasper's expression shifted to one of surprise and concern.

"We're done gabbin'," Jasper declared. "Dark magic's at play 'ere."

"Follow my lead and stay close," Jasper commanded, his voice cutting through the chaos as he charged ahead without a backward glance.

Alexandria and Aris locked eyes, a silent understanding passing between them. Despite their lingering reservations about Jasper, they knew their best chance of survival lay in sticking together. With a curt nod, they sprinted after him, dodging fallen branches and leaping over gnarled roots as they fought to keep pace with his nimble form.

The once peaceful forest turned chaotic, filled with distorted shadows and howling winds. A heavy pressure pressed on Alexandria's chest, the air thick with a sinister force. Despite her fear, she focused on the steady rhythm of her feet and Aris's reassuring presence beside her.

Aris's feline gaze burned with unwavering determination, a beacon of strength amidst the tempest. Her sleek form wove through the undergrowth with fluid grace, each powerful stride a testament to her indomitable spirit.

A thunderous boom shook the ground beneath their feet, sending shockwaves rippling through the forest floor. Jasper forged ahead, his cloak whipping behind him as he navigated the treacherous terrain with uncanny skill. Uprooted trees and jagged rocks hurtled through the air, propelled by the relentless onslaught of dark magic that sought to thwart their progress.

"Come on now, quick as ye can!" Jasper shouted, his voice barely cutting through the roar of the storm.

Alexandria gritted her teeth, determination burning in her eyes as she pushed herself to keep up with him. Aris ran beside them with effortless speed, her sleek fur rippling over powerful muscles as she surged ahead.

The air itself felt charged, crackling with an unnatural energy, as if the forest was fighting back against the darkness closing in around them. Shadows twisted and writhed between the trees, reaching out with ghostly fingers, desperate to pull them in.

Then, out of nowhere, a frigid wind tore through the trees, carrying an eerie whisper that wove itself into the electric hum of the storm. The sound wrapped around her, tugging at something deep inside. A faint green glow flickered at her fingertips, pulsing in time with the strange energy in the air.

With each step, the power inside her grew, feeling like a lost piece of herself snapping into place. Memories she tried to untangle for years revealed this magic was not new; it had always been there, waiting. As they raced through the forest, Alexandria focused inward on the awakening energy, ignoring Jasper's warnings. It was the same magic she felt on the bus when the Shadow Walkers appeared—once dormant, now reemerging.

The forest itself seemed to recognize Alexandria's awakening power, the ancient trees whispering their secrets as the spirits of nature acknowledged her abilities with reverence. Leaves hung suspended in midair, branches frozen in place, and even the shadows paused their relentless advance, as if hesitant to approach the princess.

Aris felt the shift in Alexandria's aura, the significance of this moment not lost on her. The magic that had lain dormant within the princess for so long was finally stirring, ready to be unleashed.

Jasper noticed the soft glow emanating from Alexandria's hands and slowed his pace. A grin spread across his face, his eyes sparkled with admiration. "Well, would ya look at that? Seems fate knew exactly what it was doin' when it led ya down this path, lass," he remarked as the chaos around them subsided.

In the eerie quiet that followed, Alexandria's heart raced, the newfound power surged through her veins both exhilarating and terrifying. She struggled to maintain control, her breath coming in quick gasps as she fought to steady herself.

Sensing her distress, Aris gently nudged Alexandria, a silent reassurance passing between them amidst the hushed forest. The princess could feel the ancient whispers of the trees resonating within her, a connection she had never experienced before.

Jasper took a step closer, his gaze locked on Alexandria. "Yer journey's just beginnin', lass. The path ahead is filled with great power and even greater challenges. But somethin' tells me ya already knew that."

As silence settled over the forest once more, Alexandria raised her glowing hands, the soft green light illuminating Jasper's face. A surge of courage washed over her, a determination to harness this newfound power and use it for good. "Let's keep moving," she said, her voice steady despite the uncertainty that still lingered. Aris nodded in agreement, and the trio pressed on, venturing deeper into the forest, guided by the ethereal glow emanating from Alexandria's hands.

As the day drew to a close, exhaustion began to take its toll on the weary travelers. Alexandria felt the weight of their journey bearing down on her, the chill of the wintry air seeped into her bones despite the warmth of the setting sun. Aris, ever vigilant, scanned their surroundings with a keen eye, her muscles tense and ready to spring into action at the first sign of danger. Her wolf-like instincts had served them well thus far, but the threats lurking in the shadows of the forest remained a constant concern.

"We should make camp for the night," Jasper suggested, his voice cutting through the tense silence. "We've still got a long way to go come mornin'."

Too tired to argue, Alexandria nodded, grateful for the chance to rest her aching limbs and gather her strength. She sank down onto a fallen log, the rough bark biting into her palms as she steadied herself.

Jasper rummaged through his pack, producing a meager meal of dried venison and bread. It was simple fare, but Alexandria welcomed the nourishment, the warmth of the food helping to chase away the chill that had settled in her bones. As they ate, Jasper shared his story, revealing the events that had led to his exile from Kandella. Once a member of the royal guard, someone falsely accused him of treason and banished him, forcing him to survive alone in the unforgiving wilderness.

Alexandria listened intently, her heart ached for the injustice Jasper had endured. She couldn't begin to imagine the pain and loneliness he must have faced during his years in exile. "I'm so sorry, Jasper," she said, placing a comforting hand on his shoulder.

"Ah, don't you worry about me, lass," Jasper grinned, brushing off her concern. "I've managed just fine on me own."

As the crackling fire cast dancing shadows on the trees around them, Alexandria's thoughts drifted to the events that had brought them to this point. The hand of destiny seemed to guide their every move, pulling them ever closer to the inevitable confrontation that lay ahead.

The trio settled into a comfortable silence, each lost in their own thoughts. Jasper busied himself with tending to the fire, adding more wood to keep the flames burning bright. Alexandria watched as the embers danced and swirled, casting a warm glow over their makeshift camp. Aris remained ever watchful, her eyes never straying far from the shadows that lurked just beyond the reach of the firelight. Exhaustion finally claimed Alexandria, the crackling of the fire and Aris's steady presence lulling her into a fitful sleep as she drifted off.

As dawn broke, a fierce Thundersnow approached, with ominous clouds circling overhead. Nature itself was preparing for battle, and the chill in the air intensified the sense of foreboding. Alexandria woke up shivering, her heart raced as she looked around at the gathering storm.

Jasper surveyed their camp, his eyes narrowed against the biting wind. "We've got to move fast," he called out over the rising gusts. "Thundersnows don't quit, and we can't be hanging about here."

Alexandria's breath caught in her throat as she pushed herself to her feet, her muscles tense and aching from the sudden rush of adrenaline. Her heart pounded in her chest, each beat echoing in her ears as she quickly scanned their surroundings.

The dense forest pressed in around them, shadows shifting in the dim morning light. She turned to Aris, whose piercing eyes met hers with a steady resolve. There was no need for words—she could see the determination etched into her features, the quiet understanding that danger was near.

Without hesitation, they moved swiftly, their hands working in practiced efficiency as they dismantled their small camp. Alexandria kicked snow over the dying embers of the fire, ensuring no trace remained, while Jasper secured their packs. Every rustling leaf and distant call of a bird set her nerves on edge, but there was no time for hesitation. Within moments, they were ready, their belongings slung over their shoulders as they slipped back into the forest, their footsteps light and cautious.

Chapter 9

"Visions Through Time"

THE ANCIENT FOREST SURROUNDED them, its tall trees providing sanctuary amid chaos. Finnegan moved into the shadows, eyes scanning for any pursuers. The echoes of the destroyed village lingered, a haunting reminder of their narrow escape—O'Connor's Pub, once filled with laughter, now in ruins.

With a fluid motion, Finnegan dismounted, his well-worn boots sinking into the soft, damp earth. He reached out a steadying hand to Theodora, his brow creased with concern as she stumbled slightly. "Ye holdin' up alright, Princess?"

"I'm managin'," she replied. "Titles be damned in a place like this. Just call me Theo."

With a quick nod, Finnegan led them deeper into the heart of the forest, the dense canopy overhead casting dappled shadows across their path. Each step carried the weight of the unknown, a fragile balance between the promise of safety and the lurking dangers that awaited them. The rustling of leaves and the distant cries of unseen creatures formed a primal symphony, a reminder of the untamed power that surrounded them.

Unable to bear the heavy silence any longer, Theodora spoke, her voice wavering between desperation and a profound yearning. "Finnegan, what do ye know of me parents? Any tales or whispers ye might've heard?" Her words carried the weight of an unspoken plea, a desperate hunger to unravel the mysteries of her own past.

Finnegan paused, his bronzed features drawn in contemplation as he mulled over his response. "Truth and legend often blur together," he said at last, his words measured and enigmatic. "The stories I've gathered over the years be a tangled web, lass."

His piercing gaze met hers, a flicker of something ancient and knowing in their depths. "When the time is right, the magic within ye will reveal what ye seek." His tone carried the reverence of one who had witnessed the true power that shaped their world, a subtle warning that the answers she craved might come at a cost.

"Time be a luxury we don't have," Theodora countered, her voice edged with a mixture of frustration and raw determination. "Me mind feels like an endless abyss, swallowing up everything I once knew."

A shadow passed over Finnegan's face, a flicker of empathy in his eyes as he nodded in understanding. He knew all too well the anguish of lost memories, the suffocating feeling of being untethered from one's own history. "The past has a way of resurfacing when ye least expect it, lass," he said, his words carrying a bittersweet undercurrent of experience.

As they ventured deeper into the wild embrace of the forest, each step became a gamble, a test of faith in the face of the unknown. Majestic Sycamores, Poplars, Rowans and Hazels loomed over them like ancient guardians, their branches reaching skyward as if to shield them from the perils that lurked beyond.

A twig snapped suddenly underfoot, shattering the eerie tranquility; the sound reverberated through the stillness like a gunshot. Theodora's horse reared up in panic, sending her tumbling to the ground. Instinctively, she thrust out her hands to break her fall, her fingers sinking into the cool, moist soil.

As the world spun around her, fragmented memories assaulted her mind, crashing against her consciousness like relentless waves. Through the haze, she caught fleeting glimpses of her parents, their eyes blindfolded and their hands bound, being dragged away by the merciless Shadow Walkers. The brutal truth of their fate shattered the illusion of security she had clung to, the weight of it threatening to crush her.

A strangled cry tore from Theodora's throat as she clawed her way back to the present, the vision still searing behind her eyelids. Her thoughts whirled in a frenzied maelstrom, each one a raging tempest that threatened to drag her under. She grappled with the line between truth and delusion, desperate to make sense of the revelation that had seized her.

With trembling limbs, Theodora hauled herself up from the forest floor, her mud-stained hands a mirror of the chaos that raged within her. She gulped in ragged breaths, fighting against the deluge of emotions that threatened to overwhelm her.

"Theo, what's wrong? Are ye hurt?" Finnegan's voice pierced through the haze of her anguish, his concern palpable in the charged air between them.

Tears welled up in Theodora's emerald eyes as she grappled with the enormity of what she had just witnessed. "I saw them, Finn. Me Ma and Da... They were taken by those blasted Shadow Walkers..." Her voice cracked, raw with disbelief and a desperate, fragile hope. The vision defied everything she had been led to believe, forcing her to question the very foundation of her existence.

Finnegan's face softened, his eyes brimming with compassion as he watched Theodora grapple with the enormity of her vision. The ancient forest seemed to echo her turmoil, the rustling leaves a gentle whisper of empathy.

"Ye saw 'em, lass?" Finnegan asked, his voice barely above a reverent murmur. In all his years guiding young magic-wielders, he'd never witnessed such a potent vision manifesting in one so new to the craft.

Theodora nodded, her auburn locks cascading around her face. "Aye, Finn. As real as you standin' before me now. But I don't understand... how can this be?" Her voice wavered, confusion and desperate hope warring in her eyes.

Finnegan placed a comforting hand on her shoulder, his touch grounding her amidst the emotional upheaval. "What ye saw, Theo... 'tis a rare gift, a window into the great weavin' of fate. The magic you speak of is called retrocognition. It's the ability to see things that happened in the past. It's said objects soak up the energy around 'em, and when someone with the gift lays a hand on that object or place, they catch a glimpse of the past."

Theodora shook her head, disbelief etched across her features. "But Ms. Whoo... she said they perished at sea, years ago. Why would she lie to me like that?"

Finnegan sighed, the weight of understanding settling on his broad shoulders. "Ye know Ms. Whoo, lass. She had her reasons, misguided as they may have been. Not lies, but a veil meant to protect ye from those who'd use the truth to hurt ye."

Theodora clenched her jaw, hot tears stinging her eyes as the betrayal cut deep. "Protect me? By lettin' me believe they were dead?" The words tore from her throat, raw and anguished.

"In her mind, 'twas the only way," Finnegan replied, his voice a soothing balm to her fractured heart. "She wanted to keep ye safe 'til ye could stand on yer own two feet, 'til yer true powers awakened and ye were ready to face yer fate."

The revelation hit Theodora like a punch to the gut, leaving her reeling. She teetered on the brink of despair, struggling to reconcile the love she held for Ms. Whoo with the bitter sting of deception.

But amidst the maelstrom of emotions, a fierce resolve took root in her heart. "I won't rest until I find 'em, Finn. Whatever it takes, whatever I have to face... I'll bring 'em home."

Finnegan met her determined gaze, a flicker of pride sparking in his eyes. "Aye, lass. And I'll be right there beside ye, every step o' the way. 'Tis my sworn duty to guide ye, to see this prophecy through and reunite yer family once more."

He cast a wary glance at the lengthening shadows, a sense of urgency settling over him. "But fer now, we best keep movin'. Those blasted Shadow Walkers won't stop 'til they have ye in their clutches."

Theodora nodded, squaring her shoulders as a newfound strength surged through her veins. The path ahead was fraught with peril, but she was no longer alone. With Finnegan by her side and the love for her parents burning bright in her heart, she knew she could face whatever challenges lay in wait.

Side by side, they ventured further into the forest's enigmatic heart, towering trees keeping watch as they delved deeper into the unknown. The wind carried foreboding whispers through the rustling leaves above, and a veil of uncertainty hung heavy before them.

"I don't like this one bit, Finn," Theodora muttered, her eyes darting warily between the shadowed trunks. "Feels like the very trees are hidin' something."

Finnegan nodded grimly. "Aye, lass. There be ancient secrets in these woods, and not all of 'em friendly. Best keep our wits about us."

Despite the mounting sense of trepidation, one unwavering truth burned bright in Theodora's heart—she would never surrender, not until she uncovered the truth and rescued those she cherished, whatever the cost.

"I'll turn over every damn leaf in this forest if I have to," she declared. "Me family's out there, Finn. I can feel it in me bones."

Finnegan laid a reassuring hand on her shoulder. "And we'll find 'em, Theo. You've got me word on that. But we gotta be smart about it, take things one step at a time."

With each stride, they drew closer to a fate that threatened to upend the very foundations of their world. Yet in that moment, united by the bonds of loyalty and a shared purpose, they found the strength to push onward, ready to face whatever trials lay ahead.

An unnatural hush blanketed the forest as they crept through the undergrowth, their footsteps muffled by a thick carpet of moss and decaying leaves. Tendrils of shadows writhed between ancient trunks, their sinister dance hinting at the arcane secrets lurking in the woodland's depths. Finnegan's hawk-like gaze swept over their surroundings, his battle-honed senses sharp for any sign of danger.

The deeper they ventured into the forest's shadowy heart, the more Theodora's unease grew, gnawing at her insides like a restless beast. Then, without warning, Khadall burst through the trees, his piercing eyes scanning the area with fierce intensity.

"Khadall, where've ya been all this time?" Theo demanded, unable to hide the worry that edged her voice.

The owl landed gracefully on a dead tree branch. "Aye, lass, I've been keepin' a keen eye on them Shadow Walkers since ye departed Primrose," Khadall replied gruffly. "They've been lurkin' in the shadows, biding their time, waitin' for the right moment to strike."

Finnegan's jaw tightened. "We'd best find a hidin' spot 'fore they catch up," he muttered, almost to himself. "Somewhere they wouldn't even think to look, ya know?"

Theodora nodded, the gravity of their situation settling like a lead weight in her gut.

As they pushed deeper into the eerie forest, a rich voice emanated from the ancient trees, stopping them in their tracks. "Ah, per'aps I can be of some assistance, Finnegan, me lad!" The air shimmered between two weathered rowans as a portal took shape, revealing a striking figure within.

The mysterious stranger stepped forth, his aquamarine eyes glinting in the portal's fading light. Tapered ears peeked out from beneath a mane of lustrous cobalt hair, and his flowing sapphire robes billowed around him like the currents of an enchanted stream, lending him an undeniably otherworldly presence.

In a flash, Finnegan drew his sword, the razor-sharp blade gleaming as he raised it in challenge. Muscles coiled and ready to strike, he positioned himself in front of Theodora, shielding her smaller form with his own.

"Easy now!" Finnegan warned, sword at the ready. "Who might ye be, stranger?"

The stranger held up his hands in a placating gesture. "Peace, Finnegan. I am Killian, a halfling of Isidore." His melodious voice held a note of authority that commanded attention.

Theodora's eyebrows shot up in disbelief. "A halfling? I thought yer kind only existed in fairy tales?"

Killian chuckled, his eyes sparkling with amusement. "Aye, Theodora, there's often more truth to legends than most would believe. I can promise ye, I'm as real as the dirt beneath yer boots and the breeze that dances through the trees."

He flashed a crooked grin. "We halflings might be outcasts, but we've carved out a realm of our own in Isidore, tucked far from pryin' eyes. And now, looks like fate brought our paths together."

Finnegan kept his sword raised, eyeing the unexpected visitor with suspicion. "I've heard tales of yer kind in the taverns, but I never believed 'em to be more than drunken ramblings."

Killian chuckled, a melodic sound that seemed to dance on the breeze. "Seein' is believin', me friend. We halflings may hail from a different realm, but our loyalty to the Royal Family and the Kingdom of McKuilly remains unshakable." He swept into a graceful bow, his sapphire robes shimmering in the ethereal light.

"Isidore will provide sanctuary for ye, Princess Theodora," Killian assured her, his cloak fluttering as if touched by an unseen force. "The Shadow Walkers' sight cannot penetrate the veil that separates our worlds. Come, let me guide ye to safety."

As they followed Killian through the shimmering portal, Theodora felt as though she had stepped into a vivid dream. A delicate, floral aroma suffused the air in Isidore, filling Theodora's lungs with each breath. Gone was the damp, earthy scent of the Monaghan forest, replaced by the sweet perfume of an eternal spring.

Beneath her feet, the ground transformed from the soft, yielding soil of the woods to a lush carpet of grass, each blade a vibrant emerald hue. The colors seemed to pulse with an inner radiance, as if the very essence of life flowed through every leaf, petal and stone.

Theodora found herself standing at the edge of a vast meadow, awash in a golden light that seemed to emanate from the land itself. The sky above was a breathtaking azure, unmarred by even the faintest wisp of clouds. In the distance, majestic waterfalls cascaded down rocky cliffs, their mists catching the light and casting prismatic rainbows across the horizon.

Overhead, birds of every imaginable hue soared on iridescent wings, their melodious songs filling the air with a symphony of joy. Mist draped the towering mountains around the meadow in gossamer veils, giving them an air of mystery and grandeur.

Everywhere Theodora looked, she saw wonders that defied belief. Exotic flowers with luminous petals dotted the landscape, their gentle glow adding to the enchantment of the scene. Motes of golden pixie dust drifted on the breeze, settling on her skin and hair like a sprinkling of living stardust.

Finnegan remained close by her side, his keen gaze sweeping their surroundings for any sign of danger. Despite the breathtaking beauty of Isidore, the druid's instincts remained as sharp as ever, honed by a lifetime of battles fought and perils faced.

As Killian led them deeper into the heart of the realm, Theodora felt a profound sense of peace settle over her, unlike anything she had ever known. It was as if the very essence of Isidore was a soothing balm, easing the fears and doubts that had plagued her for so long.

They soon came to a shimmering lake, its surface as smooth and clear as the finest glass. Its tranquil depths mirrored the breathtaking beauty of the sky and surrounding landscape. A delicate mist rose from the water, wreathing them in a soft, ethereal haze.

Killian turned to face them, his aquamarine eyes aglow with an inner serenity. "Isidore is a safe haven, untouched by the darkness that lurks beyond," he said. "Within these borders, evil holds no sway."

Finnegan's hand remained on the hilt of his sword, his stance relaxing only slightly. "Even the fairest of realms can hide unseen dangers," he warned, ever the cautious guardian.

Killian inclined his head, acknowledging the druid's wisdom. "Aye, you speak true me friend. But in Isidore, the light of the ancient magic that flows through this land safeguarded us. Here, we walk in peace and safety."

As Theodora gazed out over the tranquil beauty of Isidore, she felt a flicker of hope kindle in her heart. For this one perfect moment, despite the uncertain path ahead, she believed anything was possible.

The journey continued, their path winding through the vibrant landscape. As they moved further from the lake, the terrain began to change. The ethereal glow of the flowers dimmed, replaced by the soft gleam of crystal structures in the distance. Theodora's heart fluttered at the sight, her mind filled with wonder at what lay ahead.

Soon, they reached the capital, a magnificent city of carved crystal spires and silver filigree that sparkled under the sun. Killian guided them through the streets crowded with fey folk who stared at Theodora with curious eyes. At the city's heart stood the palace, a gravity-defying marvel of halflings' advanced magics. Towers twisted impossibly skyward.

Killian's footsteps echoed against polished crystal floors as he escorted Theodora through the sunlit halls. Shimmering tapestries adorned the opulent chamber, depicting ancient battles and mystical creatures. Halfling elders observed Theodora with reverence and intrigue, their faces etched with untold secrets.

Queen Seraphina enveloped Theodora in a warm embrace, her ethereal gown shimmering like starlight. "Ah, Theodora, at last! Welcome to Isidore, dear lass. Consider this yer home for now, and us yer family." She stepped back, her azure eyes twinkling with affection. "Together, we shall help unravel the secrets of yer past and guide ye on the path the fates have laid before ye."

Theodora dipped into a deep curtsy, her heart swelling with gratitude. "Thank ye, Yer Majesty. Yer kindness means more than I can say."

As the wise ones murmured amongst themselves, their ancient eyes filled with a knowing light, as Killian cleared his throat. He moved to Theodora's side, his brow furrowed with concern. "Forgive me, Princess, but I must ask - has anyone ever spoken to ye of yer heritage? Of the magic that flows through yer veins?"

Theodora's eyes widened, a flicker of uncertainty passing over her face. "I... No, not really. Ms. Whoo began ta explain that I had magic in me veins, and I had a great fate ahead of me, but that was all."

Killian exchanged a meaningful glance with Queen Seraphina, a silent understanding passing between them. He turned back to Theodora, his voice gentle but earnest. "Then it seems, lass, that we have much to discuss. The truth of yer past and the power ye wield may come as quite a shock, but fear not - we shall be with ye every step of the way."

Theodora settled into her seat before Queen Seraphina, her heart pounding at the mere mention of her magical abilities. The memory of the shadowy figure that had materialized in her chambers the previous night came rushing back, its enigmatic words reverberating through her mind. Taking a deep, steadying breath, Theodora met the queen's gaze and began to recount the unsettling encounter.

"Last night, a dark silhouette appeared in me room, Yer Majesty," Theodora explained, her voice unwavering despite the intensity smoldering in her eyes. "It was faceless and eerie, shrouded in shadows. The figure spoke of me destiny and hinted at the role I'm meant to play in some grand scheme. But it vanished before I could get any real answers, leavin' me with nothin' but more questions."

Meeting Killian's gaze with determination, she continued, "Ms. Whoo... she's been me nanny since I was a wee lassie. Today, she revealed that she shielded me from Valendor's prying eyes and blocked me memories." Despite her inner turmoil, Theodora's voice remained steady. "She knew the truth of me past and me powers, but feared what would happen if Valendor discovered them."

Finnegan spoke with regret in his voice and empathy in his eyes. "I should've been more understanding when we first met, lass. Your destiny is a burden no one should face alone."

"No need to be sorry, Finnegan," Theodora replied, adjusting her cloak. "We were both taken aback for different reasons."

"Let's start from the beginning," Killian suggested. As he spoke of unveiling hidden truths and ancient prophecies, Finnegan and he shared knowing glances. Their mission was clear: guide Theodora to discover her true purpose and unlock her dormant powers.

Finnegan cleared his throat, a determined glint in his eye. "Nine cycles have gone by, those blasted Shadow Walkers tried to snuff out the life foretold by prophecy. Their goal: to prevent a destined king and queen from sparking life within the queen's womb."

"The prophecy," continued Finnegan, his voice low but commanding, "spoke of twins. The destined pair weren't just meant to have one wee babe, but two. Two princesses born under the crescent moon's light, bound together like blood sisters. One with a fiery spirit as fierce as the sun's blaze, the other with a sharp mind as cunning as silver in the moon's glow. Together they'll shatter Lord Valendors' wicked plans and usher in a new age of brightness." He grimaced, "But that black-hearted bloke tried to wipe this truth from existence, for he knew that he couldn't stand against the power of these twins."

"Ah, sorry Finnegan," interjected Theodora. "Yer prophecy mentions siblings I don't 'ave. This fate can't be mine."

"Aye, Princess," Killian replied. "Why would the sorcerer send hellhounds after ya if yer words were true? Does he lack foresight?"

His question hung in the air, weighted with implication. "What's that supposed to mean?" Theodora asked.

"I'm sayin' that he's got the gift o' seein' through fate's tangled threads; his visions never stray from truth's path."

Theodora's head spun as she tried to make sense of it all.

"The Shadow Walkers will hunt ya down, Princess," Killian urged. "Lord Valendor's thirst for yer blood won't ease until yer heart stops beatin'. Whether ye embrace yer role in the prophecy or turn from it, he'll come for ya just the same. He'll leave nothin' to chance."

Killian's ominous warning echoed in her mind, shattering any illusions of safety. Lord Valendor's relentless pursuit would know no bounds, prophecy be damned. She'd forever be glancing over her shoulder, jumping at every unexpected noise. The very foundation of her existence had crumbled, leaving her adrift in a world turned hostile and unrecognizable.

"Ye mean to tell me," Theodora said, her voice quivering with emotion, "that no matter what I do, he will never stop huntin' me?"

Killian nodded. "I'm afraid so, lass. his obsession with the prophecy has consumed him. He'll stop at nothin' to see ye dead."

Theodora clenched her fists, a mixture of fear and anger coursing through her veins. "Then what am I supposed to do? Spend the rest of me life runnin'?"

"Nay, Princess," Finnegan interjected, his tone firm but reassuring. "Ye've got to embrace yer destiny, learn to harness the power within ye. Only then can ye hope to stand against the likes of Valendor and his minions."

Theodora drew in a shaky breath, the weight of her fate pressing down upon her like a suffocating burden. Her once-simple life had been torn away, replaced by a terrifying new reality where each shadow hid a looming threat.

For a long moment, silence hung heavy in the room. Theodora stared at the stone floor, her mind racing. Then, slowly, she lifted her gaze to meet Finnegan's. Her eyes held a new resolve, her fear now tempered with defiance. "Alright," she said, her voice steady. "I'll fight."

"Princess Theodora, might I be so bold as to try something? We may just find the answers you seek and put an end to these doubts," Killian's voice reverberated through the stony chamber, its lilting tone hushing the very air.

Theodora's gaze locked onto him, her eyes unblinking. "And what would ye have me do?"

"Clear yer mind and let yer spirit take flight back through the veils of your memory," Killian's words flowed over her, rich and melodic, dispelling the tension that clung to her like cobwebs. "Go back to the night those Shadow Walkers came, when the frigid darkness snatched yer parents away."

As Theodora closed her eyes, allowing Killian's soothing words to guide her, fragments of that fateful night began to flicker in her mind. Shadows danced in the moonlight, their inky tendrils coiling around her parents like serpents. She grasped at the shattered memories, desperate to piece together the puzzle of that horrific evening.

Killian's presence was a gentle anchor, his hand a feather-light touch on her forehead as he guided her through the twisting labyrinth of her past. Through the swirling fog, a silhouette emerged—a spectral guardian who had stood by her side, a silent sentinel against the darkness.

Theodora's eyes fluttered open, pools of emerald wide with revelation. "There was another there that night," she said, her voice quivering. "Someone right by me side."

Killian nodded, his gaze encouraging her to delve deeper. With his support, Theodora allowed herself to sink back into the memory. The fragmented images slowly wove together like the threads of a tapestry. A warm hand clasped hers, a beacon of comfort amidst the encroaching shadows. The figure beside her stood tall and resolute, a pillar of unwavering strength.

As Theodora honed in on the enigmatic figure by her side, the haze of uncertainty dissipated, revealing a startling truth. The mysterious companion bore an uncanny resemblance to Theodora herself, with the same cascading auburn tresses and vibrant emerald eyes that seemed to pierce through the very fabric of reality.

"Alexandria..." The name fell from her lips like a prayer. Tears traced glistening paths down her cheeks as the realization struck her with the force of a thunderbolt. The figure beside her, the spectral manifestation of her own essence, was none other than her twin sister.

Finnegan and Killian shared knowing glances, affirming the truth that had been concealed for so long. Theodora felt a surge of emotions—grief, joy and an overwhelming sense of connection—as the memories of shared laughter whispered secrets and an unbreakable connection flooded back to her.

"Princess," Finnegan said. "The bond between you and Alexandria is unbreakable, lass. It's a tether that can withstand any darkness and bind your fates together. Embrace it, for it shall be your greatest strength in the battles ahead."

Theodora emerged from the depths of her memories, her heart racing with newfound understanding. The realization that her twin sister, Alexandria, had been by her side all along filled her with a profound sense of emotion. She wiped away the tears that lingered on her cheeks, her gaze unwavering as she focused on Finnegan and Killian.

"Thank ye, Finnegan," she whispered, her voice filled with gratitude and strength. "I now understand the depths of me connection to Alexandria and the power it holds. Fate has torn apart us, but our bond endures."

Finnegan's eyes softened as he beheld Theodora's resolve. "Aye, lass, and together ye two will be unstoppable. Lord Valendor may seek to tear ye apart, but as long as ye stand together, no darkness can prevail."

Killian nodded in silent approval, his eyes reflecting a deep sense of respect for Theodora's newfound resolve. "The bond between ye and Alexandria is a beacon of hope in these dark times," he remarked, his voice carrying the weight of certainty. "United, ye hold the power to thwart Lord Valendor's malevolent schemes and bring back light ta the shadows that seek to engulf Kandella."

Theodora met their gazes. Her eyes were alight with determination. "We must find her," she said. Her voice remained steady despite the tempest of emotions within. "Together, we'll face whatever challenges lie ahead and put an end to Lord Valendor's reign of terror."

As the trio stood united, a ripple of ancient magic echoed through the chamber. It was a tangible manifestation of the prophecy that had set their fates in motion. Theodora felt the weight of destiny upon her shoulders, but she knew she would no longer face it alone. With her newfound allies and the flicker of power within her, she was ready to embark on a quest to shape the future of Kandella.

Theodora stood before Queen Seraphina, her heart pounding with a mixture of anticipation and trepidation. The queen's ancient eyes sparkled with wisdom as she spoke. Her voice acted as a soothing balm to Theodora's weary soul. "Child of prophecy, your journey is just beginning. The path ahead will be fraught with challenges, but you are not alone."

Theodora nodded, her resolve solidifying with each passing moment. She glanced at her new friends, gratitude welling up inside her for their unwavering support. Taking a deep breath, she braced herself for the journey ahead.

A soft hoot drew their attention to Khadall, perched on a nearby stone ledge. His intelligent eyes gleamed with understanding. With a graceful movement, he spread his wings, urging them to follow his lead.

Theodora approached her animal guardian, hand outstretched. "What is it, Khadall?"

As they stood there, Ms. Whoo emerged from the shadows. Her eyes sparkled with otherworldly wisdom. "Princess Theodora, ya journey thus far has been just a warm-up fer yer true calling. Ya were raised and molded, forged through trials and tribulations into the fierce leader ya were born to become."

Theodora's heart swelled with gratitude. "I'll forever be thankful fer yer guidance, Ms. Whoo."

The wise owl inclined her head, a smile playing upon her face. "It's been an honor, me dear. But now, it's time fer ya to continue yer training and fully embrace yer destiny."

Killian stepped forward. Determination filled his eyes. "Princess Theodora, Finnegan and I will be guiding ya. We'll be helpin' ya fine-tune your magical abilities and sharpen yer defensive skills. Together, we'll be gettin' ya ready for the challenges ahead."

Theodora nodded. A flicker of concern crossed her features. "I left me bow and arrow behind when I fled the castle."

Killian reassured her with a warm smile. "Don't ye fret. We've got everythin' ye need right here. Tomorrow mornin', we'll start yer trainin'. But for now, rest up and gather yer strength."

As they left the castle, the crisp evening air greeted them, carrying the scent of Sycamore and earth. Vibrant hues of pink, orange, and red painted the sky. Jagged peaks stood in sharp contrast against the celestial canvas, their rugged silhouettes commanding a sense of majesty and wisdom.

Killian led them to a humble stone cottage nestled on the forest's edge. Its thatched roof and soft lantern light beckoned them closer, a haven of simplicity amidst the uncertainties that lay ahead.

Inside, Theodora settled onto a cot, her mind haunted by lingering images of her captured parents. Although her new allies showed kindness, she knew she needed to be cautious in a world where shadows hid both friend and foe.

As she drifted off to sleep, shadowy figures crept into her thoughts. The sense of looming danger lingered, a steady reminder of what lay ahead. She still had to find her missing sister—and somehow rescue her parents and reclaim their homeland. However, with the help of her faithful companions and the spark of magic inside her, she remained resolute in facing whatever obstacles may come her way. She was determined to protect her kingdom and those dear to her at all costs.

Hours passed as they trudged through the snow-covered forest, fueled by desperation and a burning sense of purpose. Alexandria struggled to keep up with Jasper's relentless pace, her lungs burning with each labored breath. The cold seeped into her bones, threatening to slow her down further.

"How much farther?" she asked between gasps for air, not daring to hope for a simple answer from his grim expression.

"We still have a fair bit of ground ta cover before we reach the mountains," he replied. "The bloody storm is dragging us down, but we can't afford to dawdle."

Aris surged forward, her frost-covered pelt a meager shield against the biting cold. Alexandria soldiered on, determination fueling her every step as she refused to let exhaustion or dread derail their critical mission.

"We need to get out of this storm soon," Aris warned, her voice a gruff rumble tinged with urgency.

Jasper shook his head, his eyes never leaving the treacherous path ahead. "No can do. We gotta press on, no matter what this blasted tempest throws our way."

Alexandria gave a curt nod, the gravity of their quest propelling her onward despite the bone-chilling cold seeping into her core.

An ear-splitting crack rent the air, followed by a barrage of snaps as overburdened branches gave way, crashing to the ground. The ancient trees shuddered and swayed, their limbs creaking under the onslaught of winter's fury. Undeterred, the trio forged ahead, their pounding hearts keeping time with their muffled footfalls.

With each step, the forest grew denser, the shadows deepening and closing in around them. An eerie stillness descended, broken only by the sporadic, distant howls of a wolf. As they delved deeper into the heart of the woods, Alexandria felt the weight of their mission bearing down upon her, the very air heavy with foreboding anticipation.

Without warning, the forest's tranquility shattered, replaced by a discordant cacophony of howls and shrieks that reverberated through the trees. Alexandria's heart raced, adrenaline surging through her veins as she exchanged an uneasy glance with her companions.

Otherworldly sounds, harsh and unidentifiable, wove through the animalistic chorus, as if the forest itself had come alive with an alien symphony. Every fiber of Alexandria's being thrummed with unease, an instinctive warning that raised the hairs on the back of her neck.

As they pressed forward, the unnerving noises grew louder, echoing through the underbrush and seeming to keep pace with their own rhythmic footsteps.

Aris, typically unflappable, edged closer to Alexandria, her ears flicking back and forth as she scanned the shadows for any hint of danger. Jasper's hand drifted to the hilt of his sword, his eyes narrowing as he scrutinized the darkness ahead.

"We've got company," Aris growled, her words sending a chill down Alexandria's spine.

Jasper gave a grim nod, his gaze sweeping the surrounding area. "Stay close, lass," he warned, his tone brooking no argument.

They pushed onward, the tension ratcheting up with each passing moment. The forest itself seemed to warp and twist around them, as if manipulated by an unseen force. Fleeting shapes darted at the periphery of their vision, vanishing into the gloom before they could identify them.

They reached a small clearing where the source of the chilling sounds revealed itself—a colossal obsidian wolf. Its fur shimmered with an otherworldly iridescence, while its crimson eyes blazed with ancient, mystical energy. The magnificent beast stood atop a snow-covered boulder, its muscles rippling beneath its glossy coat, poised to strike at a moment's notice.

The trio dropped low, concealing themselves behind frosted bushes to avoid drawing the creature's attention. The air crackled with tangible energy, the tension of an imminent confrontation hanging heavy in the frigid atmosphere.

Jasper, his gaze unwavering, signaled for Alexandria and Aris to remain hidden, his expression a mixture of wariness and resolve. The wolf prowled restlessly, its keen senses attuned to the slightest disturbance as it surveyed its domain.

Alexandria's heart hammered in her chest, fragmented memories surging to the surface - flashes of adrenaline from a mundane school bus ride now intermingling with this surreal encounter.

A deafening crack of thunder shattered the stillness, accompanied by jagged bolts of lightning that cast an eerie glow across the clearing. Aris tensed, her feline form bristling as the storm's chaos descended upon them.

The wolf's head snapped skyward, its ears flattening against its skull as it unleashed a chilling, otherworldly growl. The trio watched, transfixed, as the tempest intensified, the very air crackling with elemental fury.

"We need ta get out o' here," Jasper hissed, his voice nearly lost in the maelstrom's deafening roar.

The wolf whirled around, its piercing gaze fixating on their hidden location. An unearthly howl erupted from its throat, the sound reverberating through Alexandria's core like a seismic wave.

As their eyes locked, Alexandria glimpsed a flicker of recognition in the wolf's crimson depths, a realization that sent a shiver down her spine. But before she could dwell on the implications, a blinding bolt of lightning struck mere feet away, the accompanying thunderclap so deafening it seemed to shatter the very sky above them.

Another jagged bolt of lightning struck, the deafening crack making their hearts race. Alexandria felt the magic brewing within her, an untamed power surging through her veins.

"We've gotta get out of here, now!" Aris snarled, her feline eyes flashing with urgency in the darkness. "This storm will be the death of us if we don't move!"

Jasper nodded, his face set in unshakable resolve. In one swift motion, he vaulted from their hiding spot and sprinted forward, his feet tearing across the treacherous terrain. Aris was right behind him, her agile form cutting through the blizzard like a blade, never missing a step on the icy ground.

Alexandria turned to her companions. "Get going, I'll take care of this!" Her voice was calm and commanding, belying the dread coiling in her gut. As Jasper and Aris tore ahead, she spun to confront their pursuer.

Her hands began to emit an ethereal glow as magic thrummed through her body. Acting on instinct, she thrust her palms forward, summoning the raging winds to her aid. The gale-force gusts swirled around the monstrous black wolf, crackling with lightning and static. The beast let out an agonized howl, its fur standing on end as the electric charge engulfed it. Adrenaline surged through

Alexandria's veins, her heart pounded with a dizzying mix of terror and exhilaration as she bent the storm to her will. Never had she experienced such raw, unbridled power.

The wolf thrashed and convulsed, fighting desperately against the onslaught of wind and lightning. With one final, ear-splitting roar, the creature burst apart, dissolving into wisps of indigo smoke that vanished on the howling winds. Alexandria slowly lowered her trembling hands, her breath coming in ragged gasps as the magnitude of what she'd just done began to sink in.

"Alexandria!" Aris's voice cut through the haze of her racing thoughts. "What in blazes was that?"

She glanced over to see Aris and Jasper emerging from the underbrush, soaked to the bone but miraculously unscathed. She opened her mouth to respond, but faltered. Would they look at her differently now? Would they be afraid of what she could do?

"I..." She swallowed hard. "I think I called the storm."

Jasper's eyes grew wide as saucers as he took in the aftermath of the tempest, then turned his stunned gaze to Alexandria. "You did this? Summoned the bloody storm itself?"

The wind died down to a gentle breeze, carrying a scattering of leaves and debris. Aris circled Alexandria, her golden eyes shining with a mix of awe and concern.

"I always sensed the magic within you," she murmured soothingly. "But to wield the very elements like this... it's a power beyond anything I've ever seen."

Alexandria met Jasper's astonished stare, her own eyes shimmering with unshed tears. "I never imagined I was capable of something so intense. It's overwhelming," she admitted, her voice shaking.

An eerie calm settled over the forest, broken only by the soft patter of icy rain on the leaves above. Alexandria looked imploringly at her companions, desperate for their acceptance.

"I'm so sorry," she choked out. "I had no idea I could do that. Even when Diana said my abilities would return, I never thought...." Her words dissolved into a sob.

Aris was the first to break the heavy silence. She placed a reassuring paw on Alexandria's shoulder, her gaze unwavering. "You have nothing to apologize for," she said. "Your power is a gift, not something to fear."

Jasper nodded in solemn agreement, the shock in his eyes replaced by a fierce loyalty. As Alexandria looked between them, she felt a rush of profound relief. They didn't see her as a monster. They still stood by her side, united in their shared purpose.

The waning light cast dappled shadows across the forest floor as they journeyed deeper into the dense woods. Alexandria nibbled her lip, her mind awhirl with uncertainty. How could she possibly hope to master these wild new abilities that surged within her?

Jasper noticed her troubled expression and gave her shoulder a comforting squeeze. "Chin up, Alex. We'll figure this out, you and me. Together." His steady assurance helped calm the butterflies in her stomach.

The burble of a nearby stream drew them onward. Alexandria found solace in the river's constant flow, a reminder that change was a part of life's journey. She took a deep breath, letting the tranquility of nature soothe her frazzled nerves.

Though the weight of her growing powers felt like a burden, the soft breeze, and her loyal companions helped ease her apprehension. Aris trotted ahead, her tail raised like a flagpole of courage.

When they reached the riverbank, Jasper crouched down and scooped up a handful of the clear, cool water. "We ought to make camp here for the night," he advised, his tone gentle but resolute. "Traveling after nightfall is asking for trouble, 'specially with your magic being a bit... unpredictable at the moment."

Alexandria couldn't argue with that. Her body cried out for rest after the day's arduous trek.

They followed Aris along the water's edge until the trees parted, revealing a stunning view of rolling hills and distant, mist-shrouded peaks.

A small clearing tucked among the towering evergreens proved the perfect spot to set up camp. While Jasper ventured off to gather firewood, Aris prowled the edges of their site, ever watchful for any hint of danger.

As the sun slipped below the horizon, painting the sky in a brilliant array of colors, they settled in for the evening. The crackling campfire bathed their faces in a warm glow, but it couldn't fully chase away the underlying tension that hung in the air.

Jasper rummaged in his weathered pack and produced a simple meal of hard bread, aged cheese, and a handful of wrinkled fruits.

He spread the fare out on a flat rock for them to share. They fell upon the food eagerly, the quiet broken only by the crunch of the bread and the occasional appreciative murmur. Jasper stared pensively into the dancing flames while Alexandria gazed off into the distance, her forehead creased with worry.

Long into the night they discussed the path ahead, the gravity of their mission weighing heavily on each of them.

When at last the fire had died down to glowing embers, Alexandria crawled into her bedroll. She lay there, eyes fixed on the flickering flames, her thoughts consumed by memories of Theodora. Years had passed since cruel fate had ripped them apart, scattering them to the winds. The once vivid recollections of their carefree childhood days in the castle had dulled with time, like the fading brushstrokes of an ancient painting.

"I miss her so much it hurts," Alexandria murmured, her voice nearly lost beneath the fire's crackling. "I miss sneaking out together to go stargazing, how she could always make me laugh, even when everything seemed hopeless."

Aris snuggled close beside her, a warm and reassuring presence. Jasper glanced up from honing the edge of his blade, compassion softening his rugged features.

"Aye, lass, I know the feeling all too well," he said, his words laced with old pain. "When those bastards exiled me from Kandella, I lost everything. My home, my kin, my very purpose. But I never stopped believin' that someday I'd find a way to clear me name and take back the life they stole from me."

Alexandria met his eyes, and in their depths she saw a flicker of something that rekindled her own hopes. "Do you truly believe we can find her?" she asked, hating the tremor in her voice.

Jasper nodded with conviction. "I'd stake me life on it, Alexandria. There's a strength in ya, fierce as any warrior. I've seen it. And with Aris by your side and me knowledge of these lands, nothing in this world can stop us from bringin' you and yer sister back together again."

As the velvet cloak of night drew in around them, they traded tales of their pasts and whispered of the futures they dreamed of building. Alexandria listened with rapt attention as Jasper spoke of his days as a royal guard and the betrayal that had sealed his cruel fate. She shared precious memories of her adventures with Theodora, of the mischief they'd made and the secret dreams they'd spun beneath the stars.

With each passing moment, the barriers between them seemed to melt away, baring the vulnerable, beating hearts that lay beneath their battle-hardened veneers. And as the last embers winked out, and the stars glittered overhead, Alexandria felt a new fire ignite within her breast - the unquenchable flame of hope.

Come what may, she would find her again. With Aris's unshakable loyalty and Jasper's hard-won wisdom to guide her, she knew there was no force in this strange, new world that could stand against them.

Chapter 10

"Awakening the Storm"

As Alexandria slipped into sleep, her breathing slowed, her body relaxing into the quiet hush of night. Her mind drifted first to warmth—sunlight spilling over the high stone walls of the fortress where she and Theodora once played. They'd made up stories then, spun wild tales of dragons and destiny with nothing but sticks and imagination. Laughter had echoed off those ancient stones.

But the dream turned, as dreams do.

The brightness faded, swallowed by a creeping dusk. The fortress melted away, replaced by a dense, gnarled forest cloaked in shadows. The trees loomed above her, impossibly tall, their twisted limbs clawing at the sky. Wind whispered low, like a voice just out of reach.

She moved through the woods, barefoot and breathless, the silence pressing in. Every step stirred leaves that didn't rustle, and every branch seemed to bend just slightly toward her. She called out—first softly, then louder—searching, not for the fortress, but for something she hadn't realized she was missing.

For Theodora.

Her sister's name echoed unanswered into the void.

Then, something changed. The shadows thickened. The air grew colder. A presence stirred, like something ancient had awakened and taken notice.

A voice, low and rough, unfurled from the dark.

"Alexandria..."

She turned sharply, eyes scanning the trees. "Who's there?" Her own voice sounded small, distant.

No answer. Only the sudden, sharp snap of a branch underfoot that didn't belong to her.

And then—movement. A figure stepped into view, not from behind a tree, but out of the darkness itself. Cloaked in black, his face shrouded, only his eyes were visible—burning, unnatural, gleaming with malice.

Alexandria stumbled back. She tried to summon her magic, to draw on the light within her, but it faltered—like trying to grasp smoke. The man's presence seemed to drain it from her, just by being near.

"I know you," she whispered, the words trembling out of her before she could stop them. She didn't know how, but she did.

He smiled, teeth sharp, wrong. The woods around him seemed to wither, as if they recognized what he was and recoiled.

"You fear me," he said simply, his voice like cracking stone. "You should."

She took a shaky breath and lifted her chin. "I don't." The light sparked again, faint but real, flickering in her palms. "I won't."

The glow pushed against the dark, and the figure hissed, his form rippling like smoke in the wind. "Not yet," he growled, retreating into the trees. "But soon."

She woke with a start, heart pounding, the remnants of the dream clinging to her like cobwebs. The morning air was sharp against her skin, and she realized she was outside, not in her bedroll. Around her, the ancient ruins that encircled their camp pulsed with a faint, ethereal glow. It shimmered from the stones as if responding to the fear still racing through her, the light mirroring the rhythm of her heartbeat.

She sat up slowly, brushing hair from her face, her mind replaying every detail. That forest. That voice. The man cloaked in shadow.

She didn't know his name.

But she knew this much—he was real. Not just a dream. And he knew her.

Somewhere in her bones, she could feel it: her journey was no longer just about finding Theodora.

It was about surviving what waited in the dark.

"Alex?" Aris stirred beside her, her voice soft but tense. The cat blinked up at her, golden eyes wide. "What's wrong?"

Alexandria shook her head slowly. "Just a nightmare. But something about it felt... real. Like a warning."

Jasper was already sitting up, scanning the woods, muscles tense. "A warning of what?"

"I'm not sure," she said quietly, eyes still fixed on the pulsing stones. "But I have a feeling our journey is about to get a lot more complicated."

The moon climbed higher, its pale light casting long, twisting shadows through the dense forest. A haunting melody drifted on the breeze, a sound both delicate and unnerving, catching Jasper and Aris's attention. Jasper's fingers curled around his sword hilt, his instincts sharp as he scanned the darkness beyond their camp. Beside him, Aris stood rigid, her fur bristling, ears flicking at every subtle shift in the air. Her eyes gleamed with an ancient wisdom, as if she could sense something moving beyond the veil of night.

Then, the woods began to stir. Eerie whispers wove through the trees, an indistinct murmur carried by the wind. The air felt thick with anticipation, as if the entire forest was holding its breath. A chill ran down Jasper's spine. The melody faded, swallowed by an unsettling silence—one that didn't last long.

A faint rustling broke the stillness. At first, it was soft, barely more than a brush of leaves, but then it grew, moving in unnatural patterns, circling them. The branches above trembled, and Jasper's eyes darted around the campsite, catching glimpses of shadows. His breath hitched as movement flickered at the edge of his vision—something quick, vanished behind a thick tree trunk before he could make out its shape.

Aris let out a low, warning growl, muscles coiled as she tracked the unseen presence. Jasper's grip tightened on his sword. His pulse pounded in his ears. Something was out there. Watching. Waiting.

Suddenly, a figure emerged from the shadows, moving with impossible grace. Moonlight revealed its body covered in shimmering scales that glittered like starlight on water. As it unfurled a pair of delicate, gossamer wings, the forest floor danced with swirls of color, and for a moment, it felt like time itself had stopped to marvel at the sight.

Alexandria, Jasper and Aris stared in wonder at the ethereal being. The creature's presence was both mesmerizing and comforting. Jasper's grip on his sword loosened, sensing no threat.

"I am Elara," the being said, its voice echoing. "Guardian of these woods. Princess Alexandria, your quest has reached my ears, and I offer you my guidance."

"We welcome your presence with deep respect, Elara," said Jasper. "How may we be of service?"

Elara's wings rustled softly. "I seek an alliance of purpose," she said.

"Our fates are linked, Princess," Elara continued. "You face great danger, but also great promise. Lord Valendor's grip on Kandella tightens with each passing day, but hope remains."

In the heart of the enchanted woods, Jasper struggled to follow Elara's words as they washed over him. He frowned, caught on the title she'd used - Princess Alexandria. He glanced at Alex, wondering why she hadn't mentioned this before. Each revelation from Elara only spawned more questions, leaving him scrambling to keep up.

The guardian spoke of destinies and ancient powers, but nothing quite aligned with what he thought he knew about his traveling companion. He tried to connect what Elara was saying to the Alex he'd come to know, but the pieces simply wouldn't fit together. The more he listened, the more confused he became, a nagging sense of unease settling in his gut.

Alexandria listened to Elara's words. A deep sense of responsibility stirred the embers of courage within her.

"We stand at a crossroads, Princess Alexandria," Elara intoned, her voice carrying the weight of ages. "The balance of Kandella hangs in the balance, teetering on the edge of darkness and light. Your journey will test your resolve, your loyalty and your courage in ways you cannot yet fathom."

A surge of determination welled up inside Alexandria, the magic in her veins awakening with the intensity of a dragon unfurling from an age-old slumber. Her heart brimmed with renewed hope, its luminous glow warding off the shadows that loomed threateningly around them. With Elara steadfast at her side—a formidable ally and friend—Alexandria's courage deepened, her spirit ready to confront any challenges their treacherous path presented.

"We'll fight to free Kandella from Lord Valendor's torment," Alexandria declared. Beside her, Jasper stood resolute, chin held high, eyes blazing with purpose.

Elara nodded, strange symbols glowing on her skin. "Then we'll join our strength against the darkness," she said.

Alexandria gazed at Elara, her curiosity piqued. "If you don't mind me asking, what kind of being are you?"

"I'm a Celestial Seraphina, a guardian tasked with maintaining the delicate balance of the cosmos," Elara explained. As she spoke, her form began to shift and change before their very eyes. Feathers sprouted from her skin, wings unfurled from her back, and a halo of light crowned her head. She stood before them in her true, radiant form - a Phoenix Seraphina, waves of magical energy rippling off her like heat from a flame.

They stared in amazement at this legendary being. An awed hush fell over the group, senses overwhelmed by her transformation. They knew challenges awaited, but with such power on their side, hope burned bright within.

As Elara guided the trio deeper into the glade's heart, moonlight danced with renewed vigor, weaving a tapestry of shimmering reflections upon a crystal-clear pond. The water stirred in soft waves, carrying the faint scent of blooming 'night flowers' that filled the air with their intoxicating fragrance.

Surrounding the pond, emerald moss glistened like spun silk under the moon's caress, inviting weary travelers to rest upon its verdant embrace. Ancient trees stood tall, their gnarled branches reaching skyward, etched with intricate patterns that seemed to shift in the moonlight.

Elara turned to the trio, her seraphic form casting a soft, iridescent glow over the glade. "Rest now," she murmured, her voice like a gentle caress. "Morning will come soon enough, and with it, we shall continue our journey."

Alexandria sank onto a bed of moss, her muscles aching from the day's trials. Jasper lingered at the clearing's edge, his gaze fixed on Elara with a mix of reverence and wariness.

As campfire flames flickered, Alexandria felt an unexpected wave of gratitude wash over her. Despite the dangers that loomed ahead, she found solace in this moment of respite, surrounded by companions both old and new.

Elara sang her gentle tune among the trees. Alexandria's eyes grew heavy, and she drifted into slumber. In the peaceful hush of the night, she found a sense of serenity, as if it were a brief calm before the storm they were about to face.

As the first rays of dawn pierced through the canopy, Alexandria stirred from her slumber, her senses instantly alert. The air around her thrummed with an energy she couldn't quite place. She blinked away the remnants of sleep, her eyes adjusting to the soft golden light that bathed the glade.

The world around her seemed to awaken all at once, a symphony of life unfurling before her very eyes. Delicate blooms, their petals still heavy with dew, unfurled in a mesmerizing dance. Alexandria watched, transfixed, as vibrant hues of amethyst, sapphire and emerald burst forth, painting the clearing in a burst of color.

She took a deep breath as the intoxicating scent of night-blooming flowers mingled with the crisp freshness of dawn. The fragrance wrapped around her like a comforting embrace, momentarily chasing away the weight of their impending quest.

Beside her, Jasper shifted, "Ya feel it too, don't ya?" he murmured.

Alexandria nodded, her throat tight with a mixture of anticipation and dread. "It's like the very air is alive," she replied, her fingers tracing the intricate patterns on her bracelet. The metal felt warm against her skin, pulsing with an energy that seemed to resonate with the forest around them.

Aris padded silently to Alexandria's side, her golden eyes scanning the treeline. "The forest is awakening," she said, her voice a low rumble. "It recognizes the importance of our quest."

As if in response to Aris's words, a gentle breeze whispered through the glade, carrying with it the faint echoes of an ancient melody. Alexandria felt her heart quicken, a surge of power coursing through her veins. She glanced down at her hands, startled to see them emitting a soft, ethereal glow.

"What's happening?" she gasped.

Elara's melodic voice cut through the morning air. "Your powers are growing stronger," she said, her iridescent form shimmering in the dappled sunlight. "The forest recognizes you as its rightful protector."

Alexandria swallowed hard, the weight of responsibility settling heavily on her shoulders. She thought of Theodora, wondering if her sister was experiencing the same feelings.

"We should move," Jasper said, his eyes darting between the trees. "The Shadow Walkers won't be far behind."

Alexandria nodded, pushing herself to her feet. As she stood, she felt the ground beneath her hum with energy, as if the very earth was lending her its strength. She took a deep breath, steeling herself for the journey ahead.

"Lead the way," she said, her voice steadier than she felt. "It's time we headed out."

As they prepared to leave the sanctuary of the glade, Alexandria couldn't shake the feeling that every step forward was bringing them closer to a confrontation that would change everything. The magic within her surged, a reminder of the power she now possessed and the responsibility that came with it.

With one last glance at the haven that had sheltered them, Alexandria stepped forward into the unforgiving forest, ready to face whatever challenges lay ahead in their quest to save Kandella and reunite with Theodora.

The morning sun had been warm on their backs as they set out, but the air carried a lingering chill, curling around them in ghostly wisps. It never fully faded, even as the sun climbed higher. The forest had been alive then—birds calling to one another, leaves whispering in the breeze. They had walked for hours, the sunlight shifting from golden morning light to the muted glow of late afternoon. Exhaustion weighed on their limbs, and the air, once crisp with the scent of earth and pine, grew heavy.

As they trudged through the forest, an eerie stillness hung in the air. The temperature plummeted, and Alexandria shuddered as a sense of foreboding washed over her. She glanced up at the darkening sky, ominous clouds gathering overhead like a billowing cloak of doom.

"This doesn't look good," Alexandria muttered, hugging her arms around herself as the frigid air bit into her skin. Aris stayed close by her side, offering silent comfort. Jasper's eyes narrowed, his carefree demeanor replaced by a grim intensity as he surveyed the treacherous path ahead.

The heavens unleashed their fury, pelting them with icy shards that stung like a thousand needles. The once-clear trail vanished beneath a treacherous blanket of frozen rain, each step a gamble. Alexandria's heart pounded in her chest as she fought for balance, her soaked hair clinging to her face in icy tendrils.

Lightning split the sky, illuminating the twisted landscape in stark flashes. Gnarled branches clawed at them like skeletal fingers, and ancient roots writhed underfoot, threatening to ensnare the unwary. The storm's rage battered them relentlessly, nature itself seeming to conspire against their quest.

Jasper threw up a hand, halting their progress as he spotted movement in the swirling mists ahead. Spectral figures materialized from the gloom, their forms flickering like candlelight in the wind. Malevolent eyes glinted with otherworldly hunger, and Aris snarled, her hackles raised in warning as she placed herself between Alexandria and the unknown threat.

"Stay close," Jasper warned, his voice tight with tension. Gone was his usual calm confidence, replaced by a grim determination seen on the young warrior's face.

Alexandria set her jaw, calling upon the fledgling magic that stirred within her. An emerald aura enveloped her hands, casting an ethereal light into the darkness. She squared her shoulders, ready to face whatever nightmares the storm had unleashed. With Jasper and Aris at her side, she stepped forward ready to confront the ghostly figures.

Aris's fur bristled, a low, menacing growl rumbling from deep within her chest. The wolf's golden eyes gleamed with fierce protectiveness, muscles coiled and ready to spring at a moment's notice. Alexandria could feel the heat radiating from her companion's body, a stark contrast to the biting cold that nipped at her exposed skin.

As the figures drew closer, their features twisted into grotesque masks of malevolence. Hollow sockets blazed with an eerie, otherworldly light, casting long shadows that seemed to writhe and reach for them. Each step they took sent tremors through the earth, a palpable dread seeping into Alexandria's very bones.

Jasper's grip on Alexandria's arm tightened, his calloused fingers digging into her flesh. She glanced up at him, expecting to see fear etched across his face, but his gaze remained unwavering, jaw set with grim determination. His presence beside her was both comforting and terrifying - a reminder of the gravity of their situation.

"Stay behind me," Jasper murmured. He shifted his stance, placing himself between Alexandria and the approaching threat.

Alexandria swallowed hard, her throat dry and constricted. "Not on your life," she croaked out, surprising herself with the steadiness in her voice. "We face this together."

Jasper's eyes widened for a fraction of a second before a faint smile tugged at the corner of his mouth. "As you wish, Princess," he replied, drawing his sword with a metallic hiss.

The nearest shadow walker lunged forward, its clawed hand slicing through the air. Alexandria's instincts kicked in, her body moving before her mind could catch up. She thrust her palm outward, a burst of energy erupting from her fingertips. The creature recoiled with an unearthly shriek, its form rippled like smoke in the wind.

"Well done!" Jasper shouted over the cacophony of battle, deflecting a blow from another attacker. "Keep it up!"

Alexandria's heart soared at the praise, a surge of confidence flowing through her veins. She pivoted, facing the next shadow walker that dared to approach. This time, she didn't hesitate. The magic within her responded to her call, flames engulfing her hands as she met the creature's hollow gaze.

"You want me?" she challenged, her voice ringing out clear and strong. "Come and get me."

The Shadow Walkers' advance slowed, parting to reveal a tall, hooded figure gliding towards Alexandria. She felt her body stiffen, rooted to the spot as a chillingly familiar voice cut through the chaos.

"Well, well, Princess Alexandria," the figure drawled, his tone dripping with mockery. "Still chasing after your dear sister, I see. How quaint."

The words hung in the air, sharp as icicles and just as cold. Alexandria's breath caught in her throat, her mind racing to place the voice that seemed to freeze the very storm around them.

Alexandria's jaw clenched at the mention of her sister, her resolve hardening like steel. "Malachai." she said, her voice steady despite the adrenaline coursing through her veins.

He took a step closer, flanked by his menacing companions. "Good. You remember me." he replied, his eyes gleaming with malevolent glee. "I'm here to ensure that you never reach your sister."

Aris emitted a deep, intimidating growl, her body coiled and prepared to attack. Jasper's grasp on Alexandria's arm became tighter, his face showing both worry and determination. "Yer not layin' a finger on her," Jasper declared in a firm tone, positioning himself defensively in front of her.

Malachai chuckled darkly, the sound echoing like a sinister melody. "Foolish boy. You underestimate the power at my command," he taunted, his eyes flickered with dark magic. With a swift motion of his hand, shadows coalesced around him, forming dark tendrils that reached out towards the trio.

Alexandria's pulse quickened as she raised her hands, magic surging with newfound intensity. "We might not have the numbers," she called out, her voice cutting through the howling wind, "but we've got something stronger - each other, and a damn good reason to fight."

Aris sprang into action, her white fur a blur as she lunged at the nearest shadow walker. The wolf's teeth flashed in the dim light, tearing into the creature's smoky form with surprising ferocity.

Jasper drew his sword with a fluid motion, his stance steady, and his eyes fixed on their foes with unwavering focus. The clash of steel rang out in harmony with the howling wind, a symphony of battle unfolding amidst the chaos.

Alexandria unleashed her magic with fierce determination, jolts of lightning thrusted outwards to meet the encroaching shadows. The air bristled with raw energy as light and darkness collided in an explosive display of willpower and defiance.

Malachai sneered, his laughter cutting through the tumultuous sounds of battle as he unleashed a torrent of dark magic. Shadows writhed and twisted around him, forming a seemingly impenetrable barrier.

Drawing upon the very essence of the storm, Alexandria's magic surged forth in a dazzling display of emerald brilliance. The shadows recoiled and wavered under her onslaught. Their malevolent energy sizzled and dissipated against the radiant force of her will. Even Malachai's sneer faltered for a fleeting moment, his confidence shaken by the unexpected strength of her resolve.

Aris darted and weaved with uncanny agility, her white form a blur of motion as she circled their foes with calculated precision. Her fangs flashed like slivers of moonlight, striking true against the phantom forms that sought to ensnare her companions.

Jasper's sword danced with deadly grace, each strike finding its mark with a skill born of training and determination. His movements were fluid and controlled, a mesmerizing dance of combat that kept their adversaries at bay.

As Malachai's lips curled into a contorted grimace, his spell began to unravel under the fierce onslaught. The darkness around them flickered and retreated, their ghostly forms dissipating like mist in the face of her relentless attacks.

Alexandria's fingertips crackled with sparks, illuminating the surrounding trees with each strike. With a final flourish of her hands, bolts of lightning shot out from her palms, blinding the remaining shadow walkers.

Jasper's sword danced through the air, glinting silver in the moonlight as he effortlessly cut down the smoky beasts. But during battle, a massive branch snapped off and crashed down, pinning Jasper beneath its weight and knocking his sword out of reach in the dense underbrush.

"Jasper!" Alexandra cried out, eyes wide with panic. But he lay still, the weight of the massive branch crushing the life from him.

Suddenly, from the corner of her eye, Alexandria spotted a figure emerging from the shadows. It was Elara, her body radiating an ethereal light that cut through the darkness like a blade. As she stepped forward, the light around her intensified, casting long shadows around Malachai and his minions. Alexandria felt a surge of hope as she realized they might escape this nightmare after all.

Chapter 11

"Bow and Destiny"

Theodora's eyes fluttered open, her heart pounding as the remnants of her nightmares clung to her like cobwebs. The soft light of dawn filtered through the cabin's window, painting the room in hues of lavender and rose. She sat up, her fingers trembling as she pushed her wild auburn curls away from her face.

The sorcerer's twisted appearance lingered in her mind, his bitter laughter echoing in her ears. Theodora shuddered, wrapping her arms around herself as if to ward off the chill that had nothing to do with the morning air. She could still feel the shadow walkers' icy touch, their smoky tendrils reaching for her even in her dreams.

As she swung her legs over the side of the bed, the wooden floorboards creaked beneath her feet. The sound startled her, and she froze, her breath catching in her throat. *Get a grip, Theo,* she chided herself. *Ye're safe here... for now.*

She stood, her legs unsteady as she made her way to the small washbasin in the corner. The cool water on her face helped to chase away the last remnants of sleep, but did little to quell the unease churning in her gut. As she dried her face, she caught her reflection in the small mirror above the basin. Her emerald eyes stared back at her, wide and haunted, a stark reminder of the burdens she now carried.

A gentle knock at the door made her jump, her heart leaping into her throat. "Princess, are ye awake?" Killian's familiar voice called from outside.

Theodora took a deep breath, willing her voice to remain steady. "Come in," she replied, forcing a lightness into her tone she didn't feel.

The door creaked open, and Killian stepped inside. Theodora's eyes widened as she took in his appearance. His once cerulean locks had transformed overnight into a vibrant shade of amethyst, the color shimmering in the early morning light.

"Good mornin', Princess," Killian said, a hint of amusement in his voice as he noticed her stare. "I trust ye slept well?"

Theodora opened her mouth to respond, but the words caught in her throat. How could she explain the terrors that had plagued her dreams? The weight of her destiny that seemed to press down on her with each passing moment?

Instead, she managed a weak smile. She said, "Doin' about as well as anyone might've expected, I suppose," her voice barely rising above a whisper."Yer hair... it's different."

Killian's hand went to his head, a sheepish grin spreading across his face. "Aye, it seems our moods and magic are more intertwined than we thought," he explained.

Curiosity sparked within Theodora as she observed Killian's amethyst hair, pondering the implications of such a phenomenon. "Does it happen often? Can ye control it?" she asked, her green eyes alight with fascination.

"Sometimes," Killian replied. "When we feel powerful emotions, they can manifest in our appearance. I've seen warriors' armor shimmer brighter when they're filled with courage, or healers' hands glow with warmth when they're tending to others."

"So, are ya ready to get started then?" Killian smoothly transitioned to another topic.

"As ready as I'll ever be," Theodora replied, steeling herself for the training that lay ahead.

They met Finnegan for a hearty breakfast of fresh fruits, warm muffins filled with sweet jelly, and savory ham slices straight from the spit, washing it down with fresh goat's milk. Afterward, they made their way down the grassy hill to the archery shop.

The archery shop buzzed with an ancient energy, its wooden walls lined with bows of every shape and size. Torchlight danced across the polished wood, filling the air with the scent of pine and beeswax.

Her fingers glided over the soft leather of a quiver, appreciating the detailed Celtic designs. As she continued to explore, her footsteps created a gentle echo, blending with the sporadic sound of a bowstring being plucked.

Killian guided her to a secluded corner where smaller, magical bows awaited. "These are perfect for beginners like yerself," he explained. "Go on, find one that calls to ya."

Theodora reached out, her fingertips brushed against the smooth wood of a bow adorned with delicate silver vines. The moment she grasped it, a jolt of energy coursed through her.

"Ah, the Bow of Lachesis," Killian said. "Its arrows never miss, and the quiver's always full. Legend says the Fae made it themselves."

Theodora marveled at the bow's craftsmanship, feeling a connection to its past wielders. The silver vines seemed to pulse with life beneath her fingers.

"I've never witnessed such a profound connection between an archer and their weapon," Killian murmured. "That bow's chosen you, Theodora."

The trio exited the shop and made their way to the shooting range, Theo found herself captivated by her new bow and arrows. Killian prepared the targets while Finnegan led Theo to her designated spot on the range.

With newfound confidence, Theodora stepped onto the range, free from the doubts that had plagued her. As she took her place, a variety of arrows appeared before her in a dazzling display of color and power. Some arrows, wreathed in flames, were ready to ignite her enemies. Others glinted with an icy sheen, capable of freezing opponents in their tracks. There were even arrows crackling with electricity, primed to strike down foes with pinpoint accuracy. Theodora marveled at the endless possibilities presented before her.

Her fingers trembled as she nocked an arrow, the smooth feathers brushing against her cheek. The weight of the bow felt foreign in her hands, a constant reminder of the monumental task that lay ahead. She drew back the string, muscles straining with the effort, and tried to focus on the target before her.

The first arrow flew wide, embedding itself in the grass several feet from the target. Frustration bubbled up inside her, hot and insistent. She gritted her teeth, pushing down the urge to throw the bow aside and storm off.

"Easy now, lass," Finnegan's gruff voice cut through her tumultuous thoughts. "Ye've got to relax yer shoulders. Let the bow become an extension of yerself."

Theodora took a deep breath, willing her tense muscles to loosen. She pictured Finnegan's steady hands, the way he seemed to meld with his weapon as if it were a part of him. Closing her eyes for a moment, she tried to channel that same sense of oneness with her bow.

When she opened them again, the world seemed to sharpen into focus. The target no longer felt impossibly far away, but like a challenge she could overcome. She nocked another arrow, the familiar motion already becoming smoother with practice.

This time, as she drew back the string, she felt a subtle shift. The bow hummed with energy, almost as if it were alive in her hands. A tingling sensation spread from her fingertips up her arms, and for a brief moment, Theodora could have sworn she saw faint silver threads of light connecting her to the target.

She released the arrow, and time seemed to slow. The projectile cut through the air with unerring precision, a streak of silver in its wake. With a satisfying thud, it buried itself in the center of the target.

Theodora blinked, daring to believe what she'd just witnessed. "Did ye see that?" she breathed, turning to Finnegan with wide eyes.

The druid's weathered face broke into a rare smile. "Aye, lass. That's the magic of the Bow of Lachesis, workin' in harmony with yer own power. Ye're startin' to tap into somethin' special."

A warmth bloomed in Theodora's chest, a mixture of pride and excitement. For the first time since fleeing Donaglen Castle, she felt a glimmer of hope. Perhaps she could rise to meet the destiny forced upon her.

"Again," she said, her voice steady with newfound determination. She reached for another arrow, the silver vines on the bow seeming to pulse with anticipation. As she nocked it, she felt the same surge of energy, stronger this time.

The world around her faded away—the rustling leaves, the distant chatter of birds, even Finnegan's watchful presence. There was only Theodora, the bow and the target. She drew back the string, every muscle in her body singing with tension and purpose.

With each arrow she released, her confidence grew. The bow seemed to respond to her, its magic flowing in sync with her own energy. Hours passed in this rhythm of draw, aim, release; the world beyond the clearing and her past troubles forgotten for a while. Theodora felt a strange sense of peace in this routine, a calmness that she had not experienced in a long time.

After a hearty lunch, they resumed training as the afternoon wore on. Theodora drew back the bowstring, poised to release an arrow, when an unexpected jolt of energy coursed through her, sending shivers down her spine.

In that instant, something extraordinary happened. Theodora's connection to the bow deepened, awakening a hidden enchantment. Without warning, she vanished, leaving only a faint shimmer where she once stood. Killian and Finnegan gaped at each other, stunned by her sudden disappearance.

Theodora found herself adrift in a strange realm, surrounded by swirling colors and echoing whispers. Panic gripped her as she floated helplessly, bombarded by unfamiliar sights and sounds.

Back at the range, Killian, and Finnegan called out, searching for their missing companion.

As abruptly as she'd vanished, Theodora reappeared. The air crackled with residual energy, and a faint glow clung to her skin.

"What in the blazes just happened?" Theodora gasped, her voice a mix of excitement and fear.

Killian shook his head, bewildered. "I've no idea, lass. Are ye alright?"

"I think I was... somewhere else," Theodora said, her words tumbling out. "It's hard to explain, but it felt real!"

The ethereal light that had trailed her during her disappearance now lingered around her, weaving intricate patterns of luminescence that seemed to pulsate in harmony with her very essence. It was as if she had tapped into a wellspring of magic transcending physical boundaries.

She ran her fingers over the bow's engravings, which now pulsed with a soft light. "Saints preserve us, Killian! I never knew I had this in me."

Killian's eyes widened as realization dawned. "By the gods, ye've unlocked the Shadow Step! It's a rare gift, Princess. This changes everything."

Theodora felt a surge of power flowing through her veins. "I feel... different. Stronger, somehow."

"Ye must learn to control it," Killian warned, his tone serious. "With practice, ye could move unseen, strike before yer enemies even know ye're there."

Finnegan, who'd been uncharacteristically quiet, finally spoke up. "Aye, and it'll take more than a wee bit of practice. This kind of power... it's not to be taken lightly."

Theodora nodded, a mix of determination and apprehension in her eyes. "I understand. I'm ready to learn, no matter how difficult it might be."

As night began to fall, the trio headed up to dinner. Theo's mind whirled from their training. She was becoming more confident now that she had a bow that was made for her, and two teachers to learn from.

The dining hall hummed with lively conversation as they claimed their usual spot. Savory scents of roasted meat and freshly baked bread wafted through the air, making Theodora's stomach growl. Candlelight flickered, throwing shifting shadows across the walls adorned with tapestries of legendary battles and fantastical creatures. Finnegan eyed the spread with approval, while Killian's amethyst hair caught the warm glow, a reminder of the day's magical revelations.

As they recounted the day's events, Theodora's fingers traced the bow's intricate patterns, feeling an almost living connection to the weapon. Killian beamed with pride as he described her progress, his usual composure softened by genuine warmth. Finnegan listened intently, his sharp blue eyes reflecting a mix of interest and approval.

A lively melody that filled the hall interrupted their meal. The sound of pipes and drums wove together in an irresistible rhythm that caught Theodora and Finnegan's attention.

A group of halflings burst from the shadows, their faces alight with mischief. They wore colorful outfits adorned with elaborate designs that caught the candlelight. Their quick feet moved in perfect sync with the music, creating a dizzying display of movement and laughter that swept through the hall.

Theodora watched, mesmerized, as the halflings danced with incredible skill and obvious joy. To her surprise, she noticed Finnegan's eyes light up, his usual gruff demeanor giving way to delight at the unexpected performance.

One of the halflings extended a hand towards Theodora, a mischievous gleam in their eye. "Care to join us?" they called, their voice filled with an infectious energy.

Theodora glanced at Finnegan and Killian, a spark of excitement igniting in her chest. Without waiting for their response, she placed the bow aside and took the halfling's hand, allowing herself to be pulled into the heart of the dance.

The music enveloped her, guiding her movements as she twirled and stepped in time with the other dancers. Laughter bubbled from her lips, a carefree sound that seemed to banish the shadows that had clouded her thoughts earlier.

Finnegan watched with a mixture of surprise and amusement, a rare smile graced his features. He exchanged a knowing look with Killian, who simply chuckled and shook his head in fond exasperation.

As the dance reached its climax, Theodora found herself spinning under the warm glow of the candlelight, her worries momentarily forgotten in the joy of the moment. The halflings around her clapped and cheered, the music filled the hall with an infectious energy that seemed to pulse through Theodora's veins.

When the dance finally ended, Theodora returned to Finnegan and Killian, her cheeks flushed with exhilaration. There was a lightness in her spirit that had been absent for far too long.

"Thank you," she said breathlessly, her eyes shining with gratitude. "That was... incredible."

Finnegan chuckled, a rare warmth in his gaze. "Ye have a talent for more than just archery, lass."

Killian nodded in agreement, a smile tugging at his lips. "Aye, 'twas a sight to behold. Ye move with the grace of the wild fae themselves."

Theodora beamed at their praise, the weight of her responsibilities momentarily forgotten in the togetherness of the moment.

As the evening wore on, the trio shared stories and laughter, the tension of their earlier training giving way to a sense of camaraderie and connection. Theodora felt a bond with Finnegan and Killian that went beyond mere mentorship; they were her allies, her friends.

As the night grew late and the hall began to empty, Killian bid Theodora and Finnegan goodnight. She clutched the bow close to her chest, feeling its familiar weight anchoring her to reality as they made their way to the cottage.

The cool night air greeted them as they walked down the path towards the lake. Stars twinkled overhead, casting a soft glow on the winding path. A symphony of chirping crickets and rustling leaves filled the air, creating a serene backdrop for their quiet conversation.

Silence enveloped them momentarily, each lost in thought. Theodora couldn't shake off the sense of wonder and amazement that still lingered from the day's events. Finnegan walked beside her in his stoic expression softened by a hint of warmth in his gaze.

As they approached the cottage, Finnegan paused, turning to face Theodora with an unusually thoughtful expression. "Well, lass," he began, his gruff voice softened by a hint of wonder, "ye've shown us a thing or two today. That 'Shadow Step' of yours? Not something ye see every day. And that bow..." He nodded towards the weapon, a rare smile tugging at his lips. "It's chosen ye, sure as the sun rises."

Theodora felt a rush of emotions - pride, excitement and a twinge of nervousness. She knew this was just the beginning, and the path ahead was far from clear.

The next morning, after filling their bellies with a hearty breakfast, the trio set off for the practice field. Theodora's new bow rested comfortably on her back as they walked through Isidore's verdant landscape. The morning air was fresh and invigorating, filled with the sweet scent of wildflowers and the distant sound of flowing water. As they strolled, Theodora couldn't help but feel a spark of anticipation for the day's training ahead.

Killian's voice filled the air as they walked, regaling Theodora with tales of Isidore's past. "See those cliffs there?" he pointed eastward. Warriors fought many a battle beneath their shadow. Legend has it, the noble warrior Aoife once held off an entire army from atop those very rocks."

Theodora listened, enraptured by the stories. Her eyes traced the landscape, imagining ancient warriors clashing swords where wildflowers now bloomed.

The eastern border loomed ahead, its weathered cliffs a testament to time's passage. Falcons circled above, their keen eyes surveying the land below.

As they approached the practice field, Theodora's pulse quickened. Neatly trimmed grass stretched before them, bordered by tall hedges adorned with fluttering ribbons. She gripped her bow, its familiar weight both comforting and thrilling.

Killian gave her an encouraging nod. "Show us what ye've got, lass."

At the shooting line, Theodora took a deep breath. She nocked an arrow, the world narrowing to just her and the target. Drawing back the string, she focused on the distant circles painted on wood.

The arrow flew true, striking the bullseye with a satisfying thud. Applause erupted around her as she lowered the bow, a mix of relief and exhilaration coursing through her.

Killian's laughter boomed across the field. "By the gods, Theodora! That was a shot for the history books!" His eyes shone with pride.

Even Finnegan's stern expression softened. "Well done," he said, the hint of approval in his voice warming Theodora's heart.

A rustling in the nearby bushes caught their attention. Theodora's breath caught as Kimi Rei, her faithful companion from Donaglen, emerged. The Unari's fur shimmered in the sunlight, its seven tails trailing behind like ribbons of light.

Theodora knelt, overcome with joy as she ran her fingers through Kimi Rei's soft fur. The creature's presence stirred memories—her mother's laughter, the scent of castle gardens, her father's gentle touch.

A sudden vision appeared before her, revealing a luminous figure presenting her with a shining bow. "Ye are destined for greatness, lass," the figure's voice resonated. "The fate of our realm rests on yer shoulders."

As swiftly as it came, the vision vanished. Theodora blinked, a new sense of purpose taking hold within her. The Bow of Lachesis was meant for her, she realized. This journey wasn't about sharpening her skills or seeking her family—it was about becoming who she was born to be.

Killian crouched, offering his hand to Kimi Rei. The Unari sniffed cautiously before allowing him to scratch behind its ears. "A grand creature ya have here, Theodora," he said, admiration evident in his gruff voice.

Finnegan observed the scene, his eyes narrowing. "Aye, the Unari's not just any beast. It's a powerful ally, and rare at that."

Kimi Rei pranced around them playfully, its seven tails swishing through the air. Theodora felt a wave of gratitude wash over her, thankful for her friends and the mystical creatures that had become part of her journey. She stood up, filled with a renewed sense of purpose. The vision she'd experienced moments ago echoed in her mind, hinting at the path that lay before her.

With a nod to Killian, Theodora turned her attention back to the gleaming bow in her hands. She took a deep breath, steeling herself for more training. The air seemed charged with energy, matching her own determination to face the journey ahead.

As daylight faded, Theodora pushed herself harder than ever before. Each arrow she fired was a testament to her growing skill and focus. Every hit boosted her confidence, a tangible reminder of how far she'd come.

Killian's earlier warnings about the 'Shadow Step' rang in her ears. She used the technique sparingly, aware of how quickly it could drain her. Theodora knew that true mastery meant understanding her limits as much as pushing past them.

The setting sun cast long shadows across the practice field. Theodora stood tall, silhouetted against the dimming light. Her arrows flew true, each one bringing her closer to unlocking her full potential. As darkness fell, Theodora felt a fire ignite within her. She was more than just an archer now - she was a warrior in the making, honing both her body and mind. Every shot spoke of her determination and courage, preparing her for the trials that lay ahead.

As the days passed, Theodora found herself wrestling with a maelstrom of emotions. Fragmented memories haunted her, chipping away at the trust she'd begun to build with Killian and Finnegan. During training sessions, she began to reveal snippets of her biogenesis abilities, but a nagging voice in her head urged caution. She held back, afraid to expose the full extent of her powers.

In quiet moments after training, Theodora sought solace in Kimi Rei's presence. The creature seemed to understand her struggle, offering silent comfort and gentle encouragement.

One evening, as they sat around a crackling fire, Killian's gruff voice cut through the silence. "Ye know, lass, we're here for ye. Whatever's weighin' on yer mind, ye can share it."

Theodora met his gaze, her heart pounding. She wanted to confide in them, but fear held her back.

Finnegan, often stoic, relaxed his expression. "Aye, Princess. Ye've got gifts beyond measure. No need to hide 'em from us."

Kimi Rei circled the group, its tails swishing. The creature's presence seemed to bridge the gap between them, offering a wordless reassurance.

Theodora took a deep breath, feeling the weight of her decision. She looked from Killian to Finnegan, seeing not judgment but genuine concern in their eyes. In that moment, she trusted–to let them in, bit by bit.

"I... I think I'm ready ta show ya more," she said.

As night settled over the training grounds, Theodora felt a flicker of hope. She wasn't alone in this journey, and with her companions by her side, she could face whatever challenges lay ahead.

Chapter 12

"Through the Mist"

THE WIND'S HOWL CUT through the night, accompanied by Aris's urgent instructions. "We must go, now!"

Alexandria grunted, heaving Jasper onto the wolf's back. Elara's ethereal glow led them deeper into the forest, its dense canopy swallowing them whole.

Aris forged ahead, weaving through twisted trees that seemed to reach for them. Fear's acrid taste mingled with the forest's damp scent. Shadows flickered ominously around them.

Alexandria pushed on, her legs screaming in protest. 'One more step,' she chanted, clinging to her faith in Aris.

Ahead, an ancient Rowan tree stood sentinel, its red berries gleaming. As they neared, Aris's fur began to shimmer, responding to arcane markings on the bark. She pressed her muzzle to the trunk, uttering guttural sounds. The ground shook, revealing a hidden entrance.

"Quickly!" Aris nudged them towards the opening. Alexandria hesitated, then steeled herself and plunged in.

They descended, feeling their way along smooth walls. Elara's light revealed intricate carvings as they spiraled downward. At last, they emerged into a vast cavern, its ceiling adorned with glittering crystal formations.

The cavern's heart held two stone altars, surrounded by scattered furniture. "Lay him here," Aris commanded, her focus already shifting to Jasper's wounds. Alexandria gently lowered him onto the cool surface while Aris rummaged through shelves, selecting herbs and potions.

With practiced movements, Aris mixed her concoction. Vials clinked as she worked, dried leaves crumbling between her paws. The air grew thick with earthy scents and a faint, tingling energy. She spread the mixture over Jasper's injuries, her touch steady and gentle.

"Hang in there, Jasper," Alexandria whispered, her eyes darting between Aris's skilled paws and Jasper's pale face. As the wolf worked her healing magic, the cavern seemed to cocoon them, muffling the forest's distant sounds.

Gradually, color returned to Jasper's cheeks, his breathing evening out under Aris's care. Alexandria found her gaze drifting, taking in their sanctuary. Overhead, crystalline formations cast a soft, ethereal glow.

Alexandria's gaze wandered across the cavern, her eyes drawn to a weathered mural etched into the rough stone wall. The flickering light from Elara's ethereal glow cast dancing shadows over the ancient scene, bringing it to life before her eyes. Warriors locked in eternal combat, their faces frozen in expressions of fierce determination and anguish. Light and darkness clashed, a timeless struggle captured in worn grooves and faded pigments.

Her fingers reached out, almost of their own accord, tracing the outline of a figure wielding what looked like a bow of pure light. As her skin contacted the cool stone, a jolt of energy surged through her, making her gasp. The cavern around her seemed to fade, replaced by fleeting images that flashed through her mind with dizzying speed.

Alexandria stumbled back, her heart pounding in her chest. The visions faded as quickly as they had come, leaving her breathless and disoriented. She blinked, trying to make sense of what she had just experienced. Were these memories? Or something else?

"Alexandria." Aris's voice cut through the fog of confusion, grounding her back in the present moment. The wolf's golden eyes fixed on her with concern. "He'll live, but he needs rest to fully recover."

Alexandria's gaze snapped back to Jasper, guilt washing over her as she realized she had momentarily forgotten about his dire condition. His chest rose and fell, color slowly returning to his pale cheeks. Relief flooded through her, mingling with the bone-deep exhaustion that threatened to overwhelm her.

She sank into a nearby chair, its ancient wood creaking beneath her weight. Her limbs felt like lead, her eyelids growing heavier with each passing second. As she fought against the encroaching darkness of sleep, fragments of the vision continued to dance at the edges of her consciousness.

In her dreams, Alexandria found herself back in a familiar, terrifying scene. She and Theodora huddled behind the mirror, clinging to each other as if their lives depended on it. Their hearts raced as they peered out, witnessing the horror unfolding before them. Theodora's breath hitched, and Alexandria's grip tightened, her knuckles turning white.

The sisters watched, frozen in fear, unable to tear their eyes away from the nightmarish scene. Just as all hope seems lost, a figure emerged from the shadows. In the eerie silence that followed, Ms. Whoo appeared, whisking Alexandria and Theodora away to safety.

Alexandria stirred, the remnants of her dream fading as a gentle warmth pulled her from sleep's embrace. She blinked awake, her eyes adjusting to the soft glow of the crystals overhead. Aris sat vigilant by Jasper's side, a silent guardian in the tranquil chamber.

Gratitude welled up in Alexandria's chest as she gazed at Aris, the loyal companion who had guided them through their darkest hours. She pushed herself up from the couch, wincing as her battered body protested the movement.

As she approached Jasper, Aris turned to meet her gaze. A silent understanding passed between them in the hushed cavern. Alexandria saw the depth of her guardians' commitment reflected in those wise eyes - not just to Jasper, whose breathing had steadied under the wolf's care, but to their shared mission.

Concern creased Aris's brow as she spoke, her voice low and troubled. "We need to figure out how those shadow walkers tracked us down." Alexandria nodded, mirroring the unease etched across her face. The wolf's next words sent a chill down her spine. "It's as if they have an uncanny insight into our every move and decision."

Aris paused, lost in thought for a moment before continuing, her voice heavy with worry. "There aren't many possibilities here. Either we're dealing with a traitor in our midst, or they've developed some kind of advanced tracking magic. Neither option bodes well for us."

Several hours passed before Jasper's eyes fluttered open, his vision swimming into focus. The first thing he saw was Alexandria's face, her emerald eyes wide with concern. A dull ache throbbed through his body, but the sight of her brought a weak smile to his lips.

"Thank ya," he whispered, his voice hoarse. The words seemed inadequate for the gratitude that welled up inside him, but it was all he could manage.

Alexandria's face lit up, relief flooding her features. "Jasper!" she cried, leaping from her chair and rushing to his side. Her auburn hair caught the dim light of the cavern, creating a fiery halo around her head. As she reached him, her expression shifted, guilt clouding her eyes.

"This... this is all my fault," she murmured, her voice thick with emotion. "That falling branch... if I hadn't summoned the winds ..." Her words trailed off, and she dropped her gaze, unable to meet his eyes.

Jasper's heart clenched at the sight of her distress. He wanted to reach out, to comfort her, but his limbs felt like lead. Instead, he forced his voice to work, pushing past the dryness in his throat.

"Now, now, lass," he said, his words soft but firm. "No need for blame. Ye were only tryin' to save us."

Alexandria's eyes snapped back to his face, glistening with un-shed tears. She nodded, a trembling smile tugging at the corners of her mouth. "I'm just relieved you're alright," she whispered.

Before Jasper could respond, a warm, furry presence pressed against his side. Aris had padded over, her golden eyes fixed on him with an intensity that seemed to pierce through to his very soul. In her mouth, she held a small vial filled with a shimmering liquid.

"This potion will hasten your recovery," Aris explained. She set the vial down beside him. "It's imbued with healing magic to soothe your pain."

Jasper eyed the vial with caution, but the pounding pain in his body pushed him to try it. With Alexandria's help, he propped himself up on one elbow and reached for the potion. The glass was cool against his fingers as he brought it to his lips.

The liquid slid down his throat, tasting of honey and moonlight. Almost immediately, a soothing warmth spread through his body, chasing away the lingering aches. Strength flowed back into his limbs, and the fog in his mind began to clear.

As the potion worked its magic, Jasper took in his surroundings for the first time. They were in a vast cavern, its ceiling adorned with glittering crystal formations that cast a soft, ethereal glow throughout the space. Magical energy hummed from the pages of ancient tomes and scrolls scattered about.

"So where are we exactly?" he asked, his voice stronger now.

Aris, who had been rifling through a stack of dusty books, looked up. Her tail swished back and forth as she padded over to a large map spread out on a nearby table.

"Welcome to the Veil," she said, her voice tinged with pride. "For generations, my family has used this sanctuary as a place to study and safeguard magic," she said.

Alexandria leaned in, her eyes tracing the intricate lines of the map. "And where should we begin our search for Theodora?" she asked, a hint of eagerness creeping into her voice.

A mischievous glint flickered in Aris's eyes. With deliberate steps, she padded towards a specific location, her tail flicking against the parchment for emphasis.

"Primlow," Aris declared, her feline voice carrying a note of satisfaction. "Home."

The word hung in the air, heavy with promise and the weight of their quest. Jasper felt a surge of anticipation, mixed with a twinge of apprehension. They were one step closer to finding Theodora, but what dangers lay ahead?

Before Jasper could voice his thoughts, Aris's whiskers twitched, and she turned her gaze to Alexandria. "Now, enough talk, princess," she said, a purr rumbling in her chest. "Shall we prepare a feast fit for royalty in the kitchen?"

Her face lit up, a genuine smile chasing away the last traces of guilt and worry. "I'd love to help," she said, her stomach growling as if on cue. "I'm famished."

As Alexandria followed Aris towards what Jasper assumed was the kitchen, he found himself torn between the desire to join them and the need to process everything that had happened. The scent of healing herbs still lingered in the air, mingling with the musty smell of ancient books and the earthy dampness of the cavern.

Jasper's fingers traced the edge of the map, his mind racing with questions. What other secrets did this hidden sanctuary hold? And more importantly, what new challenges awaited them on their journey to Primlow? The weight of their quest settled over him like a heavy cloak, but as he listened to the distant sounds of Alexandria and Aris in the kitchen, a flicker of hope kindled in his chest. Whatever lay ahead, they would face it together.

Though the night stretched on, Jasper became engrossed in the ancient tome detailing Carrantou's lore. Candlelight flickered, casting eerie shadows across his face as he traced intricate illustrations with a mix of wonder and determination.

Elena approached cautiously. "What about Carrantou captivates you so?"

Jasper looked up, his eyes reflecting awe and trepidation. "These pages hold secrets, Elena. Secrets crucial to our quest," he whispered.

Elena's heart skipped a beat at his words, her mind racing with possibilities and uncertainties. "And what do these secrets entail? Do they foretell of dangers ahead?" she pressed, her eyes searching for answers.

Jasper looked up from the book, his expression a blend of excitement and uncertainty. "There's something... something significant in these pages. I can feel it in me bones," he murmured, his words hanging in the air like a veil of mystery.

Meanwhile, in the kitchen, Aris, and Alexandria moved with practiced precision. As they chopped vegetables, stirred pots, and seasoned meats, the air filled with the aroma of spices and herbs. They were preparing a lavish feast fit for royalty, working together in a whirlwind of culinary expertise.

Amidst this flurry, Aris flashed a reassuring glance at Alexandria. "Don't fret. Jasper will recover. We've faced worse together."

Aris murmured. Her eyes reflected a silent understanding and her words carried a sense of steadfast resolve.

Despite Aris's words, concern tainted Alexandria's resolve. "I know, but seeing him like this... it reminds me how fragile our journey is."

After the meal, Aris filled the room with tales of her heroic adventures. Jasper hung on every word, while Elena watched him from the shadows. As stories mixed with the lingering taste of the meal, the night stretched on.

Later, as Alexandria cleared the table, Elena joined her, eyes distant with thought. Alexandria studied her, recognizing the weight of her friend's fatigue. At her request, Aris readied for their journey to Primlow.

That night, as Jasper pored over the Carrantou book, their impending travel seemed shrouded in uncertainty. The weight of destiny compelled them forward—an inescapable burden. Elena's concern for the dangers ahead was palpable. Their journey was about to become more perilous than they could ever imagine.

Dawn had barely broken when they stirred, packing their belongings in silence. Outside, Aris's arranged mounts awaited - powerful steeds with coats that caught the dim light. Alexandria felt a thrill of excitement as she swung into the saddle, her hand resting on its worn leather.

Aris turned, her silver fur rippling. "Stay alert," she warned, her voice a mix of caution and reassurance. "As we go deeper, we'll need to trust our instincts more than ever."

Jasper nodded, his eyes mirroring Alexandria's determination. "We stand together," he stated, his voice steady despite the unease permeating the forest. "Whatever comes, we'll face it as one."

In the crisp morning air, the horses exhaled. Their warm breath created wispy clouds that drifted upwards and dissolved into the sky. Alexandria sat astride her chestnut mare, her posture straight and vigilant. Her eyes darted from one darkened corner to another, taking in every rustle of leaves and flicker of movement among the trees, as she carefully surveyed their surroundings.

Hours had passed since they had left the Rowan tree behind, its crimson berries now a distant memory. The forest had grown wilder, the undergrowth thick with tangled roots and thorn-laced vines. The air had turned frigid, biting through their cloaks and seeping into their bones. Snow lay in uneven patches where it had drifted through the canopy, a ghostly sheen over the dark earth. Their breath curled in the air, vanishing into the gloom as the last light of day began to fade.

The path narrowed as they pressed on, winding through dense foliage and gnarled vines that clung like grasping fingers. Massive trees loomed overhead, their ancient trunks scarred and knotted, their branches swaying in a wind that whispered of secrets. Leaves rustled in uneasy murmurs, brittle with frost, and somewhere in the distance, a branch snapped—too deliberate to be by chance.

Shadows danced between twisted trunks, casting the path in an eerie gloom. The air had turned damp and sharp, thick with the scent of snow and decaying wood. Alexandria's muscles tightened, a chill running deeper than the cold itself. She felt watched—an unseen gaze pressing against her, testing, waiting. Her knuckles whitened on the reins, every sense sharpened by an instinctive warning that prickled at the edges of her mind.

Then, without warning, a piercing howl shattered the silence. It echoed through the trees, drawn out and unnatural, carrying a note of hunger that turned her blood to ice. The horses reared, eyes rolling with panic, hooves churning up the thin crust of snow. Aris reacted in an instant, stepping forward with a low, rumbling snarl, fangs bared and hackles bristling. The wolf's golden eyes burned with a warning—whatever lurked beyond the trees had found them.

Spectral wolves emerged from the undergrowth, their eyes like flickering candles in the gloom. They moved with an unnatural grace, forms wavering as they drifted between trees. The lead wolf paused, nose twitching as it sniffed the air. Its glowing eyes narrowed, fixing on Alexandria with an unsettling intelligence.

Her heart pounding, Alexandria drew her dagger. The wolves' raw power was palpable, and her palms grew slick with sweat at the thought of facing them.

Jasper unsheathed his sword beside her. Aris stood guard, fur bristling as she bared her fangs at the encroaching pack.

"Enough!" An unseen voice echoed through the forest.

The wolves froze, ears pricked toward the command's source. A figure in a flowing purple robe stepped from the shadows, face hidden beneath a hood. Magic hummed in the air as they raised their hands, an invisible force sweeping through the clearing and holding the wolves in place.

The spectral creatures whimpered, cowering against the power that restrained them. The figure's voice was calm yet authoritative as they ordered, "Leave now." Released from the spell, the wolves slunk away, vanishing into the forest.

Alexandria lowered her dagger, though her muscles remained tense. She didn't trust easily—especially not here, in a forest that seemed to breathe with its own sentience. The man stood calmly in the clearing, hood shadowing his face, his silence almost more unnerving than any threat.

"Who are you?" she demanded, her voice cutting through the cold like a blade.

The figure stepped forward and, with slow purpose, pushed back his hood. His face was lined and weathered, but not weak. The kind of face carved by years of magic, solitude, and knowing too much. His long silver hair caught the faint light filtering through the trees, and his gaze—sharp, clear—rested gently on her.

"I am Elder Gaelan," he said, voice low and calm. "Guardian of these woods and protector of those who pass through."

Before Alexandria could respond, Aris shifted without warning into her feline form and stepped forward, her tail flicking side to side. Her golden eyes narrowed with curiosity as she approached the stranger.

Alexandria's breath caught.

She trusted Aris's instincts more than most people's words.

Gaelan didn't flinch. He slowly crouched, extending a hand. Aris leaned forward, brushing her head against his palm. He combed his wrinkled fingers through her fur, his smile warm and almost wistful.

"You have nothing to fear from me, dear Aris," he murmured. "I'm here to guide you on your quest."

The words settled over Alexandria like a shift in the wind. She blinked, lowering her weapon fully now. Every part of her was still on edge, but something about him... it was hard to describe. Like his presence belonged to the forest as much as the trees.

She dismounted, the crunch of snow beneath her boots grounding her in the moment. Her breath left her in a visible cloud. "We're looking for my sister," she said carefully. "Princess Theodora."

Even now, saying the name aloud felt strange—too familiar for someone she didn't really remember, too distant for someone she couldn't stop thinking about.

"Can you help us find her?"

At the mention of the name, Elder Gaelan's expression shifted. His smile faded into something more solemn. His gaze drifted past them for a moment, as if peering into a place none of them could see.

"Then you must be Alexandria," he said slowly.

She hesitated, then gave a single nod. "Yes. I am Alexandria."

He stepped closer, his eyes locking onto hers. She stood her ground, though his presence seemed to press against something inside her—like he wasn't just seeing her but *recognizing* her. Not for who she was now, but for what she was meant to be.

"You and your sister are the key," he said, voice dropping. "Kandella's balance hinges on your choices and actions. But be warned—shadows stir in the realm's darkest corners. Forces long buried begin to rise. They will seek you. They will try to divide you. The prophecy has already begun."

Jasper moved up beside her, hand instinctively resting on the hilt of his sword. "What do ya mean, 'the prophecy'?"

Elder Gaelan turned slightly, his gaze rising to the branches above, now gently swaying as if reacting to his words.

"There is an old telling," he said, "older than most believe. It speaks of twin princesses born under the crescent moon. Children of starlight and storm. Meant to wield the elemental powers once fractured by war. Meant to bring balance back to a realm that has long forgotten what it means to be whole."

Alexandria's heart pounded. Every word landed with eerie weight. *Twin princesses. Elemental power. Balance.* It didn't feel like prophecy—it felt like *expectation* pressing down on her.

"But I don't remember her," she said quietly. "I only started dreaming about her after I left the mortal world. Flashes, moments... but her face was never clear. Just a feeling. And then Diana told me the truth. That I had a sister. That she was waiting."

Her voice faltered, but she pushed through.

"I don't know how to be who I'm supposed to be. I barely know who I am now."

Gaelan stepped forward and placed a calloused hand on her shoulder. His touch was surprisingly warm, grounding. "Trust in the journey, Princess. You may not know the way—but the way knows you. Every step you take is waking what lies dormant. Every choice you make draws the world closer to what it was meant to be."

Alexandria looked around. The forest was quiet again—but not empty. It felt like the trees were listening, like the earth itself was aware of what stood in its midst.

The weight of it all pressed against her chest.

A lost sister. A magical destiny. A kingdom that had lived without her.

But she wasn't the girl she used to be.

She wasn't lost anymore.

She looked up at Gaelan, then over at Jasper. He gave a small nod, offering silent support.

Her gaze returned to the old man. "Then we keep moving," she said. "We find her. And we finish what was started."

Gaelan bowed his head slightly. "You already are."

Snow began to fall again, soft and slow, blanketing the earth in silence. The trees whispered overhead, their branches swaying in rhythm with something ancient and unseen.

And somewhere in the distance, beneath that same sky, Theodora waited.

The fire crackled gently in the small clearing beneath the ancient trees. Shafts of pale sunlight filtered down through the high branches, catching motes of dust and snowflakes in the air. It was early afternoon, but in this dense part of the forest, time seemed to move slower—quieter. The light had a muted, golden quality, like the forest itself was keeping its secrets under a veil.

Alexandria sat close to the fire, elbows resting on her knees, her bracelet glowing faintly against her wrist. The warmth from the flames helped, but the chill of the realm lingered in her bones. Across from her, Elder Gaelan sat in stillness, his weathered features composed, eyes half-lidded as if listening to something only he could hear. Beside her, Jasper leaned back against a tree trunk, ever alert, his sword resting across his legs, one hand idly brushing snow from the hilt.

They had stopped for rest, but no one truly relaxed.

The silence between them stretched, thoughtful and heavy, until Alexandria finally spoke.

"Can I ask you something?"

Gaelan's eyes opened slowly, and the quiet turned attentive. "Of course."

She hesitated for a beat. "You talk about the prophecy like it's not just history. Like it's something you carry."

He nodded once. "Because it is."

Reaching into his cloak, he drew out a small pendant and held it up. The sun caught on its worn surface—an old symbol, nearly faded, of a crescent moon cradling a flame.

"This was given to me when I took my vow beneath the Yarrow Tree," he said. "A promise to serve the balance between forces—light and dark, magic and life. Before kingdoms ruled and maps were drawn, the land itself was our guide."

He paused, his gaze sweeping the fire, then the trees, as if seeing beyond all of it.

"I was born in the Ashen Vale, raised by druids who listened to the wind more than words. When I was a boy, I saw glimpses—twin daughters, born under the crescent moon. One would wield flame, the other storm. Together, they'd restore what had been broken. I didn't understand it then... but I do now."

Alexandria felt her heartbeat slow. "Me and Theodora."

"Yes," Gaelan said gently.

Jasper stirred beside her, his voice steady but wary. "But someone tried ta stop it?"

"Valendor," Gaelan replied, his voice dipping low. "A name now spoken with fear—though it wasn't always so. Long ago, he and King William were... close. As boys, they grew up within the same court, trained by the same mentors, dreaming of shaping Kandella into something better. In those early years, there was kinship. Trust."

He let that sit in the air before continuing.

"But Valendor... changed. Or perhaps the hunger for power had always been there, waiting to take root."

Gaelan's gaze drifted to the snow-dusted treetops, eyes distant.

"One day, he vanished. Left his post, his oath, and his name behind. No warning. No goodbye. For years, nothing but whispers—rumors he'd made his home on the island of Carrountou. A place of jagged cliffs, storms, and a dark castle carved into the rock. Cursed ground, even before he claimed it."

He looked back at Alexandria.

"And for a time, we thought he was gone. Until the prophecy resurfaced—until he learned you and your sister had been born."

Alexandria's breath caught.

"You were nine," Gaelan said quietly. "Both of you. Still young, but the magic already lived in you—too faint for most to feel, but Valendor... he sensed it."

Jasper's jaw tightened.

"He sent his Shadow Walkers," Gaelan continued. "Not in secrecy, but in force. They tore through the castle under cover of night—flooding the halls with smoke and shadow, their eyes like cinders. They searched every room, every corridor."

He paused, then added with a solemn edge, "But Queen Amara was faster."

Alexandria leaned in.

"She hid you both behind the mirror in the royal bedchamber," Gaelan said. "An old mechanism, passed down through the queens of Kandella—a narrow passage tucked between stone walls, concealed behind enchanted glass. She wrapped you in silence and locked the hidden door just moments before the Shadow Walkers burst through."

Alexandria could almost see it—the mirror, the cold of the stone passage, her mother's hands on her shoulders, trembling and fierce.

Gaelan's voice lowered. "They couldn't find you. So they took your parents instead. Dragged them screaming from their chambers. They were taken across the sea to Carrountou. Locked away in the dungeons beneath Valendor's keep."

Her chest tightened.

"What happened to us?" she asked.

"Ms. Whoo came," Gaelan said. "She was one of the last to remain loyal to the old ways—and to your family. Once the castle had fallen into silence, she returned to that hidden room. She found you, huddled together in the dark."

He looked at her, voice heavy. "She knew Valendor would never stop hunting you. So she did the only thing she could."

"She used magic," Alexandria murmured.

He nodded. "A powerful spell. She separated you. Blocked your memories. Cloaked your presence so deeply that even the Shadow Walkers couldn't sense them. You, Alexandria, were sent to the mortal world. Far beyond his reach. And Theodora remained here—hidden within Donaglen Castle, protected and raised in secret by Ms. Whoo herself."

A long silence fell.

"And the winter?" Jasper asked.

Gaelan's eyes dimmed. "After the King and Queen were gone, Valendor sealed the realm. He laid a curse over Kandella—one of stillness and silence. A winter without thaw. A season without end. He believed that if time stood still, the prophecy would fade."

"That *you* would never return." He added glancing over at Alexandria.

Alexandria looked down at her bracelet. The green glow still pulsed faintly, steady and alive.

She looked up, sunlight slipping through the trees. "Diana told me who I was," she murmured. "But long before that... I felt her. Theodora. I didn't know her face, but I knew she was real."

"She felt you too," Gaelan said, his voice softening. "That thread between you—magic and memory—it's waking now."

Jasper shifted beside her. "Valendor won't let it happen."

"You're right," Gaelan nodded. "However, his hold is weakening. The land is starting to push back against him. With every step you take, the balance is beginning to shift."

Above them, wind whispered through the trees, carrying light through their canopy. Snow shimmered faintly in the early afternoon sun, and somewhere in the stillness, a bird called out.

Alexandria stared into the fire.

"We'll find her," she said. "We'll finish what he tried to bury."

Gaelan's eyes met hers. "You have already begun."

And in that quiet, golden light—where magic stirred and truth slowly thawed—the frozen heart of Kandella beat once more.

Alexandria sat in silence, her hands resting in her lap, the soft pulse of her bracelet steady against her wrist. The fire's warmth licked at her skin, but her chest felt tight, a quiet ache pressing against her ribs.

Everything Gaelan had told her swirled through her mind—her parents' desperate sacrifice, the hidden room behind the mirror, Ms. Whoo's spell, the separation. Nine years old. She could barely remember what she'd been like then. Just scattered pieces. A laugh. A voice. A pull she couldn't name.

Theodora had stayed. Alone. Carried the weight of silence while Alexandria grew up in a world that wasn't hers, haunted by a sister she couldn't see.

She blinked hard, forcing the sting in her eyes to settle. Grief and guilt twisted in her chest, but beneath it all was something deeper. Fiercer. Resolve.

She stood slowly and turned to Elder Gaelan, her voice rough but steady. "Thank you… for telling me the truth. For all of it."

Gaelan inclined his head. "You deserved to know. And Kandella needed you to remember."

Alexandria looked to the trees where slivers of light poured in through bare branches, soft and golden in the early afternoon haze. "We have to go. I've wasted enough time not knowing who I was. She's out there somewhere, and I won't leave her to carry this alone."

Gaelan watched her with quiet reverence, then stepped forward and gently placed his hand on her shoulder. "Then trust the path. Follow the western trail until it forks near the frostroot stones. From there, take the leftward bend through the pine run. It will bring you to Primlow. If you keep a steady pace, you may reach the southern rise by the day after next."

Alexandria nodded, committing every word to memory. A lump sat in her throat, thick and unmoving. It all felt real now—realer than ever.

"Elder Gaelan…" she hesitated, then looked him in the eye. "I don't remember everything. But I know what I feel. And I know I need to find her—not just for Kandella, but for us."

"And you will," he said. "You carry the blood of a line born from magic and fire, but more than that—you carry love. That will guide you when all else fails."

She offered a faint, grateful smile. "You've done more than guide us. You gave me back a piece of myself."

"That piece never left," Gaelan replied. "It was only waiting."

Jasper rose beside her, his expression solemn, jaw set. He said nothing, but his presence was steady—like an anchor against the tide of everything that had shifted.

Aris padded forward, brushing softly against Gaelan's leg before settling at Alexandria's side, golden eyes watching her with quiet intensity.

With a last look at the fire, Alexandria turned toward the trail ahead.

Each step away from the clearing felt heavy at first, like walking through the past. But with each stride, her shoulders straightened, her chin lifted.

No more shadows. No more guessing.

The truth had found her.

And now she would find Theodora.

Chapter 13

"Fate's Silent Whispers"

T HE SUN DIPPED BELOW the horizon, painting the sky in fiery hues. A cool breeze whispered through the grove, sending a shiver down Theodora's spine as she stepped into the clearing. The air was thick with the scent of earth and wildflowers, pollen dancing in the fading light.

Towering trees stood watch, their branches swaying softly. Theodora's heart raced as she reached the center of the grove. She took a steadying breath, preparing to unleash her raw power before her friends.

Hazy memories flickered at the edges of her mind, offering tantalizing glimpses of a forgotten past. These fragments made her wary of her growing abilities.

"Ye've got this, Theodora. We believe in ye," Finnegan said, his eyes filled with quiet confidence.

Theodora's pulse quickened. Her mouth went dry as she called forth her inner energy. Electricity crackled at her fingertips, arcing into brilliant bolts lit up the grove. Her body trembled with the effort of controlling the surge. Killian gaped in amazement, while Finnegan watched intently.

"By the gods, lass. That's some powerful magic ye've got there," Finnegan said, his voice a mix of awe and concern.

Theodora met his gaze, her eyes still sparking with residual energy. "I'm done bein' afraid. Whatever this path holds, I'm ready t'face it."

Killian nodded, his usual sharpness softening. "Ye won't face it alone, Theodora. We're with ye every step of the way."

A sense of unity settled over them, stronger than any words could express. Theodora felt a rush of gratitude for her companions, their unwavering support grounding her in these uncertain times.

As night fell, they gathered around the campfire, its warmth a welcome comfort after the day's events. Killian broke the peaceful silence.

"That was somethin' else today, Theodora. Never seen anythin' like it," he said, genuine admiration in his voice.

Theodora smiled, a hint of shyness in her expression. "Couldn't've done it without ye two," she replied honestly.

Finnegan poked at the fire, sending sparks skyward. "Aye, we make a good team."

The crackling flames filled the quiet that followed, each lost in their own thoughts. Theodora felt a swell of determination, bolstered by her friends' faith in her.

"I never expected t'find friends like ye," she said, looking between them. "Thank ye for stickin' with me."

Killian grinned. "Wouldn't have it any other way, lass."

As the fire cast flickering shadows, Theodora felt a new sense of resolve. The road ahead would be difficult, but with her friends by her side and her powers growing stronger, she felt ready to face whatever challenges lay ahead.

Isidore's sunrises heralded new beginnings and adventures. Theodora honed her magic under Finnegan's guidance and Killian's watchful eye during their final days. Finnegan's lessons echoed as she practiced, sparks dancing at her fingertips.

Theodora's heart raced as she focused on a small orb of light in her palm, brow furrowed in concentration. The glade seemed to hold its breath, ancient trees standing guard as she worked on her newfound talents.

A sudden snap broke her focus. Theodora stumbled back, eyes wide. Killian's sword was out in a flash, scanning for threats. Finnegan stood ready, weapon in hand.

"Lord Valendor?" Theodora whispered, unease in her voice.

Killian frowned. "Unlikely. Our ancestors' magic protected this land for ages. He couldn't just waltz in."

Theodora's mind raced. What if Valendor had found a way? The thought chilled her.

Killian sighed. "Though, there might be some truth to that." He met Theodora's gaze, acknowledgin' their uncertain future.

Finnegan's eyes softened. "We can't be lettin' fear rule us," he said. "We must be trustin' in Isadore's protection."

Theodora nodded, taking a deep breath. She closed her eyes, focusing inward on her magical core. The world faded away as she concentrated on the surge of power within.

A faint scent of ozone filled the air as she called forth her magic. A soft glow emanated from her palms, forming a tiny, pulsing sphere of light.

The orb grew brighter, illuminating the area around them. It burst in a flash of light. Theodora stumbled, shielding her eyes.

"You alright, lass?" Finnegan steadied her.

She nodded, staring at where the orb had been. "What happened?"

"Too much energy at once," Killian explained. "Ye'll need to learn control."

Determination burned in Theodora's eyes. She'd master this magic—lightning crackled at her fingertips, wild but hers to command.

Finnegan gave her a measured look. "Power like that takes time, lass."

"Aye, but I won't be wastin' a second of it," Theodora shot back, sparks snapping at her fingertips. Her magic was raw, untamed—but she'd bend it to her will. She had to.

Killian exhaled, setting a hand on her shoulder. "Rest now."

Theodora clenched her jaw but said nothing. She knew they had to leave Isadore behind, to continue their journey, but it didn't sit right. The safety, the warmth—it had been a brief refuge, one she wasn't ready to abandon. Still, she swallowed the lump in her throat and gave a stiff nod.

"We leave at dawn," Finnegan added, his tone firm.

Theodora turned away, fists tightening. Tomorrow, they'll move forward. Whether or not she was ready.

Theodora jolted awake, breath ragged, her mother's face still burned into her vision—eyes wide with terror, lips forming silent words she couldn't quite catch. Her nightgown clung to her skin, damp with sweat, and her heart thundered like a drum. She pressed a shaking hand to her chest, trying to steady herself, to pull back from the edge of the dream that had felt too close, too real.

Before she could gather her thoughts, a soft knock came from the other side of the cloth partition.

"Theodora?" Finnegan's voice was low, careful.

"Aye?" she managed, her throat dry and raw.

"Can I come in?"

She hesitated, then pulled the blanket tighter around her shoulders. "Come on in, then."

Finnegan stepped through, the dim lantern casting flickering shadows across his weathered face. He moved quietly, sitting beside her bedroll with a softness that contrasted the usual strength in his posture. His eyes scanned hers, seeing more than she wanted to show.

"Heard ye screamin'," he said gently. "Still havin' those nightmares?"

She nodded, biting the inside of her cheek. "They're gettin' worse." Her voice dropped, eyes fixed on the ground. "This time, I was back in the castle. But it wasn't just the memory. It was like I was there, really there, watchin' it happen again... only different."

Finnegan leaned in slightly. "Different how?"

Theodora looked up, her eyes glassy with lingering fear.

"She looked right at me—me mother. Not like before, not like when she was taken. This time, she was trying to say somethin'. Like she knew I was there. Like she was warnin' me."

Finnegan's brow furrowed, the weight of her words settling between them. "You think it was more than a memory?"

"I don't know," she whispered. "But I felt it. Somethin' dark was movin' through the castle. Not just the soldiers... somethin' colder. Somethin' ancient. And it saw me."

He didn't speak right away. Instead, he took her hand gently, thumb brushing over her knuckles with quiet reassurance. "I can't imagine what yer goin' through, lass. But whatever it is... ye're not facin' it alone."

She stared at him for a long moment, reading the quiet tension behind his calm. "Do you have nightmares too, Finnegan?"

He exhaled, his eyes dropping to the floor. "Aye," he said after a pause. "More than I care to admit. Some memories... they don't let go. And some of 'em feel like more than memories. Like echoes of somethin' not finished."

She leaned in closer, voice soft. "What haunts ye?"

Finnegan hesitated, then looked past her, eyes distant. "There's things in me past I'm not proud of, Princess. Choices made in anger and grief..."

Theodora squeezed his hand. "Ye can tell me, if ye want. I'll listen."

Gratitude and hesitation flickered in his expression before he nodded slightly. His voice was quiet, heavy with old pain.

"When I was young, I was already trainin' t'be a druid. I'd left home for the Circle, eager t'prove meself. Thought I had all the time in the world," he said, his jaw clenching. "But while I was gone... enemies came. A sorcerer an' his men. They stormed the village, burned it all t'ash. Me family... all of 'em... gone."

Theodora's breath hitched, but she said nothing, letting him continue.

"I wasn't there ta protect 'em. And that guilt—by the gods, it nearly drowned me. I couldn't live with the weight of it, so I turned ta dark magic. Not for justice. For revenge. I thought if I had enough power, I could make 'em pay."

She listened, her heart aching not just for what he'd lost, but for the boy he'd been—full of hope, then hollowed by grief.

"Thing is," he said, voice lower now, "revenge doesn't bring peace. It just... eats at what's left o' ya. Took me years t'claw me way back t'the light. Years."

She reached out, placing her free hand over his. "Ye've overcome so much," she said softly. "Yer strength, yer goodness now... that's what matters."

Finnegan met her gaze, something raw and open passing between them. "Thank ye, lass. Yer faith... it means more than ye know."

The silence that followed wasn't awkward or heavy—it was still, steady, the kind that said I see you. I've got you.

A sudden rustling of wings stirred the quiet.

Both looked up as Khadall glided soundlessly through the open window, his broad grey wings catching the lantern light in fleeting silver flashes. The great owl landed on the wooden beam above them, his amber eyes watching with calm, ancient knowing.

He dropped gracefully to the ground, talons quiet on the stone, and stepped toward Theodora. She reached out instinctively, brushing her fingers along the soft feathers of his chest. A shimmer passed through him then, not a change of form, but a subtle shift—his presence deepening, like a spirit fully stepping into its vessel.

Finnegan watched, awe softening his features. "I've seen many strange things," he murmured, "but never a bond like that."

Theodora smiled faintly, resting her hand on Khadall's side. "He's more than a guardian. He's part o' me. Family."

Finnegan nodded, and for the first time that night, the weight of their pasts didn't feel so impossible. Whatever shadows waited ahead, they would face them—together.

Dawn broke over the horizon, painting the sky in hues of pink and gold. Theodora, Finnegan and Killian set out towards the portal leading to the Forest of Monaghan, each step taking them further into unfamiliar territory. The rustling leaves seemed to whisper secrets as they passed.

Riding through lush fields and along winding riverbanks, Theodora felt a pang in her chest. The peaceful scenery was a stark contrast to the weight of their mission. As she guided her horse with practiced hands, she couldn't shake the feeling that destiny was pushing her forward, deepening her understanding of the world with each passing moment.

"Finnegan," Theodora asked, breaking the silence, "what's so special about these Crystal Caverns?"

Finnegan's eyes lit up with reverence. "Ah, lass, it's not just some magical cave," he said, his voice low and respectful. "Those caverns hold ancient treasures and knowledge that time's all but forgotten. Secrets just waitin' to be uncovered."

As they neared the portal back to Monaghan, Theodora felt a chill run down her spine. Shadows seemed to dance at the edge of her vision, and she tightened her grip on the reins, fighting back the creeping fear.

Killian took the lead, his face set with determination. With a wave of his hand, he called forth the portal. The air shimmered and rippled, slowly revealing a swirling vortex of colors.

Theodora's heart raced as she stared into the portal. Doubt gnawed at her, threatening to overwhelm her resolve. She took a deep breath, steeling herself against the fear.

With newfound determination, Theodora urged her horse forward. She crossed the threshold, clinging to her belief in their mission.

The journey through the portal was disorienting, reality bending around them in a dizzying display. When they emerged, Theodora found herself right back where they'd first encountered Killian.

Finnegan's hand on her shoulder steadied her. "Remember, Theodora," he said, cutting through her confusion. "True strength isn't about never bein' scared. It's about facin' those fears head-on."

The portal shimmered, its golden light flickering before vanishing with a final pulse. Darkness pressed in, thick and unyielding. Theodora, Finnegan and Killian stood motionless for a moment, the weight of their journey settling over them like a heavy cloak. Behind them, the sanctuary of Isadore was gone—its warm fires, protective wards and familiar voices now a distant memory. Ahead, the Forest of Monaghan stretched in front of them. Its towering trees cast tangled shadows beneath the pale moonlight.

The scent of damp earth and moss filled the air as the trio stepped forward, their boots sinking slightly into the soft forest floor. Monaghan was not just an ordinary forest. It was old, restless, and full of secrets. The wind that whispered through its branches carried hints of voices—some real, others tricks of the mind.

Finnegan pulled his cloak tighter around his shoulders. "Best we keep movin' now, eh? No sense standin' round like lost lambs. Portal's gone, and there's no goin' back."

Killian adjusted the strap of his satchel, gaze fixed on the dark path ahead. "Aye, the Crystal Caverns are a day's travel at least. Wouldn't shock me if somethin' foul' lay in wait, watchin' for the likes of us."

A distant howl echoed through the trees, low and guttural. Theodora met Finnegan's gaze, reading the same unease in his eyes that she felt in her chest. There were things in Monaghan that did not sleep, creatures that had no fear of the dark.

She exhaled sharply and started forward. "No time like the present, then. Let's move."

Without another word, they pressed on, the path ahead winding deeper into the ancient wood.

Chapter 14

"Silent Shadows Rise"

Elder Gaelan's directions had led them deep into a forest blanketed in white. Snow coated every branch, and the crisp scent of pine clung to the air. Their breaths curled visibly in front of them as they traveled, and the only sounds were the soft crunch of hooves and boots in the snow.

They'd pressed on well into the late afternoon, the sun dipping behind a pale curtain of clouds. The world around them had grown quiet—eerily still, as if the trees were listening.

Ahead, Aris moved in her feline form, gliding over the snow with practiced ease. Alexandria rode just behind, her cloak wrapped tight around her shoulders, the chill doing little to distract her from the storm of thoughts in her head. Jasper kept close behind, always watchful.

When the trees finally gave way to a clearing, they paused. In the center was a frozen pond, still and glassy like crystal, its surface catching what little light remained and reflecting it back in muted silver and violet hues.

Jasper reined in beside her and scanned the space. "Let's stop here for a while," he said, his brogue quiet but firm. "Bit of food, rest our legs. We'll push on after."

Alexandria nodded, though her mind was elsewhere.

She dismounted, her fingers stiff with cold, and wandered toward the edge of the pond. The clearing had a strange peace to it, like it had been untouched for a long time. It made her chest ache.

Behind her, Jasper got to work quickly, building a fire from what dry wood he could find. Soon, the crackle of flames cut through the silence, and the smell of herbs and salted meat filled the air. He stirred a small pot suspended over the fire—simple fare, but enough.

Alexandria sat near the warmth, watching the flames dance, but her thoughts were miles away. Bits of memory stirred—Theodora's laughter, sunlight through tall windows, bare feet racing over stone floors. It all felt like a life half-remembered.

She rubbed her hands together, trying to shake the heaviness pressing down on her. She understood why Ms. Whoo had done it—why they'd been separated. It had kept them safe. But understanding didn't fix the hole in her chest. It didn't make up for the years they'd missed or the bond that had frayed in silence.

They'd been nine. Just nine.

Would Theodora even remember her? Would she still be the sister Alexandria saw in fleeting dreams and half-formed memories—or someone entirely different now?

Jasper handed her a bowl, the steam rising in curls. "It's nothin' fancy," he said, "but it'll warm ya up."

She gave a quiet "Thanks," and took it. The warmth helped, even if her appetite was thin.

He sat beside her with his own bowl. "You alright?"

She gave a short laugh, tired and raw. "No idea what that even means anymore."

He didn't press. Just nodded and took a bite.

The quiet settled around them again, save for the fire and the occasional snap of a branch somewhere in the woods.

When she'd finished eating, Alexandria leaned back against a large, snow-dusted boulder, her breath steadying. A soft shift of movement beside her made her glance down.

Aris had returned, curling up close to her side, silent and steady. Alexandria reached down and ran her fingers through the big cat's thick fur, grounding herself in the presence of something that had always felt constant.

"We're close," she murmured, voice barely above a whisper. "I don't know how I know it, but I do. She's not far now."

Jasper looked over at her, his eyes catching the firelight. "Ya sure yer ready for what comes next?"

Alexandria didn't answer right away. She kept her eyes on the flames.

"No," she said finally. "But I've come too far to stop now. I have to see this through—for her. For both of us."

Jasper nodded. "Then we keep goin'. Side by side."

She glanced over, a faint smile tugging at the corners of her mouth. "Together."

The fire had burned low, its warmth fading into the quiet afternoon air. Around them, the forest remained still, snow settling in soft mounds as if the world itself were holding its breath.

After some time—just enough for their limbs to rest and their bellies to settle—Jasper stood and began kicking snow over the dying embers. Alexandria followed his lead, brushing the last traces of soot from her cloak as she cinched her pack. The brief pause had given her body relief, but her mind hadn't slowed once.

Without a word, they mounted up again, Aris taking the lead. The trail ahead narrowed between frost-covered trees, the light now golden and soft, stretching shadows long across the snow.

For a while, no one spoke. The only sounds were the rhythmic crunch of hooves and the occasional rustle of wind through the branches.

Then Aris broke the silence, her voice calm and certain. "I know you miss your sister," she said, trotting alongside Alexandria. "But have faith in your journey. Your bond is strong enough to bridge distance, time... even magic. You'll find each other again."

The words landed deep. Not overly reassuring. Just true.

Alexandria's grip on the reins loosened slightly. She glanced down at Aris, then reached out and ran her fingers gently through the cat's thick fur.

"I do miss her," she murmured. "Even before I knew she was real... I missed her. It was always there, like a part of me was out of place."

Aris looked up, golden eyes steady. "That ache you've carried all your life? That was her. Even when you were apart, that connection never left."

Alexandria let out a slow breath, watching it curl into the air. "I just worry she won't remember me. Or worse—that she's changed so much, there won't be anything left between us."

"She's changed, yes. Just as you have. But what matters has endured," Aris said. "She's waited—whether she realizes it or not."

Jasper, just ahead, cast a glance back over his shoulder. He didn't speak, but the look said he'd been listening—and agreed.

The path grew denser as they moved deeper into the woods. The trees here stood older, closer, their limbs reaching like silent sentinels. Snow clung to every branch, and the light dimmed to a soft, bluish glow beneath the canopy.

Still, Alexandria pressed on, heart pounding with quiet determination. She didn't know what the reunion would look like, or what words she'd even say when she saw Theodora's face. But she didn't need to know yet.

For now, she could feel it.

A presence.

A pull beneath her skin.

Not fear, not hope—something more certain. A knowing.

They were moving in the right direction.

And no matter how long the path stretched, she would not stop until she reached her.

The forest thickened as night fell around them, the last traces of light swallowed by the canopy overhead. Snow glistened faintly underfoot, the path now little more than a narrow ribbon of frost between towering trees. Each breath clouded in the air, every step seemed to echo just a little too loudly.

Alexandria tugged her cloak tighter around her shoulders, the warmth of their campfire already a distant memory. Her horse moved steadily beneath her, but her mind wandered—drawn to something she couldn't quite name.

The deeper they went, the stronger the feeling grew. Not fear, exactly. Not yet. But something was off.

She glanced toward Aris, who had been pacing beside her in feline form. The great cat slowed, ears tilting back, muscles taut beneath her sleek coat. Without a sound, Aris began to shift—bones reshaping, limbs extending—until the form of a wolf trotted out from the shadows of her magic, silent and alert.

Alexandria watched the transformation, her pulse quickening. Aris didn't shift for no reason.

"Do you feel that?" she asked quietly.

Jasper pulled up beside her, his eyes sweeping the dark beyond the trail. "Aye," he murmured. "The woods've gone too quiet."

Even the wind had stilled.

Alexandria's skin prickled. She turned in the saddle, scanning the trees behind them, her eyes searching the darkness for movement—but the forest gave nothing away. Just snow. Just silence.

But she knew they weren't alone.

Unseen among the trees, a cloaked figure moved like a shadow between the trunks—silent, precise, predatory.

Lord Valendor watched from a distance, his form barely more than a ripple in the darkness. His eyes, cold and colorless, followed every movement of the trio below as they wove their way through the snow-laden path. Alexandria rode at the center, flanked by the swordsman and the shapeshifter—loyal, determined, unaware.

A curl of satisfaction tugged at the corner of his mouth.

He kept his distance, his presence masked by layers of illusion and old magic, but he needed only to watch. To wait.

They were heading exactly where he wanted them to go.

So close now. Closer than they knew.

His gaze lingered on Alexandria just a heartbeat longer. The girl radiated the old power—quiet for now, but rising. The bond to her sister had begun to stir, and with it, the prophecy that had haunted him for decades.

Let them chase it. Let them believe in fate and reunion and hope.

He would take it from them, piece by piece.

Soon, both sisters would belong to him—and with them, the key to unseating every last force that dared stand against his rule. Kandella would freeze beneath his will, forever still, forever his.

As their forms disappeared deeper into the trees, Valendor turned without a sound, fading back into the forest like smoke pulled by the wind.

Alexandria urged her horse forward, the quiet crunch of snow beneath its hooves the only sound breaking the stillness. The trail narrowed again, branches reaching low overhead like gnarled fingers, dusted with frost.

Aris moved just ahead in her wolf form, nose to the ground, ears flicking back now and then. Jasper kept pace on the other side, silent, focused. None of them spoke—but they didn't need to.

The feeling hadn't left her. If anything, it had settled deeper into her skin.

Something was wrong.

Not immediate. Not visible. But it was there, hovering just beyond what she could name. A pressure at the edge of her awareness, like the forest had shifted around them and forgotten to breathe.

She glanced over her shoulder for the third time in ten minutes.

Nothing but trees.

Still, her stomach wouldn't settle.

"I don't like this," she muttered, mostly to herself.

Jasper heard. "Ya feel it too?"

"Yes." Her voice came out quiet, taut. "Like we're being fol-lowed. But there's no sound. No sign."

Jasper's hand dropped to his sword hilt. "That's worse."

Aris stopped abruptly, her body stiff, one paw lifted mid-step. Her head swiveled back toward the path behind them, ears high, her growl low and constant.

Alexandria pulled her horse to a halt.

The air seemed to shift—just slightly. A ripple through the cold.

Nothing came out of the trees.

But whatever had passed through this part of the forest had left a mark. The trees looked older here. Wilder. And for a moment, Alexandria swore the branches trembled, though there wasn't a breeze to move them.

She rubbed the back of her neck, then pressed her hand to her chest, where her bracelet lay beneath layers of wool and leather.

It hadn't glowed since earlier—but the space around it felt... tight. As if it was bracing for something.

"Keep movin'?" Jasper asked, his voice low.

Alexandria gave a single nod. "We don't stop. Not here."

Aris didn't need to be told. She turned and began trotting ahead again, staying low, ears sharp.

And as they pushed forward through the narrowing trail, Alexandria didn't look back this time.

But she felt it.

Something had been watching.

And even though it was gone now, its shadow lingered—like the echo of a breath drawn in and never exhaled.

They hadn't spoken much after that—after the feeling of being watched pressed against their backs like a hand they couldn't see. The presence had passed, but it left something behind. A heaviness in the air. A silence that felt like it was listening.

When the forest finally opened into a shallow glade, Jasper pulled his horse to a halt and scanned the area. A stream trickled along the far edge, barely more than a ribbon of ice in the fading light. Snow clung to the branches above like frost-laced lace, and the clearing was ringed with pine trees, their needles dark and dense.

"This'll do," he said, voice low. "We've enough cover and some clean water—so long as it doesn't freeze solid 'fore mornin'."

Aris gave a soft huff in her wolf form before shifting back into her feline body and prowling around the edges, ears twitching. Satisfied, she dropped into a crouch near the base of a tree, tail flicking.

Alexandria slid from her saddle, her boots crunching softly in the snow. She could smell the damp earth beneath the frost, the sharp bite of cold pine sap in the air, and beneath it all, the lingering smoke of their earlier fire, still clinging to her cloak.

They moved with quiet efficiency—Jasper gathering dry wood from beneath thick pine boughs, Alexandria pulling out food and supplies. She stacked the cloaks and gear, fingers stiff from the cold but practiced. The chill cut through her layers, but the forest was still, the snow absorbing sound and softening everything.

"Smells like storm's holdin' off for now," Jasper said, setting kindling in a tight pile. "But don't trust skies like this. They look peaceful till they spit snow in yer eyes at dawn."

"I'll take peace while I can get it," Alexandria replied, brushing a strand of hair from her face. "Even if it's pretend."

He gave a short laugh as he struck flint against steel. "Pretend peace's better than none at all."

The fire caught quickly, flames licking up and casting a soft, golden glow. The smoke curled upward, sharp with pine and dry bark, wrapping around them like a veil.

They sat close, warming their hands and eating a quiet meal of dried meat and bread. The simple warmth of the fire was enough to ease the tension, if only for a while. Aris eventually returned to Alexandria's side, curling up nearby in her feline form.

They didn't speak much after that. The quiet between them was a kind of understanding.

The stars blinked into view above the trees, sharp and cold against the dark sky. The fire had burned low, casting a soft, golden flicker that danced along the snow-covered ground. Around them, the forest had fallen into a hush—not just quiet, but still. Like even the trees were holding their breath.

Alexandria sat close to the fire, her knees tucked in, hands cupped together for warmth. She stared into the flames, her thoughts distant, turning over everything they'd seen, everything still ahead.

Jasper sat a short distance away, sharpening his blade in slow, thoughtful strokes. Neither of them spoke. They didn't need to. The silence between them wasn't heavy—it simply was.

Eventually, Jasper stood, brushing snow from his cloak. "We should get some rest," he said, voice low. "Still a good stretch ahead of us come morning."

Alexandria nodded. The cold had crept into her limbs, but it was the weight of her thoughts that made her feel heavier. She rose quietly, her movements slow, deliberate.

Aris padded over and settled beside her, shifting into her feline form, her thick coat brushing against Alexandria's leg like a silent promise that she was near.

They each found a spot close to the fire, the warmth reaching just enough to take the edge off the night. Alexandria wrapped her cloak tighter, her gaze lifting once more to the stars overhead.

She let her fingers brush the edge of her bracelet, its presence a small comfort against the uncertainty pressing at the edges of her mind.

She didn't know what tomorrow would bring—or what they might find waiting for them.

But they were together.

And that was enough, for now.

Birdsong cut through the silence, sharp and clear in the cold air. Alexandria stirred as dawn broke, its pale light filtering through branches and casting long shadows across the snow. She opened her eyes, the fog of sleep lifting slowly as she adjusted to the morning's brightness. Whatever dreams had followed her through the night scattered as reality settled back in—the chill in her bones, the weight of the journey ahead, and the persistent pull toward something still unseen.

Nearby, Jasper crouched beside the fire, coaxing sizzling strips of bacon in a pan. The aroma mingled with wood smoke and frost, comforting and grounding. Aris, back in her feline form, lounged nearby, one paw lazily draped over the other, golden eyes fixed on Jasper with something between amusement and approval.

"Mornin', sleepyhead," Jasper called over his shoulder, flipping the bacon with a bit of flair. "Hungry?"

Alexandria laughed, voice still rough from sleep but bright in the quiet morning. "Starving. Please tell me there's coffee."

"What kind o' camp would this be wit'out it?" Jasper grinned, gesturing toward a tin mug already steaming near the fire.

She accepted it gratefully, cupping the warm metal in her hands. The rich scent of coffee, faintly laced with cinnamon, filled her nose. She took a slow sip, letting the heat spread through her chest.

They took their breakfast down to the lake's edge, legs dangling over the bank, the frozen water sparkling under the first touch of sunlight. Between bites, conversation flowed easily—low and warm, full of teasing and quiet camaraderie. Even Aris joined in, nudging Alexandria's side with her head until she let out a startled laugh.

For a moment, everything felt simple.

But as the sun climbed higher, the weight of their journey returned. Alexandria stood and dusted the snow from her cloak. The laughter faded from her face, replaced by a quiet determination.

"We should get moving," she said.

Jasper nodded, already rising to tend to the camp. "Aye. We've ground ta cover."

They mounted up, the horses stamping softly in the snow as Aris circled back to Alexandria's side. The trio turned toward the edge of the glade and began their ride, following the path around the lake's perimeter.

Snow crunched beneath their hooves, and their breaths misted in the air. The frozen surface of the lake mirrored the sky, still and pale. The beauty of the scene was haunting—too perfect. As if the world were holding its breath again.

Then Alexandria halted, reins tightening in her grip.

"Hold on…" she said. "Where's Elara?"

Her voice wavered with uncertainty.

Jasper pulled up beside her, scanning the trees. "Good question."

A long silence followed, broken only by the soft rustle of wind through the trees.

They waited.

Then—clear as a bell, soft as snowfall—Elara's voice rang through their minds.

"Fear not, my friends. I am with you still, though unseen. Trust in your path and in each other."

The tension in Alexandria's chest eased slightly. Jasper exhaled, shoulders dropping.

Aris's tail flicked, a soft purr rumbling from her throat. Her eyes met Alexandria's—bright, unshaken.

Elara might not walk beside them in body, but her presence was still there.

Chapter 15

"Beyond the Fury"

THEODORA'S SHOULDERS ACHED, AND exhaustion clawed at the edges of her focus as they pressed deeper into the forest. The night was thick, suffocating, the towering trees closing in like silent sentinels. Every rustling leaf, every shifting shadow felt like a warning.

Her horse snorted, ears twitching, sensing the unease that none of them dared voice. Finnegan rode ahead, his grip tightened on the reins, jaw set in determination. Killian muttered under his breath, a nervous habit that only surfaced when tension ran high.

Above them, Khadall soared through the darkness, his golden eyes scanning the landscape below. Silent and watchful, he cut through the night like a phantom, a guardian against unseen threats. Theodora took some comfort in his presence, but even he seemed restless, wings shifting as if expecting something just beyond their sight.

Then, without warning, the owl shrieked. The cry shattered the hush like glass, raw and panicked. Khadall plunged toward a dense thicket, and Theodora's mount reared in terror. She cursed, yanking at the reins, barely keeping her seat as Finnegan and Killian tore their weapons free, eyes scanning the darkness for whatever horror had set the owl screaming.

From the undergrowth emerged a creature only found in nightmares. Its form twisted and unnatural, it unleashed an unearthly howl that chilled Theodora to her core. This was no mere beast, but a manifestation of the dark forces they fought against.

Adrenaline sharpened her senses. She nocked an arrow, ready to defend herself as Finnegan and Killian engaged the beast. Their blades danced in perfect harmony, creating a deadly barrier between the creature and the princess. Theodora drew strength from their unwavering resolve.

The heat of battle awakened something within her. Magic, dormant until now, surged through her veins. She channeled this newfound power into her arrow, watching as it shimmered with verdant energy. With steady hands and laser focus, she let the enchanted shaft fly.

It struck true. The arrow pierced the creature's hide, unleashing a blast of magical force. Dark smoke erupted from the wound as the beast crashed to the forest floor. Its body convulsed, then dissolved into nothingness.

Silence fell, broken only by their ragged breathing and the rustle of leaves. Theodora's heart pounded, a mix of exhilaration and relief flooding her system. Finnegan and Killian looked grim yet triumphant. Their mounts shifted uneasily, picking up on the lingering tension. They had faced this threat together and emerged victorious, but all three knew this was just the beginning.

"That was no ordinary beast," Finnegan said, his voice low and grave. "Dark magic's at work here."

Killian nodded, grip tightening on his halberd. "Aye, and I doubt it'll be the last we see of it."

Questions raced through Theodora's mind, but she pushed them aside. They had to reach the Crystal Caverns, no matter what stood in their way.

Khadall swooped down, landing on her shoulder with a soft hoot. Theodora stroked his feathers, drawing comfort from his presence.

"We'll make it," she said, her voice steady despite her inner turmoil. "We have to."

Finnegan glanced her way, moonlight glinting in his eyes. "You've got more courage than most men I've known, lass. But courage alone won't see us through what's coming."

Theodora met his gaze, determination burning in her own. "Good thing I've got more than just courage, then."

Killian chuckled, the sound rumbling deep in his chest. "That you do, lass. That you do."

The forest's eerie calm shattered, leaves rustled and unseen creatures howled in the distance. Khadall perched on Theodora's shoulder, his amber eyes scanning the shadows for threats.

As they neared the edge of the forest, the air grew thick with tension. The oppressive silence wrapped around them like a shroud, broken only by the muffled thud of hooves against damp earth. Theodora's nerves were raw, every snapping twig making her flinch. Her fingers tightened on the reins, knuckles white, the weight of unseen eyes pressing down on her.

Finnegan rode stiffly beside her, his usual confidence replaced by rigid alertness. His hand hovered near his sword, breath slow and measured, as if bracing for a fight. Killian, quick with a jest to break the tension, said nothing. His grip on the hilt of his dagger was ironclad, his gaze darting to every shadow that stretched too far.

Above them, Khadall glided in uneasy circles, his eyes scanning the darkness. Theodora swallowed hard, forcing herself to steady her breathing. Whatever lay beyond the trees, they would face it soon.

The owl screeched, wings flapping. The horses reared, nearly unseating their riders.

"Whoa, easy," Killian murmured, steadying his mount while keeping watch.

Theodora's fingers tightened on her bow, heart racing as she peered into the gloom. The forest felt alive, watching their every move.

"Somethin's out there," she said, breaking the tense quiet.

Finnegan frowned. "What d'ya mean?"

"Can't put me finger on it," Theodora replied, eyes darting between the trees. "Just feels like we're bein' watched."

A sudden rustle of leaves had them drawing their weapons, only to find themselves facing a group of hooded figures emerging from the shadows.

"Who goes there?" Finnegan demanded, sword raised.

The lead figure chuckled, voice raspy. "We are the Guardians of Monaghan Forest."

"Guardians?" Theodora echoed, uncertain.

"We protect this land from those who'd harm it," the figure explained. "Including you, it seems."

The standoff stretched, neither side backing down. Then Killian lowered his halberd.

"We mean no harm," he said. "We seek the Crystal Caverns."

At this, the figures paused. The tallest stepped forward, lowering his hood to reveal a weathered face with piercing silver eyes and a battle-scarred cheek.

"I am Elder Bryn, leader of the Guardians," he said, voice resonating with authority. "Forgive our caution. Dark forces stir in these woods."

Theodora sensed ancient power radiating from him. She bowed her head.

"We understand your vigilance," she said. "We seek only passage to the Caverns, to complete a quest that may safeguard this land."

Elder Bryn studied them before nodding. "You may pass. But heed this warning—darkness gathers in Kandella. Not all allies are true."

With that, the Guardians melted back into the shadows.

Killian hefted his halberd and pushed forward, his steps steady but tense as the trees thinned around them. Theodora followed, her breath curling in the growing chill, Elder Bryn's warning echoing in her mind.

Then, without warning, the forest broke open. The towering trees gave way to an endless stretch of frozen, barren land, the ground shimmering with frost beneath the first hints of dawn. The sky, once suffocatingly dark, had lightened at the edges, streaked with the faintest traces of pink and gold.

As they left the shadow of the forest behind, the frozen terrain stretched endlessly before them. Theodora kept her head low against the biting wind, her breath a steady rhythm of mist in the cold air. Finnegan rode slightly ahead, ever watchful, while Killian trudged on with determined strides, his halberd resting against his shoulder.

The sky brightened with the slow rise of the sun, casting a pale glow over the icy expanse. Hours passed in silence, broken only by the crunch of boots and hooves against frost-laden ground. Theodora's muscles ached, exhaustion creeping into her bones, but she pushed forward, driven by the need to reach shelter before nightfall.

By midday, the ice, and rock began to give way to rolling hills, and in the distance, a break in the landscape revealed a valley. Though lower in elevation, it was no less winter bound. Thick snowdrifts covered the ground, and a thin layer of ice crusted the small lake at the valley's center, reflecting the pale gray sky. Frost-laden pines lined the valley's edges, their boughs heavy with snow.

Relief washed over Theodora as they reached the lake's edge. Finnegan dismounted with a tired sigh, stretching out his stiff limbs, while Killian wasted no time gathering wood for a fire.

As the sun dipped toward the horizon, flames crackled to life, their warmth a welcome reprieve from the relentless cold. Killian knelt beside the fire, murmuring a quiet incantation as he conjured a simple but hearty meal—thick stew bubbling in an iron pot, its rich aroma filling the crisp evening air.

Theodora wrapped her cloak tightly around herself, staring into the flickering flames. The tension of the past day hadn't fully left her, but here, in this quiet valley, with the scent of hot food in the air and the sound of the crackling fire, she allowed herself—just for a moment—to feel safe.

The morning broke cold and gray, mist curling through the trees as the group stirred from an uneasy sleep. Their campfire had burned low, leaving only faint embers, and the scent of damp earth filled the air. Finnegan stretched first, rolling his shoulders before nudging the others awake.

They ate quickly, their meal little more than a necessity—hardtack, dried meat, and sips of lukewarm tea. Each bite was mechanical, their thoughts elsewhere, weighed down by the journey ahead. The Mountain of Lost Souls loomed in the distance, its jagged peaks silhouetted against the dim sky. A hush had fallen over the group, not out of discomfort but from an unspoken understanding. Words felt unnecessary. Instead, they focused on the simple motions of preparation—tightening straps, adjusting gear, checking weapons.

Finnegan O'Leary adjusted the straps of his pack with a grunt. "Best be movin'," he muttered, breaking the silence. "That mountain needs climbin', and I'd rather not get caught in its shadow after dark."

They set off once more, the landscape growing harsher with every step. The path twisted upward, unforgiving and steep, forcing them into a slow, deliberate pace. The higher they climbed, the thinner the air became, each breath more labored than the last. Loose rocks shifted beneath their boots, demanding caution. Mist curled around them, snaking through the craggy terrain, swallowing sound. The mountain seemed to close in, an unseen force pressing against them, as though testing their resolve.

Killian wiped a sheen of sweat from his brow and exhaled sharply. "By the gods, this place has a feelin' to it," he murmured, his voice low. "Like it's watchin' us. Judgin', maybe."

Finnegan pressed forward, his face set with grim determination. Killian moved with practiced ease, his steps light despite the brutal terrain. Overhead, Khadall circled, his keen eyes scanning the path ahead. Theodora kept close behind, her pulse quickening—not just with exertion, but with a strange mix of fear and exhilaration. She stole a glance at Finnegan, drawing quiet strength from his steady presence.

The mist thickened. Somewhere beyond its veil, a howl rose—a low, mournful sound that sent a chill through the group. They froze, exchanging wary glances.

Finnegan's hand shifted to the hilt of his sword. "Aye," he said grimly, his voice barely above a whisper. "We're not alone. Keep yer wits about ye."

Higher up, the mist began to thin, revealing the peak ahead. There, carved into the mountainside, a massive opening yawned like the mouth of some ancient beast—the entrance to the legendary Crystal Caverns. A faint shimmer hung in the air around it, pulsing with unseen energy.

Killian suddenly halted, raising a hand. The group froze. The wind had died, the mountain eerily silent. A cold weight settled over them.

"What is it?" Theodora whispered, bow at the ready.

Killian crouched, examining the ground. "Tracks," he murmured, tracing bizarre markings. "Unlike any I've seen."

Finnegan frowned, joining him. "What manner of beast would be leavin' prints like these?"

A chill ran through Theodora as she studied the strange gouges—an impossible mix of claw and hoof.

Above them, Khadall soared high, his dark wings cutting through the pale sky. He circled once, then folded his wings and dove, wind whistling past him. At the last moment, he flared out, landing in a crouch near the markings. His feathers bristled as he studied them, a low growl rumbling in his throat.

Elder Bryn's warning echoed in Theodora's mind: "Be on yer guard."

Finnegan's voice was low yet determined. "We need t' tread carefully now. We can't be ignorin' the dangers that lurk in these parts."

They pressed on, weapons ready and senses alert. The path narrowed as they climbed higher, each step more treacherous than the last. The air grew colder, carrying an ancient power that made her skin prickle.

A bone-chilling howl pierced the silence, echoing from all sides. The group froze, exchanging tense glances.

"Company's comin'," Killian growled, eyes scanning the craggy terrain. "And fast."

A flicker of movement caught Theodora's eye. She spun around as a monstrous shape erupted from the shadows, all teeth, and claws and fury.

Its form was a grotesque fusion of various creatures, with the sleek body of a panther, twisted antlers sprouting from its massive head, and talons that gouged the very rock beneath its feet. Its breath frosted the air, an unnatural chill emanating from its twisted form.

Theodora's heart hammered as she met its malevolent gaze, centuries of hatred burning in its eyes. Finnegan's knuckles whitened on his sword hilt. Khadall screeched a challenge, wings spread wide.

The beast snarled, revealing rows of jagged teeth. Darkness seemed to seep from its very being, dimming the world around them. It moved with impossible fluidity, each motion a mockery of natural law.

"Shadowbeast," Killian breathed, recognition and dread mingling in his voice. "Guardian of the Caverns. It's testin' us."

The monstrous creature lunged forward with lightning speed, claws slashing through the air. Theodora dove to the side, narrowly avoiding its deadly strike. Finnegan met its attack head-on, his sword flashing as he deflected its razor-sharp claws.

Theodora nocked an arrow with trembling fingers, her pulse thundering in her ears. The Shadowbeast's baleful gaze locked onto her, its form a nightmare made flesh. She drew back the bowstring, muscles singing with familiar tension, but doubt gnawed at her. The beast's movements defied prediction, twisting in ways that shouldn't be possible.

She loosed the arrow, watching it whistle through the air with deadly precision. For a minute, she dared to hope. But the beast twisted impossibly, its body contorting in ways that made her stomach churn. The arrow sailed harmlessly past, embedding itself in the rocky ground with a dull thud.

A snarl of frustration escaped Theodora's lips as the creature's attention snapped to Killian. The fae warrior stood his ground, violet eyes blazing with determination. His halberd gleamed in the dim light, an extension of his very being.

The Shadowbeast charged, its massive form eating up the distance between them in a heartbeat. Theodora's breath caught in her throat as Killian raised his weapon. Fae magic crackled along the halberd's length, building to a crescendo of raw power. With a wordless cry, Killian unleashed a blinding arc of light.

The beast recoiled, its unholy roar shaking the very mountain beneath their feet. Theodora's ears rang, and she tasted blood where she'd bitten her lip. But there was no time for relief. Dark energy pulsed visibly beneath the creature's skin, a sinister reminder that this battle was far from over.

Its eyes, burning with centuries of hatred, fixed on Theodora once more. She felt the weight of its hate like a physical blow, stealing the breath from her lungs. Before she could react, the beast lunged.

It slammed into her, sending her flying. Pain exploded through her side as she crashed against the unforgiving rocks. Her vision swam, the world tilting sickeningly. She gasped, struggling to draw air into her battered lungs.

The creature loomed over her, its foul breath hot on her face. Theodora's nostrils filled with the stench of decay. Every grotesque detail burned itself into her mind—matted fur, jagged teeth, eyes that blazed with unholy fire. Her fingers scrabbled uselessly against the rock, desperate for anything to use as a weapon.

"Theodora!" Killian's shout cut through the haze of pain and terror. The beast's head snapped up, momentarily distracted.

With a roar that shook the very foundations of the mountain, Killian hurled himself at the creature. His halberd gleamed, trailing streamers of fae magic as it arced through the air. The clash was deafening, a clamour of steel on claw, magic against dark sorcery.

Strong hands grasped Theodora's arms, hauling her upright. Finnegan's face swam into focus, worry and grim determination etched in every line. "Easy now, lass," he murmured, steadying her as the world lurched alarmingly.

She leaned heavily against him, gritting her teeth against the stabbing pain in her side. Every breath was agony, but she forced herself to focus. Khadall circled above, his talons raking the air as he sought an opening to strike.

The battle raged before them, a whirlwind of violence and magic. Killian moved with inhuman grace, his halberd a blur of deadly precision. But the Shadowbeast was relentless, its form twisting and warping to avoid each strike. Dark tendrils of energy lashed out, seeking to ensnare the fae warrior.

Theodora's mind raced. They couldn't outlast this monster—not here, not like this. She closed her eyes, reaching deep within herself. The magic that flowed through her veins responded, a familiar warmth spreading from her core.

"Finnegan," she gasped. "I need... I need to get closer."

The druid's grip on her tightened. "Are ye sure, lass? Yer in no shape ta—"

"We don't have a choice, Finn," Theodora cut him off, her eyes snapping open. Determination burned away the last traces of doubt. "Help me."

Finnegan hesitated for a moment, his gaze searching hers for any sign of uncertainty. Finding none, he nodded curtly. "Aye, then. We'll do this together."

Steeling themselves against the pain and exhaustion, Finnegan, and Theodora moved forward as one, inching closer to the frenzied battle unfolding before them. Killian's strikes were swift and precise, each blow forcing the Shadowbeast back but never quite landing the killing blow.

As they neared, Theodora's magic surged beneath her skin, desperate to break free. The Shadowbeast's raw power pulsed before them, a dark force threatening to devour everything in its path.

Killian grappled with the creature, his muscles straining against its unnatural strength. The beast's form contorted, defying logic with each movement. Suddenly, it faltered, its defenses momentarily lowered.

Seizing her chance, Theodora channeled her power. The air crackled as energy burst from her palms, slamming into the Shadowbeast. It shrieked, writhing as light seared through its shadowy form. Killian pressed the advantage, his halberd carving through the darkness with renewed fury.

For a minute, victory seemed within reach. But the Shadowbeast rallied, breaking free with terrifying speed. Theodora's stomach dropped as she realized this fight was far from over.

The creature's gaze locked onto her, its eyes glowing with sickening hunger. Theodora shuddered, sensing its all-consuming desire to destroy.

"Dig deep, lass," Finnegan urged, his voice steady despite the chaos. "The magic's in ya. Use it."

Theodora closed her eyes, drawing a steadying breath. She felt the power coursing through her veins, building to a crescendo. With unbreakable resolve, she faced the beast once more and unleashed another blast of pure energy.

The beast howled in agony, reeling from the assault. Killian didn't hesitate. His halberd flashed, slicing through the dark magic binding the creature. With a final, devastating thrust, he drove the weapon into its heart.

A shockwave rocked the mountain, loosening stones and echoing ominously. The Shadowbeast convulsed, let out one last blood-curdling scream, then crumbled into ash.

Silence fell, broken only by their ragged breathing. Killian lowered his halberd, wiping sweat from his brow. "Well," he said with a wry smile, "that was a bit too close for comfort."

Exhausted and battered, they huddled together, the gravity of what they'd faced settling over them. They'd confronted a piece of the very darkness they sought to vanquish and somehow survived.

As the dust settled, they stood in the eerie silence, their hearts pounding in their chests. Theodora's magic slowly dissipated, leaving her drained and weary. Killian retrieved his halberd from the pile of ash, his eyes never leaving the spot where the beast had fallen. Finnegan moved to join them, his gaze scanning their surroundings. Their triumph was short-lived as they remembered their mission - the Crystal Caverns awaited.

Chapter 16

"Bound by Light"

They lingered only a moment longer, letting Elara's parting words settle like mist between them.

Alexandria nodded once, though her pulse thudded in her throat. The bracelet at her wrist gave off a faint warmth, like it was aware—waiting.

"Let's go," she said, her voice tight but steady.

Jasper gave a low, "Aye," and nudged his horse forward.

Aris, already alert, padded ahead in silence, her feline form gliding like a shadow between the trees, ears twitching, eyes sharp.

They followed the narrow trail curling along the lake's edge before it veered into the forest—just as Elder Gaelan had described. Snow-laden pines towered above them, their branches arching like vaulted ceilings. The wind whispered through the trees, carrying the sharp bite of frost and something old… something laced with a low thrum of magic.

The deeper they rode, the more the forest changed. The trees grew ancient, their trunks wide enough to swallow wagons whole, bark lined with silver lichen that shimmered faintly. The path beneath their horses grew firm with age-packed snow, but left no sound—only the faint pulse of enchantment buried in the roots below.

Alexandria glanced at the trees. "There's old magic here," she murmured, half to herself. "It remembers."

"Gaelan said we'd pass through the Elder's Hollow," Jasper replied, scanning the brush. "Then up the ridge ta the valley. Donaglen's just past it."

Alexandria nodded, though her gaze stayed fixed ahead. "It feels familiar… like we've walked it before—only in dreams."

Aris, now in her wolf form, growled low. "Dreams rooted in memory," she said, her voice gravelly. "This path knows your blood."

They pressed on. The light filtering through the branches had turned pale and golden, painting the snow in shades of fire and ice. Birds called faintly from somewhere above, but the air was still—too still.

Then the ridge began to rise.

The trail narrowed as they climbed, and through the thinning trees, the view opened. Alexandria pulled her horse to a stop, her breath catching.

Far below, nestled in a frozen cradle of land, stood Donaglen Castle—its towers pale and piercing, just as she remembered them from visions, dreams, and something deeper.

She stared, heart aching. "We're close," she whispered. "So close."

But before hope could settle in her chest, Aris came to a sudden halt.

Her fur bristled. A snarl escaped her throat, low and dangerous. "Stop. We're not alone."

Alexandria reined in. "What is it?"

Jasper's hand went to his sword hilt, jaw tense. "What's she smellin'?"

Aris stepped forward slowly, hackles raised. "Death. Cold magic. Bones that don't belong."

Then the earth gave a subtle tremble—just once. A sharp pulse beneath their feet, as if something had shifted far below.

The horses grew restless, stamping nervously, ears flicking.

Then came the sound—soft at first, like wind slipping through hollow wood. But it grew louder. Heavier. Rhythmic.

A dragging. A pounding.

Not hooves.

Alexandria turned sharply toward the path that led to Donaglen—and saw them.

Figures emerged from the forest, shrouded in black robes. Their forms moved with jerky, unnatural speed. Beneath their hoods, fleshless skulls gleamed in the light, eye sockets glowing faintly blue. Bony hands gripped corroded blades. Their mouths hung open in an eternal snarl, as if they'd died mid-battle cry.

Shadow Walkers.

"By the gods..." Jasper muttered.

Alexandria's breath caught. "They're not following us," she said. "They're waiting. They knew."

Aris bared her teeth, a snarl breaking free. "Valendor sent 'em. They've been guarding the way."

More shadows moved behind the first wave—dozens, spilling from the trees like smoke made flesh and bone.

Jasper's voice turned sharp. "We can't go forward. Not through that many. It's suicide."

Alexandria's knuckles whitened around the reins. The castle was right there. She could feel Theodora—close enough to touch. Magic thrummed in her bracelet again, a beat echoing her sister's. A tether calling her home.

But she couldn't reach it.

Not like this.

"We have to turn," Aris said. "East—into the gorge. Steep, narrow. They won't be able to keep up."

Alexandria's heart twisted. "But if we leave now..."

"We live," Jasper snapped. "And we find another way."

She stared at the towers one more time, chest tight with longing. Then she nodded. "East, then. Let's move."

Jasper wheeled his horse. Aris darted forward. And Alexandria kicked her mount into a gallop, snow spraying in wild bursts beneath pounding hooves.

They fled the ridge—fled the road that should have led them home.

The Shadow Walkers surged, clattering through the trees, skeletal limbs clawing at ice and stone, shrieks echoing off the rocks.

The magic on her wrist pulsed stronger now, wild and bright, as if resisting the turn. As if Theodora's soul was reaching for her across the distance.

I'm coming, Alexandria thought fiercely. *Not today—but soon.*

The path ahead twisted into the gorge. Narrow. Treacherous. But it would lead them away.

And somewhere beyond the shadows, her sister was waiting.

Behind them, the clatter of bone on stone rang louder than any battle cry. The Shadow Walkers gave no voice, no mercy—only pursuit.

Alexandria's breath tore from her lungs in ragged bursts. Her horse moved beneath her like a living storm, hooves pounding the frozen earth, mane whipping with speed. Aris led the way, darting through the snow with eerie precision, her wolf form weaving between trees like smoke made flesh.

Jasper rode close behind, sword unsheathed, his eyes sweeping constantly, ready to turn and defend if the undead gained ground.

Alexandria couldn't look back.

She didn't need to.

She could feel them gaining.

And worse—she could feel what they were riding away from.

The castle. Theodora. Home.

So close she could feel it humming through the blood in her veins. A song she hadn't heard in years was rising in her chest, half-melody, half-memory. Her twin was near. She was sure of it. The magic between them had never been louder.

And she was going in the wrong direction.

A part of her wanted to stop. Turn around. Fight her way through the horde. Reach her sister, even if it meant falling to the same shadows that hunted them now.

But another part—colder, clearer—held fast.

They couldn't help Theodora if they were dead.

Still, it tore something open in her. Something raw and deep and ancient.

Ahead, the terrain grew treacherous—rocks jutting from the snow, narrow gullies twisting between steep inclines. Aris leapt ahead, pausing at the edge of a jagged path carved through the gorge.

"This way!" she called back, her voice sharp with urgency.

Alexandria pulled hard on the reins, veering down the narrow route. The horse stumbled once but found its footing, hooves kicking up snow and shards of ice.

The sound of the undead shifted—more distant now. They were losing ground. The path was too narrow for them to follow en masse, and the walls of the gorge slowed their pursuit.

Alexandria gritted her teeth, eyes burning, as she drove her horse forward.

Her fingers clenched around the reins until her knuckles ached. The air bit at her face. Tears welled—not from the wind, but from something she couldn't explain. Anger. Grief. Fear. Guilt.

I was right there.

I saw the towers.

And I turned away.

Beside her, Jasper's voice broke through the pounding of hooves and heart. "We'll find another way, Lex. We will. But not if we're caught now."

She nodded, barely. Her jaw locked so tightly it hurt.

Aris slowed to run beside her, her fur dusted with snow. "It's not over. This path—it's not defeat. It's survival."

Alexandria blinked back the tears and forced herself to believe it. To believe this retreat wasn't the end. That turning away from Theodora now didn't mean losing her forever.

They didn't stop until the sound of pounding hooves faded into nothing, replaced by the soft crunch of snow and the ragged rhythm of their breath in the thinning air.

The gorge had swallowed them whole.

Steep and jagged, its stone walls pressed in on either side like the ribs of an ancient beast, glinting with icicles and streaked with silver frost. Shadows stretched across the path, long and still. It was quiet here—too quiet. Not the peace of safety, but the hush that comes after something has just passed... or something is waiting.

Jasper reined in beneath a jut of rock, his gaze flicking back the way they'd come. Nothing moved in the narrow cut behind them. No skeletal figures. No snapping of cloaks through the wind.

"Think we've lost 'em," he said, though he didn't sound convinced.

Alexandria slid from her saddle, her legs trembling beneath her. Her boots sank into the snow, heavier than they should have. She leaned against the rock wall, letting her breath steady, though it did little to slow the pounding in her chest.

Aris padded back along the trail behind them, sniffing the air. After a moment, she shifted, the transformation rippling across her body like a shimmer of light and fur. Her feline form reappeared, tail twitching, her voice edged with tension. "No sound behind us. No scent. They're not following—for now."

Alexandria nodded, but her shoulders didn't relax.

The ache in her muscles was nothing compared to the ache in her chest. The castle had been there. She'd seen it. Felt it. Donaglen, rising pale and sharp through the trees like a memory.

And she'd had to turn away.

"I don't understand..." she murmured, voice tight. "How did he know?"

Jasper dismounted beside her, shaking snow from his cloak. "We were either followed or listened to," he said. "Or the route was known long before we ever took it."

"No one else knew," Alexandria said. "Just us. Elder Gaelan wouldn't betray us."

Aris narrowed her eyes. "Spells leave echoes. Tracks. Especially when it's tied to prophecy. Valendor would have traced the path without hearing a word."

Alexandria didn't argue, but her chest tightened. The doubt was there anyway—small, sharp, and unwanted.

Valendor had known.

He'd known exactly where to place his Shadow Walkers.

Exactly when to send them.

Her gaze dropped to her wrist, where the bracelet sat cold against her skin. She unfastened the edge of her sleeve and pushed it back. The moment the cold touched it, a faint glow shimmered to life—soft green, pulsing in slow, steady waves.

At first, she felt relieved. The light meant Theodora was close. That their bond hadn't frayed.

But something shifted.

The warmth moved—not toward Donaglen, but east. A pull in a new direction. It was no longer a signal pointing to a fixed place. It was tracking movement.

Alexandria's breath caught.

"She's not at the castle," she said.

Jasper looked over. "What're ye sayin'?"

"She's left," Alexandria whispered. "She's not waiting at Donaglen anymore... She's moving. She's started her journey."

The realization settled like snow falling on fire—quiet, beautiful, and deeply painful.

"She's looking for me too."

For a long moment, no one spoke. The air hung heavy between them, thick with something unspoken.

Then Aris stepped close, brushing her side against Alexandria's leg. "Twins like you don't sit still once the bond stirs. The whole forest can feel it—it's alive with your connection."

Alexandria stared at the bracelet's glow, its warmth pulsing against her wrist like a second heartbeat.

The ache in her chest didn't lessen, but it changed. Shifted. What had once been grief twisted into something like hope—raw and trembling, but real.

Valendor hadn't tried to stop her from reaching Donaglen. He'd tried to stop them from reaching each other.

"We keep going." she said. "We follow this pull."

Aris turned, already heading down the next bend of the gorge. "We're not out of danger yet. But we've a lead—and Valendor's lost the advantage."

Alexandria took one more glance behind them. The forest was quiet. No more bones. No more shadows.

She wrapped her fingers around the bracelet, holding tight to its glow, and turned her back on what could've been.

Because Theodora wasn't behind her anymore.

She was ahead.

And Alexandria wouldn't stop until they were standing side by side again.

They moved through the gorge in silence, the path narrowing between high stone walls that curved like ancient ribs overhead. Ice clung to every surface, glittering in the fading light, while snow crunched beneath their horses' hooves with a steady rhythm. The air was sharp and dry, every breath rising in pale clouds.

No one spoke.

The only sound beyond their movement was the wind threading softly through the stone and the distant creak of settling frost. Even the trees above, where the gorge began to open, stood still—quiet as sentinels.

Eventually, the path widened enough to offer some relief from the tight confines. Low hills stretched beyond the gorge mouth, dotted with frost-coated trees and scattered stone. Jasper guided them into a small natural hollow, half-sheltered by a line of boulders and a crooked pine.

"We'll rest here a bit," he said, sliding from his saddle. "Give the horses a break—and ourselves."

Alexandria dismounted slowly, her muscles stiff from the ride, boots sinking into the crusted snow. Cold bit at her skin despite the layers, and her legs ached from hours of tension. She welcomed the stillness, even if only for a moment.

Aris prowled the edges of the hollow, weaving through brush and stone, tail flicking. After a slow circle, she returned and settled herself at the base of the pine, curling her tail close, eyes never still.

Jasper dug into one of the saddlebags and pulled out a few wrapped parcels. He set them on a flat top stone and unwrapped bread and dried meat, the scent of smoked salt and pepper quickly cutting through the crisp air.

"Not a feast," he said, "but it'll keep us upright."

Alexandria gave him a tired smile. "Good enough for me." She sat on a low boulder, the stone's chill grounding her more than she expected.

They ate quietly, the fire Jasper built crackling nearby, its orange light casting flickers on their faces and dancing across the snow. Aris accepted her share with a quiet hum of thanks, tearing into the jerky with deliberate care.

Alexandria held a warm tin mug in her hands, the spiced broth inside sending thin curls of steam into the evening air. The scent—clove, pine, a faint trace of dried herbs—was oddly comforting. She let the warmth soak into her fingers, her body slowly relaxing after the tense escape through the gorge.

When she looked down at her wrist, the soft green glow of the bracelet was pulsing gently through the fabric of her sleeve. Familiar. Reassuring.

She reached out and brushed it lightly with her thumb, the rhythm steady, like a heartbeat.

"She's close," she said, voice low. "I can feel her."

Jasper looked across the fire. "Aye. That bond between ye... it's not just magic. It's alive."

Alexandria nodded slowly, the weight in her chest shifting from ache to purpose. "Every step we take gets us closer."

The sun dipped behind the hills, pulling the light with it. Twilight settled in lavender and silver over the snow, and the cold deepened.

Jasper rose, dusting his gloves. "We've a few more hours before it's full dark. Let's push a bit farther, find solid ground to camp for the night."

Aris stretched and rose to her feet, eyes sharp again, body tense and ready.

They mounted up, the horses moving with fresh energy after the short rest. Snow crunched beneath their hooves as they turned east again, following the unseen thread that tugged them forward.

The air grew still again, but this time it felt different—charged, waiting. The forest loomed ahead, dark and sprawling, the trees arching over the path like watchers of something sacred.

Alexandria kept her eyes ahead, shoulders squared, hand brushing the glow beneath her sleeve.

With every mile, she knew: they were closing the distance.

They pressed deeper into the forest, twilight bleeding into night. The last golden light flickered and died behind the trees, leaving only shadows and cold.

The path narrowed further.

What had started as a trail now felt more like a tunnel—carved between towering pines and snow-laden limbs that creaked under their own weight. The trees bent inward, their gnarled branches reaching across the trail like skeletal fingers, brushing against Alexandria's cloak as she passed.

Snow clung to everything—silent, perfect, undisturbed.

Too perfect.

Alexandria's skin prickled. A low hum of anticipation vibrated beneath her breastbone. Not fear exactly, but something sharp. Something alive.

Ahead, Aris moved like smoke—her wolf form fluid and quiet against the stark white of the trail. Alexandria watched the way her companion's shoulders rolled with each step, muscle and fur working in harmony. Golden eyes swept the trees, catching glints of light that weren't there. Ears twitched. Every sound mattered.

Behind her, Jasper led the horses on foot. His boots crunched with each step, deliberate and slow. The trail had narrowed too much to ride. They'd dismounted nearly a mile back, when the branches began pressing too close and the roots clawed up through the snow like the bones of the forest itself.

The silence grew louder with every step. No birds. No rustling. Just breath and heartbeat and the dull drag of hooves through packed snow.

Alexandria gripped her dagger tightly. The worn leather hilt creaked beneath her fingers. Her hand was sweating despite the cold.

She could feel it. The pull of destiny pressing down on her, heavier than ever. Like something just ahead had been waiting for her all this time. The image of Theodora bloomed in her mind—half memory, half ache.

So close.

"You alright?" Jasper's voice cut gently through the quiet.

She glanced back at him, meeting his eyes. His concern wasn't loud—but it was real. And it cracked something in her chest.

He sees through me.

"I'm fine," she said, but her voice didn't quite hold. She forced a smile. It didn't reach her eyes.

Jasper didn't press. His brow furrowed, but before he could say more—

Aris growled.

A low, steady sound that started deep in her chest and rolled out like a storm cloud.

Alexandria froze.

Her breath hitched, cold burning her lungs as she scanned the shadows. Trees blurred. Her heart pounded loud enough to drown the world.

"Aris?" she whispered.

The wolf stood rigid, ears pinned, lips pulled back to reveal sharp, glistening teeth. Her body was coiled tight, every muscle tense.

That growl didn't stop.

It vibrated through the stillness, warning them all.

"Stay alert," Jasper muttered, the rasp of his sword leaving its sheath sounding unnaturally loud in the silence.

Alexandria's hand closed on her dagger, the weight of it suddenly heavier than before. Her palm was slick. Her breath shallow.

Just breathe.

But the forest was still. Unnaturally so.

Then—barely audible—a shift.

The softest scrape. A whisper of movement where there should be none.

Alexandria's head snapped toward the sound.

"Jasper," she breathed. "Did you see that?"

"Aye." He hadn't moved. His eyes were locked on the shadows. "Be ready."

Her thoughts raced.

Shadow Walkers? Something of Valendor's? Or something older, buried deep in this forest?

The air grew heavier. Denser. The silence felt like a presence pressing in from all sides.

Every instinct screamed that they weren't alone.

They moved forward slowly, every step muffled by snow and silence, the forest closing in around them like a secret. Alexandria's boots sank into the crusted trail, her breath fogging in the chill. Shadows thickened between the trees, each one long and reaching, cast by limbs that seemed to lean closer the deeper they went.

The air felt charged—taut and electric, humming beneath her skin like a current building toward something unseen.

Then it happened.

A warmth flared against her wrist, subtle at first—a whisper beneath her glove—but it built quickly. Not heat from the cold. Something alive. Responsive.

Alexandria stopped walking.

Her breath hitched as she pushed back her sleeve.

The bracelet glowed brighter than it ever had before. A vibrant green shimmer pulsed from its center, steady and rhythmic, casting a faint halo of light that danced across the snow. It lit the path ahead in soft flickers, the glow growing stronger with every heartbeat, like it was pulling her forward with purpose.

Jasper stepped closer, eyes narrowing on the light. "It's changin'," he said quietly. "Stronger now."

Aris padded back toward them. She paused at Alexandria's side, eyes narrowing at the glow. "It's responding to something—or someone."

Alexandria stared down at it, heart hammering in her chest. The pull was undeniable now. Not imagined. Not a symbol. A thread—real, living—stretching from her wrist toward something just beyond the trees.

Toward Theodora.

Her throat tightened.

"She's close," she whispered. "I can feel her."

The bracelet pulsed again, brighter this time, washing her hand in green light. The trees around them seemed to recoil from the magic, their branches creaking softly, shedding snow in gentle bursts as if making way.

Alexandria looked up, her voice steadier now. "We follow it. No more second guessing. It's leading us straight to her."

Jasper nodded without hesitation. "Then let's not waste a moment."

Aris turned back toward the trail, tail swaying, every muscle alert. The air around them shifted, the forest no longer just a place they passed through—but a threshold.

Alexandria adjusted her grip on her dagger, the familiar weight a comfort. The bracelet's glow guided each step, a beacon cutting through the thick dark like a promise she could finally reach.

This was more than magic.

It was memory awakening.

It was the bond between two souls finding their way back to one another.

Chapter 17

"Echoes of the Eclipse"

THE CRYSTAL CAVERNS LOOMED ahead, their curiosity undiminished by the group's recent battle. Theodora stumbled forward, her breaths ragged and her side throbbing with each step. Finnegan supported her, guiding her into the cave and easing her onto a cool rock. Killian knelt beside them, concern etched on his face.

"Ye alright, Theodora?" Killian asked, his usual gruffness softened by worry.

She forced a smile, her voice strained but resolute. "I'll manage," she said, though the pain in her side betrayed her words.

Finnegan examined her wound, his touch gentle. "That's a nasty gash ye've got there, lass," he murmured, his eyes betraying more than he said.

Killian glanced towards the cavern's depths. "We can't stay here long. Who knows what else might be lurking."

Finnegan's hand on her shoulder stopped her. "Not so fast. I'm healin' that wound first," he said, his tone brooking no argument.

Theodora started to protest, but a fresh wave of pain silenced her. She settled back, allowing Finnegan to work.

The druid muttered an incantation, his hands glowing with soft light as he pressed them to Theodora's side. Warmth spread through her, easing the pain as the wound began to close.

Theodora watched in fascination, feeling Finnegan's power flow into her. The sensation was strange but soothing, like a warm bath for her battered body.

As the healing finished, Theodora felt renewed strength coursing through her. She met Finnegan's eyes, gratitude welling up. "Thank you, Finnegan. I don't know how I'd manage without ya."

A rare smile crossed Finnegan's face. "Ye'd find a way, lass. But I'm glad ta help."

Finnegan's stoic expression softened, a rare smile tugging at the corners of his lips. "Ye'd manage just fine, lass. But I'm glad I could help."

Theodora stood, testing her newly healed side. Killian watched her closely. "Sure you're ready for this?"

She met his gaze, determination blazing in her eyes. "Nothing's stopping us now, Killian. We've come too far."

With renewed purpose, they pressed deeper into the Crystal Caverns, ready to face whatever challenges lay ahead.

The damp, musty scent of moss and ancient stone filled the air as they ventured deeper into the cave. Jagged rocks threatened their path, while stalactites loomed ominously overhead. Despite the foreboding atmosphere, an unmistakable energy pulsed through the cavern, a testament to its hidden power.

Killian lit torches along the walls, their flickering flames casting eerie shadows as they pressed on. Finnegan's voice echoed through the dim corridors, tinged with caution. His eyes darted about, ever-vigilant for unseen dangers. The weight of responsibility hung heavy on him as he led Theodora and Killian further into the mountain's depths.

"Stay close, lass," he warned. "No tellin' what we might find down here."

Theodora nodded, her calm exterior masking the unease bubbling beneath. She glanced at Killian, drawing strength from his resolute expression.

Finnegan's steps faltered slightly, old memories threatening to surface.

"You alright there, Finn?" Theodora asked, concern lacing her voice.

"Aye," he replied, his voice a touch unsteady. "Just... old ghosts. Pay it no mind. We've got work to do."

As they pressed on, the oppressive darkness began to lift. A soft, otherworldly glow emanated from the stone walls, bathing them in its light. The air grew warmer, sending a tingling sensation through Theodora's fingers. Their footsteps echoed in the vast space, accompanied by the distant sound of trickling water.

They emerged into a sprawling cavern, its ceiling adorned with countless crystal formations. The crystals pulsed with an inner light, ranging from tiny specks to massive chunks. Their rhythmic glow spoke of ancient magic.

"The Crystal Caverns," Killian breathed, his usual gruffness softened by awe.

Theodora felt a thrill of excitement as she took in the breath-taking sight. Each step deeper into the cavern quickened her pulse. The walls shimmered with iridescent hues, crystal formations jutting from every surface. The sparse light bent and refracted, creating a mesmerizing display.

Unable to resist, Theodora reached out to touch a large amethyst crystal. Its surface was cool and thrummed with energy, sending a shiver through her body. The air felt crisp and sweet, invigorating her senses.

Water droplets fell from the stalactites above, their mineral-rich taste sharp on Theodora's lips. A glowing pool nearby caught her attention. Kneeling at its edge, she watched in fascination as tiny, silver-blue creatures darted through the crystal-clear water, their fluid movements hypnotic.

Finnegan stood beside her, his eyes roaming the cavern walls as if searching for hidden truths. "This place... it's older than time itself," he murmured. "The sheer age of it..." He trailed off, shaking his head. "We'd best tread carefully, lass. There's power here beyond our reckonin'."

Theodora noticed a faint glow down a narrow hallway. She rose to investigate, feeling Finnegan's watchful gaze on her. They exchanged a look of shared wonder before Finnegan returned his attention to their path.

As they entered another room, they discovered an ancient library. Dusty tomes lined the shelves, each holding secrets from long ago. As Finnegan scanned the collection, memories of his imprisonment under Lord Valendor surfaced, bringing a flicker of fear to his eyes. He pushed the thoughts aside, focusing on their mission to uncover knowledge that might aid them.

Theodora ran her fingers over the leather bound spines, the cavern's warmth seeping into her skin. Without warning, pain lanced through her head. She cried out as visions flooded her mind, overwhelming her senses.

She stumbled, catching herself against a bookshelf. Memories crashed over her, threatening to pull her under. Her hair fell across her face, hiding the anguish in her eyes.

In the dim light, Theodora's mind became a battleground of fractured images and raw emotion. She saw her parents' terrified faces as Shadow Walkers dragged them away. Their screams echoed in her mind, piercing her heart.

"Princess!" Killian's worried voice cut through the haze. His face swam into focus, blue eyes searching hers intently. Theodora felt a rush of gratitude for his steady presence.

Killian's arms wrapped around her, anchoring her to the present. His voice grounded her as the past threatened to overwhelm. His embrace offered a moment of comfort amidst the chaos.

"Shadow Walkers," Theodora growled, seeing dark forms invading the castle. The image of her parents being taken seared into her memory, stoking a fire of loss and determination.

As Killian held her, Theodora noticed movement in a shadowy corner. Her heart raced as a figure took shape. She tensed, but as it stepped forward, she realized it wasn't a threat, but an unexpected ally.

From the shadows emerged a stocky figure, his weathered cloak hanging loosely on a battle-worn frame. A dwarf, his beard streaked with gray, leaned on a gnarled staff etched with strange symbols. Despite his unassuming appearance, an aura of power radiated from him.

"A bright morning to ya," he called, his voice echoing off the cavern walls. "Name's Nabca. I keep watch over this here Fae library and the Opalite."

Theodora's brow furrowed. "Opalite? I'm afraid I'm not familiar with that term."

Nabca's eyes crinkled with a kind smile. "No worries, lass. It's not common knowledge outside our realm. The Opalite's a special gem, see? Amplifies Fae magic somethin' fierce." He pulled out a small pendant, its surface shimmering with an otherworldly light.

As Nabca spoke, he wove a tale of Kandella's hidden mine, where the Opalite had been guarded for generations. His words painted a vivid picture of its power and importance in maintaining the balance of their world.

Suddenly, Nabca's gaze fixed on Theodora's wrist. "By the ancients," he breathed, "you've got one too!" The bracelet there pulsed in time with her heartbeat, its energy seeming to resonate with the dwarf's pendant.

"Aye, lass," Nabca said, his voice filled with wonder. "That there's genuine Opalite. Feel how it sings when it's near its kin?"

Theodora felt the bracelet's vibration intensify, a low hum that seemed to reverberate through her very bones. Its surface swirled with shifting colors, captivating in its beauty.

"With that Opalite," Nabca continued, his tone growing serious, "you've got a real chance against Valendor and his ilk. It could be the key to bringin' Kandella back to its former glory."

Finnegan, ever practical, cut in. "You seem to know a fair bit about us, Nabca. Any chance you'd be willin' to lend a hand in our fight?"

The dwarf's expression turned solemn. "Wish I could, lad. But I'm bound to these caves. Protectin' the Opalite and all this knowledge... it's my sworn duty. If I were to leave, well, the consequences could be dire."

He gestured to the cavern walls, covered in intricate carvings that seemed to pulse with an inner light. The very air hummed with the weight of ancient secrets.

Theodora listened intently, feeling the weight of responsibility settle on her shoulders. She touched the Opalite bracelet, drawing comfort from its steady warmth.

"I may not be able to join ye," Nabca said, rummaging through his cloak, "but I can offer ye this." He produced an ancient tome, its pages yellow with age. "It's full of our people's secrets. But mind ye, there are those who'd do anythin' to keep this knowledge hidden. Trust no one."

Theodora accepted the book with trembling hands. "Thank you, Nabca," she said, her voice steady despite her racing heart. "This could be the edge we need against Valendor."

As Nabca prepared to depart, he offered one last piece of advice. "Remember, lass. The bonds of love and friendship are your greatest strength. But the darkness... it'll try to use 'em against ye. Stay true to yourself, and let that love guide ye through the trials ahead."

Clutching the tome to her chest, Theodora felt overwhelmed by the magnitude of their task. Nabca's words rang in her ears as she opened the book, her fingers tracing the unfamiliar runes within. Outside, distant thunder rumbled, a fitting accompaniment to the challenges that lay ahead.

Stepping out of the cave felt like entering a frozen nightmare. A fierce blizzard raged, snowflakes whipping through the air as thunder boomed overhead. "We need to get down the mountain!" Finnegan shouted over the howling wind.

The storm battered them mercilessly. Killian and Theodora pushed forward, eyes narrowed against the stinging snow. Finnegan led the way, his broad frame offering some protection from the gale.

"The forest!" Finnegan called back, "We'll find cover there!"

Theodora nodded grimly, steeling herself for the trek. Each step was a battle against the wind and snow. Lightning split the sky, illuminating their grim faces. The thundersnow's roar seemed to shake the very mountain beneath them.

Finally, they reached the treeline. The dense branches offered some respite from the relentless storm. "Made it," Killian panted, his breath visible in the frigid air.

Their relief was short-lived as they exchanged wary glances. Was this truly safe, or just a momentary reprieve?

Finnegan surveyed the chaotic sky, his brow furrowed. This storm felt unnatural, too precise in its fury. A chilling thought struck him—Lord Valendor's magic at work, weaponizing nature itself.

He turned to Theodora, sensing a new awareness in her eyes. Somehow, she'd caught the thread of his suspicion.

"Finnegan," she said, her voice barely audible above the wind, "you're right. This isn't natural. Valendor's behind it, trying to slow us down."

Finnegan nodded grimly, his grip tightening on his sword hilt. "Aye, we're getting too close for his liking. He's thrown this in our path."

Killian cut through their exchange, urgency in his voice. "We need shelter, and fast. No time for speculation."

They scanned the snow-covered forest, but visibility was near zero.

"We can't last out here," Finnegan admitted. "Those Shadow Walkers will pick us off easily in this."

Killian's sharp eyes caught something through the swirling white. "Look! A cave!"

They hurried towards the dark opening, fighting against the wind with every step.

The cave's interior was a welcome refuge from the storm's fury. Its rough walls offered protection from the biting wind.

"I'll start a fire," Killian said, already gathering what dry kindling he could find. Soon, a small flame flickered to life, casting dancing shadows on the cave walls.

In the relative quiet, each lost in their own thoughts, Theodora couldn't shake the feeling of being watched. She knew Valendor was out there, waiting for his chance to strike.

The fire's warmth lulled her companions to sleep, but Theodora remained alert, her fingers tracing the ancient book's spine. Nabca's words echoed in her mind as she turned to page 173 with trembling hands. A chill ran through her as she read:

"Total eclipse approaches. Spell unbroken, cold never-ending. Light fades, darkness reigns."

Her mind raced. What did it mean? The eclipse, the unbroken spell - they couldn't waste time puzzling it out alone.

"Finnegan," she whispered, shaking him awake. "We need to talk."

He blinked groggily. "What's wrong, Theo?"

"Is everything alright?" Killian asked, stirring.

"No.. Yes.. Maybe?" she replied. "I've found something in Nabca's book."

Killian interrupted before more words were spoken. "Aye, we need a barrier to protect our conversations from that sorcerer and his creatures."

Understanding the urgency, Theodora nodded. Killian retrieved a small leather pouch containing a mixture of herbs and crystals prepared for such situations.

"With this protective spell," he explained, "our words will stay hidden from prying ears."

He sprinkled the contents around their chamber, forming a circle. A soft blue glow emanated, creating an invisible barrier.

"Now," Finnegan whispered, "What did ye find?"

Theodora showed them the passage. They huddled close, examining the cryptic words.

Killian's brow furrowed in concentration. He read aloud, "Total eclipse approaches... Spell unbroken, cold never-ending... Light fades, darkness reigns." The words seemed to linger in the air with an ominous energy.

"What if 'spell unbroken' means what happens if we fail?" Theodora suggested.

Finnegan leaned closer, searching her eyes. "Do ye mean breakin' the spell may be the key to defeatin' Lord Valendor?" he asked.

"Aye, but during an eclipse," Theodora replied.

Killian's excitement was palpable. He interjected, "Theo, ye might be onto somethin'!" The group exchanged glances, feeling hopeful for the first time since their journey began.

Theodora fell silent. Her brow furrowed as she contemplated something.

A moment of hopeful silence fell before Theodora spoke again. "We need to find her, ya know? Alexandria. She's out there, possibly unaware of who she is."

"But how do we find her?" Killian replied. "We've got no clues, no idea of her whereabouts."

Without warning, Theodora's bracelet flared with a vibrant emerald glow. The green light pulsed in steady waves, casting an aura around her wrist and lighting her surroundings with an otherworldly radiance.

"The crystal!" Finnegan exclaimed. "Ms. Whoo's enchantment - it'll guide us to her."

They agreed to leave once the storm passed. As they settled in for the night, Finnegan noticed Theodora shivering.

"You alright, Theo?"

"I'm fine," she lied. "Just cold."

Killian draped his cloak over her shoulders. She leaned into him, grateful for the warmth.

"Thanks," she murmured as sleep took her.

In her dreams, a golden griffin soared overhead. "Follow me," it called.

Powerless against the spectacle, Theodora obeyed. They flew over lush forests and glistening streams that caught shards of sunlight. As they climbed higher, a familiar sensation washed over her until they halted above a cliff overlooking the sea.

"Welcome to the Isle of Nau," the griffin said. "This is our home."

"Why am I here?" Theodora asked.

"Your journey leads ya here," it replied. "Across the water lies Carrantou, Valendor's island."

"Wait. Khadall, is that you?" Theodora gasped.

But before she could press for answers, her dream vanished, and reality rushed back in. She awoke, the memory of Khadall and his homeland still fresh.

"Not all who wander are lost," she recited softly, recalling Khadall's wisdom.

"What did you see?" Finnegan asked, noting her expression.

Theodora paused, processing the dream's implications. She knew the Isle of Nau awaited them after finding Alexandria. Despite her resolve, unease crept in as they prepared to face the challenges ahead.

The first rays of dawn crept over the horizon, painting the sky in hues of pink and gold. Finnegan stirred, his joints protesting as he rose from the hard cave floor. The crisp morning air bit at his exposed skin, sending a shiver down his spine. He tightened the laces on his well-worn leather boots, feeling each familiar groove beneath his calloused fingers.

As he slung his satchel over his shoulder, the weight of their provisions settled against his back - a constant reminder of the long journey ahead. Finnegan cast a glance back at Theodora and Killian, still huddled beneath their cloaks. Theodora's brow tensed even in sleep, and Finnegan felt a sharp pang of concern for the young princess.

Stepping out of the cave, Finnegan's senses came alive. The forest awakened around him, a symphony of rustling leaves and birdsong. He drew a long breath, the scent of pine and damp earth flooding his lungs. His eyes swept the treeline, alert for any sign of danger.

The clearing where they'd tethered the horses came into view, and Finnegan's heart lightened at the sight of Moonbeam and Storm grazing peacefully. Moonbeam's coat gleamed like freshly fallen snow in the early light, her blue eyes seeming to hold ancient wisdom.

"Easy now, girl," Finnegan murmured, his voice low and soothing as he approached. Moonbeam's ears flicked towards him, as she lifted her head with a soft nicker of recognition. The silky strands of her mane slipped through Finnegan's fingers as he stroked her neck, feeling the steady thrum of her pulse beneath his palm.

Storm regarded Finnegan with intelligent eyes, his dappled coat catching the light. "Aye, we've got a long road ahead of us, old friend," Finnegan said, meeting the stallion's gaze. "But ye've got the heart of a warrior, just like yer rider."

With Moonbeam and Storm settled, Finnegan turned his attention to Killian's horse, a magnificent bay mare named Shadowdancer. Her sleek coat rippled in the morning light, and her eyes held a fierce intelligence that mirrored her master's spirit. She pawed at the ground, eager to be on the move.

"Easy, girl," Finnegan said as he approached the mare. He ran a hand down her neck, feeling the power coiled beneath her skin. "We've got a journey ahead of us, and I need ye at yer best."

She snorted, as if in agreement, and nudged Finnegan's shoulder with her velvety nose. He chuckled, appreciating the unspoken bond between them. With practiced ease, he checked her saddle and gear, ensuring everything was secure for the road ahead.

As Finnegan finished preparing the horses, his mind wandered to the challenges that lay before them. The weight of their quest pressed down on him, as heavy as the storm clouds gathering on the horizon. He couldn't shake the feeling that they were racing against time, each moment bringing them closer to a confrontation with forces beyond their control.

The sound of approaching footsteps pulled Finnegan from his thoughts. He turned to see Theodora and Killian emerging from the cave, their faces etched with determination despite the weariness in their eyes.

"We need ta move," Finnegan said, his voice carrying an urgency that brooked no argument. "Those storm clouds don't bode well, and we've got ground ta cover."

Theodora nodded, her green eyes flashing with resolve as she mounted Moonbeam. "Aye, Finnegan. The sooner we find Alexandria, the better our chances against whatever Valendor's planning."

As they set off through the snow-covered forest, Finnegan couldn't shake the feeling of being watched. Shadows seemed to flit between the trees, just out of sight. He tightened his grip on the reins, every muscle tense and ready for action.

"Keep yer wits about ye," he called to the others. "We're not alone out here."

Killian rode up beside him, his hand resting on the hilt of his weapon. "Ye feel it too, then?" he asked, his eyes scanning the forest. "Like eyes in the dark, watchin' our every move."

Finnegan nodded grimly. "Aye."

A bone-chilling howl echoed through the trees, sending a shiver down his spine. The horses shifted nervously, sensing the tension in the air. Theodora's hand went to her bow, her knuckles white against the polished wood.

"Steady now," Finnegan cautioned, even as his own heart raced.

The forest fell silent, save for the crunch of snow beneath the horses' hooves. Finnegan's eyes darted from shadow to shadow, straining to catch any sign of movement. The air grew thick with anticipation, each breath feeling like it might be their last moment of peace before the storm broke.

The trail wound through dense pine and bare-branched birch, the trees whispering secrets with every gust of wind. Overhead, the pale morning light had given way to heavy grey skies, the promise of more snow hanging in the air. They rode in uneasy silence, their mounts puffing clouds of breath into the cold.

By midday, the path narrowed, forcing them to ride single file along a ridge that dropped into a deep ravine. Khadall circled above, gliding silently as their sentry. At one point, he let out a sharp cry and veered eastward. Finnegan raised a hand, calling for a halt.

"Somethin's out there," he said, voice low. "Could be nothin'... but me gut says otherwise."

Killian scanned the treeline, his knuckles white around the reins. "Ye feel that too? Like the woods're holdin' their breath."

Theodora glanced behind them, unease creeping into her chest. "We've not seen a soul since dawn. Even the animals have gone quiet."

Finnegan nodded grimly. "That's what worries me. Nature doesn't go silent fer no good reason."

They pressed on through the thinning light, snow beginning to fall again—soft, steady, relentless. By the time they reached a clearing just before dusk, the horses were tired, and so were they. Killian found a patch of flat ground sheltered by a ring of stones and fallen logs. It wasn't ideal, but it was enough.

As they dismounted, Killian pulled his cloak tighter and muttered, "If we're settlin' in here, best we be lightin' that fire fast. I don't fancy sharin' a bedroll with a snowdrift."

"Just keep yer eyes peeled," Finnegan replied. "If Khadall saw somethin'—"

"He'd've warned us properly," Killian interrupted, though his tone held little confidence. "Still... I don't like this place."

Neither did Theodora.

Night settled over the forest, its inky darkness broken only by the flickering campfire. The wind had died down, but the cold seeped in, wrapping around them like a second skin. Restlessness gnawed at Theodora as she watched Finnegan and Killian swap tales by the flames—laughing low, their faces half-lit in amber glow.

"Tell me again why we're out here chasin' ghosts an' shadows," Killian said, blowing into a tin mug of steaming broth. "Could've been warmin' me arse in a tavern somewhere."

Finnegan gave a faint smirk. "Because ghosts an' shadows don't wait politely. They come whether we're ready or not."

"Aye," Killian grumbled, "but must they always come when I've just dried me boots?"

Theodora tried to laugh, but a sudden memory flashed through her mind—sharp and strange. A sensation more than a thought, like a voice calling from somewhere just beyond hearing.

She turned her eyes to the trees. The forest had shifted. It wasn't just dark—it was *watching*.

She stood without a word, brushing snow from her cloak.

Khadall, perched high in the branches of a pine, shifted slightly, feathers ruffling, but remained silent.

Finnegan noticed first. "Where're ye goin', lass?"

"I just—" she hesitated, her voice thin. "I need to check somethin'."

Killian raised an eyebrow. "Now? At night? In *this* wood?"

"I won't go far," she said. "I promise."

Finnegan stood up, serious now. "Whatever's lurkin' out there... it already knows we're here. Don't let it catch ye alone."

Theodora gave a small nod and stepped away from the firelight. Behind her, laughter faded into the hush of the trees.

And the forest... held its breath.

Drawn by an invisible force, Theodora wandered alone, her footsteps muffled by a blanket of snow. A cluster of trees seemed to beckon her, their branches entwined in a tight embrace.

She settled at the base of one of the towering trees, feeling the rough bark pressing against her back. Closing her eyes, she allowed memories to flood her mind—her mother's warm embrace that always smelled faintly of lavender, her father's steady gaze that seemed to promise everything would be alright.

Now, these moments felt like distant echoes in her heart. Tears gathered in her eyes as she gazed up at the vast expanse of stars twinkling above. "Will I ever see them again?" she murmured to the night, her voice barely more than a breath. "Will they even recognize me now?"

The forest seemed to close in around her, shadows deepening. Theodora's voice was barely audible as she murmured, "We were a family once. Now I'm lost, surrounded by the ghosts o' the past."

Yet even in her sorrow, hope flickered. She wasn't alone - Finnegan and Killian stood with her, bound by loyalty and shared purpose.

Shivering, Theodora sat with her back against the rough trunk of an old tree, her cloak wrapped tightly around her. The cold had settled deep into her bones. Somewhere in the distance, an animal called out—low and strange—before the sound was swallowed by the trees.

She shifted, trying to get comfortable, when something caught her eye. A faint shimmer flickered between two gnarled trees ahead of her. At first, she thought it was a trick of the firelight behind her, or maybe just the stars playing tricks through the canopy.

But the light didn't fade.

It pulsed gently, like it had a heartbeat of its own. Slowly, it grew stronger, swelling between the twisted trunks, casting a pale glow across the snow-covered forest floor. It stayed there, hovering in that narrow space—silent, steady, and untouched by wind or shadow.

Theodora sat up straighter, her heart beginning to race. She couldn't look away. The light didn't move toward her, didn't threaten—but it didn't feel like it was meant to be ignored either.

She rose to her feet, hesitation gripping her.

As she watched, a figure materialized from within the portal of light, as if the forest itself had reached into her soul and pulled out the one thing she missed most. Theodora's breath caught in her throat as the familiar silhouette stepped forward—graceful, radiant, heartbreakingly real.

"Ma," she choked out, the word barely forming as her chest caved under the weight of years of grief. Tears streamed down her cheeks as she stood, her legs barely holding her.

Queen Amara opened her arms, her expression soft with love, her voice trembling on the breeze. "Me dear girl," she whispered, a smile in her tone, though her eyes glistened with unshed pain.

Theodora rushed forward, the world narrowing to that single moment. Sobs broke from her as she collided with her mother's embrace, arms thrown around her as if she might vanish if Theodora didn't hold on tight enough. She clung to her, shaking, her face buried in her mother's shoulder.

"How... how did ye find me?" Theodora asked, her voice barely a whisper.

Her mother's voice, soft and soothing, carried a tremor beneath the tenderness. "Me dearest Theodora, the bond between a mother and her child—'tis a powerful thing. Even in the darkest depths, me love for ye never faded. It guided me, helped me push through the veil that keeps our souls apart."

Theodora loosened her grip, breath hitching, and as she stood back to truly look—reality struck hard.

Her mother's face, once glowing with life, now told a different story. Scars laced across her skin like delicate threads, bruises bloomed like fading ink, and the soft glow surrounding her flickered, revealing the shadows that lingered just behind—echoes of pain that hadn't let go.

Theodora's chest tightened. "What did he do to ye?" she asked, voice shaking.

Amara's smile faltered. Her gaze dropped for a moment, heavy with everything she couldn't say aloud. Then she met her daughter's eyes again, her voice shifting, urgent and clear.

"There's not much time," she said, her grip tightening on Theodora's hands. "Ye have to listen now. I came to give ye a warnin'."

Theodora's heart thudded in her chest, breath shallow as she leaned in.

"A warnin'? Ma, what is it?" she pleaded, her voice thick with fear and hope. "Please... what are ye tryin' to tell me?"

Amara's image shimmered, flickering like a flame in the wind. As if the forest itself was trying to keep her there for just a moment more.

"You must beware," her mother's voice echoed, a whisper carried by the wind. "Lord Valendor's power grows with each passin' day, fueled by the shadows that envelope his heart. The eclipse approaches - his power will peak then, as will yours. Don't underestimate him."

Theodora felt the weight of her mother's words settle in her chest, an icy dread seeping into her very being. She clenched her fists, determination flaring in her eyes.

Her mother's form flickered, her eyes clouded with sadness. "There's great power within ye, me darling. Trust in yerself and the bonds you've forged; they will be yer greatest strength. Together with yer sister, rely on yer combined abilities fer victory. Believe in yerself, Theodora. You're never truly alone."

As the last words of guidance echoed through the air, the vision slowly dissipated. The doorway shimmered and blurred like a mirage, then vanished completely, leaving Theodora standing alone in the quiet night.

Theodora fell to her knees, tears streaming down her face. She reached out desperately, grasping at the empty air where her mother had been just moments before.

"No! Ma, don't leave me!"

She squeezed her eyes shut, willing the warmth of her mother's touch to return. But there was only the chilly night and the hard ground beneath her fingers. Though grief threatened to consume her, she refused to let fear take hold.

She lifted her gaze from the shadows to the moonlight filtering through the branches. Drawing a deep breath, she vowed not to give in to despair. The thought of her family and home strengthened her resolve. The tears on her cheeks were a reminder of all she stood to lose, but as she straightened, determination took hold. Whatever lay ahead, she would face it—for those she loved.

Chapter 18

"The Twins' Resurgence"

THE FOREST WAS UNNATURALLY quiet. No animals rustled, no breeze stirred the leaves. Only the faint crackle of the distant campfire broke the silence.

The hair on the back of her neck stood on end as a subtle vibration on her wrist drew her gaze downward. The bracelet shimmered with an otherworldly light, its glow intensifying until it bathed Theodora's face in a pale radiance. As she watched in awe, intricate runes etched into the metal band flared to life, pulsing in rhythm with her heartbeat, as if responding to her very presence.

A sense of recognition stirred within her as the symbols on the bracelet shifted and glowed, whispering ancient secrets that connected her to a power she had only begun to understand. A brief vision fluttered at the edge of her consciousness—a memory from her past just beyond her grasp.

Overhead, the leaves murmured her name, their rustling sending a shiver down her spine. But something else—something beyond the wind—prickled at her awareness. In the darkness ahead, a presence moved with unnatural precision, slipping between the trees.

Theodora stiffened. A spectral whisper brushed her ear, and she instinctively reached for her bow, fingers curling around its familiar contours. Her pulse quickened as she scanned the woods, senses sharpening, bracing for whatever lurked beyond the shadows..

"Who's there?" she called, keeping her voice steady despite the unease creeping over her. The presence lingered just out of sight, a murmur at the edge of her awareness.

Her gaze locked onto a cluster of trees, their branches twisted into a perfect circle. A knot tightened in her stomach. She stood at a crossroads—one foot planted in the reality of their dangerous quest, the other hovering on the edge of something unknown. The forest seemed to hold its breath, every shadow, and flicker of moonlight hinting at secrets waiting to be revealed.

The forest stretched around them, silent and still, yet a strange presence lingered just beyond their sight—unseen but undeniable.

Finnegan moved through the shadows, his sharp gaze sweeping the treeline. "Show yerself?" he called, his brogue steady, though a trace of unease tightened his words. "We know ye're out there."

Beside him, Killian shifted, his stance subtly adjusting as his hand closed around the worn grip of his halberd. "We felt something," he murmured, his deep voice carrying a weight of certainty. He glanced toward Theodora, his expression unreadable, but the protective set of his shoulders spoke louder than words.

Theodora's pulse quickened as she met Killian's gaze. She had sensed it first—a ripple in the air, like a held breath just before a storm. Now, with both Finnegan and Killian on edge, the feeling was impossible to ignore.

A sudden rustling in the trees drew their focus. The wind had been still moments ago. Now, the branches twisted against one another, whispering secrets in a language she couldn't understand.

From above, the beat of great wings cut through the hush. Khadall descended, landing on a thick branch with effortless grace. His golden eyes gleamed in the dim light as he regarded them with quiet intensity. "Stay vigilant," he warned, his voice a deep rumble that sent a shiver through Theodora's spine.

The trio stood in tense silence, their breath misting in the chilly night air. Theodora gripped her bow tighter, the steel pressing into her palm, grounding her against the rising storm in her chest.

The electric air crackled with anticipation as two shadowy figures emerged from the trees ahead, their movements slow, deliberate.

Finnegan shifted beside her, his hand hovering near the hilt of his sword. Killian exhaled sharply, his jaw clenched. None of them spoke. They just watched, waiting, as the figures stepped closer, the moonlight finally revealing their faces.

Then Theodora saw her.

Alexandria.

Her brown hair shimmered like a halo in the pale glow, her features achingly familiar. Theodora's breath hitched. Their eyes met, and recognition struck like an arrow to the chest. The pain, the longing, the ghosts of everything left unsaid surged through her in an instant.

"Alexandria," Theodora whispered, her voice trembling as she uttered the name that seemed both strange and familiar.

Alexandria's eyes widened, surprise etched across her face. "Theodora... is that you?" Her soft voice cut through the heavy silence of the forest.

They moved toward each other as if pulled by something unseen, something stronger than time or distance. Theodora's heart pounded, her breath coming fast. Her feet barely felt the ground—roots and leaves catching at her boots, but she didn't care. Nothing else mattered. The forest, the night, even Finnegan and Killian faded away. All that remained was this moment.

Alexandria hesitated when they were just steps apart, her hand lifting but not quite touching, fingers shaking as they hovered near

Theodora's cheek. There was a question in her eyes, a flicker of doubt, as if she wasn't sure this was real.

Theodora didn't wait. She surged forward, wrapping her arms around her sister in a fierce embrace. The moment their bodies collided, something cracked—not just in her chest but in the very air around them. A pulse of energy rippled outward, unseen but powerful, like a string snapping after being pulled too tight. The wind picked up, swirling through the clearing, carrying whispers of something ancient, something long forgotten.

Then, the memories hit.

Theodora gasped, her grip tightening on Alexandria as flashes of the past flooded her mind. A warm hearth on a stormy night. Their mother's voice hummed a lullaby. Their father's laughter echoing through the halls. And then—chaos. Flames licking at the castle walls. Shadows moving in the night. Hands tearing them apart.

Ms. Whoo's spell had kept it all hidden. It had dulled the pain, blurred the truth, made them forget. But now, it is gone, shattered by their reunion.

Theodora's knees nearly buckled under the weight of it all. She felt Alexandria shaking against her, hearing the sharp intake of breath as her sister's own memories rushed back.

Tears slipped down Theodora's cheeks, hot and unchecked. She buried her face in Alexandria's hair, inhaling the familiar scent of pine and lavender, grounding herself in something real. The ache of lost time and stolen memories was almost too much, but they clung to each other as if holding on could keep the past from slipping away again.

"You're real," Theodora whispered, her voice thick with emotion.

Alexandria pulled back just enough to cup her face, her thumbs brushing away the wetness on Theodora's cheeks. "I never stopped looking for you," she said, her voice barely more than a breath. "Not for one second."

Theodora let out a shaky, tear-soaked laugh. "Neither did I."

"I've missed ya somethin' fierce," Theodora continued, her voice heavy with emotion.

"And I you," Alexandria replied, gently pushing back a loose strand of Theodora's fiery hair. "It's like part of me was missing. And now..."

"Now we're whole again," Theodora finished for her, nodding in agreement.

Their matching bracelets pulsed in unison, glowing as if echoing their sentiments. Magic thrummed through Theodora's veins, stronger than she'd ever felt it before. It coursed through her like wildfire, leaving a warmth that seemed to spread throughout her entire body.

"Do ya feel that?" she asked in awe, staring at their intertwined hands.

Alexandria nodded. "Everything feels clearer. Brighter."

As they stood there, reunited at last, both sisters knew they had overcome incredible odds to find one another again. They had braved heartache and darkness to stand where they were now—together in the moonlit clearing.

But the moment couldn't last forever. Reality began to creep back in, and with it came the weight of their responsibilities and the knowledge that the world was far from safe. They had found each other once more, but they would have to stand together against the looming threat that still cast its shadow over them all.

A rustle in the underbrush snapped Theodora's attention away from Alexandria. Her heart, still pounding from their reunion, skipped a beat as she instinctively reached for her bow. But as the figures emerged from the shadows, relief washed over her.

Finnegan stepped out of the shadows, his face a mixture of reverence and relief. His blue eyes glistened in the moonlight, reflecting a depth of emotion Theodora had never seen before. Behind him, Killian's usual stern expression had softened, a hint of a smile playing at the corners of his mouth.

Khadall swooped down from a nearby branch, landing gracefully on a fallen log. His eyes seemed to glow with an otherworldly light as he regarded the reunited sisters, his silence speaking volumes about the significance of the moment.

"Aye, a blessin' indeed," Finnegan's gruff voice cut through the silence. He stepped closer, careful not to disturb the moment. "But keep yer wits about ya. Danger's never far in these parts."

Theodora felt Alexandria tense beside her, their shared apprehension palpable. Squaring her shoulders, Theodora lifted her chin defiantly.

"We'll face it together," she said, her voice steady despite her trembling hands.

"Always," Alexandria agreed, tightening her grip on Theodora's arm.

A movement caught Theodora's eye. A young man she didn't recognize approached, his manner cautious yet determined. Alexandria's cheeks flushed as she realized her oversight.

"Oh! Theo, I can't believe I forgot," she said, her usual composure slipping. "This is Jasper. He's been my guide since Aris and I arrived in Kandella. We wouldn't have made it without him."

Theodora studied the newcomer, taking in his striking features and the way he carried himself with a calm confidence. Curiosity mingled with wariness as he drew near.

"Princess Theodora," Jasper said, offering a slight bow. "It's an honor to finally meet ya. Alexandria has told me so much about ya."

Theodora hesitated for a moment before extending her hand. "Well met, Jasper," she replied, her tone formal but not unkind. As their hands clasped, she felt a spark of... something. Not quite magic, but a sense of connection, as if the very fates were acknowledging this meeting.

Walking towards the campfire, Theodora felt Jasper's gaze on her. His charm didn't quite mask the intensity that set her on edge.

"Thank you fer looking after me sister, Jasper," she said, her words polite but tinged with a hint of skepticism. "I know she wouldn't have made it this far without your guidance."

Jasper smiled, that effortless charm lighting up his features. "It's been me pleasure, Princess. Your sister is a remarkable young woman, and it's been an honor to accompany her on this journey."

As they settled around the fire, the dancing flames cast a warm glow over their faces, the group's conversation shifted from serious matters to lighter topics. Finnegan entertained them with tales of his druidic training in the lush forests of Kandella, weaving in humorous anecdotes about mischievous woodland creatures and his early blunders with magic. His deep laughter mingled with Alexandria's melodious voice as she shared stories of her adventures in the mortal world, painting vivid pictures of bustling cities and vast oceans that left Theodora longing to explore beyond the confines of her homeland.

Even Killian joined in, surprising everyone with a story about an ill-tempered unicorn and a bucket of glitter that had them all in stitches. The earlier tension melted away, replaced by a sense of shared purpose and friendship.

As the fire dwindled, Finnegan rose, his gaze sweeping over the group. Shadows played across his weathered face. "It's late," he said. "We've a long day ahead. Best get some rest while we can."

Theodora gazed into the dying embers, the weight of their mission settling over her once more. Rescuing her parents, saving the kingdom—it all seemed overwhelming. But looking around at her companions, their faces set with determination, she felt a flicker of hope. They were in this together, and somehow, they'd find a way.

As they laid down for the night, Theodora, and Alexandria settled side by side, fingers laced together. Aris curled up at their feet while Khadall kept watch from a nearby branch. The forest's nocturnal symphony surrounded them—the leaves rustling, an owl hooting, and the fire's dying crackle.

Despite her weariness, sleep evaded Theodora. Her mind churned with disjointed memories and vague strategies as she turned to observe Alexandria's face in the dim light. Her sister's rhythmic breathing grounded her, a reminder of their newfound connection.

As the night stretched on, Theodora sat watching the stars, their cold light stark against the fading glow of the fire. A slow chill settled over the camp, seeping through her bedroll, wrapping around her like unseen hands. The forest had fallen into an uneasy silence, broken only by the distant howl of a lone wolf. She pulled her blanket tighter, but the unease lingered.

Sleep tugged at her, heavy and insistent. The dying embers flickered, their glow softening at the edges as her eyes drifted shut. The cold faded, the sounds of the forest dissolving into something distant, dreamlike. Her breathing slowed, her body sinking into rest at last.

Morning light filtered through the trees, its golden glow cutting through the lingering mist. Theodora stirred, the scent of damp earth thick in the air as she blinked awake. Nearby, Alexandria shifted, her breath deepening as she slowly opened her eyes, taking in the quiet of their camp.

Theodora stretched, savoring the feeling of freedom. She glanced at her sister, thinking of the dangers they'd faced apart and the challenges that lay ahead. Together now, they'd face whatever came next.

"Mornin', Alex," Theodora said, her voice a mix of excitement and nerves. She ran her fingers over the silver bracelet on her wrist.

Alexandria rolled over, the early light catching her eyes. "Morning," she replied with a small smile.

They rose together, moving in sync as they prepared for the day. Birds chirped in the distance as the camp came to life around them.

Finnegan stood at the edge of camp, his hands weaving intricate patterns as he reinforced their magical protections. He focused his eyes, his gestures emitting a faint glow.

The twins made their way to the campfire, where Killian tended a bubbling cauldron. They filled their bowls with steaming oatmeal, the scent of cinnamon, nutmeg and honey rising with the steam. Nearby, freshly brewed coffee added its rich aroma to the crisp morning air.

As they ate, the warmth of the meal chased away the lingering chill. They savored the quiet, the occasional clink of spoons the only sound between them. A sense of camaraderie settled over the group, unspoken but firmly rooted.

After breakfast, they packed up and followed Finnegan through the snow-laden forest. Their boots crunched over frost-hardened ground as their breath curled into the air in soft plumes. Sunlight filtered through the towering pines, glinting off icicles that hung like daggers from the branches. They stepped into a vast clearing, the open field blanketed in untouched snow.

"This is where we'll be startin' our training," Finnegan announced, his voice carrying in the crisp air. He spread his arms, gesturing to the empty expanse.

Theodora and Alexandria exchanged glances, scanning the barren field. There was nothing—no targets, no weapons, not even a single marker to suggest a training ground. The wind whistled through the trees, rustling the branches overhead.

Killian caught their puzzled expressions and smirked. "Just wait," he said with a wink.

He raised his arms, fingers tracing symbols in the air as he muttered an incantation under his breath. The air around them crackled with energy, the snow swirling in sudden gusts as light flared from his fingertips. A wave of shimmering magic surged across the field, bending reality in its wake.

As the glow faded, the landscape transformed before their eyes. Targets now stood in precise rows, their surfaces marked with concentric rings and shifting sigils. Wooden dummies wrapped in thick ropes loomed nearby, some bound in chains, others crackling with latent enchantments. Wicker spheres hung from tree branches, swinging slightly as if waiting for a challenge. Jagged crystals jutted from the ground, pulsing with an inner glow.

The empty field had become a battlefield, alive with challenge and danger.

Moments ago, there had been only snow. Now, a training ground stretched before the twins, ready to push them to their limits. Their eyes widened in shock.

Standing at the forest's edge, they took in the sight with a mix of excitement and unease. Theodora's fingers hovered near her bow, while Alexandria's hand tightened around her dagger hilt. They had experienced a joyful reunion, but that was now over. Ahead lay trials that would challenge not only their skills but the strength of their bond as sisters.

Theodora glanced at Alexandria, noting the changes in her twin. Gone was the carefree girl she remembered; in her place stood a woman hardened by her time in the mortal realm. Still, beneath the wariness, Theodora sensed their connection, strong as ever.

Alexandria felt it too - that invisible thread linking them, even after years apart. She'd grown used to relying only on herself, yet having Theodora beside her again felt right, like finding a missing piece of herself. But doubts lingered. Could they work as one after so long apart?

Finnegan watched the sisters, his face unreadable. He knew this training would reveal more than just their magical abilities. It would show if they could overcome their individual fears and truly unite.

"Listen well, lasses," he called out, his gruff voice carrying across the field. "Yer strength lies not just in yer individual talents, but in yer bond as sisters. Trust in each other, trust in yerselves. That's where the real magic happens."

The twins shared a look, years of unspoken understanding passing between them in an instant. Without a word, they stepped onto the training ground together, ready to face whatever challenges lay ahead.

"Well then," Theodora said, a hint of her old mischief in her voice, "shall we show 'em what we can do, sister?"

Alexandria's lips quirked in a small smile. "Let's."

"Ah, lasses," Jasper called out, his voice carrying across the training ground. The twins turned to face him, curiosity piqued. Finnegan and Killian glanced over, their attention drawn by Jasper's commanding tone.

"If ye are to train as warriors, ye must also dress the part." Jasper continued. "Proper warrior princesses need proper gear. Killian, if ye would?"

Killian stepped forward, his purple hair catching the sunlight. He positioned himself between the twins, a look of concentration on his face. "This might feel a bit strange," he warned, raising his hands. Altering reality was no easy feat, but he was determined to help the sisters. His face etched with concentration, he assessed the twins.

On the sidelines, Jasper watched anxiously, grinning as he recognized the potential in this situation. The thought of enhancing the girls' clothing intrigued him greatly.

The air around them began to crackle with energy. Theodora and Alexandria exchanged excited looks, trusting Killian's magic implicitly.

Killian's hands began to glow with a soft, ethereal light, the energy of his fae magic swirling and dancing around him like wisps of lavender smoke. With a deep breath, he closed his eyes and focused on the essence of each twin, seeking to capture their unique strengths and vulnerabilities in the garments he was about to create.

A surge of electricity crackled in the air around Theodora, the power within her responding to his touch. Her auburn hair shimmered with an inner light as she stood, anticipation building within her. Her eyes met Killian's, reflecting a mix of curiosity and trust.

With a flourish of his hand, Killian spun threads of crackling lightning into Theodora's garments, imbuing them with an essence that thrummed like a symphony of magic. The fabric undulated and metamorphosed, adopting a streamlined and safeguarding nature that reverberated with strength. Elaborate symbols pirouetted along the hems of her outfit, casting a gentle luminescence under the sunlight.

As the radiance dimmed, Theodora gasped, her gaze widening in awe. Her newfound attire gleamed with an ethereal luminescence, pulsating with a potency that harmonized with her very essence. She trailed her fingertips across the sleek tunic, admiring its resilient texture. The material offered a cool caress while exuding a soothing warmth that seeped into her very core.

Intricate silver runes danced along the edges of her sleeves and collar, their delicate patterns shifting and changing as she moved. Theodora traced one with her fingertip, feeling a gentle tingle of magic beneath her skin. The runes seemed to whisper ancient secrets, their meaning just beyond her grasp.

Her leggings, a deep forest green, hugged her legs like a second skin. As she flexed her muscles, she felt the fabric move with her, offering both protection and freedom of movement. A belt of interwoven silver and leather encircled her waist, adorned with small pouches perfect for storing herbs or other necessities.

But it was the cloak that took her breath away. It flowed from her shoulders like liquid moonlight, its color shifting between deep purple and midnight blue. As she swirled it around herself, she caught glimpses of constellations woven into its fabric, twinkling stars that seemed to pulse with their own inner light.

"By the gods," Theodora breathed, her voice filled with awe. She met Killian's gaze, gratitude shining in her emerald eyes. "How did ye manage this?"

Killian smiled, a hint of pride in his violet eyes. "Fae magic, lass. I wove yer very essence into the fabric. It'll grow stronger as ye do, offering protection and enhancing yer natural abilities."

Theodora flexed her fingers, feeling the surge of power coursing through her veins. The outfit seemed to amplify her connection to the magic within her, making her feel more alive than ever before. She took a deep breath, inhaling the scent of ozone and fresh pine that clung to her new garments.

"It's incredible," she murmured, her mind already racing with the possibilities this new attire offered. She glanced at Alexandria, eager to see what Killian had planned for her outfit. As their eyes met, Theodora felt a surge of excitement.

Alexandria stood tall, her heart racing with anticipation as Killian turned his attention towards her. The air around them crackled with elemental magic, a swirling vortex of earth and wind that made her skin tingle. She could feel the power emanating from Killian's hands, pulsing in rhythm with her own heartbeat.

As his fingers began to weave their spell, Alexandria gasped. The fabric of her clothing seemed to come alive, rippling and shifting like leaves caught in a gentle breeze. Emerald light danced across the surface, casting intricate shadows that moved of their own accord.

The transformation began at her feet, a warm sensation spreading upwards as her simple boots morphed into something extraordinary. Supple leather, the color of rich soil after a spring rain, molded itself to her calves. Delicate vines of silver thread spiraled up the sides, their tendrils seeming to pulse with an inner light. Alexandria flexed her toes, marveling at how the boots moved with her, as if they were an extension of her own body.

Her leggings shimmered, transforming into a material that felt cool against her skin yet radiated strength. Threads of gold interwoven into the deep forest green fabric caught the light, creating shifting patterns with her every movement. As she ran her hand along her thigh, she felt the fabric respond to her touch, tiny runes flickering to life beneath her fingers.

A tunic materialized around her torso, its fabric a mesmerizing blend of earthy browns and vibrant greens. It hugged her form perfectly, offering both protection and freedom of movement. Intricate embroidery adorned the collar and cuffs, depicting scenes of ancient forests and windswept plains. As Alexandria traced the patterns, she could have sworn she felt a breeze whisper across her skin, carrying with it the scent of pine and wild herbs.

A belt of intertwined leather and silver cinched her waist, adorned with pouches and loops perfect for storing herbs, small weapons or other necessities. At its center, a polished stone the color of a storm-tossed sea gleamed, seeming to pulse with its own inner light.

The cloak was the most stunning piece. It wrapped around her like a comforting hug, its hues constantly changing from earthy browns to vibrant blues. As she moved, it revealed hidden landscapes within its layers - hazy peaks, sun-drenched fields, and ancient woods. The edges danced against the ground, leaving behind no trace of her steps.

Killian's hands moved with fluid grace, weaving intricate patterns in the air as he focused on the final touches of the twins' attire. Theodora watched in awe as delicate strands of magic coalesced around her fingers, forming supple leather gloves that left her fingertips exposed. The material felt cool against her skin, yet radiated a comforting warmth.

"These'll give ye a better grip on yer bow," Killian explained, his violet eyes twinkling. "And they won't hinder yer magic none."

Theodora flexed her fingers, marveling at how the gloves moved with her, like a second skin. She could feel the raw power thrumming through them, amplifying her connection to the magic that coursed through her veins.

Beside her, Alexandria gasped as similar gloves materialized on her hands. The leather was a shade darker than Theodora's, with intricate silver runes etched along the knuckles. As Alexandria curled her fingers, the runes flickered to life, casting a soft glow in the early morning light.

"Now one final thing," Killian murmured, his brow furrowed in concentration.

Theodora felt a gentle tugging at her scalp as strands of her fiery hair began to move of their own accord. They wove themselves into an intricate series of braids, each one adorned with tiny charms that glinted like stars. She glimpsed her reflection in a nearby puddle and saw that the braids formed a delicate crown atop her head, fit for the princess she was born to be.

Alexandria's hair underwent a similar transformation, though her braids took on a more elaborate pattern. Tiny flowers and leaves seemed to sprout from the plaits, their colors shifting with each movement of her head. The effect was mesmerizing, like a living, breathing forest crown.

"These braids are more than just pretty trinkets," Killian said, his voice low and serious. "They're woven wit' protective magic. They'll help shield yer minds from dark influences an' boost yer natural abilities."

Theodora reached up, her gloved fingers tracing the intricate patterns in her hair. She could feel the magic humming beneath her touch, a constant reminder of the power that now flowed through her.

"It's incredible," she breathed, turning to Alexandria. "How do ye feel?"

Alexandria's eyes were wide with wonder as she met Theodora's gaze. "Like I could take on the world," she replied, a fierce grin spreading across her face.

The twins stood side by side, their new attire gleaming in the morning light. Theodora felt a surge of confidence coursing through her veins. The weight of their quest still loomed, but now she felt ready to face whatever lay ahead.

"Well," she said, her voice steady as she reached for her bow, "shall we show 'em what we're made of?"

Alexandria's lips curved into a sly grin, her hand moving to the dagger at her hip. "Let's give 'em something to talk about."

As they stepped onto the training ground, Theodora sensed this was just the beginning. With each step, the magic in their new garments seemed to intensify, responding to their shared resolve. Whatever challenges awaited, they'd face them together—as sisters, as warriors, as the twin princesses of Kandella.

Jasper watched with approval, nodding at Killian's handiwork. He recognized this as a turning point in the twins' training, one that would enhance both their abilities and their bond. The magical attire seemed alive, pulsing in tune with the twins' inner strength.

Finnegan approached, pride evident in his eyes as he took in the sight before him. His voice carried a hint of reverence as he spoke. "Ye wear more than just cloth, lasses. Ye wear the strength of yer bond, the very essence of magic. Let these garments remind ye of who ye are and what ye fight for. Together, there's no challenge ye can't overcome."

Jasper stepped forward, his expression a mix of satisfaction and anticipation. "Now's the time to train as true warriors—not just with weapons, but with heart and spirit. These garments aren't just for show; they reveal the magic within ye. Let them guide ye, shield ye, and strengthen ye in the trials ahead."

The training ground hummed with anticipation as Finnegan's voice rang out once more, filled with unwavering confidence. "Let's begin."

The twins shared a look, their hearts beating as one. The magic in their garments seemed to resonate with their very essence. With renewed determination, they faced Finnegan, ready for whatever he had in store.

A hush fell over the training ground. The twins, filled with shared purpose, moved forward in perfect sync. Theodora's fingers found her bow, tracing the familiar grooves. A silent understanding passed between them before they turned to face their challenges.

Theodora notched an arrow with practiced ease. The bow felt like an extension of herself as she took a deep breath, muscles coiling and releasing. Her arrows found their marks with unerring precision, thudding into the targets with satisfying finality.

Alexandria stood firm, sword at the ready. Finnegan had issued his challenge, and she was eager to meet it. Their blades met with a clash that echoed across the grounds. She moved with calculated efficiency, her innate combat skills on full display. She met his strikes with swift blocks and countered with agile attacks, her quick thinking evident in every move. Her reflexes allowed her to adapt seamlessly to each new challenge he presented.

Jasper stood at the forest's edge, his heart pounding as he watched the princesses. A mix of awe and unease churned in his gut. He'd never expected to feel this way about them - these girls he'd once seen as mere pawns in a larger game. Now, he found himself fiercely protective, ready to stand between them and any danger.

The transformation bewildered him. *When did strangers become so dear?* Alexandria's determined stance and Theodora's unwavering focus stirred something in him he couldn't quite name. It was more than admiration; it was a bone-deep certainty that their fates were now intertwined with his own.

The weight of his previous schemes and lies pressed on him. He felt a strong desire to confess, but the fear of losing their trust held him back. Still, as he observed them in training, Jasper realized he couldn't abandon them. No matter what lay ahead, he was determined to face it with them.

A rumble of thunder in the distance caught his attention. Dark clouds gathered on the horizon, mirroring the storm of emotions within him. Jasper took a deep breath, steeling himself. The choices he made now would shape not just his future, but theirs as well. There was no going back.

Killian stood apart, his keen eyes catching the tension in Jasper's stance. Though he couldn't pinpoint the cause, Killian felt the weight of Jasper's inner turmoil. He watched from afar, taking in the scene with a mix of admiration and understanding born from his own battles.

The twins' journey struck a chord in Killian. As a halfling warrior from Isadore, he knew the sting of loss. Dark forces had stolen his family years ago, leaving a wound that never truly healed. But from that pain, he'd forged himself anew. Each day, each fight, drove him to protect others from similar fates.

Killian moved through the forest, his steps purposeful. He was a blend of two worlds - human warrior and fae spirit - each vying for control. His warrior's instinct was both shield and burden, while his fae heritage added depth often overlooked by others. This internal struggle was as familiar to him as breathing.

Watching Theodora and Alexandria train stirred old memories. Their determination mirrored his own early days, and he felt a kinship in their struggles. The bond between the sisters echoed the family he'd lost, a bittersweet reminder of what was gone.

As the princesses moved in sync, Killian's mind drifted. He remembered his family's warmth, shared laughter, and his parents' embrace. His father's absence remained a constant ache. In the twins' resolve, he saw his own quest for justice reflected back at him.

Killian's eyes met Finnegan's, and understanding passed between them. They'd both seen their share of battles, carried their own secrets. Though life had led them down different paths, they shared the weight of protecting those who needed it most.

A telepathic connection hummed between the two seasoned warriors, their minds intertwining in a silent conversation.

"They've got spirit, those two," Killian murmured, nodding towards the twins.

Finnegan grunted in agreement. "Aye, that they do. Reminds me of another young warrior I once knew."

Killian's lips quirked in a half-smile. "Let's hope their path is easier than mine was."

"We'll do what we can to make it so," Finnegan replied, his voice low and determined.

Killian prowled the perimeter, senses on high alert as the forest whispered around him. He moved silently, eyes scanning for any sign of danger when a faint shimmer caught his attention. From the dense foliage emerged a figure bathed in soft light.

"I am Elara," she said, her voice gentle yet ancient, her eyes holding wisdom beyond mortal years. Killian stood transfixed, the tales of otherworldly beings he had often heard about now made vividly real.

Meanwhile, on the training field, Alexandria sensed a familiar presence and froze mid-exercise. She whirled around and spotted Killian and the newcomer, sprinting towards them with wide eyes of recognition and excitement. Elara smiled at Alexandria, her aura radiating calm. "Ah, Princess Alexandria," she said, her lilting voice carrying an old-world charm. "I've been watchin' you and your sister. The realms are out of balance, and you've a vital part in settin' things right."

Alexandria's heart raced as the weight of Elara's words sank in. She glanced back at Theodora, who had paused her archery practice; curiosity and caution mingled in her expression as Elara's presence seemed to illuminate the entire training ground. Killian stood nearby, torn between reverence for Elara and a protective instinct towards the princesses.

Finnegan and Jasper soon joined them as Elara explained her arrival two days prior to assist in their fight against the evil plaguing Kandella. She revealed that the upcoming eclipse was crucial; balance must be restored, or darkness would reign and their king and queen would be lost forever.

Theodora gripped her bow, determination, and apprehension swirling in her eyes as she absorbed Elara's words—the fate of their kingdom rested on their shoulders. Finnegan's gaze darted between Elara and the princesses, his weathered features set with resolve; his knowledge of ancient magic hinted at the gravity of their situation. The druid's loyalty to the twins burned fiercer than ever.

Killian was acutely aware of the responsibilities weighing on his shoulders, and he was constantly on guard, ready to defend those who depended on him from the ever-approaching threat. Elara's calm eyes shifted from Alexandria to Theodora. "It's time to have faith in yourselves and each other, my princesses," she declared, her words echoing through the clearing. "Only by coming together and harnessing the full extent of your magic can you restore balance and defeat the darkness."

A flicker stirred within Theodora's soul as she nodded resolutely, her fiery hair catching the light, her resolve strengthening alongside her sister's newfound courage in this pivotal moment.

Alexandria stood shoulder to shoulder with Theodora, her eyes gleaming with newfound resolve. The weight of their shared destiny was immense, but she wouldn't back down. Silently, she pledged her unwavering support to her sister, come hell or high water.

The small group around them stood firm, each harboring their own mix of hope and trepidation. They stood together to face the looming threats, fully aware that their bonds would be tested in the days ahead.

Guided by Elara's wisdom and with the forest as their witness, the twins braced themselves to face their deepest fears and unlock their true potential. They gathered their courage, ready to carve out a path that would not only shape their own fates but restore balance to the realms and protect everything they held dear.

Chapter 19

"Edge of the Tempest"

THE FOREST AWAKENED WITH the first light of dawn, a symphony of rustling leaves and birdsong filling the air. Theodora's eyes fluttered open, her body stiff from sleeping on the hard ground. She inhaled, the scent of damp earth and pine needles filling her lungs. Beside her, Alexandria stirred.

Theodora sat up, wincing as she stretched. The dying embers of their campfire cast a faint orange glow across the clearing. She glanced at her sister, a surge of warmth flooding her chest at the sight of Alexandria's peaceful face. How strange it was to feel so connected to someone she'd been apart from for so long.

"Rise and shine, lasses," Finnegan called, his voice gruff as he stoked the fire. "Breakfast's on, and we've got work to do."

Theodora's stomach growled, a sharp reminder of her hunger. She gave Alexandria a light shake. "C'mon now, Alex. Time ta get up."

As they gathered around the rekindled fire, Theodora couldn't help but notice the tension in Finnegan's shoulders, the way his eyes darted to the treeline every few seconds. It set her on edge, reminding her of the dangers lurking beyond their camp.

Killian passed out chunks of crusty bread and handfuls of ripe berries. Theodora bit into the bread, savoring its hearty flavor. As she chewed, her mind wandered to the training that lay ahead. Excitement and nerves battled in her gut.

"Ready for this?" Alexandria whispered.

Theodora met her sister's eyes. "As I'll ever be," she replied, forcing a smile.

After they finished eating, the group made their way back to the training field. A fresh blanket of snow covered the grass. Alexandria shivered, pulling her cloak tighter around her shoulders.

"Right then," Finnegan said as they reached the field's center. "Today we push yer limits. Let's see what ye can do together."

Theodora's heart raced as she turned to face Alexandria. They clasped hands, their fingers intertwining as naturally as breathing. She could feel the magic thrumming beneath her skin, responding to her sister's presence.

"Remember," Killian's voice rang out, "focus on each other. Let yer powers flow between ye."

Theodora closed her eyes, taking a deep breath. She reached out with her senses, feeling for that invisible thread that connected her to Alexandria. There it was–a pulse of energy, warm and familiar.

As they began to channel their magic, the air around them crackled with electricity. Theodora's hair stood on end, static dancing across her skin, while Alexandria felt the wind coil around her like a living thing, tugging at her cloak and whistling through the trees as if whispering secrets only she could hear.

Their fingers were tightly intertwined, grounding each other as the energy between them surged.

"That's it," Finnegan encouraged. "Now, shape it. Bend the elements to yer will."

Alexandria closed her eyes, picturing the air currents swirling faster, lifting them from the earth. A deep breath, a firm pull—suddenly, their feet were no longer touching the ground. The wind carried them higher, weightless, and she knew Theodora was rising with her.

Theodora's eyes snapped open, meeting Alexandria's wide gaze. They were floating several feet above the ground, caught in a vortex of wind and raw power.

"Bloody hell," Jasper's voice carried from below. "Would ya look at that?"

Theodora let out a breathless laugh, the thrill of it coursing through her veins. But the energy inside her wasn't just power—it was something sharper, wilder. Sparks danced along her fingertips, crackling against Alexandria's palm where they were still joined.

Theodora hesitated for only a second before she released one of Alexandria's hands, lifting her freed arm toward the sky.

The moment she did, lightning arced from her fingertips, streaking toward the heavens in jagged, brilliant flashes. Electricity hummed up her arm, filling her with raw, intoxicating power.

The sky above them darkened. The clouds churned, thick and heavy, gathering with unnatural speed. Alexandria guided the wind upward, pulling the storm into formation, willing it to dance around them. Thunder rumbled in response, deep and resonant, like the earth itself was waking up.

"Careful now," Killian warned, his voice edged with caution. "Don't lose control."

But Theodora had never felt more alive. The charge in the air sent a delicious shiver down her spine, the power thrumming in her blood. She lifted her hand higher, and another bolt of lightning split the sky, illuminating the swirling tempest Alexandria controlled. Wind and thunder obeyed one; lightning and raw energy answered the other.

Alexandria gritted her teeth, fighting to steady the raging winds. The storm had gained too much momentum. If she didn't rein it in, it would spiral beyond their control.

"Theodora, listen to me!" she shouted over the howling gale. "We're pushing too far!"

Another bolt of lightning struck dangerously close to the tree-tops. Theodora gasped, blinking as if coming out of a trance. Her fingers twitched, and for a moment, Alexandria squeezed the hand she still held, grounding her. The wind faltered just enough for

Alexandria to seize control, forcing a powerful downward gust to steady them.

Theodora's feet hit the earth, her knees nearly buckling beneath her. The lightning flickered out, the static charge dissipating into the air. Alexandria exhaled shakily, releasing the storm. The sky above them gradually lightened, the wind settling into a gentle breeze.

For a long moment, neither of them spoke. Then Theodora let out a breathless chuckle, grinning. "That was—"

"Too much," Alexandria finished, still catching her breath. But despite herself, she smiled. "But incredible."

Killian folded his arms, eyeing them both. "Aye, incredible it was. But next time, try not to nearly bring the bloody sky down on our heads, eh?"

Suddenly, a voice cut through the chaos. "Girls!"

Theodora looked for the source. Diana and Elmer stood at the clearing's edge.

"Diana? Elmer?" Alexandria's voice cracked with emotion.

"Well," Diana said with a slight smile, "looks like we arrived just in time." They slowly made their way across the field towards the group.

Without thinking, Alexandria sprinted towards them, her feet barely touching the ground. The world blurred around her, narrowing to just the two figures before her. As she reached them, she flung her arms around them both, burying her face in Diana's shoulder.

The scent of lavender and pine enveloped her, so achingly familiar it brought tears to her eyes. Diana's arms wrapped around her, warm and solid, while Elmer's hand rested on her back, a comforting weight.

"We've missed you, little one," Diana murmured, her voice thick with emotion.

Alexandria pulled back slightly, drinking in their faces. Diana's silver hair shimmered in the sunlight, her eyes as kind as ever. Elmer stood tall beside her, his rugged features softened by a rare smile.

"How... how are you here?" Alexandria asked, her voice trembling.

Elmer chuckled, the sound rumbling deep in his chest. "Did ye think we'd let ye face all this alone? We've been keepin' an eye on ye since ye left the mortal world."

A thousand questions raced through Alexandria's mind, but before she could voice any of them, she heard footsteps approaching. Turning, she saw Theodora walking towards them, her expression a mix of confusion and wariness.

"Alex?" Theodora called, her hand hovering near her bow. "Who are these people?"

She felt a pang in her chest at the uncertainty in her sister's voice. She reached out, taking Theodora's hand in hers. "Theo, it's okay," she said. "This is Diana and Elmer. They... they took care of me in the mortal world."

Theodora's eyes widened, flicking between Alexandria and the newcomers. Alexandria could feel the tension in her sister's body, the way her fingers tightened around hers.

Diana stepped forward, her movements graceful and unhurried. "It's a pleasure to finally meet you, Princess Theodora," she said, her voice warm.

Theodora's grip on Alexandria's hand loosened slightly, but her posture remained guarded. "You... you protected my sister?"

Elmer nodded, his violet eyes serious. "Aye, that we did. And now we're here to help ye both."

As the others gathered around, Alexandria felt a surge of warmth and nostalgia wash over her. The familiar scents of lavender and pine mingled with the crisp forest air, bringing back memories of her childhood in the mortal realm. She turned to face her companions, her heart racing with a mix of excitement and apprehension.

"Everyone," she began, her voice trembling slightly, "I'd like you to meet Diana and Elmer. They... they're my family from the mortal world."

Killian's eyes narrowed, his hand moving to the hilt of his weapon. "Ye're both Fae, are ye not?" he asked, his voice low and wary.

Diana's lips curved into a gentle smile. "Indeed we are, Killian. Your perceptiveness serves you well."

Elmer nodded. "Ms. Whoo chose us to protect and care for Alexandria when she went to the mortal realm."

Jasper, who had been uncharacteristically quiet, stepped forward. "So, ye knew about Alexandria's true identity all along?" he asked, his eyes fixed on Diana and Elmer. "Why reveal yerselves now?"

Elmer's expression darkened, his rugged features set in grim determination. "The balance is shiftin', lad. The darkness that threatens Kandella... it's reachin' beyond the veil. We couldn't stand idly by any longer."

Diana nodded, her ethereal presence seeming to draw everyone's attention. "We offer our knowledge, magic and support. The twins' destiny intertwines with the fate of both realms, and we intend to guide them through it."

As Diana spoke, Alexandria felt a tingling sensation in her fingertips, a familiar warmth spreading through her body. She glanced at Theodora, wondering if she felt it too. The air around them seemed to shimmer, as if the very fabric of reality was responding to the presence of so much magical energy.

Diana's attention turned to Theodora and Alexandria. "Girls," she began, her voice soft yet commanding, "what ye just experienced is only a fraction of yer true potential. But with great power comes great responsibility."

Theodora felt a shiver run down her spine, remembering the wild, uncontrollable magic that had coursed through her moments ago. She glanced at Alexandria, seeing her own mix of exhilaration and fear mirrored in her sister's eyes.

Diana continued, her tone growing more urgent. "To harness yer combined powers, ye must learn to control them. What happened earlier... it could happen again, but much worse."

Alexandria's brow furrowed. "Worse? How?"

Diana's expression darkened. "Imagine that storm ye conjured, but a hundredfold. Ye could level entire forests, dry up lakes, or worse... hurt those ye love."

Theodora's stomach churned at the thought. She remembered the rush of power, how intoxicating it had felt. The thought that it could turn so destructive terrified her.

"But how do we control it?" Theodora asked. "It felt... it felt like it had a mind of its own."

Diana's eyes softened, the silvery flecks in her irises dancing like starlight. "That's where we come in, lass," she said, her voice a soothing balm to Theodora's frayed nerves.

"Elmer and I will guide ye through this. Ye must learn to channel yer emotions, to find the delicate balance within yerselves and each other."

Theodora's heart quickened at Diana's words. The enormity of the task ahead loomed over her, a mountain she wasn't sure she could climb. She glanced at Alexandria, finding comfort in the determined set of her sister's jaw.

Elmer stepped forward, his rugged features etched with resolve. The air around him crackled. "It won't be easy," he warned, his violet eyes boring into Theodora's. "Ye'll be pushed to yer limits and beyond. There'll be times when ye'll want to give up, when the weight of it all seems too much to bear."

A lump formed in Theodora's throat, fear, and doubt threatening to overwhelm her. But then Elmer's expression softened, a glimmer of pride shining through. "But remember, the fate of Kandella rests on yer shoulders. Ye're stronger than ya know, both of ya."

Alexandria's hand found Theodora's, their fingers intertwined. A spark of energy passed between them, softer this time, like a gentle caress. Theodora drew strength from her sister's touch, feeling the steady thrum of Alexandria's pulse against her skin.

"We're ready," Alexandria said, her voice steady despite the slight tremor Theodora felt in her hand. The words hung in the air, a promise, and a challenge.

Diana nodded as she stepped forward, her presence calm yet commanding. "Girls," she began, "to harness yer true potential, ye must learn to breathe as one, to move as extensions of each other."

She took another step closer, her eyes studying them with quiet intensity. "Power alone is not enough. Control, trust—these will shape ye into what ye're meant to become."

Elmer crossed his arms, his deep voice rumbling like distant thunder. "Close yer eyes," he instructed. "Feel the rhythm of each other's hearts, the way yer magic flows between ya. Let it weave together, like threads in the same tapestry."

The air around them seemed to still, charged with unseen energy. Theodora drew a long breath, her fingers still locked with Alexandria's. She could feel the faint thrum of life beneath Alexandria's skin, a pulse that echoed her own.

At first, the connection was subtle—like a distant drumbeat just out of sync. But as she focused, as she let herself tune in to the magic between them, something shifted. The rhythm steadied, their energies brushing together, then intertwining.

"Good," Diana murmured. "Now listen—not just to yerselves, but to each other. Magic is not meant to be wielded alone."

A shiver ran through Theodora as sparks flickered between their joined hands. Alexandria's breath hitched, the wind around them stirring in response.

"Let it build," Elmer urged. "But do not force it. Let it flow as it wants to."

Theodora felt it then—pure energy, raw and untamed, humming beneath her skin. It wasn't just hers. It was theirs. The realization sent a thrill through her.

For the first time, their magic wasn't two separate forces crashing together. It was one.

Theodora drew in a slow breath, and Alexandria mirrored her. As their eyes closed, the world faded—the whisper of leaves, the distant birdsong, even the solid ground beneath them.

Only each other remained. The quiet rise and fall of their chests. The pulse of energy between them, once wild, now calm and steady.

Theodora felt it, and so did Alexandria. Their connection deepened, threading through them like a slow-moving current, patient and sure. They stood still yet fully aware, bound by something beyond themselves.

"That's it," Diana's voice floated to them, sounding far away. "Now, both of you reach out with yer magic. Feel the energy of the world around you."

They extended their senses, marveling at how different everything felt. The trees pulsed with life, their roots stretching deep into the earth. The air itself seemed alive, currents of energy swirling around them like invisible rivers.

"Breathe together," Diana murmured. "Let yer power flow as one."

Theodora drew a steady breath, feeling Alexandria's rhythm align with hers. The magic within her surged—no longer chaotic, but sharp and controlled. She felt a subtle pull, as if Alexandria guided her.

"Open yer eyes," Elmer said.

As the girls looked around, they gasped. The world had changed. Faint lines of light seemed to connect everything–the trees, the earth, even the air.

For a moment, Theodora felt as if she could see into Alexandria's very being, experiencing her emotions as her own. Their fears, excitement and determination blended, strengthening their bond.

"Now," Diana whispered, "channel yer energy. Focus on the air around ya."

Theodora felt the magic stir beneath her skin, crackling like a live current. She didn't fight it this time. Instead, she let it flow, reaching for the air around them. As she imagined movement, a breeze swept through the trees, rustling the leaves in response.

Beside her, Alexandria's grip tightened. Theodora felt the shift—their magic merging, yet distinct. While hers surged wild and electric, Alexandria's touch was precise, guiding the wind with practiced control. The breeze sharpened into a gust, whipping their hair and sending leaves swirling.

Theodora laughed, exhilarated by the raw energy sparking at her fingertips, but Alexandria remained focused, holding the wind steady.

"Careful now," Elmer warned. "Don't lose control."

Theodora exhaled, steadying herself. She let the crackling energy within her subside, trusting Alexandria to do the same. Slowly, the wind eased, the air settling once more.

As the last leaf drifted to the ground, Theodora turned, meeting Alexandria's gaze. In that moment, she knew—they were stronger together.

"We did it," Alexandria said, eyes wide. Theodora grinned as she squeezed her hand.

Diana stepped forward, her eyes twinkling. "That was just the start, lasses. Ready for more?"

The twins shared a look, their unspoken answer clear.

"Aye," Theodora said, her voice steady despite her nerves. "What's next?"

Diana smiled. "Let's try somethin' a bit more... elemental."

Suddenly, Theodora noticed warmth emanating from her wrist. Her bracelet lit up in a green glow, pulsating in time with her heartbeat. At the same moment, Alexandria's bracelet mirrored the same reaction.

"Focus on the energy between ye," Elmer instructed. "Build it, but keep control."

Theodora closed her eyes, reaching out to Alexandria. She felt their shared magic growing, powerful and almost overwhelming.

"Good," Diana said. "Now, Theodora, project that energy out. Alexandria, summon the winds."

Theodora concentrated, channeling the power through her body. It felt like fire in her veins. She thrust her hands forward, and a blast of magic erupted from her palms. The air rippled, bending grass and leaves.

Beside her, Alexandria raised her arms. The wind began to swirl around them, growing stronger by the second.

Their bracelets blazed brighter, bathing the clearing in green light. Theodora felt the magic surge through her, stronger than ever.

"Careful," Elmer cautioned over the wind. "Focus, girls."

But Theodora was lost in the rush again. She pushed harder, her energy growing. Alexandria matched her, the wind reaching gale force. Trees groaned, their branches bending.

"Theodora! Alexandria!" Diana shouted. "Ya need to stop!"

Theodora looked at Alexandria, seeing her own mix of excitement and fear. The magic was slipping away from them, growing wilder.

"Alex," she gasped. "We have to stop it!"

They clasped hands, and Theodora felt a jolt of energy. In that moment, teetering between control and chaos, they realized the weight of their power.

With a nod, they focused on stopping the elements. Their bracelets pulsed. Theodora gritted her teeth, straining to pull back the surging power.

Alexandria's eyes blazed with determination. Her connection to the wind shifted, no longer commanding but guiding. The currents slowed at her silent urging.

As the winds subsided, Theodora felt relief wash over her. The trees stilled, leaves rustling softly. Panting, she turned to Alexandria, their eyes meeting in silent victory.

Diana and Elmer approached, looking proud yet cautious. "Well done, lasses," Diana said. "Ye've shown yer potential, but remember—power without control is dangerous."

Theodora nodded, still trying to catch her breath. The magic left her feeling drained yet exhilarated. She glanced at Alexandria, who gave her a small smile.

"We understand," Alexandria said steadily. "It won't happen again."

The distant horizon darkened as sinister forms began to materialize—Lord Valendor's minions. At the far end of the field, Shadow Walkers emerged from nothingness, their flowing dark robes shifting like liquid shadow. They sat atop dreadful mounts, watching in eerie silence, their hollow eyes burning with malevolence.

For a long moment, they remained still, a foreboding presence against the golden hues of the late afternoon sun. Then, as if receiving an unheard command, they urged their mounts forward, moving in eerie unison. The pounding of hooves was slow at first, measured, like the heartbeat of something ancient awakening. Then they quickened their pace, surging toward Theodora and Alexandria.

At the campsite, the warm scent of coffee mixed with the crisp afternoon air. The fire crackled softly, its embers glowing as Finnegan and Killian sat nearby, savoring a rare moment of calm.

Killian stretched his legs out, swirling the coffee in his cup. "Feels almost peaceful," he mused.

Finnegan took a slow sip, gaze drifting to the open field. "Too peaceful."

Then—movement.

Finnegan's grip tightened around his cup. At the far end of the field, the Shadow Walkers had broken into a full gallop, their dark robes billowing like spectral banners. The tension in the air shifted, thickening.

Killian lowered his cup slightly. "That's not good."

The first Shadow Walker raised a jagged blade, its mount kicking up dust.

Finnegan didn't hesitate. He dropped his cup, the tin clattering against the ground.

Killian let out a breath. "Figures." His cup hit the dirt as well.

Then they were running.

Jasper hesitated, but Finnegan and Killian rushed in, weapons drawn, ready to meet the oncoming storm.

An electric charge surged within Theodora, sharpening her senses. She met Alexandria's gaze, an unspoken vow of unity passing between them.

A towering Shadow Walker lunged at Alexandria, its robe rippling as it raised a gleaming blade. Theodora reacted first, a crackling bolt of lightning arcing through the air and slamming into the creature's chest. It reeled back with an ear-splitting screech.

Seizing her moment, Alexandria took a steady breath and focused. The ground trembled beneath her feet. She thrust her hands forward, fingers curling like claws. The earth obeyed.

A nearby tree groaned, its massive roots breaking through the ground twisting unnaturally as if waking from slumber. With a sharp motion, Alexandria sent them lashing outward.

The first root struck a charging Shadow Walker, wrapping around its waist before hoisting it into the air. It writhed, screeching as the roots constricted.

The second root snaked toward another rider, ripping him clean off his mount. The earthbound tendrils coiled around the creature's form, crushing the darkness from its body and cutting short its shriek.

With a final jerk of her wrists, Alexandria tightened her hold. The first Shadow Walker crumpled in on itself before vanishing in a wisp of black smoke. The second followed, leaving only silence in their wake.

Elsewhere, Killian danced with death, his halberd spinning in shimmering arcs. His reckless smile taunted his opponent, inviting challenge.

A Shadow Walker struck at him, aiming for that grin—but met only air. Killian twisted, bringing his halberd around in a swift, fluid motion. The weapon's axe blade sliced clean through the creature's limb, leaving behind nothing but a dark wisp of smoke.

Finnegan was direct. His heavy sword cleaved through a charging Shadow Walker, a burst of sapphire light illuminating the battlefield. A shrill scream echoed as the creature disintegrated.

The remaining foes hesitated, then slithered back into the shadows, their hissing whispers fading into the afternoon air.

The warriors stood firm, chests heaving, weapons gripped tight. Victory was theirs—for now. But the darkness was far from finished.

Alexandria turned to her companions, her voice hoarse but determined. "What was that?"

Elmer and Diana emerged, assessing injuries with keen eyes.

Theodora's gaze flickered. "It was a bloody trap," she muttered.

Diana's somber nod confirmed Theodora's assumption.

Killian put away his halberd. "We must stay on our toes," he stated, his resolve underscoring every word.

Elmer stood firm, his voice steady as he gave the command: "Regroup. Rest. Strategize."

Finnegan barely heard him over the wind rising around them. The air had changed—thick, electric, charged with the promise of a storm. He sniffed, then exhaled sharply. "Storm's comin'," he said, loud enough for the others to hear. "We'll need proper shelter tonight. I'm headin' back ta camp ta sort it."

He turned, already striding across the field when Jasper fell in beside him. "I'll give ye a hand," Jasper said, matching his pace.

Finnegan glanced at him but didn't argue. "Good. First thing, we'll need ta fix the ground—no sense conjurin' tents just ta have 'em sink into the muck."

Jasper nodded, and the two pressed forward, the wind at their backs, ready to prepare for the night ahead.

The group gathered around the fire, their faces illuminated by its flickering light. Elmer's voice broke the silence. "The Shadow

Walkers have been keepin' a close eye, waitin' for this moment. We knew it was bound to happen."

Diana's eyes scanned the darkness beyond their circle. "Now that they've found ya, they won't give up. We must stay ahead of their next move."

Killian's gaze remained steadfast. "We won't be surprised again."

Finnegan, ever the strategist, shared his plan. "We'll fortify our defenses and lay some traps 'round the perimeter. I'll put up some stronger wards 'round the camp as well."

Alexandria added, "We've faced them before and made it through. Together, we can overcome this."

Elmer nodded. "Aye, keep in mind, they feed off of fear and mayhem. We must stay cool-headed and resolute to beat 'em."

United in purpose, the group began strategizing. Each person contributed ideas to outwit their formidable foes. As they deliberated deep into the night, Finnegan retired, planning to rejoin the discussion at breakfast. While the others retreated to their quarters, Elmer, and Diana melted into the shadows, standing watch over the camp.

A few hours later, Jasper emerged from the darkness, his troubled face illuminated by the dying embers. The forest floor muffled his approach as he neared Elmer and Diana at the clearing's edge.

Elmer's hand instinctively reached for his weapon. Recognizing Jasper, he relaxed slightly, but the young man's unease set his nerves on edge.

"What brings you out at this late hour?" Elmer asked, his voice low and cautious.

Diana's piercing gaze studied Jasper, searching for any hint of deception. Despite proving himself a skilled fighter and loyal ally, in a world where allegiances shifted like sand, trust remained a precious commodity.

"Is something bothering ya, Jasper?" Diana probed.

Jasper hesitated, his eyes darting towards the darkened forest as if the trees might overhear. When he finally spoke, his voice was barely above a whisper. "During the brawl, I caught wind of the Shadow Walkers gabbing about a turncoat in our midst. A bloody traitor who could ruin all we've fought for."

The weighty words hung in the air. Elmer and Diana exchanged a knowing glance, their expressions hardening as they processed the news. The thought of a traitor in their midst sent a chill down their spines, colder than the night air that enveloped them.

Elmer's mind raced, sifting through recent events, searching for signs they might have missed. The Shadow Walkers were cunning and ruthless, their dark magic capable of twisting even the most loyal hearts. A traitor could spell doom for their mission and the fate of the kingdom.

"Are ye sure of what ya heard? The Shadow Walkers are notorious for their mind games and trickery." Elmer pressed.

Jasper nodded grimly. "I couldn't catch any names, but their words were crystal. We have a turncoat among us, and they're scheming somethin' devious."

Diana's eyes narrowed, her mind already racing with the implications. As one of the most powerful sorceresses in the land, she knew all too well the devastation a single act of betrayal could bring.

Chapter 20

"STORMS AND SECRETS"

THE MORNING GREETED THEO with a menacing sky. Swirls of dark clouds hovered overhead, ready to burst. She stirred in her sleeping bag, her body ached from yesterday's battle.

Her eyes fell on the backpack. As she reached for her clothes, her fingers brushed against something soft. As she pulled out a blue pouch, its contents spilled out on the floor.

Herbs with forest-thick aromas tumbled out. Glass vials clinked as they rolled out onto the ground-clear, blue, and red.

But it was the folded parchment that captured her attention. Ms. Whoo's elegant script flowed across it: "Knowledge has the power to shape destinies and conquer fears. It is a radiant light that shines through darkness, guiding us towards our true purpose."

Across from her, Alexandria stirred. Seeing Theo's puzzled expression, she moved closer to see what had her confused.

"What's all this?" Alexandria asked.

Theo met her sister's questioning gaze. A moment's pause filled the air; thoughts darted within like startled woodland creatures. The parchment's weight seemed to multiply in her grasp.

"It's from Ms. Whoo," Theo whispered, motioning to the scattered items. "She snuck these in me bag."

Alexandria's brow wrinkled, suspicion evident even in the dim light. "For what, exactly?"

Theodora shrugged. "She always knew when somethin' was about ta happen, before anyone else." As she spoke, unease washed over her. "Or mayhap she knew more than she let on."

Alexandria's gaze shifted between the objects. A sudden gust rattled the tent, its eerie howl breaking the silence. The storm outside mirrored the turmoil brewing within Theo's mind.

She met Alex's probing stare. Ms. Whoo's cryptic message hung heavy between them.

"We need ta figure out what she's tryin' ta tell us," Theo said. "She wouldn't have left these in me bag unless there was a good reason." She carefully returned everything to the pouch. "We'll show these ta Killian and Finnegan. Maybe they'll have some insights on what ta do with 'em."

As Alexandria nodded, lightning illuminated the tent, casting stark shadows. Thunder rumbled close behind, a primal drumbeat echoing through the forest. Moments later, hail began to pound against the canvas like a thousand tiny fists.

As they emerged, the wind lashed at their cloaks. They raced towards Killian and Finnegan's tent, mud squelching under their boots. The scent of wet foliage filled the air. Hail stung their faces and pelted their backs as they struggled forward.

Theodora pushed aside the tent flap. Water cascaded from her cloak like a miniature waterfall. Killian turned, his expression a mix of surprise and concern.

"Finnegan," he called.

He appeared, his blue eyes locking onto the twins. "What's the craic? Somethin' wrong?"

Theodora held out the blue velvet pouch. "Ms. Whoo left these in me bag."

She emptied the contents onto a small cot. Potions and herbs spilled out. The men studied the objects, knowing Ms. Whoo's deep understanding of the dangers, especially those involving Lord Valendor.

"Finnegan, remember when she spoke about the importance of knowledge?" Theodora asked, eyebrows raised.

He nodded. "Aye, she often said knowledge was key to unlockin' our potential. Understandin' our enemies and mysteries would empower us."

She presented the parchment next, reading it aloud. Finnegan moved closer, drawn to the text. "Might I have a gander?"

The moment he touched it, energy pulsed through him. "There's more here," he murmured, handing it to Killian.

Killian's eyes narrowed as he took the paper. He felt a faint vibration in his fingers.

"You're right," he confirmed. "I sense a hidden message within these words."

"How can you tell?" Alex whispered.

Killian pointed to faint symbols hidden in the intricate handwriting. "It's a cipher."

"What's that now?" Jasper asked as he entered.

"It's a hidden code used ta veil a message from prying eyes." His gaze was fixed on the aged parchment before him, as if it held the secrets of the universe.

The twins leaned closer, expressions filled with curiosity. "Can ya decipher it?" Theo asked, eyes shining with hope and apprehension.

Killian studied the intricate symbols and patterns, his mind racing. He reached into his pocket and pulled out a small leather-bound notebook. It contained pages upon pages of transcribed codes and ciphers. Flipping through its worn pages, he found the section dedicated to deciphering messages like this one.

"I will need some time ta translate the markings."

Theodora swept the herbs and potions back into their velvet sanctuary as instructed by Killian. His words still hung in the air–a directive born of caution.

Killian had performed a spell that would keep the fire constantly lit so the girls headed to the campfire. As they sat cross-legged on the weathered logs, the flames danced and flickered, casting ethereal shadows across the ground.

The storm had raged for hours, battering the campsite with howling winds and a relentless mix of hail and snow. The once-fierce gusts had now softened to an occasional whisper through the trees, shaking loose the last bits of ice from their branches. Small white drifts clung stubbornly to the ground, glistening in the firelight.

The girls huddled close to the fire, their cloaks pulled tightly around them. The warmth seeped into their chilled fingers, chasing away the lingering bite of the storm. They had been quiet for some time, their earlier conversation fading into the steady crackling of the fire and the occasional plop of melting hail slipping from the trees.

Finnegan finally joined them, rolling up his sleeves as he crouched near the fire. With practiced ease, he pulled out a small bundle of ingredients from his pack.

"Ah, sure, ye girls must be starvin'," he said, pulling out a knife to chop some root vegetables. "A bit o' stew will do us all some good."

Finnegan glanced up, nodding toward the clearing sky. "See there now? Storm's lost its bite. Just a few last growls before it moves on."

Alexandria followed his gaze, tracking the heavy clouds as they split apart to reveal patches of pale blue. She exhaled slowly and extended her hands toward the flames. "It's about time."

Theodora, arms wrapped around her knees, letting out a tired sigh. "Feels like we've been waitin' ferever."

"Aye, patience, lass," Finnegan chuckled as he dropped a handful of chopped potatoes into the pot. "Rome wasn't built in a day, an' neither are secrets uncovered in a hurry."

As the stew simmered and its herbal aroma filled the clearing, the group huddled closer, finding comfort in the fire's steady glow. Finnegan and the girls sat in quiet anticipation, their minds drifting to the mystery ahead. They waited for Killian's return, eager to learn what he had uncovered in the note from Ms. Whoo, their faces lit by the flickering light.

Inside his tent, Killian poured over the ancient parchment with intense focus, deciphering each intricate symbol with meticulous care born from years of experience. His brow furrowed in concentration as he cross-referenced the markings against the pages of his leather-bound notebook, piecing together the hidden message from Ms. Whoo's note.

Outside, the storm had finally relented, leaving behind a calm stillness that enveloped the campsite in a peaceful embrace. The snowflakes continued to drift down from the darkened sky, their gentle descent a stark contrast to the earlier fury of the tempest.

And then, as if on cue, Killian emerged from his tent, his eyes alight with excitement and triumph. He called out to Theodora and Alexandria, his voice cutting through the late afternoon like a beacon of hope.

"Theo, Alex!" Killian ducked through the tent flap, parchment in hand, his eyes bright with discovery. "I've got it."

The twins looked up from the fire, instantly alert. They recognized that look—Killian had found something. The campfire popped and hissed as everyone gathered, their faces half-lit in the dancing light.

The parchment lay before them, its yellowed surface covered in faded markings that seemed to shift subtly in the firelight. Strange symbols lined the edges, some resembling ancient runes, others unlike anything they'd seen before. Killian leaned forward, keeping his voice low as if the trees themselves might be listening.

"These potions and herbs," he gestured towards the vials and various plants in the blue velvet bag Theo clutched, "are essential components for a powerful spell." His fingers traced the hidden code etched into the parchment, each line, and curve holding a secret meaning. "Within this encrypted cipher lies the key - the words to unlock the spell's full power."

Finnegan leaned in, his brow furrowed. "What's this spell meant ta do?"

"The instructions are specific. Only Theo and Alex can recite it, and it must be done before they confront Lord Valendor."

He read aloud the translated message, his voice filled with anticipation. "Ah, Theo, me lass. When ye and Alex chant this spell, it'll grant ye the power to fend off the dark energies Lord Valendor wields. Even them Shadow Walkers he's brought back to life. With this magic, ye'll be able to counter anythin' he throws at ya and finally defeat him for good."

Theodora and Alexandria exchanged confused glances. "But we thought our combined powers would suffice to rid ourselves of him?" Theo questioned.

Killian nodded, his eyes reflecting the weight of the revelation. "Yer powers alone be strong, but Lord Valendor's magic is ancient and twisted. He's wieldin' dark forces beyond what ye can handle now. This spell will amplify yer abilities, makin' ye his equal match."

Theodora clenched her jaw, the weight of their impending confrontation settling heavily on her shoulders. She exchanged a determined glance with her sister, a silent vow passing between them. "We can't be lettin' him keep our kingdom in his icy grasp any longer."

Alexandria nodded in agreement, her jaw set with resolve. "We must put an end to his tyranny once and for all."

Killian took a deep breath before continuing, "Recitin' this spell will require focus, unity and trust in each other. Do ye think ye'll be able to do it?"

The twins nodded, their eyes tinged with a flicker of fear. The weight of their destiny bore down upon them as they prepared to face Lord Valendor.

As Killian handed the parchment back to Theodora, urgency filled the air. The fire crackled and danced before them, casting long shadows on the ground.

Jasper's gaze flickered between the sisters and Killian, his face holding a calculating expression. He shifted uneasily on the log, his eyes betraying curiosity and apprehension.

"What if this bloody spell goes awry?" he asked.

Killian turned to Jasper, his gaze hardening, and tone unwavering. "If all else fails, this spell is our best shot at taking down Lord Valendor. It's the only other option we have ta save Kandella."

Tension filled the air as Jasper's question lingered, his doubt casting a shadow over their resolve.

Theodora felt defiance rise within her, refusing to let fear cloud her judgment. "Don't ye be worrying, Jasper. The spell will work when and if we need it."

The sky churned with dark clouds above them, heavy with the threat of another storm. A gust of wind blew through the trees, intensifying the charged atmosphere. Nature itself seemed to hold its breath for what was to come.

Theodora rose, her limbs protesting but her will unyielding. She glanced at Alexandria, who mirrored her determination.

"C'mon, Alex," Theodora urged with her thoughts.

"Lead the way," Alexandria replied as she stood up and followed her sister to the training grounds.

They headed to the practice area where targets loomed like specters in the dusk. Theodora notched an arrow, her fingers trembling slightly. But with each breath, she steadied herself. She aligned her shot with the clarity of her purpose.

"Focus, lass," Killian advised as he strode up behind her. His presence was comforting and commanding. "Remember, it's not just about hittin' the target. It's about trustin' your arrow will find its mark 'fore it leaves your bow."

"Got it," she breathed out, banishing the ghosts of doubt that clung to her mind. With a whisper of feathers against leather, she released the tension in her bowstring—and in her heart. The arrow sailed through the air, a harbinger of her growing prowess. It embedded itself in the center of the target.

"See?" Alexandria beamed, her hands aglow with summoned winds. "We are more than our fears."

"Indeed," Theodora agreed, pride swelling in her chest. "We are Carringtons. We harness the storm and command the gales. We shall not falter."

Their laughter mingled with the evening air. Every arrow loosed, every spell cast, brought them closer to reclaiming their heritage and fulfilling their destiny.

Hidden in the shadows, watchful eyes tracked the twins' every move as they trained. The sisters worked in perfect rhythm, unaware they were being observed from the tree line. Each shot Theo landed, their silent audience noted each spell Alex perfected.

"Higher, Alex!" Theo called, grinning as her sister sent a gust of wind to scatter a pile of leaves.

The twins pushed on until the last light faded, too focused on their progress to notice the occasional rustle beyond the clearing's edge. Despite the weight of tomorrow's challenges hanging over them, they found joy in their growing strength.

When the stars finally blanketed the night sky, they lowered their weapons and stood shoulder to shoulder, catching their breath.

"We're getting better," Alex said.

Theo nodded, too exhausted for words. Their muscles ached from hours of practice, minds drained from concentration. They trudged back to their tent, collapsing onto their bedrolls. Sleep claimed them instantly as darkness settled over the camp—while outside, their watchers slipped away into the night.

Yet while Alexandria slept soundly, Theodora's mind wandered into darker territory. She found herself trapped in a realm of writhing shadows that toyed with her worst fears. Standing at the edge of a bottomless pit, she felt the darkness call to her, its whispers icy against her skin.

She leaned forward, watching as twisted figures clawed their way up from the depths. Their misshapen forms seemed to pulse with malice. All around her, voices hissed words of failure and doubt, each syllable chipping away at her confidence.

Unlike the waking world, here Theodora stood completely alone. No Alexandria. No Killian or Finnegan to steady her. The burden of what lay ahead pressed down on her, making each breath a struggle, each thought heavier than the last.

The cold intensified around her, biting through her clothes. Theo's heart hammered against her ribs as she sensed something approaching—something ancient and cruel that watched from just beyond her sight, drawing ever closer with each passing second.

Her mouth opened in a desperate cry for Alexandria, but no sound emerged. The swirling mists devoured her words before they could travel beyond her lips, leaving her trapped in the dream's suffocating silence.

The nightmare tightened its grip as Theo plunged deeper. Each haunting vision dragged her further, sapping her strength to resist. Shadows coiled around her limbs, their touch like winter frost leeching the last traces of warmth as they slithered toward her heart.

Still, in the middle of all the fear and uncertainty, something broke through—a ray of hope. A memory rose to the surface, bright and solid, pushing back the darkness. She could see Alexandria's steady gaze, calm and unshaken. And she could hear the voices of her friends, their quiet encouragement steadying her when she needed it most.

Theo clenched her fists and pushed back against the nightmare's grip. Something in her—maybe stubbornness, maybe courage—refused to surrender. She drew on memories of everything they'd overcome, wielding them like weapons against the darkness.

The shadows retreated inch by grudging inch. The whispers grew fainter, their power diminishing as Theo reclaimed control.

The abyss that had seemed so vast now shrank before her determination, its edges crumbling away like rotting cloth.

Theo stood her ground until the last dark vision crumbled away. The bone-deep chill receded, and she jerked awake in their tent, disoriented. Moonlight filtered through the canvas flap, casting odd patterns that shifted with the gentle night breeze. She pulled in a ragged breath as the nightmare's grip faded, leaving only the solid reality of their shelter around her. Her pulse, which had hammered against her ribs moments before, gradually steadied as she sank back onto her bedroll.

Alexandria slept peacefully beside her, untroubled by whatever darkness had invaded Theo's dreams. Theo watched the play of silver light across the tent ceiling, letting it wash away the remnants of fear. What had seemed overwhelming in sleep now felt conquerable. She'd faced down her own demons and won—perhaps the real enemy wasn't as unbeatable as he seemed.

"Not so tough after all, are ya?" she whispered to the memory of Valendor's shadow.

With a determined nod to herself, Theo tugged her blanket up to her chin. Whatever waited for them tomorrow, they'd meet it head-on. Her eyelids grew heavy as she drifted back to sleep, this time without dark figures lurking at the edges of her consciousness—just the quiet promise of dawn and another chance to fight.

Chapter 21

"Unseen Forces Stir"

Theodora jolted awake, heart hammering, a nameless urgency tightening around her chest. The pre-dawn light filtered weakly through the tent's canvas, casting everything in a ghostly blue hue. Her fingers clutched at the rough woolen blanket, seeking any anchor to reality. The fabric scratched against her palms, grounding her in the present moment.

Her breath came in quick, uneven gasps before slowly steadying. Then she saw it—a faint, pulsing glow emanating from her battered leather backpack. The emerald light beckoned, insistent and urgent.

With trembling fingers, she reached for the pack, the familiar worn leather cool against her skin. The zipper's rasp sounded unnaturally loud in the stillness of the tent as she opened it. There, nestled among her possessions, lay Nabca's ancient tome.

The book seemed alive, its pages rustled as if stirred by an unseen breeze. The eerie green radiance spilled from between the weathered pages, casting dancing shadows on the tent walls. Theodora's throat tightened as she carefully lifted the book, its weight far greater than its size suggested.

As she opened it, the familiar scent of aged parchment and musty leather filled her nostrils. Her eyes fell upon the passage about the eclipse, the words seeming to burn themselves into her retinas. The realization hit her like a physical blow. They were running out of time!

"Alex," Theodora hissed, reaching out to shake her sister's shoulder. "Alex, wake up!"

Alexandria stirred, rubbing her eyes as she fought against the pull of sleep. "Wha-? Theo? What's wrong?"

"The eclipse," Theodora said, her voice tight with panic. "It's the day after tomorrow. We've lost track o' time."

Alexandria's eyes snapped open, instantly shaking off sleep. "Oh no," she whispered, as the seriousness of the situation enveloped her like a shroud. "We need to get going. Now."

As Alexandria went to wake the others, Theodora carefully tucked the book back into her pack. Her hands shook as she fastened the zipper, the finality of the action sending a shiver down her spine.

Outside, the sky was a seething mass of angry clouds, promising a storm to match the turmoil in Theodora's chest. The weak morning light struggled to break through, casting everything in a sickly, washed-out hue.

Finnegan's gruff voice broke the tense silence that had fallen upon the bunch as they clustered around the dying embers of their fire. His rugged face betrayed a sense of worry, and his piercing blue eyes glinted with resolve. "We've got no bleedin' choices left," he said staunchly. "The hour is at hand."

Theodora straightened her back, finding strength in Finnegan's unwavering stare. "We need ta make it to Nau," she said, her voice steady despite her nerves. "Th' griffins will take us over ta Carrantou."

Finnegan paused. "Ye're certain 'bout this, lass?"

"Yes," Theodora said. "I'm certain."

They set off, the threatening sky a constant reminder of the danger ahead. Theodora's nerves were on edge, every sound making her jump. The once-welcoming forest now felt sinister.

"We can do this," Alexandria murmured. "Together, remember?"

Theodora nodded gratefully, but doubt still nagged at her. The path ahead looked treacherous, but they had no choice. Kandella's fate hung in the balance.

After hours of travel, Killian suggested stopping for lunch and rest. Theo's heart pounded as she looked around. Tall trees lined the narrow path, their branches reaching out. An eerie silence hung in the air, broken only by distant rustling leaves. Something felt wrong.

Sitting cross-legged on the mossy ground, Theo watched Killian sort through their supplies. Unlike her, his face showed no doubt. He seemed sure of their path and mission. Theo wondered if they were truly prepared for what lay ahead.

Killian's warm voice broke into her thoughts. "Theo, look how far we've come," he said encouragingly. "Don't be lettin' yer doubts cloud yer judgment now."

Theo forced a smile. "Aye, ye're right. Everything's riding on our success."

As they ate, Theo observed her companions. Alex and Jasper were sharing a rare light moment. Finnegan sat nearby, watching the horizon intently. And Killian caught her eye and smiled reassuringly.

Moving on, the forest grew denser and darker. Tension built in Theo's shoulders with each step. The path narrowed dangerously. Suddenly, she felt a chill. Her instincts screamed a warning - they weren't alone.

The afternoon air split with an unearthly shriek as Shadow Walkers swarmed from the treeline. Their ghostly forms flickered in and out of sight, sunlight glinting off razor-sharp claws and fangs. Killian and Finnegan stood ready—Killian gripping his halberd, Finnegan's sword gleaming in the light.

The first wave hit like a storm. Killian's halberd cleaved through rotted bone, Finnegan's blade flashing as he cut down one creature after another. But no matter how many fell, more rose from the darkness.

Theodora's pulse pounded. They were being surrounded. She hurled a bolt of lightning into the horde, white-hot energy tearing through several creatures. Alexandria moved beside her, summoning wind that sent the enemy reeling before the ground split open beneath them, jagged roots dragging them into the earth.

Killian gritted his teeth. "There be too many!"

"Aye!" Finnegan growled. "And they're not slowin'!"

Theodora barely dodged a swipe from a Shadow Walker before striking it down with a surge of electricity.

Stay close!" Alexandria shouted, hurling a stream of searing blue flames at the shadow walkers. The fire roared as it engulfed the black-robed figures, their bony bodies twisting as the rotted flesh clinging to them sizzled and peeled away. The attackers shrieked and recoiled from the blaze. "We have to keep moving!"

Then Theodora heard it—Finnegan's cry.

She spun around just in time to see clawed hands, gnarled and blackened like twisted roots, latching onto his arms. Finnegan thrashed, his eyes wide with terror, but the creatures were relentless, their elongated fingers digging into his flesh. His sword clattered to the ground, the metal ringing against the stone before being swallowed by the dirt.

"Theodora!" he choked out, his voice raw with fear.

The shadows of the forest yawned open, and in a heartbeat, he was gone.

"FINNEGAN!" Her scream tore from her throat as she threw a bolt of lightning, but it was too late.

Killian roared, his halberd crashing down with brutal force. "WHERE IS HE?!" But there was no answer—only the endless wails of their enemies.

Alexandria grabbed her sister. "We have to go!"

"No!" Theodora tore free, her golden eyes blazing. "I won't leave him!"

"Ye can't save him if we all die here!" Killian snapped, grief twisting in his face. He swung his halberd with ruthless force, cutting through another Shadow Walker.

Theodora's breath was ragged, fury clouding her thoughts. She wanted to burn them all down, to chase the darkness until she ripped Finnegan free herself.

Alexandria put her hands on Theodora's shoulders. "Listen to me! We'll get him back—but we need a plan!"

Theodora exhaled sharply, then unleashed one final bolt of lightning. The sky cracked open, white-hot energy slamming into the ground. Heat rippled through the air, and the earth trembled. Shadow Walkers shrieked as their rotting flesh smoldered, hesitation flickering in their hollow eyes.

Then, one by one, they fled, their eerie wails swallowed by the night.

Silence fell. Theodora swayed, her breath unsteady. Her knees buckled, but Alexandria lunged, catching her before she hit the ground.

"I got you," she murmured, holding her firm.

Sparks still flickered at Theodora's fingertips. Finnegan was gone, torn from them like he was nothing. And those wretched things had fled, as if they hadn't just stolen him.

Her vision blurred—not from exhaustion, but from seething rage. Power crackled through her veins, restless and ravenous, aching to be unleashed.

They weren't done.

"Then let's make a plan," she said, her voice like thunder. "Because we're bringing him home."

Theodora stood frozen, her chest tight with grief. Their mission had failed, and the weight of it pressed down on her, crushing and relentless. How could they go on without their leader? Without Finnegan? The path ahead felt empty, impossible.

A shuddering breath escaped her, and suddenly, tears began to spill down her cheeks. She hadn't even realized she was crying.

A sudden rush of wind whipped around her, rustling leaves and stirring the dust at her feet. She blinked through her tears, her breath hitching as a massive shadow loomed over her.

Where her owl guardian had been just moments ago now stood something far greater—Khadall, but not as she had ever seen him.

A griffin.

His golden feathers gleamed under the afternoon sun, powerful wings tucking against his muscular frame. His sharp amber eyes met hers, unwavering and full of purpose.

"We'll get him back," he said, his voice calm but unwavering.

Theodora's breath caught.

This wasn't possible.

Khadall had been her guardian for years—her protector, her guide. She had trusted him with her life. But she had never known. Never suspected. Her mind reeled, struggling to reconcile the familiar warmth of his presence with the staggering power now standing before her.

"You... you can shift?" Her voice barely rose above a whisper.

Awe and disbelief crashed over her like a wave, momentarily drowning out her despair. The grief that had pressed so heavily on her chest loosened, if only for a moment. But as the initial shock faded, doubt crept back in.

She wanted to believe him. She needed to. But could she?

She questioned everything—her abilities, their mission, herself.

Khadall gently nudged her with his beak. "Believe in yerself, Theodora," he urged. "You're not alone in this fight."

She looked into his eyes again, drawing comfort from his steady gaze. "I dunno if I've got it in me," she whispered.

He nuzzled his head against her, and the softness of his feathers tickled her cheek. "I believe in ya," he whispered. "And I'll always be here ta support ya."

Anxiety churned in Theodora's gut as they pressed forward, searching for a place to rest. Every plan she imagined saving Finnegan felt doomed before it even began. The weight of their failure clung to her like a second skin.

The sun hung low, casting long shadows through the towering trees. The thick canopy muted the afternoon light, bathing the forest in a dim, golden haze. The air carried the scent of damp earth and charred wood, remnants of their battle still clinging to the land.

The forest stretched endlessly around them, shadows shifting between the trees. Killian finally halted in a small clearing, his sharp gaze sweeping their surroundings before he crouched. With practiced ease, he struck flint to steel, coaxing a flame to life.

The flames crackled, their glow stretching across the group. Theodora eased onto a fallen log, rubbing her arms as the tension in her chest refused to settle.

They sat in silence, exhaustion pressing down on them. But silence was dangerous. It left too much room for thoughts—for guilt.

Alexandria shattered it with a sharp breath. "We can't just sit here while Finnegan's out there in danger!"

Her words hit like a slap in the face. Theodora gripped the log beneath her, steadying herself against the emotions threatening to pull her under.

Jasper snorted, his voice sharp. "Oh, aye? And what's yer brilliant plan then? Stumble about through the woods, hopin' we trip over him?"

The fire popped, filling the heavy silence that followed. Even Alexandria, usually quick to snap back, clenched her fists in quiet frustration.

Theodora's jaw tightened. She wanted to argue, but the bitter truth sat heavy on her tongue. Charging in without a plan would only get them all killed.

Killian exhaled, his voice cutting through the tension. "That's enough." His gaze swept over them before landing on Jasper. His expression hardened.

"And where the hell were you while the rest of us were fightin' the Shadow Walkers?"

The crackle of flames filled the silence.

Jasper's smirk faltered, his fingers tapping nervously against his knee. His usual air of smug detachment wavered—just for a second. Theodora narrowed her eyes, watching him closely.

For the first time that night, Jasper looked uneasy.

Jasper exhaled sharply, shaking his head as if he couldn't believe what he was hearing. "Ah, for gods' sake," he muttered, dragging a hand through his tousled hair. "I wasn't hidin', if that's what yer accusin' me of."

Killian didn't blink. "Then where were ye?"

Jasper's fingers twitched against his knee, but his expression quickly smoothed into something more controlled. "Scoutin' ahead," he said, leaning forward slightly. "While the rest o' ye were fightin', I was tryin' to cut 'round their flank. Thought if I could find a weak spot, I could take one o' them out 'fore they noticed." He let out a slow breath, shaking his head. "Didn't work. By the time I got into position, they were already retreatin'."

Theodora studied his face, searching for cracks in his story. His usual smirk was gone, replaced with something that almost looked like regret.

Alexandria narrowed her eyes. "An' ye didn't think to call out? Let us know what ye were doin'?"

Jasper scoffed. "Aye, 'cause shoutin' in the middle of a battle is real smart. Figured I'd have a better chance o' helpin' if I kept quiet. Turns out, I miscalculated. It happens." He leaned back against the tree, crossing his arms. "Not much else to say."

Theodora exchanged a glance with Killian. It sounded reasonable. Jasper was reckless, but he wasn't a coward. An' if he had been trying to flank the enemy, it would explain why they hadn't seen him.

Killian held Jasper's gaze a moment longer before exhaling through his nose. "Fine," he said, his voice low. "But next time, ye let us know what ye're plannin' before ye run off."

Jasper gave a mock salute. "Aye, Captain."

The tension in the clearing didn't fully ease, but for now, it was enough. The fire crackled between them as they turned their thoughts back to what mattered most.

Finding Finnegan.

Killian rose from his spot near the fire, his broad shoulders tense as he paced, the flickering flames casting restless shadows across his face. His boots scuffed against the dirt, his muttering barely audible over the crackle of burning wood. He looked like a man ready to fight, but with nowhere to swing his blade.

Alexandria watched him for a moment before speaking. "What are you doin'?" she asked, her brow arching.

"Tryin' ta come up with a plan," Killian grumbled, not breaking stride.

Theodora sat still, watching him. His frustration mirrored the turmoil in her own chest—the helplessness, the anger, the gnawing uncertainty of where Finnegan had been taken.

Jasper emerged from the shadows of a gnarled oak, his expression pinched with frustration. "But we've not a damn clue where they took 'im," he said, raking a hand through his hair. "We could wander these woods fer days an' still be no closer."

Silence fell over the group, thick with unspoken fears.

Then, something clicked.

Theodora's breath hitched as a memory surfaced—one that sent a jolt through her like a spark catching dry kindling. "Wait," she whispered. "I may have an idea." Killian stopped pacing, his sharp gaze snapping to Theodora. "What are ye thinkin', lass?"

She hesitated, her fingers curling into her palms as she forced herself to say it aloud. "When I was in Monaghan forest with

Finnegan... I tripped over a root. Fell flat on me face," she admitted, a hint of something bitter in her tone. "But when I hit the ground, somethin' else hit me." She swallowed hard. "I saw our parents bein' dragged away by the Shadow Walkers."

Silence.

Killian, Jasper and Alexandria all stared at her, their faces scrunched in confusion.

Jasper frowned. "What do ye mean, like a vision?"

Killian crossed his arms, glancing between them. "Ye saw the past?"

Theodora exhaled sharply. *It's hard to explain*, she admitted, her thoughts brushing against Alexandria's mind. Can ye do it?

Alexandria's lips pressed into a thin line. *You could if you tried, Theo.*

Maybe, Theodora conceded, *but I dunno how to put it into words right now. Please?*

A moment passed. Alexandria sighed, but there was no frustration in it—only understanding. *Alright*, she replied. *I got you.*

She turned to the others. "Theo means that when she touches certain objects, she can see past events tied to them. If she touches one tree he passed by, there's a chance she could get a vision from one of them."

Jasper raised an eyebrow, skepticism flickering in his eyes, but Killian nodded, his mind already working.

"Ye think ye can track 'em that way?" he asked.

Theodora steadied herself. "I won't know 'til I try. But it's better than sittin' here doin' nothin'."

Alex added, optimism lacing her words, "If there's even a slim chance of finding Finnegan, we've got to try."

For the first time since they set up camp, the weight of helplessness began to lift. It wasn't much. But it was a start.

A tense silence settled over the group as they exchanged determined glances. Without a word, they agreed to pursue Theodora's plan.

Retracing their steps through the dense forest, Theodora felt a strange tingling sensation wash over her. The trees seemed to hum with an otherworldly energy, connecting past and present. She approached a gnarled oak, its bark rough under her fingertips as she closed her eyes and focused on Finnegan.

A sudden image flashed in her mind - Finnegan, alive but imprisoned in a vast, shadowy dungeon. Eerie runes pulsed on the stone walls, their light casting shifting shadows across the chamber.

Theodora's eyes snapped open, her voice cracking with disbelief. "Finnegan's alive!"

"Ye saw him?" Killian demanded, closing the gap between them in two quick strides. His piercing gaze bore into hers, a mix of hope and desperation etched across his face.

Theodora nodded, her words tumbling out in a rush. "Aye, in some kind of dungeon. It was dark, but these strange runes on the walls... They were glowing. We've got ta get ta him, Killian."

Killian's brow furrowed, a grim understanding settling over him. "Sounds like the sorcerer's keepin' him in the warded cells. Them runes'll keep his powers in check, but..." He paused, choosing his next words carefully. "At least we know he's still breathin'. For now."

Alexandria squeezed Theodora's shoulder reassuringly. Theo inhaled sharply, her fingers curling into fists at her sides. Her chest tightened, and she forced herself to swallow the lump rising in her throat. She turned away, staring hard at the snow covered ground as if searching for an answer. "What if I fail him again?" she whispered, her voice barely steady.

"None of that," Alex said. "We all share the blame here."

Theodora's heart clenched at Alexandria's words, a mixture of gratitude and lingering guilt swirling in her chest. She met her sister's gaze, emerald eyes reflecting a storm of emotions. The weight of Finnegan's absence pressed down on her, threatening to crush her resolve.

She wiped away the tears with the back of her hand and nodded. "Yer right, Alex. We can't let this break us. Finnegan wouldn't want that."

Alexandria squeezed her shoulder, the warmth of her touch anchoring Theodora to the present.

A gust of wind whipped through the trees, and thunder rumbled in the distance. Theodora drew a long breath, letting the crisp air clear her mind. She pulled her cloak close, the familiar weight of her bow pressing against her back.

"Come on," she said, her voice growing stronger with each word. "We need to eat and plan our next move. Every moment counts now."

The campfire crackled, its warmth a stark contrast to the chill that had settled in Theodora's bones. Killian hunched over a battered pot, stirring something that smelled of herbs and spices. The aroma mingled with the earthy scent of pine, creating an oddly comforting blend.

"Here," Killian said, passing her a steaming bowl. "Eat up. Ye'll need yer strength."

Theodora nodded gratefully, her fingers curling around the warm pottery. She took a quick sip, the rich flavor spreading across her tongue. It tasted of home and safety, things that felt impossibly far away now.

As she ate, her mind raced with possibilities and fears. The shadows between the trees seemed to grow darker, more menacing. She caught Alexandria watching her, concern etched across her face.

"Whatcha thinking?" Alexandria asked softly, leaning in close.

Theodora set down her bowl, her appetite fading. "We need ta move," she said, her voice low and urgent. "We need ta continue on ta Nau."

As they began to pack up camp, the wind picked up, howling through the trees like a mournful spirit. Theodora's hair whipped around her face, and she shivered despite the warmth of her cloak.

"Ye feel that?" Killian murmured, falling into step beside her. His hand rested on the hilt of his halberd, muscles tense and ready.

Theodora nodded grimly, her own fingers tightening around her bow. "Aye. Like we're bein' watched."

The forest seemed to press in around them, branches reaching out like gnarled fingers. Every shadow held the potential for danger, every rustle of leaves a potential threat. Theodora's heart pounded in her chest, but she forced herself to remain calm.

As they pressed on towards Nau, the sky darkened ominously. Thunder rumbled in the distance, a promise of the storm to come. Theodora felt the first trickle of hail on her face, cold and sharp.

She glanced back at her companions, their faces set with determination despite the fear that lingered in their eyes. Theodora squared her shoulders, her resolve hardening with each step.

The path stretched before them, winding into the depths of the forest. Shadows danced at the edge of her vision, and she couldn't shake the feeling that they were walking into a trap. But there was no turning back now.

Chapter 22

"Whispers of Betrayal"

Alexandria's gaze fell onto Theodora, her heart pounding as a storm of fears churned within her chest. She fought to keep her expression steady, to project an air of calm and strength—the rock her sister needed. But watching Theodora's face, etched with pain and uncertainty, tore open wounds she had long hidden. Old doubts surged to the surface, whispering subtle questions: Did she truly belong here? Could she ever prove worthy of the legacy others had given her?

Her entire life had remained firmly planted in the mortal realm, far from magic and prophecy. The weight of her newfound destiny pressed down on her like iron chains, unyielding in their demands. How could she—a girl untrained, untested, a stranger to this mystical world—stand as her sister's equal, her guide through a fate fraught with danger?

Yet she shoved her doubts into the far corners of her mind, swallowing down the raw ache that clawed at her throat. Theodora needed her to be strong, an anchor in this whirlwind of chaos. She clung to the remnants of her courage, fingers curling into tight fists as she willed herself not to break. There would be time, later, to shatter, to let her own fears pour out. But not now. Now, she must be an unyielding pillar of strength, even if she was trembling inside.

As the sun dipped below the mountains, casting long shadows across the land, Theodora felt her confidence slip. The weight of what lay ahead pressed down on her chest, cold and unrelenting. She glanced at Alexandria beside her—steadfast and fierce—but instead of reassurance, she felt doubt tugging at her heart.

"The road ahead is dangerous," Theodora said, more to herself than to her sister. "But we can't turn back now."

Alexandria's eyes narrowed, her voice sharp. "Saying we won't turn back is one thing. Surviving is another. Power doesn't mean safety, Theo. Do you really think our bond alone will protect us from what's coming?"

Theodora flinched but held her ground. "I know what ye're sayin'. Our bond isn't a shield—but it's not just that. It's everythin' we've fought for an' everything we've lost."

Alexandria crossed her arms tightly, shifting her weight from one foot to the other. Her jaw tensed, but she didn't interrupt.

Theodora took a steadying breath, her voice thick with emotion as she pressed on. "If we turn back, we lose everythin'—our parents, gone forever; Kandella frozen while Valendor squeezes the life from it." Her hands clenched at her sides, and her voice wavered under the weight of it all. "I can't let that happen. I won't."

She swallowed hard and locked eyes with Alexandria, her gaze unflinching. "Ye think I don't see the risk? I feel it in me bones. But I'd rather die with me bow in me hand than live knowin' I walked away when I could've fought. We've come too far ta let Valendor win now."

Alexandria's eyes didn't waver, but her lips parted slightly, as if searching for words that refused to come. Her breath caught in her throat, and for a second, silence stretched between them.

Raw and undisguised pain etched Theodora's face, yet beneath it burned a fierce, unbending resolve.

"D'ye doubt me, then? D'ye doubt us?"

Alexandria shook her head slowly, her chest tightening as a humorless laugh slipped out. "Doubt you?" Her voice cracked, softer now, as if the truth stung more than she wanted to admit. "Maybe I do."

She took a step back, running trembling hands through her tangled hair. "They ripped us apart before, didn't they?" Her gaze dropped to the ground, then rose, steel sharpening in her eyes. "What makes this time different?"

She stood there, shoulders stiff, a storm of emotion brewing just beneath the surface, caught between fear and something far harder to name.

Her eyes, once filled with hope, now seemed lost. "The prophecy doesn't care that we're sisters. The kingdom doesn't care." She shook her head, voice barely above a whisper. "This thing we're facing has existed for years, Theo. It crushed better fighters than us. What makes you think we stand a chance?" The fear in her voice was undeniable, a stark contrast to the anger she'd tried to mask. Each word felt like a weight pressing down on her chest.

Theodora struggled to maintain eye contact with Alexandria, feeling a mix of emotions twist within her chest. The heavy silence hung between them, charged with unspoken fears and a deep uncertainty about what might come next.

"I don't know if we do," she finally admitted, her voice low. "But I know what happens if we don't try." She swallowed hard. "Look, I'm scared too. Terrified, actually."

She reached for Alexandria's hand, half-expecting her to pull away. When she didn't, Theodora squeezed it.

"We've both lost too much ta walk away now," she continued. "This isn't about some grand prophecy anymore. It's about Finnegan. It's about our parents. This fight is not just ours ta bear, but also for those who cannae defend themselves. It's about not lettin' that bastard win after everythin' he's taken from us."

Alexandria's fingers tightened around hers. "And if we fail?"

"Then at least we went down fightin'," Theodora said, a stubborn edge creeping into her voice. "Together this time. Not alone, not separated. That's the difference." She held her sister's gaze, unflinching, as she continued, "I can't promise we'll win, but I can promise I won't leave yer side again. Whatever comes, we face it as sisters."

Something shifted in Alexandria's expression—not quite hope, but determination. She nodded once, sharp and decisive.

"Together, then," she said. "God help anyone who gets in our way."

As they continued through the forest, an eerie silence enveloped the group. Killian's battle-honed instincts prickled with unease as he observed Jasper's subtle interactions. The young man's charming facade seemed to slip, revealing a guarded demeanor.

"Is all well, Jasper?" Killian asked, his voice laced with suspicion.

Jasper's grin didn't quite stretch to his eyes as he answered back, "Aye, just keepin' me peepers peeled for trouble."

"Indeed," Killian muttered, unconvinced. His hand strayed towards his weapon, a reflex born from years of caution.

Jasper's mask faltered before he composed himself. "Just the weight of our mission, Killian," he replied, though his eyes darted towards the forest's menacing shadows.

Killian's piercing blue eyes bore into Jasper, unyielding in their intensity. The young man's veneer was cracking, revealing glimpses of hidden motives.

"Ye carry a heavy load, that's for sure," Killian acknowledged, his tone tinged with warning. "But we're all in this together. Trust is everything, especially in times of doubt."

Jasper's grin flickered before he regained composure. "Aye. Ye have me word that I'm fully committed to the cause," he assured, though his words rang hollow in the tense atmosphere between them.

Killian cleared his throat, looking around the weary faces of the group. "Let's take a breather," he said, his voice steady. "We've all had a long day, and with the road ahead, best to keep our strength up. How 'bout we grab a quick bite? Food always makes things a bit clearer, eh?"

Before anyone could reach for their packs, Khadall, perched nearby, gave a low hoot, his amber eyes gleaming with a mix of care and mischief. "No need to wear yerselves out rustlin' through bags," he cooed. "I know ye all are dead on yer feet, so allow me to whip up somethin' that'll warm ye right up."

With a graceful sweep of his wide wings, Khadall stirred the air, summoning a spark that quickly grew into a flickering fire at the camp's center. He tilted his head and muttered a few ancient words, his feathers shimmering faintly. A soft hum of energy pulsed through the clearing as a smooth stone slab materialized above the flames. Moments later, golden-brown flatbreads appeared, their crisp edges curling slightly as they cooked, releasing the warm scent of honey and spice. Beside them, a platter of ripe berries and soft cheese shimmered into existence, accompanied by slices of roasted venison, its rich aroma mingling with the warmth of the fire.

Theodora's eyes lit up, her weariness melting as she breathed in the savory aroma, while Alexandria offered a grateful nod to their feathered friend.

"Now that's more like it," Killian chuckled, settling down near the fire. "Never knew an owl with a knack for cookin'."

Khadall puffed his chest, dipping his head in a half-bow. "Ah, well, I'm not just any owl, am I?" he hooted, flaring his wings as he gracefully distributed portions of the meal. With a flick of his talons, golden-brown flatbreads floated onto wooden plates, accompanied by generous slices of roasted venison, ripe berries and soft cheese. The plates warmed their hands as they accepted the feast, each feeling a spark of renewed energy as they savored the rich flavors, the warmth of the meal settling deep into their weary bones.

They ate in a peaceful silence, the warmth of the fire and Khadall's meal lifting the group's spirits. When they'd finished, Killian lifted his canteen in a small toast. "To strength—and to friends with magical feathers," he said, casting a grateful look at Khadall.

One by one, they raised their drinks, feeling fortified and ready for the journey ahead.

As the group finished their meal, an uneasy silence settled over the camp. Killian's gaze drifted to Jasper, who sat apart from the rest, eyes darting toward the shadowed forest. Finally, he stood, stretching his limbs with feigned ease. "Need ta stretch me legs," he murmured, as if trying to justify the solitude he sought. Then, with a final, sidelong glance he slipped into the darkened woods.

Killian waited until he had vanished into the shadows, then rose quietly to follow, each step muffled by the snow-covered ground. The forest stretched around him, hushed and cold, the night air thick with an eerie silence. Moonlight filtered through twisted branches, casting a faint silvery light over the snow, illuminating his path but deepening the shadows ahead.

Jasper moved with purpose, weaving smoothly among the trees. Killian kept his distance, watching as Jasper navigated the forest with a confidence that only fed his suspicions. Then, just as Killian neared a cluster of ancient oaks, he lost sight of him in the tangle of trees and mist.

He paused, straining his ears for the faintest sound. Minutes passed in silence, broken only by the distant rustle of branches and the crunch of his own boots on frozen ground. Frustration gnawed at him as he realized Jasper had slipped beyond his reach. Gritting his teeth, Killian retraced his steps, reluctantly making his way back to camp.

As he emerged from the trees, Killian froze. Jasper was already there, sitting by the fire as if he'd never left. Every instinct screamed that something wasn't right.

"Lost yer way in the woods, Killian?" Jasper's tone was casual, almost teasing, but there was something guarded in his eyes as he looked up.

Killian forced a smile, though his mind raced. "Just takin' in the night air," he replied.

Jasper's gaze flickered, but he simply shrugged, stoking the fire without another word. Killian settled down across from him, his senses on high alert. He couldn't prove anything yet, but he knew he'd stumbled upon something dangerous. The silence stretched taut between them, as if both were waiting for the other to break.

As the fire crackled, Killian silently vowed to keep watch. Jasper's betrayal wouldn't go unchallenged—but he needed to be cautious. Too much was at stake, and he couldn't risk tipping his hand before he was certain of Jasper's intentions.

The campfire crackled softly, casting flickering shadows across the trees. Alexandria jabbed at the flames with a stick, her frustration growing with each passing moment. Across from her, Theodora sat with her arms crossed, foot tapping restlessly against the dirt. The night pressed in around them, too still, too quiet. The energy beneath their skin refused to settle.

Alexandria exhaled sharply. "I feel like we should be doing something," she muttered, tossing the stick into the fire with more force than necessary.

Theodora's eyes flicked toward the tree line. She'd noticed a small clearing earlier, just beyond the camp. The memory tugged at her now, as if calling to her.

"Come on," she said suddenly, pushing to her feet. Alexandria blinked up at her, startled. "There's a clearin' not far from here. Let's go practice our magic."

A spark lit in Alexandria's eyes, frustration giving way to anticipation. She stood without question, her pulse quickening. "Lead the way."

Theodora moved swiftly through the trees, her sister close behind. The cool night air clung to their skin as they stepped into the moonlit clearing. The space felt different somehow—charged.

"Let's focus on our own powers first," Theodora said, her voice barely above a whisper. "Feel it. Control it. Then we'll bring them together—just like Diana and Elmer taught us."

They closed their eyes.

Alexandria pulled her focus inward, steadying her breath as heat bloomed in her chest and rolled down her arms. It started small, like a spark catching dry kindling, then built into something brighter, steadier. She held it there, letting it grow.

Next to her, Theodora stood still, fingers twitching as light shimmered at her hands. Her magic moved sharper, quick and restless, but she kept it in check, guiding it like wind caught in sails.

The pressure built as their powers grew. Alexandria's magic hummed under her skin. Theodora's crackled in the air between them. Their eyes met—nervous, excited.

"Ready?" Theodora asked.

Alexandria nodded.

They let their magic reach out.

It hit at first—two forces colliding—but then something shifted. The energy twisted, caught, and began to move as one. Still wild, but aligned. Seamless in a way that felt instinctual, like it had always known how to do this.

Alexandria gasped as the force moved through her—not painful, but raw and overwhelming. Like being caught in a current just strong enough to lift her off her feet.

Just breathe, Alex. Theodora's voice cut through the noise, calm and steady.

Alexandria's grip tightened, fingers locked with her sister's as the magic under her skin stirred—bright, restless, alive.

That's it. Hold steady, Theodora said, grounding them both.

The wind picked up, swirling gently around them. Strands of hair lifted across their faces. Sparks flickered between their joined hands, soft at first, then brighter, growing with each passing second. Alexandria's breath caught. The air buzzed, not heavy, but charged—like the moment before a summer storm.

Theo... this feels different, she managed, her thoughts shaky, slipping through their connection.

Aye. Because it is, Theodora said, eyes locked on hers, lit with focus and fire.

They stood there, stunned. Breathless. Hands still clenched, power humming beneath their skin.

Theodora met Alexandria's wide stare, her own chest heaving. And for the first time, they saw it—what they were capable of. Not luck. Not fear. Not chaos.

Power. Controlled. Channeled. Theirs.

A sharp laugh slipped out of Alexandria—half shock, half thrill. Theodora blinked, her eyes stinging, heart pounding with something sharp and aching. Relief. Understanding. Maybe even fear—at how fast everything had shifted.

They reached for each other, instinctive, and wrapped their arms around one another. The magic still danced in the air around them—but slowly, it began to fade. The light dimmed. The wind stilled. The clearing settled into quiet, like the world was exhaling with them.

"I felt you," Theodora whispered, her voice thick with emotion. "Like you were right there with me."

Alexandria nodded into her shoulder. "We did that. Together."

The words landed like a vow. Quiet. Unshakable.

After a beat, Theodora pulled back just enough to look at her. "And I don't think that was even our full strength," she said. "Not yet."

The magic had gone still—but something deeper had awakened. And neither of them could ignore it now..

Nearby, Alex sank onto a fallen log, her red curls tumbling over her shoulders, catching the moon's light like molten copper. She exhaled slowly, feeling the weight of the night settle around her. The Opalite stones on their wrists shimmered, pulsing with an energy that stirred something deep within her—a sense of awakening, of possibility.

A sharp intake of breath snapped her attention to Theodora. Her sister sat rigid, eyes locked on the ancient grimoire sprawled open on the forest floor. The pages fluttered as if touched by unseen fingers, though the air around them was still.

Theodora's pulse thundered in her ears. "No," she whispered, shaking her head. "That's not possible." Her satchel lay beside her, buckled shut, exactly as she had left it. She reached for it, fingers trembling, and unclasped the flap. Inside, the space where the grimoire had been was empty.

"I didn't take it out," she murmured.

Alex leaned forward, her gaze flicking between her sister and the book. "Then how in God's name did it get on the ground?"

"I've no idea." Theodora hesitated, then extended a cautious hand toward the grimoire. The moment her fingertips brushed the edge of the parchment, a ripple of warmth coursed up her arm, like dipping into sun-warmed water. She pulled back sharply, staring at Alex.

Alex's expression was unreadable, but her eyes gleamed with something between curiosity and knowing. "Maybe it's trying to tell us something," she said softly. "Maybe there's something in there we can use. "It could be exactly what we need to understand all this."

Theodora swallowed hard. The stone on her wrist flickered in response, as if echoing her unspoken fears. The book hadn't just appeared. Someone placed it there. Or worse—it had moved itself.

She met Alex's gaze, uncertainty warring with reluctant determination. Then, with a steadying breath, she turned back to the grimoire and flipped the page.

Together, they hunched over the ancient book, studying the faded symbols with quiet intensity. Buried among cryptic warnings and instructions, they discovered a passage about the bracelets—and the dormant power they contained.

Theodora ran her finger along the weathered text, pulse quickening. "Look here," she said, leaning closer. "It says we need clear minds and strong intentions ta make these work properly. Can't be doubtin' ourselves or the magic won't respond."

Alex frowned, her attention caught by darker text further down. "There's more," she said, voice dropping to barely above a whisper. "If we lose control—if we let fear take over—these things could backfire.."

The grimoire described a ritual that demanded complete harmony between their minds and the crystals. Like before they would need to stand facing each other, hands joined, eyes closed. Then, they would have to focus on a single memory filled with love. Only then would the Opalite respond to their command. But the warning that followed was clear: once started, any disruption could break more than just the spell. The magic, if mishandled, could turn violent—potentially harming them both.

The clearing was quiet for a long moment, the hum of magic now a gentle, soothing presence around them. Theodora and Alexandria sat in the soft, glowing light, their breaths still heavy but in sync with the steady pulse of the stones. They stared at each other, a silent understanding passing between them—each of them feeling the weight of the magic, the responsibility and the fear that still lingered in the air.

Alex's eyes glistened with unshed tears, but there was a new strength in her gaze now. The raw vulnerability she'd felt moments before had been tempered by something deeper. Something unshakable.

Theodora broke the silence, her voice soft yet resolute. "Alex…" She paused, taking a breath as she studied her sister. "Ye ready to try again? We know what we need ta do now, with Nabca's words in mind."

Alex swallowed hard, nodding with a fierce determination she hadn't known she possessed. "I think… I think I am." She leaned closer to Theodora, her hands reaching for her sister's once more, the warmth of their connection grounding her.

Together, they stood up and walked back to the center of the clearing, their footsteps silent on the soft snow covered ground, each of them knowing this was their moment. They stood there, taking a breath in unison as they prepared to face the magic once again.

Theodora glanced at the opalite stones, their glow now a soft pulse, as if waiting for them to try again. "Let's start slow, like Nabca suggested. No rush. We'll build it up together."

Alex nodded, the weight of their task heavy in her chest, but now, there was a sense of calm that had settled between them. She felt the love from earlier still swirling within her, now intertwined with the steady, growing resolve she had to protect her sister, to protect everything they had left.

"Right," she whispered, her voice steady now. "Let's do this."

Fingers laced together in the quiet glade, the sisters stood still, letting the forest's sounds fade to background noise. The stones' energy pulsed through them—not just around them, but part of them now. They both knew this attempt was different. No desperation, no fear driving them forward. Just purpose.

"Ready?" Theodora whispered, feeling the opalite warm against her skin.

Alex nodded, eyes closing as she steadied her breathing. "Ready."

With each careful breath, the stones' rhythm matched their own. They thought of their mother—not the loss, but her strength, her love that somehow still felt present. The magic built slowly this time, controlled and deliberate. No wild surges or unpredictable bursts. Just steady power flowing between them, visible in the soft light that wrapped around their joined hands.

"I can feel you," Alex murmured, eyes still closed. "Like we're the same person."

Theodora squeezed her sister's hands. "That's it. Don't fight it."

The air around them shifted, charged but calm. This wasn't just raw power anymore—it was theirs to command.

They poured their thoughts into the opalite stones—love, loyalty, courage flowing from mind to crystal. The magic stirred, a warm current rising from their wrists and swirling into the air between them. Their connection strengthened with each heartbeat, as if the world itself leaned in to listen. "Can ye feel it, Alex?" Theodora whispered, barely audible above the rushing energy. "It's like we're not just us anymore. Like we're one."

Alex nodded, her breathing steadier now. Power filled her chest, exhilarating and terrifying all at once. "Yes, Theo... I feel it. Feel us, together. I can almost see it growing."

And it did. Each pulse of magic intensified, the stones' glow brightening like an approaching storm. The ground trembled beneath them. Their hands shook not from fear but from raw power. They stood firm though, eyes closed, minds locked in concentration as the energy danced between them, flowing back and forth in a living current they were learning to guide.

The air thickened suddenly, light pulsing faster as a deep hum rolled through the clearing. Theodora felt the magic swelling beyond what they'd expected, yet they held steady, fingers intertwined. Control was slipping, but not gone.

"Alex... keep yer thoughts steady," Theodora urged as the stones flared brighter. "We're not done yet. Focus!"

"I—I know!" Alex's eyes squeezed tighter as the magic took on its own momentum. She clung to thoughts of their bond, their parents, everything that mattered. Fear tried to creep in, but she pushed it away.

The magic surged again, wilder now—energy crackling from their wrists like lightning. The ground shook harder as shadows writhed at the clearing's edge. Something was shifting, slipping from their grasp.

"Theo!" Alex cried, gripping tighter. "It's—it's too much!"

Theodora's eyes snapped open, determined despite the chaos. "We can't stop now. Remember—love, loyalty, strength. We have to focus, or it'll destroy everything."

The energy pulsed and contracted, each surge threatening to overwhelm them. Their hearts raced with the storm building around them, but they refused to yield to fear.

With one final breath in unison, they channeled everything they had into the stones. Their magic flowed like light, pushing back the chaos. Slowly, the wild energy stabilized, returning to their control.

They held it—barely. But centered on their connection, they knew they could succeed. They had to.

The magic finally settled into a quiet hum. Their hands remained clasped, steady now, their bond unbroken.

They stared at each other, frozen, hearts pounding in their chests.

"Is this real?" Alex breathed, eyes wide, barely able to form the words. She blinked hard, as if trying to force reality into focus. "Tell me this isn't just... in our heads."

Theo didn't answer right away. She just stared, her gaze locked on her sister's hair—no, not just her hair. It was alive with color, deep violet strands threaded with streaks of glowing magenta that shimmered when the light caught them. The texture had changed too—silky and weightless, as though woven from magic itself. And her skin—there was a faint radiance to it now, like moonlight kissed across her cheekbones. Her eyes, once a sharp, familiar green, now held flecks of amethyst that seemed to pulse with a light of their own.

And Theo—she had changed too. Her copper curls had transformed into a vibrant cascade of pink and lavender, shifting in gentle waves down her shoulders. The colors shifted like sunlight through water, glowing with a soft inner warmth. Her freckles, always faint, now looked like constellations—tiny golden specks scattered across her cheeks and nose. Her irises, once that same vivid green, had brightened into a pale, gleaming rose-gold, rimmed with silver. There was a raw energy in her now, buzzing just beneath her skin, as if she was holding back a storm.

She reached out slowly, brushing her fingers gently against one of Alex's glowing strands. The contact grounded her, sending a warm jolt through her chest. "I think... I think it's us," she whispered. Her voice cracked. "I think this is really us."

Alex let out a shaky breath that turned into a laugh—half hysteria, half disbelief. "This shouldn't be possible," she murmured, tears glinting in her lashes now. "But Theo, it looks real. Doesn't it?"

Theo nodded, her throat tight. "It feels like it was always waitin'. Like it was just... buried under everythin'. All the fear. All the pretendin'."

They both glanced at their hands, now resting apart, no longer clasped. The magic still lingered between them, quiet yet steady. And more than that, there was a thread of something deeper, something that had always connected them even when they hadn't known how to trust it.

For a moment longer they stood like that, bathed in the strange shifting light, breathless and wide-eyed. Neither dared speak, afraid words might break the fragile wonder of the moment. But slowly, the disbelief began to ease—not vanish, but soften—as a new, fiercer truth took hold:

This was real.

This was them.

And they weren't going back.

Killian sat on the log, the firelight flickering across his face. He barely felt its warmth, too focused on the man across from him. Jasper had been restless since they set up camp, his fingers tapping against his knee, his gaze drifting toward the darkened trees.

For a while, neither of them spoke. The crackling fire filled the silence, but the tension rolling off Jasper was impossible to ignore. Killian exhaled slowly, then pushed himself up, stretching as if shaking off fatigue. He wandered a few steps away, leaning casually against a Rowan tree. From here, he could monitor both the girls in the clearing and Jasper by the fire.

Jasper shifted, his movements tight with impatience. Then, with a grunt, he stood, brushing off his coat. "Need to release meself," he muttered, his rough Irish brogue thick. "Keep an eye on things, eh?"

Killian gave a slow nod, watching as Jasper disappeared into the trees. He waited a bit, listening to the crunch of twigs underfoot, then turned his attention to the bag Jasper had left behind.

His pulse quickened as he moved toward it, senses sharp. Crouching beside it, he carefully unfastened the flap. If his instincts were right, there was more to Jasper's unease than just the silence of the forest.

"There has to be something," he muttered, fingers probing the fabric.

He discovered a hidden seam and carefully pulled it open, revealing a secret compartment. Inside lay a detailed map of their journey, marked with ominous symbols showing potential dangers ahead. Killian's grip tightened on the parchment, confirming his worst fears. Jasper was leading them into a trap.

"Jasper knows more than he's letting on," Killian thought, mind racing. "I must warn the girls before it's too late."

Killian scowled, checking the time. Jasper's "quick bathroom break" had stretched well beyond reasonable. The hairs on his neck stood on end—something was off. Without hesitation, he slipped into the forest, following the trail of broken twigs and disturbed foliage Jasper had left behind.

He moved like a shadow, each footfall deliberate, breath controlled. The forest seemed to hold its secrets close, the darkness between trees nearly impenetrable. Then he heard it—voices ahead in a small clearing. He dropped low, pressing against the rough bark of an ancient oak.

"—exactly as planned," came Jasper's voice, no longer carrying its usual affected nervousness, but smooth and self-assured.

Killian's fingers curled into a fist against the cold earth. Not a coincidence, then. He settled deeper into his hiding spot, straining to catch every word, determined to learn what game Jasper was playing before he made his move.

"They've no idea they're bein' led astray," Jasper said, his voice stripped of its feigned stammer. "The girls trust me completely."

"Good," came the bitter reply. It sent shivers down Killian's spine. "Delay them at all costs."

Killian's jaw clenched as the pieces fell into place. No proof beyond what he'd heard with his own ears, but it was enough. The traitor had revealed himself. Now he needed to get back to camp before Jasper—before Theodora and Alexandria found themselves caught in whatever trap was being laid.

Killian clenched his jaw, scanning the dimly lit forest. He needed a plan. "Think," he growled under his breath. "How do I expose Jasper without puttin' them at risk?"

His mind juggled plans and discarded each one faster than the last. Time was running short. The trap was set, and three lives hung in the balance—their safety resting squarely on what he did next.

He doubled back through the forest, placing each foot with the precision of a man who'd spent years avoiding detection. No snapped twigs, no rustled leaves. Just the ghost of movement through shadow and moonlight. One mistake and Jasper would know. One mistake and it would all be over.

Movement near camp caught his attention. Killian pivoted, muscles tensing as Theodora and Alexandria stepped into view. The words forming in his throat died instantly.

Their hair—by the Gods—their hair blazed with living color, pinks, and purples shifting and pulsing like something not of this world. The very air around them seemed to bend and shimmer with energy. Something fundamental had changed in them both.

"Bloody hell," he breathed, rooted to the spot as they drew closer. The transformation wasn't just their hair—their entire beings seemed to glow with barely contained power.

"Theo... Alex..." His voice came out rough, disbelieving. "What in God's name happened to ye?"

The sisters traded glances, something unspoken passing between them. Theodora stepped forward first, chin raised, eyes blazing with newfound confidence.

"We found it, Killian," she said, voice steady despite the wonder threading through it. "The magic that's been ours all along."

Alex nodded, blinking as if still adjusting to the reality herself. "The crystals worked when we... connected properly." She lifted her wrist, the opalite stone pulsing with inner light. "It's like Mother never left us."

Killian stared at them both, pride rising in his chest. These weren't just charges to protect—they were becoming something formidable. In a world sliding deeper into shadow, they stood as beacons.

He moved forward, reaching for Theodora's shoulder. "Ye two are incredible."

Theodora's confidence wavered, uncertainty flickering across her face. "We've got more power now, sure, but we'll need more than fancy lights to face what's comin' for us."

"And ye think I'd leave now?" Killian snorted. "Not bloody likely. Whatever's out there, we stand together."

He held out his hands, and they took them without hesitation. The contact jolted through him—not painful, but like a current finding ground. The forest seemed to pause around them, wind rustling through the leaves overhead.

Something strange passed between them—a sensation like distant voices carried on the breeze, offering guidance, warning, promise. They stood silent, drawing strength from one another, three against the encroaching darkness.

Their eyes met, and something had shifted within them—a resolve beyond mere determination. They weren't just running from danger; they'd become guardians in ways none had foreseen. As their hands separated, the power didn't vanish but settled within them like warmth after a fire, steady and lasting. The forest grew quiet around them, not a sound to be heard, as if bearing witness to something rare and important.

"Well then," Theodora said, her voice steadier than before. "Suppose we've got work ta do."

Alex nodded, a half-smile touching her lips. "Valendor won't know what hit him."

With nothing more needed between them, they headed back toward camp, their footsteps sure and steady. The fire had dwindled to glowing coals, stretching their shadows across the forest floor. At the edge of camp, Killian gave them a curt nod before ducking into his tent, the canvas swallowing him whole.

The sisters paused by the dying embers, sharing a look that contained everything words couldn't capture. Alex stretched her arms overhead, wincing as her shoulders cracked.

"Tell me again why we couldn't have just been bakers or something?" she whispered, half-joking.

Theo tucked a strand of luminous hair behind her ear, her lips quirking up at one corner. "Because ye'd have burned down the shop within a week, an' ye know it."

Alex snorted, nudging her sister with an elbow. "Fair point."

They slipped into their tent without another word, the small lamp inside casting one brief flicker before darkness settled over the camp. The night sounds continued around them—leaves rustling, creatures scurrying—but the forest no longer felt like an enemy. It was just there, watching, waiting.

Morning would come with its own troubles—Jasper chief among them—but for once, the path ahead, dangerous as it was, didn't seem unconquerable.

Chapter 23

"Fractured Loyalty"

As dawn's faint light filtered through the dense canopy, the girls began to stir in their makeshift beds. Thick humidity clung to the air, hinting at the storm brewing on the horizon. Theodora sat up first, rubbing sleep from her eyes. Alexandria followed, her hair tousled and her gaze bleary with lingering dreams. They exchanged a wordless glance—something silent, yet familiar—before slipping out of their tents. The crisp morning air made them shiver.

Aris, sleek in her feline form, stretched beside Alex's bedroll, her paws splaying in the damp earth before she moved into step behind her. Her tail flicked low as her golden eyes swept the treeline. She moved with quiet alertness.

Overhead, Khadall drifted through the branches in his owl form. His wings glided soundlessly through the misty green. He dipped lower as Theo walked beneath him, perching briefly on a crooked limb before gliding into the shadows to follow.

Despite the looming storm, Killian was already up. He crouched beside the fire like the rising wind didn't faze him. Strips of venison sizzled in a blackened skillet. They crackled beside a scatter of wild onions and mushrooms—likely foraged that morning. The scent was rich and grounding. It cut through the dampness and pulled the girls toward the fire.

A dented kettle steamed over the flames. The sharp scent of coffee curled into the air. Smoke and roasted beans mingled, warm and steady against the wild hush of the woods.

As the twins approached, Killian's silhouette came into view against the bruised sky. He looked up and offered a crooked smile that reached his eyes.

"Mornin'," he said. His voice was rough, touched with a lilting edge. "Yer, just in time. Coffee's strong enough to raise the dead. Breakfast ain't far behind."

"Top of the mornin to ya, Killian. Thanks for the grub," Theodora replied. Her breath curled in the chilly air.

They ate quickly. The storm crept closer with every passing minute. The sky darkened from silver to a heavy gray. Wind whis-tled through the branches, sending leaves spinning across their path.

Jasper leaned against a nearby tree, unreadable beneath the overcast sky.

"Looks like we're in for some wicked weather," he said. "Nau's still a good distance, but I know a quicker route. It'll be rough—but it'll get us ahead of the storm."

The group paused to consider. The twins exchanged a glance and nodded. "We should take the faster path," Theodora decided. "Time's tickin'."

They moved fast. Hands swept the plates away, and the fire snuffed out. Killian brushed soot from his hands and stepped toward the girls. His eyes rose to the sky, then shifted to Jasper. His tone stayed light, but a hard edge ran beneath it.

"Oi, Jasper," he said. "Where were you last night—after everyone turned in?"

Jasper didn't move. He met Killian's gaze with calm resolve. His jaw tightened slightly.

"Just takin' a stroll," he replied. "Making sure all was secure. Ye know how I am—always watchin'."

Killian studied him for a moment. His gaze lingered, searching for something beneath the surface. Then he gave a small nod. It wasn't quite agreement—but it was enough.

Theodora shot him a questioning look. Killian gave her shoulder a gentle squeeze before turning to help pack. Overhead, the sky rumbled—a low, ominous growl echoing the urgency rising among them.

With their gear packed and cloaks pulled tight, the group set out on the shortcut Jasper had promised. The forest closed in, thick and brooding. Branches reached from either side like skeletal fingers.

Then the storm broke.

Hail began to fall, cold and stinging. The trail turned to muck beneath their boots. Every step became a struggle—mud, roots, and fallen limbs fought against them. Still, they pressed on. The storm was here. And so was whatever waited beyond it.

Hours blurred together in bitter silence, each step heavier than the last. Boots scraped over hidden roots and caught on stones. The underbrush clawed at their legs. Shoulders hunched against the biting wind, they trudged onward—fatigued, fraying, and tangled in the weight of unspoken tension.

Alexandria kept her eyes fixed on Jasper's back. He moved with rigid purpose—shoulders squared, jaw clenched, gaze fixed ahead. Not once did he glance back. Not at her. Not at anyone.

This wasn't the Jasper who used to offer a hand over rough terrain or crack a joke when things felt bleak. This Jasper was all stone and silence, colder than the wind cutting through their cloaks.

And he hated himself for it.

Every step twisted in his chest. He was shutting her out. Shutting everyone out. And that wasn't who he was. But his father's voice echoed in his mind: Stay focused. Don't let emotions compromise the mission. You're not here to make friends.

He'd learned the cost of disobedience. He wouldn't forget it.

So when Alexandria's voice finally cut through the cold quiet behind him, it landed sharper than expected.

"Hey," she called. "You gonna tell me what's going on, or do I have to keep chasing your shadow all day?"

His stride faltered, barely noticeable—but she saw it. He didn't stop.

"Nothin's going on," he said, the words flat and bitter on his tongue.

"I don't believe you," she shot back. "You've barely spoken since we left. You're acting like none of this—none of us—matters."

He slowed, turned slightly. The tension in his jaw was unmistakable, his eyes guarded. "I'm just tryin' to keep us movin'."

"No," Alexandria said, stepping into his path. "You're shutting down. That's not helping anyone. And that's not you."

For a moment, snowflakes spun between them, catching in their hair, melting on their shoulders. Jasper stared at her too long. She searched his face, eyes full of quiet worry, and for just a second, he nearly told her everything—that he hated this distance, that he was sorry.

But he couldn't. Wouldn't.

"People change," he said instead, his voice hollow.

"Yeah," she murmured. "But not overnight. Not without a reason."

He looked away. His jaw clenched. And then he stepped around her, moving forward with even stiffer resolve.

Alex stood frozen, snowflakes gathering on her lashes as she watched him walk away. When had things broken between them? Or had it been building all along?

Jasper trudged ahead, shoulders hunched against more than just the cold.

She caught up in three quick strides, anger and hurt sharpening her focus. "Where exactly are we headed?" she demanded, studying his face. His eyes darted to the horizon then back to the path, too quick, too nervous.

"Trust me," he said, attempting a smile that failed completely. His jaw tensed like he was biting back words. "I know where we need ta go."

His pace never slowed, boots dragging heavy tracks through the snow.

Killian's voice cut through the silence. "There it is again—'trust me'," he spat, not bothering to hide his anger. "He's been sayin' that fer miles, and where are we? Trippin' over rocks in the arse-end o' nowhere."

He yanked his hood down and shook snow from his hair with a frustrated swipe. His eyes scanned the treeline, alert and wary. The forest was unnaturally quiet.

"Careful now, Jasper," Theodora said, pulling her cloak tighter. Her voice stayed calm but carried a dangerous edge. "Ye've a fair tongue, but words won't carry us much farther. We're runnin' on nothin'. We need more than blind faith."

She didn't need to accuse him directly. The weight of her words hung in the air between them.

Jasper said nothing. His gaze dropped to the ground, shoulders visibly tensing under the scrutiny.

For a moment, it looked like he might speak.

Instead, he turned away without a word.

Killian swore and crouched down, digging through his pack until he found a worn leather map. He spread it across his thigh, his frown deepening as he studied it.

"Hold on now," he muttered. "This... this ain't right."

Everyone stopped.

Boots shifted in the snow as they gathered around, drawn to the urgency in his voice.

"See this bend we just took?" Killian jabbed at the parchment. "It's not marked. Should've gone east at the ridge. Instead, we're stuck in this hollow—and another mile forward, we'll be walkin' straight into a feckin' ravine."

Theodora moved closer, her voice dropping to ice. "Did ye know?" she asked Jasper directly. "Did ye know we left the path?"

Jasper remained silent.

Alex watched him carefully. Something in his stance betrayed him—a slight shift of weight, a hesitation, the smallest tremble.

He knew.

"Why would we leave the trail?" she asked, her voice cracking with tension. "Why lead us this way?"

Killian stood quickly, stuffing the map back into his pack. "This ain't just a wrong turn," he said, voice hardening. "He's takin' us off course. And I've a bad feelin' we won't like where it ends."

The wind picked up, whistling through the trees. Snow fell in gentle spirals, but no one moved. It felt like the entire world was holding its breath.

Jasper's hands curled into fists at his sides.

His head bowed slightly. His chest rose and fell with a deep, painful breath.

Then he turned away again and kept walking, each step looking like it took all his strength.

Alex's heart pounded against her ribs. The suspicion, the hurt—it all burned to clear to ignore.

She went after him, her steps quick and determined.

"Jasper," she called. He didn't acknowledge her.

"Jasper!"

Still, not a glance.

She caught up beside him, voice low and tight. "If you don't start talking, I swear I'll shake the truth out of you with my own hands."

But he didn't answer. He just kept walking, jaw clenched so hard she could see the muscle twitching, as if silence might shield him from whatever was coming.

Alexandria felt something inside her crack—sharper than the cold that bit through her cloak.

Her eyes narrowed, heart hammering against her ribs. The pieces clicked together with terrible clarity. She opened her mouth—

—but Theodora beat her to it.

"Jasper," she said, her voice stripped of warmth, hard as iron. "What else haven't ye told us?"

Jasper stopped dead.

Alexandria sensed it—that shift in the air between them. His silence wasn't empty. Words he couldn't bring himself to say filled the silence, pressing down and fighting to escape.

Her breath clouded in front of her face.

"Enough," she said, each word precise. "We trusted you. That ends now—unless you start talking."

He didn't turn. Just stood there, snow collecting on his shoulders, wind pulling at his coat. Their stares weighed on him, heavy and waiting. Then—

He let out a breath.

Long and ragged, like something inside him had finally broken.

"Alright," he murmured, barely audible. "Ye deserve the truth."

The silence hung, razor-sharp.

His shoulders rose and fell. Slowly, he turned to face them. Each step looked painful, boots crunching through snow with deliberate heaviness. When he finally stood before them, his eyes stayed fixed on the ground.

"I haven't been honest," he said, forcing each word out. "Not about... where me loyalties lie."

No one spoke.

Jasper's hands fidgeted at his sides, opening and closing like he was grasping for something that wasn't there. He looked up briefly, and the expression in his eyes hit Alexandria like a physical blow.

Guilt. Fear. Something like a plea.

"I'm not who ye think I am," he said.

Theodora cut in, "Spit it out, then. No more dancin' around it."

His jaw clenched tight, lips parting only to close again. He swallowed hard, the confession lodged in his throat.

Then, finally:

"Me name is Jasper Valendor," he said.

The words fell heavy in the silence.

His voice was steady but hollow. "I'm... I'm his son."

Theodora stumbled backward, her hand instinctively grabbing Alexandria's arm.

Alex stood motionless. Her face revealed nothing, but her eyes turned cold—colder than the snow piling around their boots.

Behind them came the sound of steel shifting. Killian's knuckles whitened around his halberd, his stance rigid with restraint.

"Ye're tellin' us," Killian growled, each word tight with fury, "that ye're the son of the bastard we've been fightin' all this time? The one who's hunted us like animals?"

Jasper's face was drained of color.

His breath caught. One hand lifted slightly, trembling, a futile gesture of peace.

"It's... it's not what ye think," he stammered, voice cracking. "I never wanted to lie. But me father—ye've no idea what he does to those who defy him. No idea how far his influence reaches."

He looked between them, eyes pleading.

"I thought—" His voice broke again, rougher now. "I thought I could help ye. Be better than him. Different from him. But I was wrong, wasn't I?"

Alexandria answered without hesitation.

"Yes," she said. "You were."

Jasper stilled completely, as if her words had struck something vital.

She continued, her voice level despite the hurt beneath it. "You thought you could lie to our faces and still walk beside us. That we'd not discover the truth. That your secrets wouldn't matter in the end. But they do matter, Jasper. And we're already paying the price."

"I'm sorry," he whispered, the words hollow in the cold air. "I know it means nothin' now."

But the damage was done. His confession had shattered what trust remained between them. The silence that followed wasn't empty—it was filled with anger, hurt, betrayal.

Thunder rumbled overhead, no longer distant but closing in. The storm gathered strength. Snow began to fall in earnest, icy flakes swirling around them.

The wind cut through the clearing, scattering snow, and dead leaves, as if the forest itself rejected his presence.

Alexandria broke the silence first. Her voice was hard, unflinching. "We need to figure out what to do with him."

The warmth that once softened her features was gone. She looked at Jasper as if he were a stranger.

"Can we risk trusting him again?"

Theodora hesitated, glancing between her sister, Killian and Jasper—who seemed to shrink beneath their scrutiny.

"I... I dunno, Alex," she said softly. "But we can't be makin' another mistake. Too much depends on us gettin' this right."

Her uncertainty lingered between them, caught between loyalty and the fear of what other secrets Jasper might be keeping.

Killian stepped forward. His hand never left his weapon, grip unwavering. Every line of his face hardened with distrust.

"He's lied ta us before," he said. "What's ta stop him from leadin' us straight ta Valendor? For all we know, his father's watchin' us right now."

Jasper backed away, his face ashen. His hands shook. The people who'd been his companions—his family—now looked at him with suspicion and fear.

"I know I've broken yer trust," he said, barely audible above the wind. "But I wanted none of ye hurt. Please..."

He looked directly at Alexandria, then Theodora.

"Ye must know I wouldn't harm ye."

Killian barked a laugh, harsh and bitter. "Believe ye? After what ye just told us? Yer Valendor's son. Ye've been playin' both sides from the start, and we were fools not to see it."

Alexandria remained still, arms wrapped tightly around herself as if holding something together. Her eyes weren't angry—they held something deeper, more painful.

Then she spoke, each word quiet but final. "Trust doesn't just come back because you want it to. Not now. Not with everything at stake."

She turned her back on him. The motion was small. But it hit like a blade. It was distance. It was a dismissal.

Jasper opened his mouth to speak, but no sound came. His throat tightened, choking back the words that refused to come out.

He turned to Theodora, voice shaking. "Theo—please—ye know me. Ye know me."

She half-reached for him, then faltered. Her hand fell back to her side like something withered.

"Maybe..." she said, the word uncertain. "Maybe he stays. Proves himself. We've all done things we regret, haven't we?"

Killian rounded on her, his voice a low warning. "Don't be so naïve, lass. Look around us—lost, cold, in danger. He's led us here on purpose. We can't be harborin' a snake."

"No—wait—" Jasper stepped forward, something breaking in his expression. "One more chance. That's all I ask. I'll do anything. Face whatever trial. Just don't—" The rest caught in his throat.

The silence pressed in from all sides.

Even the wind died down, as if listening.

Alexandria stood motionless. Her shoulders rose with a deep, steadying breath.

"I'm sorry, Jasper," she said, voice quiet but firm. "We can't take that chance. You need to go."

He froze.

The fight drained from him visibly—hope, resistance, everything—gone in an instant.

"No," he whispered. "No, Alex—ye can't mean that—"

She didn't turn.

His lips parted again, then pressed together. A single nod was all he managed. Small. Defeated.

"Aye," he said. "I understand."

He turned away before anyone could respond.

The storm met him with full fury—wind howling, snow cutting across his face. He didn't shield himself. Just walked. Head down. Shoulders hunched against more than just the cold.

The forest consumed him with each step. His footfalls vanished beneath fresh snow.

No one moved.

No one spoke.

He never looked back.

Alexandria finally turned, drawn by something deeper than instinct—something she hated acknowledging. Her movements were wooden, shoulders stiff with a resolve that was already crumbling. She watched him go, each heartbeat hollow in her chest. Despite everything, part of her still waited for him to look back, to say something that might soften this brutal severing.

But he just kept walking.

Her chest constricted. She'd told herself this was right, necessary, unavoidable. Yet as his figure blurred into the whiteout, all she felt was their history crashing down—battles fought side by side, secrets whispered in darkness, trust built and betrayed.

Her hands trembled. She couldn't fill her lungs properly.

The snow swallowed him bit by bit until nothing remained. Just white. Just wind. Just cold.

Where certainty should have been, she found only emptiness.

Beside her, Theodora clutched her cloak tighter, as if it might shield her from more than just the chill. Her gaze remained fixed on the spot where Jasper had vanished, eyes wide with stunned disbelief.

"He was our friend," she whispered, her voice just barely rising above the wind. "After everythin' we've been through... he was one of us."

Alexandria's jaw clenched tight. Her fingers curled into fists, fighting the ache climbing up her throat. She'd trusted him. Relied on him. Believed in him. Now that trust lay shattered at her feet.

"I wanted him to be different," she said, words carried away by the storm. "To choose us over his father... to fight alongside us, not against us."

Theodora's hand found her sister's shoulder, her touch steady even as her voice roughened with grief. "I wanted that too, Alex. But some things..." She swallowed hard. "You can't mend some things once they're broken."

Silence fell between them, heavy with all they couldn't say. Thunder rolled across the valley, punctuating their fractured thoughts. Wind swept through the pines overhead, dislodging snow that fell around them in soft, mocking flurries.

They stood together—yet alone. Theodora shifted her weight, snow crunching beneath her boots. Killian's breath clouded and dissolved into nothing.

Alexandria stared at the empty path where Jasper had disappeared, her expression unreadable. Without a word, she turned away, taking measured and deliberate steps through the deep snow that carried her further from what they had lost. Ahead lay the war they had come to fight, while behind them lingered the one they had never seen coming.

Chapter 24

"Journey Toward Nau"

THE SKY WAS A black void, heavy, and crushing, as the storm howled, tearing at their cloaks and driving them forward with violent force. Thunder cracked overhead, booming like the wrath of gods, reminding them of how small they were beneath the vast heavens.

Above, Khadall soared, his powerful wings slicing through the violent squalls as he circled, a lifeline reminding them they weren't entirely alone in this brutal landscape. Each step was a battle, their bodies worn and weary, struggling against nature's fury. Hail struck like shards of ice, stinging their faces and freezing them to the bone. The wind nearly dragged them off their feet, their fingers grew numb, and each breath was a struggle in the biting cold. Yet, they pressed on, defying exhaustion as if sheer will could conquer the storm.

Something was in the storm. Not just wind and snow—it felt like something was watching, moving in the cracks between thunder and lightning. You couldn't see it, but you felt it. Like a breath on the back of your neck. Like a voice that wasn't quite yours whispering inside your head.

Turn around. This is a waste. You'll never make it.

The storm didn't scream at them—it nudged, soft and steady, wearing them down thought by thought. And for a moment, just a moment, giving up almost felt like a mercy.

But they kept walking. Not because they were brave. Because stopping meant dying.

They clung to what they had left—each step, each breath. The storm could beat the hell out of their bodies, but it was after their minds. That's where it hit hardest. There was something wrong in the wind. Like it wanted them broken, not just cold.

Theodora's foot caught under the snow and she pitched forward with a shout, grabbing at whatever she could. Her hand latched onto Alexandria's shoulder, holding tight like the ground had tried to swallow her. She said nothing—the wind would've drowned it out anyway—but her grip said enough.

Alexandria winced but didn't shake her off. She felt the same pull, like the storm was trying to tear her apart. She could barely feel her legs. Her jaw ached from clenching it so long. Her mind drifted—Is this how Valendor fought? No blood. No blade. Just… slow defeat.

Aris was barely keeping shape, flickering between cat and wolf, like the storm was reaching inside her and tugging at the seams. She slunk close, her usual swagger gone. No jokes. No grin. Just ears flat and tail down.

She looked up, voice tight and low. "Khadall? You up there?" No answer. Just wind and dark.

The silence beneath the storm was worse than the storm itself. Like the world was holding its breath, waiting for them to give in.

They were hanging on by threads. Four of them. Cold to the bone. Heads down. Hope stretched thin.

Then Killian's voice cracked through it, rough and sharp.

"Oi! Ye listenin' to that voice in yer head? The one tellin' ye to lie down and freeze?" He spat into the snow. "That ain't you. That's the feckin' storm. And I'll be damned if I let it win."

He pushed ahead, waving a hand. "We're not stoppin' here, not now! Nau's still out there—we get there—we don't give up!"

Aris barked a laugh—more breath than sound—but it was something. "You heard the man. Stick together. Don't let the wind split us."

Theodora nodded, lips pressed tight. Her grip loosened, but she stayed close. The storm was still howling, but something shifted.

Killian took the middle, shoulders squared like he could hold the wind back by sheer stubbornness. On one side, Theodora walked quiet, haunted. Jasper's betrayal still stung—every step forward was a fight not to think about it.

On the other side, Alexandria moved with that same weight. Her anger was quieter than her sister's, more like a bruise than a burn. But it was there. It kept her upright.

Step by step, they pushed through. The storm didn't ease up. But neither did they.

Killian held his halberd, his eyes scanning the storm's swirling shadows. He felt the heavy burden of responsibility, driven by a powerful urge to protect the two princesses, willing to put himself in danger if necessary. I'll ensure you both remain safe, he vowed silently, his jaw clenched in defiance against the storm's unyielding wrath.

The storm clawed at them like it meant to peel the skin from their bones. But it wasn't the cold or the wind that hit Killian hardest—it was the memory. Sharp. Sudden. Unrelenting.

Smoke filled his lungs again. Not from this storm, but from another night long ago. He could smell it, thick and choking. He could hear it—the crackling of flames devouring his village, the screams slicing through the dark. People he knew, people he loved, burning and running and falling.

He was just a boy. And they came without warning.

The Darkling Court.

Whispers turned flesh—fae twisted by greed and old power. No mercy, no warning. Just ruin. Their leader, hidden in shadow, was more myth than man. No face. No voice. Just dread. No one said his name out loud. Not if they wanted to sleep again.

His father stood in their way—sword drawn, shouting for Killian and Agaela to run. So they did. Or tried.

But there was nowhere to go.

One of the darklings came out of the smoke and snatched his sister, wrapped her in clawed hands like she weighed nothing. She screamed his name, and Killian screamed back, lungs tearing.

"No! Let her go!"

He ran at the creature. Rage swallowed fear. He didn't think—he lunged. And something inside him broke loose. Light—or was it fire?—erupted from his hands.

The darkling staggered but didn't fall. Agaela was still screaming and reaching for him as they dragged her away.

And Killian... he just stood there, shaking, staring at his hands.

Magic. Fae magic. In him.

He didn't know what it meant. Only that it wasn't enough.

He dropped to his knees as the forest swallowed her up.

"I'll find ye," he whispered, voice cracking. "I swear on my life—I'll find ye."

Even now, the words echoed. Even now, her tear-stained face wouldn't leave him.

The wind snapped him back. The snow. The cold. The weight in his chest. He blinked hard, clenched his jaw, grounded himself in the here and now. In the storm. In the fight.

He had a promise to keep. And nothing—storm, darkling or demon—was going to stop him.

Not again. Never.

They trudged deeper through the forest, each step heavier than the last. Darkness pressed in around them, the twisted branches overhead reaching down like grasping fingers. Theodora's pulse quickened at the prickling sensation of being watched. Something in those shadows was tracking them. She shivered and grabbed Alexandria's hand, finding it as cold as her own.

"You holding up?" Alex asked, concern cutting through her exhaustion.

"I'll be fine once we find Nau," Theo answered, voice steadier than she felt.

The trees thinned gradually, and Theodora glimpsed patches of open sky between the branches. For the first time in hours, something besides dread stirred in her chest. A flicker of possibility. Not quite hope yet, but close enough.

They moved forward without speaking, shoulders bumping. The weight of everything—Jasper's betrayal, the cold, the fear—seemed less important now. What mattered was getting to Nau. What mattered was the kingdom waiting for them. The people counting on them not to fail.

Each step through knee-deep snow was defiance. Each ragged breath was refusal—to give up, to turn back, to listen to that voice in the wind telling them they couldn't make it.

Then suddenly, they broke through the treeline.

The storm had weakened, though wind still cut through their layers and tugged at their cloaks. Behind them, bare branches scraped against each other as if waving them off.

Ahead stretched an empty field blanketed in pristine snow, undisturbed and silent beneath the moon's pale glow.

Theodora paused, breathing hard, taking in the open expanse. No more forest closing in. No more shadows pressing at their backs.

Just emptiness. Just sky.

Scattered dead trees standing alone like forgotten watchers broke the stark white landscape. From somewhere across the field came a wolf's cry—lonely and sharp, yet somehow right in all its wild sorrow.

Khadall dropped from the sky in a wide arc, wings beating hard against the wind. He landed beside them with a heavy thud, snow kicking up around his talons. The gust from his descent sent cloaks flapping and stung exposed skin with fresh cold.

He folded his wings and exhaled a slow plume of steam. "Nau lies just beyond that hill," he said, raising one wing toward the distant mountain, a dark shape on the horizon. "It's hidden. Enchanted."

Silence enveloped them. The wind slithered through seams and collars, nipping at their skin and sapping heat from their bones. Ahead lay a vast, barren expanse—only snow, wind, and quiet. Just the lengthy trek separating them from the looming mountain ahead.

Killian stepped closer to Khadall, lowering his voice. "What kind of enchantment?"

Khadall didn't meet his eye. "The kind that pays attention."

Killian said nothing, just pulled his hood tighter.

Theodora exhaled steadily, arms crossed over her chest for warmth. She glanced at Alexandria—cheeks raw from wind, eyes locked on the mountain. Steady. Unshaken.

Without a word, Alexandria started walking.

The others followed.

With each step, the mountain loomed larger, its summit lost in swirling mist. It wasn't menacing—just vast. Watchful. Patient.

As they continued, something subtle changed in the air around them. The fear that had been their constant companion began to recede. The stillness felt different now—not threatening, but acknowledging. As if the very land recognized them, permitting their passage through its domain.

Yet the silence carved out space for thoughts they had pushed aside in their exhaustion.

Theodora's fingers ached beneath her gloves, but it was the weight in her chest that troubled her most. Doubt, coiled quiet and persistent, pressed at the edges of her resolve. She walked anyway, unwilling to be the one who broke.

Killian kept his eyes on the snow, jaw clenched. Every step reminded him of what they'd left behind—and who. He wanted answers. Vengeance. But the closer they came, the more hollow that want began to feel.

Alexandria walked ahead of them all, unwavering, but not untouched. She could feel the cracks beneath her calm—the grief, the pressure, the fear of failing them. She held it all like a blade's edge, sharp and quiet.

Moonlight bathed the snow in silver, making every crystal sparkle. Even the dead trees no longer seemed foreboding up close, but like guardians keeping vigil. Their silence felt almost welcoming.

They pressed forward, numb with cold yet somehow fortified by each other's presence. The quiet that surrounded them now carried something new—possibility.

At the base of the mountain, they stopped.

The peak was gone, swallowed by thick clouds swirling high above. The mountain rose before them like a wall, vast and unmoving. They just stood there, chests rising and falling in the cold, staring upward.

Then the winds softened to gentle whispers, and the group began their ascent, a hush falling over them as if the very air demanded reverence. Scattered trees lined the path, spaced out and twisted by time, their bare branches swaying with a quiet, almost sentient grace. They didn't block the way—they seemed to mark it, subtle guides watching silently as the group passed. It felt as if even the mountain had acknowledged them.

The climb had been longer than any of them expected. The narrow dirt path twisted up the mountainside, carved by time and weather, more suggestion than trail in some places. Loose stones slipped underfoot, and dust rose with every step, coating their boots and clinging to their skin. The air grew thinner the higher they went, making each breath feel like it had to be earned. Muscles ached. Throats were dry. But none of them stopped.

"Didn't think it'd be this high," Killian said, casting a look over the drop beside them. "Feels like we're climbin' into the bloody sky."

"Feels like we've been climbin' half the world," Theodora replied, breath short but steady. "But we're close now. I can feel it in me bones."

Alexandria nodded, her eyes locked on the trail ahead. "We're finally going to see it. After everything... Nau's just over the next ridge."

They all felt it—something waiting just beyond the next rise, just past the next bend. The knowing that settled in your bones before your mind could name it.

They walked in silence for a while after that. The only sounds were their footfalls, the wind brushing against the rocks, and the occasional call of some unseen mountain bird. The world was still. Sacred, almost. Like the mountain was holding its breath.

Then Alexandria slowed. Something had shifted.

She looked down at the ground, then around at the cliffs rising around them. The air was heavier now, not with heat, but with presence. It prickled across her skin.

"Do you feel that?" she asked, voice barely a whisper.

Theodora stopped beside her. Her face had changed—eyes wide, the usual edge in her expression softened by something close to reverence. "Aye," she said softly. "It's like the mountain knows we're here. Like Nau itself is watchin'."

Killian didn't speak, but he scanned the rocks around them, shoulders tight, as if expecting the stones to move.

They kept going, their pace slower now, more deliberate. No one joked. No one complained. The climb had become something else—a passage. And when they reached the peak, everything below them shifted.

Their breath caught.

Not from exhaustion—though the climb had been brutal—but from the sight before them. Silence passed between the three as they stepped into the open, eyes wide, shoulders slack. A hush fell over them that no one dared break. It wasn't just awe. It was a relief. It was the aching release of hope held too long, too tight.

Alexandria let out a sound that was half-laugh, half-sob. Theodora just stared, blinking hard, like the city might vanish if she looked away. Even Killian stood still, jaw clenched, but eyes soft.

Nau was real.

Even from this distance, it was clear: Nau wasn't like any city they'd ever seen. It belonged to something deeper, older. A realm of magic.

"Sweet Jaysus," Killian breathed.

Theodora stood still, the tension gone from her shoulders. Her gaze lingered on the city like she was afraid to blink.

Alexandria felt her chest tighten—not with fear, but something more raw. Wonder. Relief. And something just beneath it, stirring.

"We made it," she said, soft and certain.

But she knew, even as the words left her mouth, that reaching Nau wasn't the end of the road.

It was only the start.

Khadall came up beside them, his gaze fixed on the valley with a mixture of pride and sorrow. His voice, strong and commanding, softened as he spoke. "Welcome to Nau. It is more than land or stone—it's sacred ground, a place woven with ancient magic. For centuries, it has been the sanctuary of my kind, the griffins. We have called this valley home for longer than human history can remember."

Crystal structures rose elegantly from the snowy ground, their transparent walls catching the moonlight and refracting it in a dazzling array of colors. Each building shimmered as if alive, its facets casting rainbows across the city. Spires of delicate, crystalline towers reached skyward, appearing almost weightless as they floated just inches above the earth, held aloft by some unseen magic. The structures sparkled in hues of blue, lavender and soft gold, their surfaces so smooth and clear that they seemed to glow from within.

Alexandria gasped, one hand rising to her mouth as she took in the sight. "It's... it's like stepping into a dream," she whispered, awe flooding her voice. "How can such a place exist?"

Theodora, usually calm and composed, found herself momentarily speechless. Her eyes widened as she took in the floating bridges crisscrossing above the city, suspended in mid-air without support. They twisted and curved in impossible shapes, some leading toward distant cliffs while others seemed to dissolve into mist. It was as if the laws of nature had been rewritten here, bending to the will of an ancient, powerful magic.

Killian shook his head slowly, his voice hushed with wonder. "I've seen many cities, but nothing like this. It's as if the city itself is alive... breathing."

Khadall stood beside them, his sharp gaze sweeping over Nau with both reverence and pride. "The ancient ones of my kind and our allies—creatures who lived with magic rather than wield it crafted the city. Each crystal structure grew, not built, shaped over centuries by the collective will of griffins, humans and others who once called this place home."

Alexandria's eyes tracked the glinting pathways that seemed to pulse with soft light, like veins carrying some luminous energy through the city. "It feels alive," she murmured. "Like it knows we're here."

Khadall nodded. "She is indeed alive, in a way. The enchantments that bind it have a spirit of their own. They sense us, recognize us as part of its purpose. These bridges, these structures... they exist to guide and protect. Only those meant to walk these paths can cross them." He gestured to a bridge ahead of them, its surface shimmering with an inviting, gentle glow. "Those bridges once connected Nau to other realms, places that exist now only in the memories of the ancient ones."

Theodora squinted, spotting glimmers of translucent, ethereal figures shifting within the crystal walls, moving like echoes from another time. "Are... are those spirits?" she asked, a shiver crawling down her spine.

"Not exactly. Those are echoes—traces of the people who once lived here. The crystal holds their essence. When you walk through Nau, you're walking through the lives of everyone who came before."

Killian's eyes sparkled with awe. "So the city remembers them."

"Aye," Khadall agreed, his voice deepening with the weight of his own memories. "It holds every moment, every triumph, and sacrifice of those who dedicated themselves to protecting it from outsiders. My ancestors wove their lives into these walls. They wanted Nau to live on, even as their own lives faded."

A moment of silence fell over the group as they took in the depth of what lay before them. It wasn't just a beautiful city; it was a place of immense legacy and purpose, a testament to countless lives and countless generations dedicated to guarding its sacred magic.

"I can feel it—the strength, the beauty, the sorrow. It's like everything they were is still here, waiting." Alexandria said.

As they descended towards the city, each step filled Alexandria with wonder. Streets lined with tall crystal buildings that seemed to glow from within. Magical symbols etched into every surface pulsed with faint light.

A burst of movement caught her eye as she turned to see an approaching group of griffins. As they neared, the striking resemblance between Khadall and these unknown beings became clear - his long-separated kin.

"Khadall!" One figure called out. Her voice, akin to a joyful tune, seemed to lighten the very air around them. Their laughter meshed with the patter of raindrops and a distant roll of thunder as they embraced.

"By all heavens above, we feared we'd lost you forever," another sibling whispered.

Tears glistened in Khadall's eyes as he embraced his sister, Sariya. His voice thick with emotion, he whispered, "I never thought I'd see you again." His gentle gaze filled with deep gratitude. "But lo-and-behold, we are back together, united at last."

Alexandria watched the reunion unfold, a bittersweet pang tugging at her heart. Would she ever experience such pure, unadulterated happiness again?

Theo sensed her thoughts and reached out, squeezing her hand. It was a silent reminder of the bond they shared. Alexandria met her sister's gaze, and the tension in her body softened.

Khadall turned to his companions, pride shining in his eyes as he introduced them to the two griffins standing nearby, their eyes gleaming with warmth and recognition. "Sariya, Rashid—meet Alexandria, Theodora and Killian," he said. "They've become my family in the outside world, and together, we've faced countless trials."

Sariya dipped her head in a graceful nod, her feathers glinting with traces of silver that suggested her proficiency in magic. She had left Nau years before to study ancient enchantments and gain knowledge to strengthen the city's wards. Now, with the threats to Nau growing stronger, she had returned to lend her skills and reinforce its magical defenses.

Rashid, his gaze calm, and kind, stepped forward as well. Soft, earthy tones marked his feathers, a sign of his healing abilities. Having trained as a healer in distant lands, he had come back to Nau when he sensed that both his family and his homeland needed him. Now, he stood ready to heal and protect all who sought sanctuary within these sacred borders.

As the siblings greeted Khadall's companions, the bond between the three griffins was clear—a deep, unbreakable connection that had endured through their years apart. For Sariya and Rashid, returning to Nau was more than a duty; it was a homecoming, and a promise to protect the land they held dear.

Sariya smiled warmly, her eyes brimming with gratitude. "You've brought our brother back to us, and for that, we're forever grateful."

"It's a pleasure to meet you both," Alexandria greeted, reciprocating the kind gesture.

Theo nodded in agreement. "Khadall has told us so much about Nau and its people. It's an honor to be here."

"We've been following your adventures," Sariya added, her voice tinged with excitement.

"It's wonderful to finally meet you all face-to-face," Rashid said, his calm demeanor unwavering. "But before we head to Carrantou, please join us for a meal and some rest. You all look like you could use it."

As the group crossed a floating bridge, Theo instinctively reached out to touch the elaborate handrail. It felt cool yet emanated an undeniable warmth. She exchanged awed glances with Alex and Killian.

"Can you feel it?" Theo whispered. "The energy here is like nothing I've ever experienced."

Alex nodded, her voice hushed. "It's as if Nau is the very essence of magic."

Descending to the ground level, the trio marveled at the ornate details adorning each structure. Intricate carvings depicted mythical beasts and heroic battles, their forms brought to life by the interplay of light and shadow. Theo traced her fingers along a crystal pillar, sensing a faint thrum of magic pulsing beneath.

The group wandered through Nau's tranquil streets, marveling at the lush greenery and ethereal landscape. Vibrant flowers bloomed in every hue imaginable, while earthy herbs released intoxicating aromas. Crystal-clear lakes sparkled under the sun, and majestic griffins soared overhead.

Theo felt transported into a fairy tale. "How is this place real?" she asked, wonder shining in her eyes.

Khadall's pride resonated as he replied, "Nau has always been a haven for magic and nature. The spirits blessed our ancestors to create this sanctuary."

Alexandria inquired, "Why keep this magnificent city hidden?"

Khadall's expression turned somber. "Centuries ago, outsiders sought to exploit our resources and magic. Their greed caused discord and devastation within our once-harmonious city."

Sariya added, "Since then, we've kept Nau hidden to protect ourselves and our way of life."

"You've seemed to have found balance now," Killian observed.

Rashid smiled warmly. "Indeed, we've calibrated our hearts toward forgiveness and opened doors for those worthy of entering our city's heart."

Theodora nodded, understanding the weight of such responsibility. "It must have been a tough decision. But I see why you did it. Nau is special and deserves protection."

Khadall's gaze softened. "Your understanding means a great deal, Princess."

Chapter 25

"Tides of Tranquility"

As they continued through the shimmering streets of Nau, ethereal melodies drifted through the air, delicate yet resonant, like voices from another world. The sound seemed to dance and flow around them, each note reflecting off the crystal buildings and reverberating in waves of pure, shimmering beauty. A nearby group of musicians, griffins, and humans, caught their attention; their hands and talons moved gracefully over crystal instruments.

"Music is woven into Nau's fabric," Khadall explained, his voice barely above a whisper, as if unwilling to disrupt the magic of the moment. "It speaks to the soul and echoes the harmony of our realm. Here, it is more than sound—it's part of the very life of Nau."

Theodora closed her eyes, letting the music wash over her, each note filling her with a sense of calm and belonging she hadn't felt in a long time. It felt as though the melodies reached deep into her heart, brushing away the exhaustion, fear and burden of their journey, replacing them with warmth and peace. For the first time in days, her mind was still, her spirit at ease.

Beside her, Alexandria watched her sister with a soft smile, grateful for this rare moment of tranquility in their relentless quest. She felt the music wrapping around her too, filling her with a quiet strength, as if each note whispered reassurance and courage. For a fleeting moment, all the uncertainty and danger they had faced seemed to melt away, replaced by a deep sense of connection to this ancient place.

Killian exhaled, releasing tension from his shoulders as the music swept him away. The melodies reminded him of the calm before battle, a sacred pause that allowed him to remember who he was fighting for and why. This wasn't merely music; it was a lifeline, a reminder of hope and the beauty they were fighting to protect.

It wound around them, its rhythms like the heartbeat of Nau itself, alive with memory and promise. As they listened, each of them felt renewed—strengthened by the city's song and the shared understanding that this place, so full of history and harmony, was worth any battle they would face.

Theodora's heart raced as they approached Khadall's family home. In the living room, Khadall's youngest sibling Layla waited patiently. Her eyes sparkled with a mischievous twinkle, and a playful grin tugged at her lips as she watched them enter.

The house blended with its surroundings, its walls built from sturdy tree trunks etched with intricate carvings. A canopy of branches and leaves stretched overhead, forming a natural shelter.

Inside, Theodora marveled at the spacious interior flooded with natural light. The polished wooden floors felt cool beneath her feet despite the warmth outside.

Theodora admired the quiet rhythm between Sariya and Rashid as they moved through the house, their coordination so seamless it felt like a well-rehearsed dance.

They all gravitated toward the kitchen, where the pair worked with a practiced ease that spoke of years spent in harmony. Soft light from crystal sconces bathed the room in a gentle glow, casting amber reflections across the polished stone countertops. Even the simplest tasks seemed to carry a kind of reverence, as if each movement echoed something much older than the room itself.

Sariya stood over a bowl of firm, unripe fruit. She murmured something under her breath, and her paw shimmered with golden light. As she passed it over the bowl, the fruit transformed—colors deepened into jewel tones, skins softened, and the air filled with a sweet, intoxicating fragrance.

Just beyond the open door, Rashid knelt beside the garden bed, his fingers brushing the soil. His voice was a quiet chant, rich with age. The earth shimmered as the young plants responded to his call—sprouting faster than nature should allow, leaves uncurling toward the sky like dancers greeting a spotlight. Tomatoes blushed into vibrant reds, cucumbers stretched to their glossy fullness, and Rashid, with the care of a seasoned grower, harvested each ripened vegetable, placing them gently into his woven basket.

Back inside, Sariya gave a flick of her paw, and a roast appeared on a silver platter—its skin golden and crisp, its fragrance wafting into the room, rich with herbs and spice. It mingled with the scent of sun-warmed fruit and fresh-cut vegetables, creating an aroma that made everyone's mouth water.

Theodora and Alexandria stood watching, awe written plainly across their faces. The kitchen thrummed with quiet magic, alive and welcoming.

"This is incredible," Alexandria whispered, eyes fixed on the feast. "I've never seen anything like it."

Rashid's expression was warm, his voice gentle. "Here, magic is woven into everything—into the land, our meals, our daily rituals. Every dish is a celebration of life and the people we share it with."

Killian leaned back against the counter, visibly impressed. "Even the food feels... alive. Like it carries the magic in every bite."

Sariya nodded, her tone thoughtful. "We honor the spirit in each ingredient. Magic doesn't just make things grow—it reveals their essence. This is the land's gift, shaped by our hands and guided by respect."

Theodora closed her eyes for a moment and took in a deep breath. The warmth, the scents, the unspoken care threaded through every action—it wrapped around her like a blanket. For the first time in days, the knot in her chest loosened. She felt safe. She felt at peace.

Before long, the table was brimming with dishes of every color and texture—each one a masterpiece in its own right. The kitchen pulsed with a kind of quiet joy, a sense that they stood at the heart of something wonderful.

As they gathered around the table, Theodora lifted her fork, her hand trembling slightly as she took her first bite. The moment the food touched her tongue, the room fell silent—each flavor unfolded with depth and clarity, a symphony of taste that spoke of care, tradition, and love.

Conversation soon returned, flowing naturally between them, interspersed with laughter and shared stories. The air turned light with camaraderie, and the weight they'd carried began to lift, one smile at a time.

Killian watched his companions closely and noticed the weariness settling into their movements, heavy and undeniable. "We should get some rest," he said, his voice low with a soft lilt. "We've earned it."

Everyone agreed without hesitation, their silence more telling than words. Relief washed over the group as they began to drift apart, grateful for the promise of rest in this strange, magical place.

Sariya stepped forward, silver-flecked feathers catching the soft crystal light. Her tone was light, her words smooth as water over stone. "We've a place ready for ya. Come on now, this way."

Alexandria blinked, surprised. "But... how did you know we were even coming?"

Layla, perched nearby, tilted her head with a soft smile. Her voice was airier, more musical. "The winds told us, they did. Whispered of yer comin' long 'fore ye set foot here."

As they followed Sariya through winding halls of crystal and carved wood, Theodora felt the last of her energy slipping away. Her limbs grew heavy, and her eyes stung with fatigue. She glanced over at Alexandria, who looked just as drained. The corridor glowed faintly, lit by walls pulsing with soft, golden light. The air was rich with the scent of night-blooming flowers and something deeper—something ancient, like forgotten magic lingering just beneath the surface.

"Here we are," Sariya said, stopping in front of an ornate door. She waved her paw, and the door opened on its own with a quiet breath.

Theodora stepped inside and stopped short. The room was a perfect harmony of nature and enchantment. Living vines climbed the walls, their leaves giving off a gentle glow. Two beds stood side by side in the center of the room, their wooden frames grown from the very floor. Iridescent blankets, shimmering like morning dew, layered each bed.

"It's... incredible," Alexandria whispered.

Khadall padded in behind them, his golden eyes sweeping over the sisters with a look that held both pride and quiet concern. His voice, deep and rough. "Rest now," he rumbled. "Ye're safe here, so ye are."

Theodora sat on one bed, the soft surface rising to cradle her body. The tension began to melt from her shoulders, and for the first time in what felt like forever, she felt warm. Safe.

"Khadall," she murmured, fighting sleep, "what's next? We've still got so far..."

The griffin's eyes softened. "Don't worry about tomorrow. Tonight, just rest. Remember, you're not alone. We're in this together, ready for whatever comes."

Theodora felt a surge of strength at his words—not physical, but a renewed sense of purpose, like a flicker of light in a long, dark tunnel. She met Alexandria's eyes across the small space between their beds, seeing the same fire reflected there—tired, but unbroken.

The room around them was quiet. Shadows danced across the stone walls, and the weight of the day slowly began to lift.

Unspoken thoughts—fear, hope, the ache of their losses, and the quiet, growing bond they were finding in each other—filled the silence between the sisters as they lay down.

Alexandria slowly reached out her hand across the space. Theodora hesitated only a moment before extending hers, their fingers meeting and curling together.

"Together," Alexandria whispered, her voice trembling with emotion.

"Together," Theodora echoed, her throat tight.

Between their palms, a soft glow sparked to life—faint, but steady—proof that even in their weariness, the magic they shared was still alive.

As sleep claimed her, Theodora's last thought was of the battle ahead. But for once, she wasn't afraid. Here in this magical refuge, surrounded by allies, she felt ready to face whatever challenges awaited.

Chapter 26

"Crossing into Darkness"

T HE FIRST RAYS OF dawn crept over the horizon, painting the sky in soft hues of lavender and gold. Theodora's eyes fluttered open, her heart pounded as reality set in. Exhaustion weighed heavy, but she pushed it aside, focusing on Alexandria's sleeping form beside her. Her purple and magenta hair framed her face like a halo, her chest rising and falling with steady breaths as she stirred from sleep.

"Time to rise and shine, Alex," Theodora whispered, gently shaking her sister.

Alexandria groaned, rubbing her eyes. "Already? Feels like I just fell asleep."

Theodora managed a weak smile, masking her own fear. "I know, but we can't be lingerin' here any longer. Every moment counts now."

She slid out of bed, the cool floor a stark reminder of their unfamiliar surroundings. Stretching her sore muscles, Theodora walked to the window.

In the distance, Nau's waters sparkled in the morning light, a beautiful sight at odds with the danger they faced. Her fingers traced the intricate patterns etched into the windowsill, feeling the thrum of ancient magic beneath her touch.

"It's gorgeous," Alexandria said, joining her. "Almost makes you forget what we're up against."

Theodora nodded, her throat tight. "Aye, but we can't forget. Not for a second."

A knock startled them. Killian's voice came through the door: "Ye up, lasses? We need to be movin' soon."

"We're up," Theodora called back, her voice steadier than she felt.

As they dressed and gathered their meager belongings, Theodora's mind raced with all that lay ahead. The journey to Carrantou, Lord Valendor's fortress, loomed before them like an insurmountable mountain. But they had no choice. The fate of Kandella, of their parents, rested on their shoulders.

They found Killian waiting outside, worry etched on his face. "Ye both alright?"

Theodora nodded, squaring her shoulders. "We're ready."

Killian's expression softened slightly. "Good. Let's go then."

As they made their way through the winding halls of the house, Theodora's senses were on high alert. The air hummed with magic, making her skin tingle. She could feel the power within her responding, like a slumbering beast stirring awake.

They stepped onto a wide balcony overlooking the sea. Below, the beach stretched out in soft grays and golds, touched by the first light of dawn. The tide rolled in slow and steady, the waves gentle as they kissed the shore. Everything was still—no wind, no voices—just the quiet hush of the world waking up.

Mist clung to the sand, wrapping around rocks and driftwood with stubborn persistence. The sky warmed slowly, brushed with hints of pink and amber. Carrantou waited somewhere beyond the horizon. For now, the beach remained still, expectant.

They descended the cliffside path, their boots crunching against damp stone. Salt and seaweed scented the air, a cool touch against their skin—present but not harsh. Theodora's heart beat heavily. They stood at the precipice of something significant.

Near the shoreline waited Khadall and his siblings, imposing and still as ancient monuments. Their feathers caught the growing light, their golden eyes following the trio's approach.

Theodora paused as they reached the sand. Despite everything they'd been through, the sight of the griffins still took her breath away. They possessed something otherworldly—something that made this moment feel decisive.

Alexandria joined her silently. Killian followed, adjusting his shoulder strap, his face set with grim determination.

Khadall stepped forward, talons sinking into wet sand. "It's time," he said, voice deep and certain. "Are ye ready to fly?"

Theodora looked between her sister and Killian before nodding. "Aye. We're ready."

They mounted the griffins. Theodora settled onto Khadall's back, fingers winding through the thick feathers at his neck. Alexandria climbed carefully onto Sariya. Killian mounted Rashid with practiced efficiency, eyes already fixed on the horizon.

Khadall shifted beneath her. "The skies are calm now," he said as his wings rustled. "But when we near Carrantou, the winds will turn fierce. Brace yerselves."

Theodora nodded. "We'll be ready."

Behind them, Nau rested in quiet stillness beneath the morning light. Before them stretched the sea, smooth as polished glass—until the horizon, where dark clouds loomed.

"Hold tight," Khadall said. "We fly now."

Theodora's stomach lurched as Khadall's powerful wings beat against the morning air. Wind stung her face, drawing tears from her eyes as she blinked, struggling to maintain focus.

The coastline of Nau vanished behind them. Below, the sea gleamed, golden near shore, deepening to steel blue as they flew outward. With each wingbeat, Theodora felt the weight of their mission pressing harder against her chest.

"Ye alright there, lass?" Khadall's voice rumbled through her grip on his feathers.

"Aye," she replied, voice barely audible against the wind. "Just... takin' it all in."

She glanced sideways, catching sight of Alexandria astride Sariya. Her sister's face was a mask of determination, jaw clenched, fingers buried deep in the griffin's feathers. Their eyes locked for a moment—no need for words between them now.

Khadall's powerful wings beat as they soared farther from shore. Sunlight faded as clouds thickened ahead, casting long shadows over the sea below. The water darkened, its surface churning with increasing violence.

"There," Killian shouted over the wind, gesturing toward the horizon. "That shadow—that's Carrantou."

Theodora narrowed her eyes, her chest tightening. The island appeared as though someone had spilled ink across the water, shrouded in clouds that coiled like smoke. Even at this distance, something about it felt wrong—the air grew colder, heavier.

"Gods, it's depressing," Alexandria said to herself, her voice thin against the strengthening wind.

Theodora couldn't tear her gaze away. A shiver ran through her despite the warmth of Khadall beneath her. The island wasn't just dark—it felt malevolent.

"Brace yerselves," Khadall barked, his voice sharper than usual. "Crosswinds comin' in hard!"

He didn't even get the words out before the storm hit.

A savage gust slammed into them like a wall. Khadall bucked midair, wings straining, his body jerking sideways. Theodora's stomach dropped—gone in an instant—like the ground had vanished beneath her. She wrapped her arms tighter around his neck, fingers tangled in his feathers, clutching so hard her hands went numb.

The sky had turned a deep, churning black. Not just dark—wrong. The air was heavy, like they were flying through smoke or breath. Something unseen was watching. Waiting.

Then—

"Theo!"

Alexandria's scream cut through the wind, high and terrified.

Theodora twisted around, heart slamming against her ribs. Alexandria was sliding sideways, one leg off Sariya's back, her body tilted too far. Her fingers scrambled at the leather harness, barely catching hold. Sariya was spiraling, wings thrashing, fighting the gale with all her strength—but it wasn't enough. She dipped, and Alexandria slipped farther, her boots kicking at open air.

"She's slipping!" Killian shouted from Rashid's back, his voice raw. He was already moving, unstrapping himself, leaning far over as the griffin flew closer. "Alex—take my hand!"

Alexandria's fingers fumbled, one hand already gone, her other arm trembling with the effort of holding on. Wind ripped her scream away as her grip broke—she dropped—

And Killian caught her.

He snatched her wrist in both hands, teeth bared in a shout of effort. Alexandria swung beneath Rashid's belly for a second, wind battering her like a plaything. Rashid shrieked and flailed, struggling to balance under the new, uneven weight. His wings wobbled, his body dipped hard—but he didn't fall.

"I got you!" Killian yelled, muscles straining as he hauled her up inch by inch. Alexandria kicked, scrabbling for anything solid. Her foot hit Rashid's flank—slipped—then found a foothold.

With one last pull, Killian yanked her up and over, dragging her fully onto Rashid's back. They collapsed together, gasping. Alexandria's jaw clenched, fingers buried deep in the griffin's feathers, shaking.

Rashid screamed again, wings flapping erratically, struggling to recover—but after a few gut-lurching dips, he found the air current and steadied. His muscles bunched, then smoothed. He soared again.

"Rashid's good—he's got us," Killian breathed, holding Alexandria close, eyes darting toward Theodora.

Theodora was still watching, knuckles white on Khadall's feathers, her breath coming in short bursts.

"You okay?" Killian called.

She nodded stiffly, but her voice came out hoarse. "Yeah. Yeah."

They didn't say the rest.

They didn't need to.

The wind roared against them as Carrantou's jagged cliffs and fortress loomed closer. Deep within her, Theodora felt her magic stir—responding to the island's presence like a cornered animal sensing danger.

As they approached through the screaming gale, Theodora knew without doubt: nothing had prepared them for this.

The island's cliffs formed a dark ring around the shoreline, rising like broken teeth against the sky—a warning etched in stone. Before they even landed, Theodora sensed it—something wrong seeping from the rocks themselves, threatening everything they'd fought for. Her heart tightened as the malevolence washed over her. After Nau's peaceful shores, this place felt like a slap across the face, and she knew they faced their greatest challenge yet.

Khadall descended, and the ground rushed up. Theodora dismounted, her boots sinking into wet sand that shifted treacherously. Wind blasted her, whipping her hair across her face, feeding the anxiety gnawing at her nerves. She fought against it, struggling for balance.

The beach stretched before her—dead and empty. A distant wail carried on the wind, thin and mournful. The sand beneath her felt strange, as if it held memories best forgotten.

Behind Theodora, the others began to land.

Sariya came in first, her claws hitting the sand harder than usual. Her wings flared wide to steady herself, but it wasn't a graceful landing—a more controlled crash. She crouched low, feathers ruffled, sides heaving. Her head turned quickly, searching the sky.

She let out a low, anxious trill the moment she spotted Alexandria clinging to Rashid as he descended. Her body tensed, eyes locked on the pair.

He came in fast, fighting the weight of the two riders. His wings beat hard, kicking up a spray of sand as he touched down. He staggered a few steps, then steadied. His chest was rising quick, feathers puffed from the strain, but he'd done it. He got them both down safely.

Killian dismounted in one smooth motion, his boots hitting the ground before Rashid fully stopped. He turned and reached up, steadying Alexandria as she slid off behind him. Her legs buckled slightly, and she gripped his arm until she found her footing.

She looked over at Sariya. The griffin had already taken a few slow steps toward her, eyes wide, head low.

Alexandria crossed the space between them and reached for her, fingers brushing over damp, wind-ruffled feathers. "You tried," she said. "You did try."

Sariya leaned in, pressing her beak gently against Alexandria's shoulder, a soft sound rumbling from her throat. She hadn't been strong enough to carry her all the way down, and she knew it—but her rider was safe. That was enough.

Alexandria rested her forehead against Sariya's brow, eyes closing for a moment. "It's okay," she murmured.

Behind them, Rashid gave a quiet, tired call—his version of a sigh, maybe. Killian reached out and ran a hand along his neck in thanks. The griffin gave a slight nod and folded his wings in tight, finally still.

Killian turned to the shoreline, hand already on his halberd. His eyes scanned the beach, his cloak snapping in the wind.

Alexandria stood beside him, wind whipping her hair around her face.

"Something's wrong here," she said, voice low, almost lost in the crash of waves.

"Eyes open," he said, voice low and controlled. "This place isn't what it seems."

Theodora nodded. "Shadow Walkers could be anywhere."

Silence fell between them, heavy with unspoken fear.

The wind howled fiercer now, carrying the stench of brine and decay. Each gust flung sand against their skin like tiny needles. Above them, the sky had darkened to a lifeless gray.

Sariya's feathers bristled with unease, and even stoic Rashid snorted a warning.

Theodora's fingers tightened around her bow. Her heartbeat pounded in her ears.

"Move," Killian said simply.

They obeyed, pressing forward into the wind, toward the waiting treeline that seemed ready to devour them whole.

The wind began to die as they entered the forest—not all at once, but in strange, stuttering breaths, like the storm had lost interest in chasing them further. The gusts tapered off into a heavy stillness that pressed in from all sides.

Above them, the sky hung low and dark, a dull grey blanket that smothered any hint of sunlight. There was no brightness left—just a flat, lifeless glow that made the trees look even more distorted. Nothing golden reached through the canopy. The forest seemed to drink in what little light there was and give nothing back.

The trees closed around them, tall and ancient, their twisted branches locking together high above. Shadows clung to everything—too still, too deep. Every step forward felt like sinking into something colder, more unwelcome.

The air changed too. Damp, heavy, and stale, like it hadn't moved in years. It wrapped around them like a wet shroud, dragging on their clothes and stealing heat from their skin. Even the birds had fallen silent. No rustling, no calls. Just the sound of their own breathing, too loud in the quiet.

Theodora rubbed her arms, eyes darting through the gloom. "It's so... alien," she whispered. Her voice barely rose above the silence, swallowed almost instantly.

Alexandria stepped closer, gaze moving slowly over the gnarled trunks and blackened bark. "It's dead," she murmured. "The trees... they're standing, but there's no life in them."

Killian, who had walked ahead in silence, stopped dead. His body shifted—looser in his shoulders, but tight in his stance. He reached back, fingers brushing the shaft of his halberd.

His voice was low and certain. "We're bein' watched."

No one questioned him.

As they ventured deeper into the forest, an eerie stillness settled around them. Theodora felt her pulse quicken, every shadow seemed to conceal potential danger.

Suddenly, she felt a surge of energy coursing through her veins. The ancient magic of Carrantou called to her, its whispers carrying echoes of long-forgotten secrets. Theodora's movements became graceful and deliberate as she channeled the swirling forces around her.

Tiny orbs of light materialized at her fingertips, responding to her silent commands. Her once wild power now bent to her will, creating a shimmering aura of vibrant hues that enveloped her like armor.

"Theo?" Alexandria's voice was laced with worry.

Killian squeezed Alexandria's shoulder. "She's tappin' into the magic 'ere," he murmured, his eyes fixed on Theodora.

A soft hum filled the air as Theodora wove intricate patterns of energy. Without warning, her eyes flew open wide. "Valendor," she gasped, her voice strained. "He knows we're 'ere."

Alexandria edged closer to Killian, her eyes darting between the shadows. The forest's eerie silence set her nerves on edge as she scanned for any sign of movement.

Suddenly, the air filled with snarls and mocking laughter. Cloaked figures emerged from the darkness - Shadow Walkers sent by Valendor himself.

"Ready?" Theodora whispered, her voice barely audible over Alexandria's pounding heart.

"As I'll ever be," Alexandria replied, feeling magic pulse through her veins.

Killian nodded grimly, his hand on his halberd. "Stay close," he murmured.

As the Shadow Walkers crept closer, the trio braced themselves. They knew what was at stake - there was no turning back now.

Theodora and Alexandria joined hands, their bracelets glowing. Power surged between them, sending out a shockwave of blinding light.

The forest erupted into chaos. Killian's blade flashed as he cut down foes with practiced skill. The twins' magic lit up the gloom, driving back the shadows.

Theodora felt something awaken inside her - a wellspring of untapped power. With a cry, she unleashed it. Lightning arced from her hands, striking down Shadow Walkers left and right.

Alexandria watched in awe as her sister's newfound strength turned the tide of battle. Pride and determination welled up inside her.

The wind began to swirl around Alexandria, lifting her hair and forming a protective whirlwind. With a determined gleam in her emerald eyes, she summoned the earth to aid her. The ground trembled beneath her feet as vines erupted from the forest floor like serpents, entangling the Shadow Walkers.

"Feel the power of Kandella!" she shouted, her voice carrying a command that resonated with authority.

Theodora fought with a fierce grace, her movements fluid and precise. Bolts of energy crackled around her, illuminating the darkness with bursts of light. An equal force of elemental magic repelled each strike, pushing back their assailants.

Killian moved like a force of nature among the chaos, his halfling strength matched only by his unwavering determination to protect the princesses. His weapon sang through the air, a deadly dance that kept their enemies at bay.

Together, the trio fought as one - a symphony of earth, air and lightning swirled around them in a dazzling display of power. The Shadow Walkers, taken aback by the ferocity of the Carrington siblings and their steadfast ally, found themselves outmatched.

The forest echoed with the clash of steel, the crackling of magic, and the pained cries of the shadowy assailants. The ground trembled beneath their feet as the twins' combined magic surged, driving back the encroaching darkness.

With a final burst of energy, Theodora unleashed a blinding wave of light that consumed the remaining Shadow Walkers in its radiant embrace.

As the last echoes of battle faded, an eerie quiet settled over the forest. The twins stood side by side, chests heaving as they caught their breath. Theodora's hands still crackled with residual energy, while Alexandria's hair settled from its wind-whipped frenzy. Killian scanned the area for any lingering threats.

"Well," he said, breaking the silence, "that was a bit of excitement."

Theodora let out a shaky laugh. "Just a bit?"

Alexandria said, her eyes wide. "That was just practice for the main event."

The forest floor was littered with fallen Shadow Walkers, their dark forms already beginning to dissolve into wisps of smoke. The air hung heavy with the scent of ozone and earth, a testament to the elemental forces the twins had wielded.

Killian clapped a hand on each of their shoulders, his touch grounding them after the chaos. "Ye did well, lasses," he said, pride mingling with caution in his voice. "But don't get too comfortable. This was just Valendor testin' the waters. He'll not take to us thrashin' his welcoming party."

The adrenaline of battle faded, leaving them exhausted. Aches spread across their bodies, a stark reminder of the fight they'd just survived.

Killian's keen gaze swept the forest, his body tense. Satisfied they weren't in immediate danger, he turned to the sisters, his gruff exterior softening. "Let's catch our breath 'ere for a bit. No point pushin' on if we're runnin' on empty."

The sisters gathered firewood while Killian dug a fire pit. Soon, a small blaze crackled to life, throwing warmth and light into the cold gloom. They huddled close, exhausted but alert, each of them listening for sounds the forest might offer—or hide.

Late morning brought no light—just a blanket of dark grey clouds pressing low over the trees. The fire still burned strong, its flames steady against the chill. The air was heavy, still. Unsettling.

Then came the rustle—sharp, sudden, and too close.

Theodora grabbed her bow. Alexandria was on her feet in a blink, muscles tensed. Killian stepped in front of them, jaw tight, eyes locked on the trees.

Silence followed, thick and waiting. Theodora's fingers clenched the bow hard enough to hurt. Her heartbeat thundered in her chest. She didn't blink. Didn't breathe.

A figure burst through the underbrush—and collapsed.

Theodora's breath caught. Finnegan.

He hit the ground hard, face pale, clothes torn, blood soaking through the fabric. He didn't move.

For a second, no one did.

Then Theodora dropped to her knees beside him. The smell of blood hit her—sharp, metallic. Her stomach turned, but she forced it down. "Gods," she whispered. "Finnegan..."

She touched his face and gave him a light shake. He lay unconscious, his chest rising and falling in shallow, uneven breaths.

"Hold on," she said, voice cracking. "We've got ye. Just hold on."

Killian knelt beside her, lifting Finnegan's head with both hands. The rough edge in his voice was gone. He looked down at the pale, battered face, eyes searching for some sign of life.

Alexandria stood watch, blade drawn, eyes on the trees.

No one said it out loud, but the thought hung there between them:

If Finnegan made it out... something else might've too.

Chapter 27

"Dusk Before Doom"

Finnegan slept for hours, unmoving but breathing steady. The trio kept close, watching over him, speaking in low tones, weapons within reach. When he finally stirred, it was slow—his eyes fluttered open, clouded with pain but aware.

Alexandria was the first to lean in. "Finnegan," she said. "How do you feel?"

He blinked, struggling to focus. "Like I got trampled by a warhorse," he muttered, voice gruff but laced with the barest trace of humor.

Killian shifted closer, eyes scanning Finnegan's battered face. "How in blazes did ye get out?" he asked, voice low and tight with concern.

His eyes, though heavy, held a flicker of defiance. Each word was a struggle. "Hidden passage," he rasped between ragged breaths. "In the dungeons. Led to... the sea cliffs."

Without thinking, Theodora's hands moved to him, magic already rising. A soft glow bloomed at her fingertips, spreading as she pressed her palms to his wounds. The warmth flowed through him, easing the pain, coaxing torn skin and broken tissue to mend.

"Ye're safe now," she murmured, though the words felt brittle. They weren't safe—not really. Enemy territory pressed in from all sides.

His gaze met hers. "Had to jump," he said. "Prayed I'd survive the fall. The sea... it was so far down."

She shuddered, the image clear in her mind—Finnegan, battered, bloody, and still choosing to leap into the unknown. Admiration and heartbreak tangled in her chest. What he'd done to get back to them... she didn't think she'd ever forget it.

"We'll stop Valendor," Alexandria vowed, her voice hard. "We will prevent any more lives from being lost to his cruelty."

As Finnegan's worst injuries faded, Theodora's magic deepened, drawing on ancient power. Each pulse of energy brought renewal.

"Rest now," she said. Alexandria offered water while Killian kept watch, alert for any threat.

Finnegan's eyes fluttered open, filled with gratitude. "Thank ye," he croaked. "Ye saved me life."

Theodora shook her head, a small smile gracing her lips. "We're all in this together. Ye would've done the same for any o' us."

Her mind raced as she realized the implications of Finnegan's escape—it changed everything. Not only might he possess crucial information about Valendor's defenses, but his unexpected return filled a void she hadn't even recognized was there. Their mentor had returned against all odds, and as Theodora tended to Finnegan's wounds, a spark of hope ignited in her chest. They were together again, their little band complete, and that unity brought a strength they would need for the battle ahead.

Finnegan let out a groan as he started to wake, his eyes flickering open. Theodora quickly knelt beside him, her hands moving over his shoulders and down his arms, searching for any additional injuries she might have overlooked. Everything seemed intact. No sign of blood. A wave of relief washed over her.

Their eyes met. No words—just a tight, silent exchange that said everything.

"Y'with me?" she asked, voice low but urgent.

He nodded slightly struggling to sit up. "Aye," he croaked. "Still breathin'." His gaze shifted to the imposing outline of the castle, and his jaw tightened.

A few feet away, Killian and Alexandria sat near the low-burning campfire. He leaned forward, elbows on his knees, sharpening a blade in steady strokes. She sat with her hands out, fingers stretched toward the flames, jaw tight, eyes distant. No one spoke.

Then it hit—the silence.

Killian's hand paused. Slowly, he straightened, eyes lifting skyward. Alexandria followed his gaze, rising to her feet just behind him.

He stepped forward, boots crunching over dry leaves. His gaze locked upward. He raised his arm and pointed.

"It's begun," he said, voice low and grim. "The eclipse."

Above them, the moon crept over the sun, slow and deliberate. Shadows bled across the forest. Light dimmed to a sickly dusk. Theodora's breath caught in her chest.

Then the ground began to tremble beneath them—subtle at first, like the forest exhaling. But it grew. A low groan rumbled through the trees as their ancient trunks began to sway and moan. Wind slammed into them, sudden and sharp, tearing leaves from branches and throwing dust into the air.

Theodora's heart hammered. Her hair whipped across her face, stinging her eyes. She shielded them with a hand, squinting through the rising storm. Finnegan stood rigid beside her, eyes scanning the horizon. Alert. Braced.

In the distance, a roar echoed up from the valley below—the ocean. They turned as one, watching the ribbon of water churn violently. Its banks burst, sending white spray high into the air. The river surged like a beast waking from a nightmare, tearing through the land with a mind of its own.

Alexandria froze, her eyes wide. "Sweet stars," she whispered.

Then—a sharp crack, like the sky itself splitting open. Lightning clawed through the dark, followed by thunder so violent it rattled the ground beneath their feet.

Killian's voice rang out, cutting through the chaos. "To our mounts! Move! Now!"

Overhead, the griffins came—wings outstretched, eyes glowing, slicing through the storm like arrows loosed from the heavens.

Khadall landed in front of Theodora with a shriek, wings flaring, golden eyes locked on hers.

She stepped forward without hesitation, bow already slung over her shoulder. She met his gaze. "We fly."

He knelt. She swung onto his back, legs gripping tight, breath sharp, and shallow in her chest. She looked back.

Finnegan hadn't moved.

He stood there, jaw clenched, eyes fixed on the maelstrom ahead. Waiting.

She stretched out a hand, arm trembling. "Finnegan," she called, her voice louder now, firm and clear over the wind. "Ride with me."

His eyes flicked to hers. For a second, they held.

Then he took her hand, pulling himself up behind her. Khadall shifted with a grunt, wings unfurling. Theodora leaned forward, bracing for flight.

Killian mounted Rashid in one fluid motion. Alexandria was already airborne, her griffin screeching into the storm.

Theodora's grip tightened as Khadall surged upward. The ground dropped away. Wind screamed past her ears. Her cheeks burned with cold, her body pressed against the warmth of Finnegan behind her.

Below, they watched as the ground tore itself apart.

Cracks split the forest floor. Trees fell like matchsticks. The earth buckled and groaned, ripping itself open in jagged lines.

Ahead, Alexandria pointed toward the dark mass rising on the horizon—the sorcerer's fortress, stark against the advancing eclipse.

Her voice came hard, fierce. "We end this. Before the eclipse finishes."

Killian's eyes narrowed. "Or there won't be a damn thing left to save."

In the distance, Lord Valendor's castle loomed, a jagged silhouette against the storm-hung sky. Its towering spires clawed at the heavens like the fingers of something long dead but not yet buried. The sight alone made their stomachs tighten. It wasn't just a fortress—it was a warning.

The wind grew colder as they neared, carrying with it the sour tang of decay and something older—magic warped by time and cruelty. Theodora's heart pounded against her ribs. The air itself felt heavier, as if the castle's presence was reaching out, pressing down on them.

She leaned forward and wrapped her arms around Khadall's neck, burying her face for a moment in his warm feathers. His breathing was calm beneath her, steady and sure. Finnegan sat behind her, arms braced around her waist, but his gaze stayed locked on the dark horizon.

Below, the land writhed with ruin. Cracks split the ground like open wounds, trees twisted at impossible angles, and the storm overhead howled with fury. Lightning carved through the clouds, thunder cracking close behind—louder, nearer.

But as they drew closer to the ominous fortress, the chaos began to fade. The thunder grew less frequent. The lightning came slower, softer. Winds that had screamed now whispered through the air like breath held too long. Still tense, still wrong—but quieter. Like the world was waiting.

Killian rode Rashid to their right, one hand clenched tight around the base of the griffin's neck feathers. His face was grim. Alexandria stayed low against Sariya, her fingers curled into her mount's thick mantle, jaw set.

"We're almost there," Killian said, voice low, tension threading each word.

"Aye, and it's quietin' down too fast," Finnegan muttered, eyes narrowed, scanning the ground. "That's not peace—it's a trap settin' in."

He leaned in closer to Khadall's neck and spoke low. "Take us down. Forest's edge, just there—nice and soft."

Khadall gave a subtle grunt of acknowledgement and adjusted his wings, angling them into a smooth descent. Alexandria and Killian followed without a word, eyes fixed on the castle as it crept larger in their view.

The griffins landed in a muted flurry, talons digging into the soft earth and damp leaves at the forest's edge. Around them, the wind died down to a slow crawl. Rain had threatened but never came. The clouds remained, heavy and bruised, but the fury of the storm had ebbed. In its place, a silence bloomed—uneasy and absolute.

Over the hill ahead, just barely visible through the gaps in the trees, the tops of Valendor's towers pierced the dark sky. Distant, but close enough to feel.

Finnegan slid off Khadall first, crouching low as his boots touched the ground. His voice was low but firm.

"We walk from here," he said, scanning the slope ahead. "Keep quiet. They'll be eyes on the ridge."

Theodora followed him down, hand still brushing Khadall's feathers. Killian dismounted silently, already pulling his hood low. Alexandria slid off Sariya's back, her eyes lifting immediately to the dark hill beyond. She stared toward the towers for a long, still moment.

"He knows we're here," she said. "I can feel him already."

Theodora's eyes didn't leave the jagged towers rising beyond the hill. "Let him," she said, her voice steady. "We didn't come this far ta hide."

The words cut clean through the silence, firm, and resolute.

"We'll split up," she continued, glancing between them. "Finnegan, Killian—ye'll free our parents. Alex and I will deal with Valendor."

Finnegan's eyes met hers, sharp and uncertain, a storm of emotion flickering behind them. He didn't speak. Didn't have to. She saw the hesitation clear on his face.

She reached out and squeezed his arm, fingers brushing the tension knotted beneath his sleeve.

"I know this be troublin' ye," she said softly, but her tone left no room for argument. "It has to be us. Alex and me. We're the ones meant to face him."

A beat passed. The wind stirred the treetops. Then Finnegan gave a quick nod, rough and reluctant.

"Right then," he muttered, jaw tight. "We'll handle the dungeons."

The group leaned in closer. No one spoke. Even the griffins were still.

Finnegan's voice dropped to a whisper. "'Tis a secret passage," he said, low and fast, the weight of it pressing into the space between them. "Hidden deep. Not marked. Stick close now and keep an eye peeled for guards. If they spot us before we're in, we've no chance."

Theodora's grip tightened around her bow. Every word etched itself into her mind. Next to her, Killian shifted, checking the straps on his pack, quiet but focused.

Finnegan took a breath and stepped forward, his movements silent. The forest swallowed him easily, his dark hair and cloak melting into the shadows. The rest followed in tight formation.

The air grew thicker with every step—heavy with damp and rot. The scent of old, dying things clung to the undergrowth. Leaves brushed their legs like grasping fingers. Even the trees seemed to lean in, listening.

Theodora's heartbeat thudded in her ears. Every snapped twig beneath a boot, every rustle of wings above made her flinch. Her senses sharpened. She scanned the darkness, muscles taut, ready to react.

They moved carefully, one foot at a time, each placement deliberate. Finnegan moved like he'd done this before—quick, quiet, knowing. Theodora kept her eyes on him, letting his path guide hers.

The shadows deepened as they pushed further. Light barely touched the ground now. What did filtered through came in flickers, like something was shifting above them—clouds or something worse.

Then, ahead, a twisted tree rose out of the gloom like something torn from a nightmare. Its bark was dark and split, ridged like old scars, and its gnarled branches stretched upward like clawed hands frozen in place. The air around it felt heavy—thick with old, silent magic.

Finnegan stopped, boots crunching on dead leaves. He turned back to the others, his face tight, set like stone.

"We're 'ere," he said. "Through the roots. Passage runs under the ridge—takes us right below the walls."

He looked at each of them, pausing just long enough to make it clear—this was it.

"Once we go down, there's no comin' back up," he said. "So if ye've got doubts, settle 'em now."

No one answered. They didn't have to. That moment had passed.

Killian glanced up—and one by one, the rest followed. Above the tree's twisted limbs, the sky was churning. Thick grey clouds rolled overhead, and behind them, the sun was being swallowed. The eclipse had blacked out half the sun, like a coin sliding in front of a flame. The light was strange. Shadows stretched long and thin. The air had gone still.

Finnegan turned back to the tree. He reached out and traced a jagged spiral etched into the bark. The symbol pulsed faintly, like it was waiting. He pressed his palm against it.

The tree groaned, a deep, slow sound that vibrated through the ground. Its roots twitched, then started to shift—writhing like something alive, pulling apart to reveal a narrow stairwell spiraling into the earth. A dim orange glow flickered from below, steady and slow, like a heartbeat.

For a moment, no one moved.

Then Finnegan stepped in first.

The others followed, one by one, leaving the fading light behind.

As they navigated through the twisting tunnels, memories clawed at Finnegan's mind. Each step echoed with ghosts he'd tried to bury. The cold stone walls were too familiar, the damp air too much like before.

He'd been a prisoner here once. The darkness of the dungeon, the bite of chains on his wrists, the way Valendor's voice had slithered into his head, forcing him to betray others—it all rushed back. His breath caught suddenly, and he stumbled, one hand bracing against the wall.

"A moment," he muttered, the others stopping behind him.

Theodora moved closer, brow furrowed. "Finnegan? Are ya alright? Ya seem... troubled."

"I..." He swallowed hard, eyes fixed on the ground. "These tunnels hold memories I'd rather forget."

She reached for his arm, her touch steady, warm. "We're here for ya, Finnegan."

He nodded, jaw tight as he forced the memories down. He had work to do. The tunnels felt like they were closing in, the air thick with a heaviness that seeped from the very walls. It weighed on him, threatening the resolve he'd built.

His gaze found Theodora, her face half-lit by torchlight. Even here, she stood straight, unwavering. She'd always had that about her—that quiet strength. Now he could see the worry behind it too, and something protective stirred in him.

"I know ye're worried," she said softly, meeting his eyes. "But we're in this together. United, we're stronger than any darkness Valendor can throw at us."

He nodded, her words steadying him. The deeper they went, the colder it grew. The scent of damp earth mixed with distant sea salt as they pushed forward.

When his thoughts threatened to drag him under again, he focused on his companions—their determination a lifeline pulling him back to the present. Their footsteps echoed in grim rhythm as they hurried through the passages, exchanging looks that said more than words could.

Valendor's tower waited somewhere above, unseen but felt.

Chapter 28

"Twin Flames Rise"

Finnegan stopped at a junction where the passage split. Shadows danced across the ancient stones as the torchlight flickered. Theodora and Alexandria stood beside him, tense and ready.

"Lassies, the high tower's passage is just ahead," he said. "We'll be splittin' up from here."

The sisters exchanged a glance. Finnegan's face hardened with concern.

"The path ta the tower is crawlin' with guards," he warned. "Keep yer wits about ye. Trust each other. It won't be pretty."

Alexandria's fists clenched at her sides. "We'll find a way through."

Finnegan gestured toward a narrow gap in the wall ahead. "That's yer path. Through there." His voice dropped lower. "Stay together. All of Kandella's countin' on ye whether they know it or not."

"We'll see ye when our parents are free," Alexandria said, voice firm.

"Aye, that ye will." Finnegan's mouth curved into a quick, tight grin. He turned to Killian with a nod. "Let's be off then." They headed down toward the dungeons, soon swallowed by darkness.

Theodora watched them disappear, then turned to her sister. "For our family. For Kandella. We can't fail."

Alexandria nodded, her eyes gleaming in the flickering torchlight. "We won't," she replied, her voice steady despite the gravity of their task. With a shared look of resolve, they approached the passage Finnegan had shown.

Shadows hid the entrance, its stone walls etched with intricate designs that seemed to shift in the dim light. The sisters exchanged a wordless glance, their bond palpable. As they stepped inside, a chill crept over them, and an eerie silence fell.

Theodora's pulse quickened, the weight of their mission settling heavily upon her. She glanced at Alexandria, who offered a reassuring smile.

Suddenly, footsteps echoed through the passage, growing louder by the second. Alexandria's eyes widened as she grabbed Theodora's arm, pulling her into a hidden alcove. They pressed against the cold stone, scarcely daring to breathe.

"Guards," Alexandria whispered, her body tense as she peered out.

Theodora's senses sharpened, her heartbeat thundering in her ears as the footsteps drew near. The torchlight cast long, dancing shadows along the corridor. She steeled herself, gripping her bow.

The guards came into view, their dark armor clinking with each step. Their dark metal armor covered them, and their helmet visors hid their faces. Theodora felt Alexandria's grip tighten as they willed themselves to meld with the shadows.

"Spread out and search every corner," the lead guard barked, his gruff voice sending a shiver down Theodora's spine. She squeezed her sister's hand, silently reaffirming their resolve to remain hidden.

As the guards fanned out, one approached their alcove. Theodora's breath caught in her throat as the guard's shadow loomed over them.

"Hear somethin'?" the guard asked, his voice cutting through the silence.

The girls remained motionless, willing themselves to become one with the darkness.

The guard leaned closer, his gaze sweeping the alcove. The torchlight flickered, casting strange patterns on the walls.

Just as Theodora braced herself for their imminent discovery, a distant shout echoed down the corridor. "Intruders in the eastern wing! All units mobilize!"

The guard swore under his breath. "We're needed elsewhere," he called to his companions. With a final glance at the alcove, the guards hurried away, their footsteps fading into the distance.

The sisters exhaled slowly, tension draining from their bodies. They shared a look of relief before cautiously emerging from their hiding spot.

"We need ta move," Theodora whispered. "That distraction won't buy us much time."

Alexandria nodded, her expression set. "Let's get to the tower before they come back."

They pressed on alert for any sign of more guards. The air grew thick and oppressive, and shadows seemed to dance along the walls, setting Theodora's nerves on edge.

Rounding a corner, they stepped out of the narrow passage and into a vast chamber bathed in an otherworldly blue glow. The contrast hit them immediately—the cramped, suffocating tunnel gave way to open space, cold air and silence so deep it felt alive.

Ancient murals covered the walls, their faded pigments still clinging to scenes of long-forgotten battles and legends. Warriors with burning swords, cities swallowed by waves of fire, a crowned figure standing alone atop a mountain of bones. Theodora slowed, her eyes tracing the jagged lines of a crumbling fresco.

Alexandria moved a few steps ahead, eyes sweeping the chamber. "The high stair has to be here somewhere," she murmured. "It's the only way up to the tower."

Theodora nodded but didn't speak. Her chest was tight. The hum of magic here wasn't just in the air—it was in the walls, the floor, even the light itself. That copper tang was back on her tongue, sharp and bitter.

They moved deeper into the room, boots crunching over debris—splintered stone, shattered glass, rusted fragments of armor left behind by someone who'd never made it back. The ceiling stretched far above, lost in shadow, and for a moment, Theodora felt like something up there was watching.

"There," Alexandria said, pointing past a toppled statue near the chamber's edge. "There it is—hidden, but that's the stairs, sure enough."

As they approached it, Theodora hesitated. "An' what if he's already waitin' for us?" she asked, voice low.

Alexandria glanced at her, jaw tight. "Then we face him head on. We didn't drag ourselves this far just to stop at the door."

Theodora forced a breath through her nose, nodded. They looked up the staircase—tight, steep, disappearing into darkness.

"Let's end this," Alexandria said, her voice low but steady."

And together, they began to climb.

They moved in silence, side by side on the narrow, winding staircase. Each step sent a faint echo spiraling into the darkness above, as if the tower itself was listening. The air grew colder with every turn, the walls tightening around them.

Theodora kept her hand on the stone as they climbed, grounding herself. The rough surface pulsed beneath her fingers—alive with the same twisted energy that buzzed beneath her skin. It felt like the tower was breathing, waiting.

What if we can't stop him? The thought came uninvited, sharp and cold. *What if we're too late?* Theodora clenched her jaw, but the questions kept coming. *What happens if we fail? Who will protect Kandella then?*

Her chest tightened. She could still see it—home. The fields just beyond the northern wall, the rooftops in the early morning light, the sound of bells echoing through the narrow streets. People who didn't know their lives were hanging by a thread.

Alexandria didn't slow. Even though her steps and breathing stayed steady and controlled, Theodora noticed tension in her shoulders and stiffness in her movements. She was holding it all in—fear, anger, whatever memories were clawing at the back of her mind.

Theodora wanted to speak, to say what was eating at her, but the words stuck. So she kept moving. One foot after the other.

As they climbed higher, the light from the chamber below faded completely. Only the faintest glow seeped through the cracks in the stone—blue and pulsing, like a heartbeat. Theodora blinked, her eyes straining, her body tightening with every turn of the stairs.

They had to be close now. The air was so heavy it was hard to breathe, thick with the scent of ash and something older—decay.

Then, the stairs ended. They stepped onto a narrow landing facing a massive door. It loomed before them, black and veined with the same glowing blue that lined the walls below. The wood was ancient, twisted in unnatural ways, the ironwork etched with runes that shimmered in the gloom.

Beyond it, the tower's spires reached toward the sky.

Theodora froze. That crawling sensation spread across her arms and neck like a thousand invisible insects. Her mouth filled with the sharp taste of copper, stronger now, almost choking.

Valendor's magic.

It was here. Right on the other side.

She looked at Alexandria. Her sister's hand hovered over the door, fingers curled but steady.

"You ready?" Alexandria asked without looking back.

No. Not really.

But Theodora nodded anyway. "Yeah."

They faced the door.

Elsewhere in the castle, far below the tower's looming shadow, the air was colder, thicker—heavy with centuries of secrets.

While Theodora and Alexandria prepared to face Valendor in the high tower, Finnegan and Killian moved in silence beneath, navigating the underbelly of the keep with the urgency of men who knew time was running thin.

Finnegan and Killian slunk through the castle's bowels, their footsteps barely audible against the damp stone floor. The dungeon reeked of mildew and something worse—the lingering scent of fear. Rusted cells lined the narrow corridor, most empty save for a few that housed grim evidence of previous occupants—scattered bones, deep scratches in stone, dark stains on the floor.

Finnegan halted, the hairs on his neck rising. "Magic," he breathed, barely audible. Beside him, Killian's hands trembled slightly, his own power responding to the corrupted energy that hung in the air like poison.

They rounded a corner and froze. At the corridor's end stood a massive wooden door inscribed with arcane symbols that pulsed with sickly light.

"Watch yerself," Finnegan murmured. "One misstep here and we're finished."

Killian nodded, his face tight with concentration. Finnegan squeezed his shoulder once, then stepped back. Killian drew a steady breath, focusing his power. The wards resisted, ancient and cruel, but he worked methodically, teasing apart each strand of protection. One snapped with a hiss. Then another. The door shuddered and, with a reluctant groan, swung inward.

The stench hit them first—waste, rot and hopelessness. Two figures huddled in the corner, skeletal and filthy. King William and

Queen Amara, once regal, now reduced to hollow-eyed prisoners in tattered clothes. Recognition sparked in their exhausted faces.

Queen Amara made a broken sound. "Finnegan?"

Two strides and he was there, blade flashing down on their chains. Metal shattered against stone with a jarring clang. Killian lunged forward to catch the king as he wavered, each breath a visible struggle.

Relief washed through the cell, raw and palpable. The queen gripped Finnegan's arm with fingers like twigs, her lips quivering as if she couldn't believe he was real.

"Thank the stars," she whispered, voice scraped thin by thirst.

"We thought... we didn't think anyone was comin'," King William rasped, clutching Killian's arm for support. "How—how did ye find us?"

Killian glanced at Finnegan. "It was Theodora."

"Aye," Finnegan confirmed. "Had a vision in Monaghan Forest. Saw shadow walkers draggin' ye both from the castle. Knew it was Valendor's work. Knew where they'd taken ye."

The queen stared. "She knew?"

"She's got the gift," Finnegan said. "Sees the past. Powerful visions."

"She's somethin' else," Killian added, voice low.

The king's gaze hardened as he looked between them. "Where is she? The girls—where are they?"

Finnegan's jaw tightened. "They went for Valendor."

"Theodora's decision," Killian explained. "Said ye needed freedom—that was our task. But her and Alexandria... they're the ones from the prophecy. Said only they could end him."

"Her exact words—'Get them out. We'll handle the rest,'" Finnegan added.

Horror crept into Amara's expression. "They shouldn't face him alone."

"They're not alone," Finnegan countered. "They've each other. We've trained them hard since this all began. Combat, stealth, magic—everything we could pack into days."

Amara shook her head. "A week's trainin' isn't enough."

"They're ready," Killian insisted, unexpected fire in his voice. "I've never seen anythin' like them. Theodora's courage, Alexandria's quick thinkin'—they balance perfectly. Your Majesty, they're unstoppable together."

"Aye," Finnegan agreed. "The way they fight, the way they think—it's somethin' else."

The queen and king exchanged a look, understanding dawning through their exhaustion.

"Then we trust them," Amara said, a newfound strength in her voice. "They are our daughters."

William straightened despite his weakness. "And if anyone can destroy Valendor, it's them."

"We still need to reach them," the king continued, voice thin but determined. "They might need our help before this ends."

Finnegan glanced toward the corridor, listening for guards. "We move now, before they discover ye're gone. Time's runnin' short."

William pushed himself up with visible effort, his eyes fierce despite his frail state. "What are we waitin' for then?"

"High Tower," Finnegan said. "Valendor's there. So are the twins."

"To the High Tower," Killian confirmed, helping the queen stand. "We find the girls and end this."

"Quiet and fast," Finnegan warned. "Once they find this cell empty, every guard in the castle will be huntin' us."

No one questioned him.

Sword at the ready, Finnegan took point. They pushed forward, muscles burning, lungs heavy, exhaustion pulling at their limbs. Only raw urgency kept them moving. With every step, the castle seemed to shift, its hallways twisting unnaturally, dark magic thrumming through stone.

The need to reach the girls drove them, but the deeper they went, the clearer it became that Valendor wouldn't make it easy. They turned a corner, the passage narrowing and Finnegan's instincts flared. He halted, hand raised to stop the others, eyes sharp as he listened.

"They know we're comin'," he said grimly, barely audible.

Killian's jaw tightened. "Then we give 'em hell."

An echo down the next corridor. Shuffling footsteps. Many of them.

"Brace yerselves," Finnegan muttered.

The sound swelled—rhythmic and heavy. Shadows stretched toward them, flickering in torchlight.

Guards.

A small army of them.

They didn't hesitate.

Steel rang against steel as blades crossed and magic crackled through the corridor. The narrow space made every sound sharper—fire hissing, metal clashing, men shouting in pain.

"Left flank!" Finnegan called, thorny vines erupting from the floor to snare two charging guards. They howled as barbs pierced their armor.

Killian rolled through the fray, quick and deadly. "On it!" he shouted, leaping over a fallen guard and hamstringing another as he landed. "Bloody hell, Yer Majesty—aim that ice away from me face!"

The queen stood her ground, hands glowing with frost and wind. "Duck faster then," she retorted, sending a blast of freezing air that caught three guards mid-charge, locking their legs in ice. She flashed Killian a smirk.

William blocked a heavy blow with his battered shield, the impact jarring his weakened arms. He countered with a savage swing. "Not exactly the homecoming I pictured," he grunted.

"No fancy feast waitin' for us, that's for sure," Killian shot back, sidestepping a blade.

The guards faltered. Fear crept into their ranks as they realized these weren't helpless escapees. One backed away. Another looked ready to run.

Finnegan caught Killian's eye. A nod between them.

"Now!" Finnegan shouted.

They surged forward as one. Moments later, it was finished. The last guard fell, and silence returned, broken only by their harsh breathing and the dying crackle of spent magic.

"Everyone still standin'?" William asked, lowering his weapon.

"More or less," Amara answered, scanning for threats.

"We need ta move," Finnegan said, wiping blood from his cheek, worry plainly in his eyes.

Killian nodded. "Aye, those girls are waitin' on us."

Finnegan sealed the passage behind them with a wave of his hand. They slipped into a hidden alcove, all four shivering as they felt the twins somewhere ahead—in Valendor's domain.

William straightened, meeting Finnegan and Killian's eyes. Despite his haggard face, determination hardened his gaze.

"We've no time ta waste," he said, voice rough but commanding. "Those girls are facin' the devil himself, and every moment matters. We move now."

Far above, the tower seemed to pulse with dark energy, like a living thing awakened. Theodora and Alexandria stood at its heart, the massive iron door before them like a final threshold. Every second dragged like a weight, the silence pressing in around them, as if the stones themselves held their breath.

Their allies were coming—but not fast enough.

Theodora felt a wave of malevolent energy emanating just beyond the massive iron door. She exchanged a determined glance with Alexandria, their resolve evident.

Taking a deep breath, they tapped into their telepathic link. Together, they pushed open the heavy door and entered the tower. An eerie silence enveloped them, broken only by their soft footsteps echoing on the cold stone floor. The air was thick with dark magic, wisps of mist curling around their ankles.

Theodora surveyed the chamber, a chill running down her spine. The tower thrummed with an otherworldly energy. Faded tapestries hung on the walls, depicting ancient battles. The musty scent of old books and incense permeated the air, mixed with the tang of magic that made their skin tingle. Faint whispers seemed to echo from the walls, urging them deeper into the tower's mysteries.

As the girls cautiously advanced through the chamber, their senses sharpened and attuned to every creak and whisper in the oppressive stillness. The air grew colder, laden with a sense of foreboding that seemed to seep into their bones. A faint metallic taste touched their tongues, sharp and unnatural. The very stones beneath their feet vibrated with a low, pulsing hum—like a heartbeat tethered to something ancient and cruel.

Exchanging a knowing look, the twins felt their shared magic pulsing between them like a steady rhythm. The bond kept them grounded as they ventured further, passing between towering obsidian columns that gleamed with an unnatural sheen. Stone gargoyles leered from shadowy corners, their grotesque faces appearing to follow the sisters' every move. Flickers of movement danced in their peripheral vision—shadows that disappeared the moment they turned to look.

Alexandria gripped Theodora's arm, her voice barely above a breath. "He's here... I feel him, Theo. It's like his shadow's crawling over my skin."

Theodora's gaze swept the room, her jaw tightening. "I know. This place reeks of his magic."

"It's thick... like he's watching, waiting," Alexandria murmured, her voice laced with unease.

A sudden gust of cold air rushed past them, whispering in a voice not quite human.

Theodora met her sister's eyes, her tone firm. "Let him watch. We're not leavin'."

"Together, then?"

"Always," Theodora said, fire flickering in her eyes.

"'Tis about time our guests decided t' grace us with their presence," a voice drawled from the shadows, smooth as oil over broken glass.

The air grew still.

From the gloom, Lord Valendor stepped forward like a specter slipping free from the bones of night. He moved with unnatural ease, each step deliberate, his form gradually taking shape until he stood fully revealed beneath the dim torchlight. His robes, black as a starless sky, clung to him like sentient smoke. The runes embroidered along the fabric shimmered faintly, whispering in a tongue that scratched at the mind.

A silver chain hung around his neck. Its sapphire centerpiece pulsing with an eerie, unnatural glow—like it held something alive.

His gaze swept past the sisters and fixed on the sliver of eclipse visible through the tower window. A slow smile curved across his face, cold and knowing.

"Ah, the eclipse," he said softly, like he was savoring the taste of the words. "A celestial dance markin' the end of an age and the dawn of a new reign. Fittin' that ye, Princess Theodora—and yer dear sister Alexandria—should witness it from within me domain."

Theodora's jaw tightened. His presence distorted the room, made the torchlight flicker and the stone seem colder beneath her boots. Even the silence felt strained—like the tower itself was holding its breath.

"We're not here to witness yer twisted ambitions, Valendor," Theodora snapped, voice low but firm. "We're here to put an end to 'em."

Alexandria stepped forward to stand beside her sister. Despite her smaller stature, she radiated fierce determination, her emerald eyes burning with quiet rage.

"Your reign of terror ends tonight," she said, though fury edged each word. "Starting with what you did to our parents."

He chuckled, a dark, hollow sound that echoed across the chamber. It wasn't loud—but it carried weight. A promise of cruelty.

"Brave words," he said, his tone laced with contempt. "Two little girls who think they can storm a tower and overthrow a king."

He stepped closer, the shadows bending with him.

Theodora's heart pounded, but she held her ground. Her fingers itched for her bow, for the familiar draw of the string, for the surge of power that came when her magic aligned with her will. The air around her crackled faintly. Her pink and lavender locks stirred as if touched by an invisible wind.

"King?" Theodora said, her voice like a drawn blade. "You're no king. Just a coward clingin' ta illusions and borrowed power."

The words landed hard, echoing in the charged silence of the tower.

Beside her, Alexandria didn't move. She didn't need to. Her stillness was its own kind of strength—controlled, sharp, unyielding. Her emerald eyes burned steady. When Theodora glanced her way, there was no fear there. Just fire.

"We're not afraid of you," Alexandria said, voice calm, but carrying. "And we won't let you destroy what's left of Kandella."

Valendor's smile twitched.

"We may be young," she continued, her tone sharpening with each word, "but don't mistake youth for weakness. Our strength isn't in titles or blood—it's in the fire you tried to snuff out... and failed."

The chamber held its breath.

Then came the shift.

Valendor raised a hand. Shadows surged, ripping from the walls like smoke given form. Runes across his robes lit in blood-red pulses, the sapphire at his throat flaring like a heartbeat soaked in malice. The very stone beneath their feet seemed to groan as darkness swelled.

But Theodora didn't flinch.

She stood firm, drawing strength from the steady presence of her sister beside her.

Her hand moved to her bow—new, but already a part of her. It had chosen her barely a week ago in Isadore, but their connection was fierce, unshakable. Not forged over years, but sealed in battle and blood. The moment her fingers touched the smooth wood, it responded—warm, alive, ready. The bowstring hummed like a live wire, echoing the power thrumming in her veins.

Beside her, Alexandria's hands ignited with a searing glow. Magic sparked at her fingertips, threads of light twisting into sigils midair. The energy in the chamber shifted—brighter, sharper—pushing back against Valendor's encroaching dark.

The sorcerer snarled, and the first wave came.

Tendrils of void magic screamed through the air, jagged and furious, reaching for the sisters like claws. Theodora moved first.

She loosed an arrow.

It soared, trailed in fire and lightning, and struck the first shadow mid-air. The explosion lit the tower in a sudden burst of gold and blue. Another arrow followed—ice-tipped, then wind-bound—each one singing with elemental magic, each one landing true.

Alexandria stepped forward, planting her feet, hands raised.

She unleashed a wave of radiant energy that cut through the shadows like dawn tearing through mist. Beams of blinding light burst from her palms, colliding with Valendor's spellwork in explosive flashes that lit the stone walls like a storm of stars.

The tower shook.

The clash of magic rattled its bones, echoing through its spine. Light met shadow again and again, neither side giving ground. Valendor roared, casting bolts of dark fire, wind laced with decay, illusions that clawed at the mind.

But the sisters didn't yield.

Theodora's arrows flew, fast and furious—guided by instinct, powered by will. The bow bent to her, and she to it. They moved as one.

Alexandria's magic flared brighter. Her voice rose into a spell, words glowing on her lips. The light she wielded was no longer just magic—it was conviction made manifest.

The darkness surged in one final wave, massive and all-consuming, meant to crush them whole.

Then—

a low rumble cut through the chaos.

At first, it was subtle. Like thunder rolling through the bones of the tower. The stone beneath their feet trembled. Theodora's eyes snapped to the far wall. Alexandria froze mid-motion, her magic flickering as the sound grew louder.

Even Valendor turned, attention wrenched from his attack.

The towering chamber doors began to glow—soft at first, then blinding. Lines of golden light raced across the surface, carving cracks in the ancient wood. The runes etched into the arch pulsed once—twice—then shattered.

Boom.

The doors exploded inward.

Chapter 29

"When Shadows Fall"

The blast tore through the tower, splinters of wood and iron rained down as the doors shattered.

Through the swirling dust and smoke stepped King William—alive, whole, and burning with fury. He moved slowly, every step deliberate. Even after years locked up and tortured in Valendor's dungeons, he stood tall. Though he was thin, his clothes torn and bloodied, his eyes blazed like a storm barely held in check. His magic rolled off him in shimmering waves, golden light cracking across the broken stones.

At his sides, Finnegan, and Killian moved like shadows, weapons drawn, faces set with grim determination. Finnegan's sword caught the light as he shifted it in his hand, the steel steady, his knuckles white around the hilt. Beside him, Killian drove the spike of his halberd into the cracked floor with a low thud, anchoring himself, a living wall between the king and whatever came next. They came in ready, standing with their king and the twins, loyalty carved deep into every step they took.

Valendor staggered back, shock flashing sharp across his face.

"William," he rasped, like the name itself poisoned his mouth. "No... That's not possible."

His gaze darted to Finnegan and Killian, and his lip curled in bitter understanding.

"They freed you..." he hissed, the realization souring into fury.

The tension in the room wound tighter, the air vibrating with it.

But William didn't waste words.

"I'm here ta end this madness."

His voice struck the air like a hammer's blow.

Valendor's face twisted. Shadows slithered at his feet, coiling like hungry beasts. "Still the self-righteous fool," he spat. "Ya never understood real power. Not then. Not now."

William's voice sliced through the air. "Power ain't about control. It's about protection—but that was lost to ya long ago."

Behind him, Theodora and Alexandria backed away. The air had changed—more charged, more dangerous. Theodora's fingers curled around her bow, her posture taut. She was ready to move if needed, but her gaze never left her father.

Finnegan and Killian moved closer to the twins, silent and ready to defend. They flanked the girls without a word, a wall of steel and loyalty at their backs.

William stepped in front of them, his broad frame a living shield.

Theodora held her bow, her breath shallow. Alexandria stood rigid beside her, energy burning just under her skin—earth, air, fire and water clawing to be released. She clenched her fists to hold it back, knowing the time wasn't yet right.

Watching and waiting.

The wind tugged at the ends of Alexandria's hair, carrying the scent of smoke and stone. Energy sparked under her skin, alive and restless. She felt Valendor's fury, raw and reckless—a wildfire barely contained—and her father's steady resolve, unyielding, a fortress against the storm.

His face twisted, rage blooming hot and fast.

He thrust both hands forward. A violent wave of shadows exploded from his palms, slamming toward William with a force that made the tower groan and the walls shudder.

"A kingdom needs strength!" he bellowed. "Somethin' you'll never have!"

William didn't move. A radiant shield of golden light flared from his hands, catching the surge midair and tearing it apart into smoke and sparks.

"Strength comes from honor and loyalty," he snapped back, his voice cutting like a blade. "Both of which ya threw away."

The impact shook the chamber. Dust rained down from the ceiling. Stones cracked under the weight of clashing power. Magic screamed against magic, ripping the air raw.

Valendor snarled like a cornered beast. "Pretty words," he spat. "They won't save ya."

Magic flared again. Light and darkness collided in a brutal burst, shaking the tower to its foundation. The ground split in jagged lines beneath their feet.

"We could've ruled together, ya fool!" He roared, voice ragged with rage.

The words hit like a slap. Alexandria blinked, a cold ripple running through her.

What was he talking about? she thought, heart hammering. What ties could there possibly be between them?

Theodora shifted beside her, jaw tightening. Confusion twisted sharp and ugly in her gut, but she stayed silent, watching, trying to piece the madness together.

"Ye chose power over duty," William shouted back. "Ye destroyed everythin'."

Theodora and Alexandria exchanged a glance, their hands twitching at their sides. Doubt and dread tangled inside them, knotting tighter with every breath.

"You cast me aside," Valendor growled, voice shaking with fury. "But our fates are linked, whether ya like it or not."

The words landed heavy. Alexandria's stomach twisted. She wanted to move, to speak, to demand answers, but the storm of magic was too thick, the moment too fragile to break.

"I'll never bow to yer madness," William said, his gaze locked, unflinching.

Valendor let out a raw, guttural scream. The magic around him thickened, suffocating, swallowing the air itself. He hurled everything he had—his rage, his hatred—in a final, violent wave of darkness.

It tore across the chamber like a living storm, shadows screaming as they rushed forward, crackling and wild.

The tower shook to its core. The ground split wide, stones ripping free. Pillars buckled. Darkness raced to devour everything, swallowing light, air and hope itself.

Theodora and Alexandria braced, their power surging to the surface, hearts pounding as the world around them threatened to come crashing down.

Beyond the shattered doorway, heavy footsteps pounded the stone.

Jasper charged down the corridor, heart hammering against his ribs. He barely slowed as he hit the wreckage, skidding through the remains of the shattered door.

"Gods..." he breathed, the word torn from his throat.

Without thinking, he scrambled over the splintered wood, boots slipping as he fought for footing. His eyes locked onto the scene inside—Valendor's magic already tearing through the air, a dark spear racing toward King William.

And behind it all—his father.

Valendor stood, eyes alight with power and cruel purpose, hand still raised from the casting. There was no hesitation, no flicker of remorse. Only hunger—for domination, for destruction. He meant to end the king where he stood.

No.

Jasper froze for a heartbeat, horror flooding him. *That's my father. That's the blood in my veins.*

But even as the thought struck, another rose like a flame inside him.

That's not who I am. Not anymore. I have to prove it—to them, to me.

He wasn't going to be Valendor's echo. Not now. Not ever.

The air was thick, heavy with magic that clawed at his skin. Darkness, alive and writhing, twisted through the room, and Jasper knew that a moment's hesitation would mean the king's death.

He didn't hesitate.

Digging in hard, he launched himself forward, cutting straight into the heart of the storm. The shadows twisted, sensing him—but he was already moving, reckless and fast.

Valendor's voice cut through the chaos, low and venomous. "Jasper," he snarled, "what do ye think ye're doin'?"

There was no surprise in his tone—only fury. As if Jasper's defiance was not betrayal, but insult.

But it was already done.

With a shout, Jasper hurled himself between Valendor's blast and the king, throwing his body wide to shield William.

The dark wave slammed into him mid-air. Jasper took the full force of it square in the chest, his body jolting violently. The impact ripped the breath from his lungs, pain lancing through his ribs like fire.

The force hurled both him and William back into the far wall. Stone cracked. Dust and debris rained down like a hailstorm.

Jasper hit the ground hard. A sharp crack sounded deep in his side, and for a long second, he didn't move.

Pain roared through him, raw and overwhelming. His limbs felt leaden, his chest burning with every shallow gasp. Blood filled his mouth, coppery and hot, and he turned his head to spit it out onto the broken stone.

For a moment, the world tilted and blurred. Every part of him screamed to stay down.

But with a ragged breath, he gritted his teeth and forced himself upright. His arms shook violently as he dragged himself up the wall, each movement sharp, brutal. Every breath felt like a battle he was losing.

Across the chamber, the sisters froze.

"Father!" they cried out in unison.

Theodora started forward, but Alexandria caught her arm, holding her back.

"We can't, Theo," she said, voice breaking. "The eclipse is fading. We have to end this now."

Jasper slumped against the wall, blood trailing from the corner of his mouth. He had lifted himself once, dragging his battered body into position to shield the king, but now he sagged where he sat, head lolling to the side, eyes closed.

At his side, King William lay sprawled across the cracked stone, unconscious.

They remained there—still, broken, unmoving—in the wreckage.

Finnegan was the first to move, dropping to one knee at William's side. He pressed a hand to the king's chest, searching desperately for a pulse. For a long, brutal second, he felt nothing—then William drew in a shallow gasp.

Relief flickered across Finnegan's face, but he didn't slow. He pressed his hands over the king's chest, golden healing magic sparking to life beneath his fingers. His jaw tightened in focus, shutting out everything else.

Killian hesitated a beat, torn between the two men lying in the rubble. His gaze shifted from William to Jasper—between his king and the fool who had thrown himself straight into death's path.

The magic hit him full force, tearing and burning his shirt and bruising and scorching the skin beneath. Blood streaked his mouth, and his breathing was shallow, strained.

Killian cursed under his breath and scrambled to Jasper's side, dropping hard to his knees. He grabbed Jasper's shoulder and eased him forward, searching for any sign of life.

His hands hovered for a moment, taking in the damage—burns and bruises marred his ribs, smoke still curling from the scorched cloth clinging to his skin. Jasper's chest rose and fell—just enough to show he still breathed.

Killian just stared at him, confusion twisting in his chest. Why had Jasper shown up at all? After everything—after revealing he was Valendor's son—why now? Why throw himself into the blast meant for King William? Why turn on the very man he once defended?

None of it made sense.

And yet... even after all the betrayal, here he was—broken, burned—because he'd chosen to protect the king. Whatever his reasons, whatever had changed, Killian couldn't ignore what was in front of him.

"Hold on, ya stubborn bastard," Killian muttered, voice low and rough. He pressed both hands over Jasper's wounds, a faint, strained glow of healing magic flickering beneath his palms. It was weak, but steady. He poured everything he had into keeping Jasper breathing, jaw clenched, heart pounding.

The room held its breath.

Then, like a wire snapping, the sisters turned.

They faced Valendor, eyes burning, Killian's magic throwing sharp shadows. Theodora's fists clenched, nails biting skin.

"You'll pay for what ya did to our father," Theodora snarled, her voice shaking as she locked eyes with him.

"You won't get away with this," Alexandria said coldly, stepping up beside her sister.

Valendor straightened slowly, a cruel smile tugging at his mouth. He looked them over like they were nothing more than children playing at war.

"Proud little things," he said, voice thick with contempt. "But ya know nothin'. Absolutely nothin'."

Theodora's hands curled into fists. "We know enough," she spat. "We know yer a coward. We know yer nothin' like our father."

Valendor's grin widened, slow and poisonous. He leaned forward slightly, just enough that the sisters could see the glint in his eyes.

"That's where yer wrong," he said, his voice dropping to a near whisper, heavy with satisfaction. "We're more alike than ye realize."

The air tightened around them, the weight of his words pressing down, waiting to drop.

He let the silence stretch, savoring every second. Then, like a knife twisting between ribs, he said:

"Yer king and I—we're brothers. Twins."

The words slammed into them.

Theodora staggered a half-step back. Alexandria's breath caught. The world seemed to hold still.

Valendor's laughter broke the silence, sharp and ugly, echoing off the stone walls.

"Aye," he said, relishing the words. "Two princes, born together, destined to rule as one. But the crown fancied him—their perfect son. Their golden heir. And me?" His smile turned wild. "They wanted me forgotten, they did."

Theodora shook her head, heart hammering against her ribs. "Yer lying," she snapped, her voice raw.

Valendor took a slow, mocking step closer.

"Would he tell ya, lass?" he said, voice thick with venom. "Would yer shining father admit he had a brother like me? A brother he abandoned?"

Theodora's fists trembled at her sides. "Stop," she whispered, but the doubt was already digging in, sharp and relentless.

Valendor sneered. "Ah, it'd be much easier ta just erase me, wouldn't it? Bury the shame. Pretend I never even existed."

Memories swarmed up—the quiet arguments behind closed doors, the names no one dared to say. Alexandria felt her stomach turn, the cracks forming faster than she could stop them.

"Shut up!" Theodora shouted suddenly, the sound ripped from her throat.

Valendor's smile only widened.

"Hurts, doesn't it?" he said softly. "To know yer precious daddy couldn't even look at what he left behind."

"Shut your mouth!" Alexandria snapped, stepping forward, rage burning in her eyes. "You don't get to speak about him!"

Theodora was shaking, fury and betrayal colliding inside her until she thought she might break from it. Her vision blurred, fists aching with the urge to strike, to make him pay for every word.

Valendor just stood there, smiling, feeding on their fury like it was the sweetest thing in the world.

And something inside the sisters finally broke.

Across the chamber, stunned silence fell.

Finnegan and Killian stood frozen, the blood draining from their faces. Finnegan's jaw locked tight, his hands curling into fists, while Killian sagged forward, clutching at Jasper's side, the healing magic flickering between his palms.

Jasper stirred, a low groan escaping him as the words sank deeper into the haze clouding his mind.

He forced his eyes open, blinking at the scene before him. Theodora and Alexandria stood rigid, radiating fury. Valendor faced them, smiling like a man who had already won.

The words filtered through Jasper's dazed thoughts, each one cutting sharper than the last.

Brothers.

Twins.

Family.

Jasper's chest tightened as the truth crashed into him. His gaze drifted from Valendor to the king, and the full weight of it hit like a hammer.

The twins he had spent time with, the ones his father ordered him to capture or kill, were his family. His blood.

His cousins.

A sick, hollow feeling opened in his gut. He looked at Theodora, then Alexandria, and guilt crushed the breath from his lungs. He had followed his father's orders without question, without doubt, blind to the truth.

He had tried to destroy his own blood.

Jasper struggled to push himself upright, but his battered body barely responded. His hands trembled with the effort as he turned a stricken gaze toward the sisters, shame burning hotter than any wound.

Valendor had manipulated them all. Used them. Cared for nothing but his own ambition.

And yet there stood Theodora and Alexandria—battered, betrayed, and still willing to fight for what they loved.

For their family.

For a kingdom Jasper had nearly helped tear apart.

He swallowed hard against the guilt rising in his throat, knowing deep down there might be no forgiveness for what he'd done.

Somehow, he found himself reaching for it.

Chapter 30

"Breaking the Chains"

JASPER SAGGED AGAINST THE wall, the fight bleeding out of him along with everything he thought he knew. Finnegan stood rigid beside him, fists clenched, while Killian pressed harder against Jasper's wounds, both of them frozen by the truth still echoing in the chamber.

But the sisters didn't look back.

Their focus had already shifted forward.

To him.

To the man who had shattered everything.

Theodora stepped forward, her voice cutting through the thick, heavy air like a blade.

"Ya may share our blood," she said, steady and sharp, "but that means nothin' now."

Alexandria's hand found hers, a quick, fierce squeeze grounding them both.

"Together," Alexandria said, voice firm but quiet, "we're stronger than you'll ever be."

A low hum answered her words as their magic stirred—Theodora's heat crackling outward in sharp, snapping bursts, sparks of electricity crawling along her arms. Alexandria's breath frosted in the air, cold swirling around her as the earth trembled at her feet, her elemental power gathering low and steady.

Valendor's smile twitched—the first crack in his mask.

He raised his hands, and dark magic bled from his fingertips like ink swirling in water. The air thickened, buzzing and heavy. Sparks flashed and spat across the floor, lighting the broken stones in brief, brutal bursts.

"Ye're just wee children playin' at power!" Valendor snarled, voice raw and straining to sound sure.

Theodora's mouth twisted into a grim smile. Electricity snapped at her fingertips. "He's tryin' to get in our heads," she muttered, the air around her warping with heat.

"Won't work," Alexandria said, ice biting at her words.

They moved together—measured, deliberate, unstoppable.

Their magic slammed forward—Theodora's electricity lancing out in bright, sizzling bolts, Alexandria's elemental power rising in a sharp blast of frozen air and shattered stone. Fire and frost collided against his dark shield with a deafening crack. The ground shuddered, fractures splitting the stone beneath their feet.

Valendor staggered, just a step—but it was enough.

"Don't give 'im a breath!" Theo barked, sparks crackling around her fists.

Snarling, he fought back, standing tall, fire flashing in his eyes. He hurled shadows from his hands, sharp and wild, dark magic clawing through the air.

"Ye think this'll scare us, do ya?" Alex shouted, twisting her hands through the air, drawing up shards of stone and whips of wind.

Valendor struck again and again, each blow meant to crush, to overwhelm. A grin twisted his mouth. "Pathetic," he spat. "You've no idea what you're meddlin' with."

Theo threw out a wave of searing heat, the air between them shimmering. "We know enough," she said, steadying her stance, bolts of lightning crackling across her arms. "Enough to end ya."

Valendor pressed harder, shadows tearing through the air in thick waves. For a moment, he was certain he'd break them. Another flick of his wrist, another blast—

But for the first time, his spells didn't rip through them.

The sisters held their ground, weaving fire, lightning, ice and earth into a barrier he couldn't break. Their movements were sharper now, cleaner, every strike biting deeper, chipping at his power, forcing him back a step at a time.

Valendor's sneer faltered, twisting into a grimace of frustration. "You'll break, same as the rest," he snarled, though the heat behind the words was slipping.

Alex grinned, teeth flashing. "Not today!"

He realized he wasn't fighting children.

He was fighting the heirs of the kingdom—and they weren't backing down.

Valendor's grimace deepened as he stumbled back another step, his dark magic cracking against the sisters' combined strength.

This wasn't how it was supposed to go.

Theodora glanced briefly at their allies before refocusing on the fight. Alexandria's power flowed into hers, strengthening their shared magic.

"For our family," Alexandria called out. "For Kandella."

Pain shot through Theodora's body, but she held firm. She caught her sister's questioning look.

"Keep goin'," she said through gritted teeth.

Valendor snarled, rage surging through him. Then he thrust a hand upward, clawing at the air as if ripping it open.

Above them, the last light of the fading eclipse pulsed.

The temperature of the chamber dropped sharply, the shadows deepening. The dying remnants of the eclipse twisted and funneled toward Valendor's outstretched hand, the very air shuddering under the weight of it.

Theodora and Alexandria faltered for half a heartbeat, feeling the change, the wrongness crawling down their spines.

"He's pulling from the eclipse!" Alexandria shouted, throwing up a thicker wall of ice as the shadows clawed toward them.

Valendor's laughter echoed through the chamber, raw and desperate.

"Ye thought this was all I had?" he rasped. His voice sounded warped, stretched thin by the dark power filling him. His skin seemed to ripple under it, his eyes darkening to bottomless pits.

The ground trembled harder now. The cracks splitting wider across the floor, and a low, bone-deep hum filled the air, rattling in their teeth.

He wasn't just fighting with magic anymore.

He was trying to tear the castle around them apart.

Valendor drove both hands into the ground, unleashing a shockwave of stolen power and dark flame.

Theodora barely anchored herself, sparks whipping violently from her arms as she steadied the shield between them.

Alexandria gritted her teeth, summoning the strength of the earth beneath her, roots cracking through the broken stone to hold them steady.

The eclipse's last breath howled around them, and for the first time, Valendor's face twisted into something closer to madness.

He had thrown away everything—blood, kingdom, even his own body—for power.

And he would not stop until he either destroyed them—

—or destroyed himself.

The sisters stood unmoved.

Side by side, they raised their arms. Their magic flared brighter, hotter, colder—bigger than before.

Theodora's electricity snapped outward in a blinding storm, but now it wasn't just lightning. Fire ignited in its wake, flames roaring to life around her hands, swirling with searing heat.

Alexandria's frost thickened into spears of ice that shattered across the floor, and the ground itself answered her call—jagged stone rising in sharp, brutal spikes.

Element met element, crackling and alive.

Valendor screamed, a raw, broken sound. He hurled a final blast of shadow toward them, dark tendrils writhing through the air.

The sisters didn't flinch.

Their magic struck first.

Theodora's lightning speared through the darkness, splitting it apart in a flash of blinding white. Flames followed, searing the air black. Alexandria's frost surged in behind it, freezing the twisted magic midair before shattering it into glittering shards, and the earth itself buckled forward, battering Valendor's shields.

He staggered, forcing more dark power into the attack, clawing at the air, trying to rebuild his defenses—but it was useless. Their combined strength hammered him, relentless, tearing through every shield he tried to raise.

Piece by piece, they broke him down.

He fought to the last breath—grappling with the raw forces tearing him apart, spitting curses and throwing everything he had at them—but it wasn't enough.

Theodora's final surge of electricity wrapped around him like chains, locking him in place, while fire flared at his feet, pinning him there.

Alexandria's frost crept along his body, locking him in a cage of shimmering ice, and the ground rose, binding him from below.

And then, with a final pulse of unstoppable power, the sisters crushed him.

Valendor's form twisted violently, unraveling at the seams. His body turned to ash before their eyes, scattered by the force of their will.

They poured everything they had into the attack, holding it steady until only silence remained.

As the dust settled, they stood in the ruined chamber, shoulders touching.

For a long moment, neither spoke.

Their eyes met—tired, battered, but unbroken—and in that look, they shared the same unspoken truth: it was finally over.

The air felt lighter now, as if the room itself was breathing again. Only wisps of magic hung there, mixed with the faint scent of singed herbs and incense. Somewhere in the distance, water dripped steadily, a quiet reminder that life went on.

The cool floor grounded them as the last traces of power faded away.

And for the first time in what felt like forever, they stood free.

For a long moment no one moved.

No one spoke.

No one dared.

Across the chamber, Finnegan let out a shaky breath he hadn't realized he was holding. His fists unclenched slowly, the blood drained from his knuckles.

Killian sagged to his knees beside Jasper, exhausted magic sparking at his fingertips before fading out altogether. He leaned heavily against Jasper's side, blinking hard against the sting in his eyes.

Jasper stared at the spot where Valendor had stood. Now there was only an empty, scorched stone. His heart hammered against his ribs, guilt and awe twisting together it hurt to breathe. He had tried to break them—and they had stood stronger than anyone he'd ever known.

Theodora and Alexandria stood at the center of it all, shoulders touching, heads bowed slightly, breathing hard but unbroken. They looked like queens already.

A soft creak from the entrance broke the heavy stillness.

The sisters turned, tense at first, magic still humming in their blood.

Standing in the archway was Queen Amara—regal even in her weakened condition.

Theodora's breath caught in her chest.

Though captivity had worn her down, her strength shone stubbornly through the exhaustion on her face. Her tattered emerald gown hung loosely on her frame. Her once-flowing auburn hair now fell messily around her shoulders. But her green eyes—those fierce, familiar eyes—still burned with the unyielding fire they remembered.

The sisters exchanged a glance, a thousand unspoken memories passing between them—lazy afternoons in the garden, laughter drifting under the shade of ancient oaks, their mother's steady hands brushing hair from tear-streaked cheeks.

For a minute, it was almost like they were little girls again.

But reality snapped back into place as they truly saw her—worn, battered, but resolute.

Without a word, Theodora, and Alexandria rushed forward.

They flung their arms around her, pulling her close, feeling the thinness of her frame, the strength still humming in her bones. Their mother's warmth wrapped around them, chasing away the lingering chill of the chamber.

For a long moment, they just stood there, clinging to each other.

Queen Amara's breath shook against her daughters, the steady beat of her heart grounding them both. She pulled back slowly, hands lingering on their faces as if afraid they might disappear. Her fingers brushed over bruises, tucked stray strands of hair behind their ears, her touch full of aching relief.

Together, the sisters gently held her up. The broken floor was treacherous beneath their feet, littered with cracked stones and scorched debris, but together they moved carefully, supporting her between them.

Ahead, King William slumped against the wall, barely conscious.

As they approached, Finnegan, who had been kneeling nearby, rose to his feet and stepped aside to give them space. He said nothing, just dipped his head in quiet respect.

Queen Amara sank to her knees with a soft groan, reaching out to her husband. Her hand, though trembling, found his with certainty.

"Will," she whispered, voice raw but steady.

At her voice, he stirred. His eyes fluttered open, clouded with pain, but clearing when they met hers. His fingers tightened around hers, dragging her hand to his chest, holding it there like an anchor.

And in that fragile, broken moment, surrounded by the wreckage of what once was, something whole began to knit itself back together.

Behind them, Killian moved carefully, slipping his arm under Jasper's shoulders. With a grunt, he lifted him, and Jasper staggered upright, leaning heavily into him for support. His body protested every movement, while his gaze locked onto the sight before him. The royal family, battered but alive—and he couldn't look away.

Killian helped him forward until they stood beside Finnegan.

At that moment, a large white wolf padded into the room, her gleaming coat catching the low light as her amber eyes scanned the space sharply. A warning growl rumbled deep in her chest, but it quickly faded when she recognized the figures gathered there. Aris moved with silent grace, her presence serving as a comfort more than a threat.

Above her, a grey owl glided soundlessly through the broken archway. It was Khadall in his owl form, who circled once overhead before settling on a fractured pillar. As he perched, his eyes swept the chamber, keenly observing every detail within.

Aris padded forward, brushing her side lightly against Alexandria's leg in silent reassurance. She reached down instinctively, fingers brushing through the wolf's soft fur.

A low hoot echoed from above as Khadall tucked his wings tighter against his body, keeping quiet watch.

They were together again.

For a moment, nothing else mattered.

The rawness of survival hung thick in the air, but so did something stronger—something more enduring.

Finnegan cleared his throat softly, drawing Queen Amara's attention.

"What happened, Your Majesty?" he asked, voice low, rough from the strain of battle and fear.

Queen Amara straightened slowly, lifting her chin, fire flickering in her eyes despite the tremble in her limbs.

"I got separated in the scrap with the guards," she said, raw from exhaustion. "The eejits tried draggin' me back to that bloody dungeon, but I wasn't havin' it."

Her fists clenched briefly at her sides, a spark of iron flashing through her words.

"I used the last bit of elemental magic I could muster," she continued, her voice gaining strength. "Set the stone floor ablaze behind me, I did. Ran through half the castle, blastin' walls and freezin' doors shut. Must've looked like a madwoman—but pure stubbornness got me here in the end."

A tired, crooked smile ghosted across her lips.

The twins exchanged a glance, a quiet pride burning in their eyes. Their mother—tattered, worn, but as unbreakable as ever.

At her side, King William stirred again. His grip on Queen Amara's hand tightened, and with a grunt of effort, he shifted, trying to rise.

The movement was slow and shaky, but full of stubborn will.

Finnegan reacted first, stepping quickly to his side. Killian was right behind him, dropping to the other side, each man slipping an arm under the king's shoulders.

"Easy now, Your Majesty," Finnegan said.

Together, they lifted him—carefully, steadily—until he was on his feet.

He swayed for a moment, his legs trembling under the strain, but with Finnegan and Killian bracing him, he stayed upright.

His breath came hard and fast, but when his eyes found his daughters, they burned with pride.

"Me girls," he rasped, voice thick with emotion.

He looked at them—Theodora with her fierce, unyielding fire, Alexandria with her quiet, steady strength—and his chest tightened painfully.

"Ya both fought so bravely," he said. "Ya've saved us all."

Theodora blinked hard against the sudden sting in her eyes. Alexandria lowered her gaze for a heartbeat, steadying herself against the flood of feeling those words stirred.

Around them, Finnegan, Killian, and Jasper gathered closer, forming a circle.

Worn. Scarred. Alive.

The weight of everything they had endured pressed down on them—yet for the first time, it didn't crush. It bound them together.

They had survived.

Chapter 31

"Rising from the Ashes"

Alexandria's breath caught suddenly. Her eyes turned toward the far side of the chamber, toward the shattered balcony doors, and a memory flared sharp and clear in her mind—the eclipse.

"The eclipse," she said softly, almost to herself. Then louder, steadier: "The eclipse!"

She pointed, and every head turned to follow her gaze.

For a long moment, no one moved.

Then, slowly, as if pulled by something stronger than pain, the group began to walk across the broken floor.

King William leaned heavily against Finnegan and Killian, his breath ragged, each step a battle—but he walked. Jasper limped beside them, battered but stubborn, jaw set tight as Killian kept a steadying hand at his back.

Theodora and Alexandria flanked Queen Amara, close enough to catch her if she faltered. Neither spoke; they didn't need to. Their strength flowed into her through every step, every breath.

Aris padded ahead, paws soundless on the cracked stone, her fur catching the faint, rising light. Outside, Khadall soared, a dark shape etched against the clearing sky.

Together, they slowly followed the others.

Step by step.

Towards the open archway.

The broken doors hung off their twisted hinges, groaning in the morning breeze. Beyond them, the world stretched wide—and changed.

They glanced upward as they neared the threshold.

The eclipse, the dark symbol of their worst hours, was retreating at last. The sun bled through the edges, brilliant and unyielding, peeling the shadow back like old skin.

Theo swallowed against the lump in her throat, her fists clenching and unclenching. She had almost forgotten what real light looked like.

Alexandria felt her chest tighten, not with fear this time, but with something sharper, deeper—hope.

When they reached the archway, the sunlight hit them full in the face.

Outside, Carrantou was not whole.

The battered towers cast long, broken shadows across the ground. Trees lay snapped and scattered like kindling. Deep cracks split the earth, dark veins running through the wounded fields. Smoke drifted from the blackened edges of the forests.

It was scarred. It was battered. But, it was still standing.

Brilliant oranges, bruised purples, and molten golds spilled across the sky, touching every corner with light. A soft, forgiving glow bathed the scorched ground and shattered stones.

Jasper let out a breath. Killian's hand tightened on his shoulder, grounding him.

Queen Amara lifted her chin, just a little, just enough.

Theo blinked hard, the sting behind her eyes sharp and sudden.

Alexandria stepped forward, tasting the air—still heavy with ash, but no longer choking.

Behind them lay wreckage.

Before them, a broken island ready to heal.

The air itself seemed different—lighter, sharper, alive in a way it hadn't been in years.

They stood together, breathing in the first true breath of freedom. It filled their lungs and burned a little, raw and clean after so many years spent breathing the bitter cold.

Hope stirred in their chests—bright, unfamiliar, a fragile spark in a place long emptied of light.

The worst was over.

The future—the light—was theirs to claim.

They stepped onto the battered balcony, and the world opened before them, vast, broken, and achingly beautiful.

The towers, shattered and leaning, caught the first gold of sunrise on their jagged edges. The stones below, cracked and blackened, shimmered where the light kissed them. The earth, scarred and hollowed by years of darkness, stretched wide, battered but unbowed—waiting.

The air shifted, growing softer, warmer, as if the land itself exhaled. The sharp, bitter edge of winter, once all they had known, began to pull away like a tide going out.

They could smell the change—wet stone, thawing earth, and the faint, stubborn sweetness of green life pressing through the ruins.

Below them, the snow that had blanketed the island in silence began to melt. Thin rivulets of water ran down the broken stones, carving shining paths through the rubble. The sound of it—small, steady, alive—sank deep into their bones.

The earth, long frozen under the weight of darkness, breathed again, a low, shuddering sigh, as if Carrantou itself was waking from a nightmare it had nearly forgotten how to escape.

For a long moment, they stood there, hearts aching with the weight of it all—the warmth on their faces, the damp air on their skin, the wild, unbearable rush of what might come next.

And for the first time in years, they didn't just hope.

They believed.

From the edge of the light, a figure began to take shape.

At first, just a shimmer, a flicker against the brightening sky. Then, slowly, Ms. Whoo emerged from the shadows, her midnight cloak swirling around her slender frame. The rising sun caught in her crystalline hair, making it glitter like morning frost.

Her dark blue eyes, bright and clear, found Theodora first, and a slow, proud smile curved her lips.

"Nine winters of darkness end today," she said, her voice low and steady. "Ya both have shown more strength than I could've hoped for."

Even as her words settled in the warming air, another figure coalesced beside her.

Elara, in her full majestic phoenix form, materialized in a rush of golden flames. Her wings radiated intense heat and light, casting long, vivid shadows across the balcony. The brilliance of her presence seemed to drive away the last remnants of darkness clinging to the stones.

The two stood side by side—guardian and guide—outlined against the light of dawn.

Theodora and Alexandria stepped forward, hearts thudding against their ribs.

Ms. Whoo opened her arms without hesitation, and Theodora moved into her embrace, the familiar scent of herbs and morning dew wrapping around her like a second skin.

"You're here," Theodora whispered into her shoulder.

"Course I am, lass. Took ya long enough," she murmured.

She pulled Theodora in tighter before easing back just enough to see her face. Her hands framed her cheeks, her thumbs brushing away the tears she didn't bother to hide. Up close, her blue eyes were glassy with unshed emotion.

For a moment, she couldn't speak. She just held Theodora's gaze, her throat working around the words.

When she finally found her voice, it was low and rough. "It's you, love," she said, her smile trembling at the edges. "You're the one who found the way. I just showed you where to start."

Theodora blinked hard, but she only smiled wider, nodding once, fierce and proud.

Nearby, Alexandria found herself drawn into the shelter of Elara's fiery wings. The warmth of the phoenix wrapped around her, chasing away the cold that had burrowed deep into her bones and refused to leave.

Elara's voice resonated in her mind, low and steady, a heartbeat against her thoughts. *"You have risen higher than I ever dared to dream, little one."*

Alexandria swallowed hard, the sudden burn behind her eyes almost blinding. She gripped a fistful of Elara's brilliant feathers, grounding herself against the rush of feeling that threatened to tear her apart.

"I couldn't have done it without you," she whispered, voice shaking.

The phoenix lowered her head, and their foreheads touched—full of a pride too large for words. Heat bloomed between them, not just from Elara's fire but from something deeper—an unbreakable bond, forged in trials neither of them had expected to survive.

When Elara finally pulled back, Alexandria remained, pressing her forehead into the lingering warmth for one more stolen moment.

Her gaze found Ms. Whoo. Without thinking, she crossed the space between them. Her steps were shaky, unsteady, but driven. She threw her arms around her nanny, clutching her like a lifeline.

She gave a startled laugh, soft and breathless, before wrapping her feathery arms tightly around her in return. She pulled her close, like a mother welcoming a lost child back into the fold.

"Ah, there's me girl," she murmured, voice thick and cracking with emotion. "Back where ya belong."

For Alexandria, the embrace wasn't just comfort. It was a tether to something real. She had spent her whole life in the mortal world, raised by her fae guardians, Diana, and Elmer, hidden away from the Shadow Walkers and Valendor so they couldn't find her. They had loved her like their own, but even then, a piece of her had always felt missing—some unseen thread tugging her toward a place she didn't remember.

Now, in Ms. Whoo's arms, that final piece slid quietly back into place.

Theodora moved closer without a word, pressing into their nanny's side, slipping one arm around Alexandria and the other around her. Ms. Whoo held them both, murmuring something low and wordless, as if trying to soothe them the way she had when they were small.

For a fleeting moment, it felt like the world had stilled.

Then the ground trembled.

It was slight at first, a subtle shiver beneath their feet, easy to miss in the cocoon of warmth and memory. But then the stones beneath them gave a deep, rumbling groan.

Then the tower shuddered.

The ground buckled again, harder this time. Loose stones clattered down the walls, and the sisters instinctively clung tighter, feeling the old, wounded structure strain around them.

The tremors suggested something still stirred below—something not yet vanquished.

"The magic," Theodora muttered against Ms. Whoo's shoulder, her voice tight with dread. She turned her head just enough to catch Alexandria's wide, alarmed eyes. "It might not be over."

She loosened her grip, pressing a swift kiss to both their heads before nudging them gently toward the others.

"Stay close," she said, low and fierce. "Stay strong."

The sisters moved, hands still brushing against each other's sleeves, not fully willing to let go.

Around them, the others had gone still, senses sharpened, muscles tensed, waiting.

A heavy silence fell, thick and suffocating, laced with the sharp, metallic scent of old magic and fear.

Unspoken worries threaded through the group, curling into the fresh morning light like smoke.

"We face an uncertain path," Alexandria whispered, her voice tight with resolve and trepidation, as if speaking the words aloud could steady her.

Theodora caught her hand, squeezing hard, grounding her. Her eyes burned with fierce determination as she looked to others, the ones who had bled and fought beside them.

"Indeed," she said. "But we'll face it together. We'll rebuild Donaglen—our kingdom—all of it. And we'll make sure the darkness stays buried this time."

King William watched his daughters from where he stood, exhausted but unbowed. His chest swelled with pride, and though his voice was rough with emotion, it carried clearly over the broken stones.

"Ya've given our people hope again," he said. "You've proven yourselves true leaders... in every sense of the word."

Though they won the battle, the fight to restore their home was only beginning.

Theodora stood rooted in place as the morning wind cut through the haze hanging over the ravaged landscape. The blackened stumps of trees and cracked earth told their own story of what had happened here. She looked at her companions—family by blood and family by choice—and felt something tighten in her chest. They'd been through hell together, and it showed on every face, in every scar. Each of them carried marks of what they'd sacrificed, yet here they stood, alive and unbowed.

Side by side. She looked to her sister, then her parents, then the others who had fought beside them. Alone, they might have fallen. Together, they stood unbreakable. Their strength wasn't just in numbers—it was in the bonds between them, forged in fire and tested beyond breaking. Theodora knew, with bone-deep certainty, that whatever came next, this was how they would face it.

Overhead, the sun pushed higher into the sky, climbing slow and steady, burning away the last shadows of the night.

Alexandria brushed her hair out of her face. She glanced at Theodora and gave a crooked, tired smile.

"Can you believe it?" she said. "He's gone."

Theodora shifted the bow on her back, her mouth twisting into a wry smile.

"Thought he'd haunt us 'til our last breath," she said. "But he's gone, Alex. And he's not comin' back."

Alexandria let out a breath, almost a laugh. "Kandella's free."

"Aye," Theodora said, pulling her sister into a brief, fierce hug. "Free. And ours again."

They stood there a moment longer, letting it sink in — all those years of cold and snow, the blood spilled, the stolen lives — all finally ending here. The land was broken, but it will heal.

Their family gathered around them — her mother, wounded but proud, blinking hard against tears; her father, nodding, his hand tight around his sword hilt; their friends, exhausted and bloodstained, some holding each other upright. The air was thick with grief, relief and something close to joy. It felt fragile, like if anyone spoke too loudly it might shatter.

Alexandria's voice cut through the heavy stillness — soft, sure, and trembling at the edges.

"Let's go home," she said.

The words seemed to ripple through them all — pulling a sharp breath from her mother, a quiet sob from one of their friends. Even her father, stoic as stone, bowed his head for a moment, as if the weight of what they'd won finally settled.

Theodora swallowed hard, her chest tight, then managed a fierce smile.

"Aye," she said, her voice rough. "Home."

She turned, rallying herself and the others, her voice steady now.

"Right then. No time for lingerin'. We've a kingdom to put back together."

With the sun beating down on their faces, and the ruins of the past behind them, they moved forward — toward broken hills, the waiting future, and the battles still to come.

Behind them, Jasper stayed a moment longer, his gaze locked on the shattered remains of his father's castle.

From the blackened stones, something stirred — not a whisper, but a voice, low and cold, slipping through the cracks like smoke.

"Blood calls to blood..."

The sound barely brushed the air, but Jasper flinched as if struck. His hand curled into a fist at his side.

He didn't look back again.

Without a word, he turned and followed the others into the rising sun, the weight of something unseen settling over his shoulders.

Stay Tuned

KINDLED BOND

Book Two of *The Carrington Chronicles*

T HE CURSE IS BROKEN. The sisters are reunited. But peace in Kandella was never meant to last.

Something ancient stirs beneath the Cradle Spires. The leylines bleed. Magic twists and unravels. As Alexandria and Theodora face the rising storm, a forgotten war awakens—and a voice calls from the mortal world, one Alexandria thought she'd left behind.

Not all shadows stay buried.

Not every bond is safe.

And destiny never forgets.

Stay tuned for the next chapter in *The Carrington Chronicles*.

Sign up at jennifer@jklaneauthor.com for updates, sneak peeks, and exclusive extras.

Join the Magic. Never Miss a Tale.

Sign up for J.K. Lane's Fantasy Newsletter

Be the first to hear about:

- *Exclusive short stories*

- *Behind-the-scenes lore from Kandella*

- *New releases & cover reveal*

- *Reader giveaways*

- *Special bonus content just for subscribers*

Email me: *jennifer@jklaneauthor.com*

Thank You For Reading

If you enjoyed *Shadowed Past*,
leaving a review is a great way to share the love.
It helps new readers find the book,
and I always enjoy hearing your comments.

About J.K. Lane

J.K. Lane is a young adult fantasy author from Northeast Ohio, where her love of storytelling began beneath the tree in her backyard with a stack of books and a wild imagination.

Shadowed Past is her debut novel, marking the beginning of a richly woven fantasy series filled with magic, mystery, and heart. Lane is known for crafting immersive worlds and unforgettable characters that resonate with young readers. Her work draws inspiration from authors like V.C. Andrews, C.S. Lewis, Sarah J. Maas, and Leigh Bardugo, as well as beloved fantasy films such as *The Chronicles of Narnia*, *Twitches*, *The NeverEnding Story*, and *A Wrinkle in Time*.

When she's not writing, she enjoys painting, quiet walks, and spending time with her family and grandchildren. Through her stories, she hopes to spark imagination, stir emotion, and remind readers of the hidden magic still waiting to be found.

www.ingramcontent.com/pod-product-compliance
Lightning Source LLC
Chambersburg PA
CBHW022250310726
48973CB00001B/23